Doodleville
ART ATTACKS!

CHAD SELL

ALFRED A. KNOPF ✦ NEW YORK

THIS IS A BORZOI BOOK PUBLISHED BY ALFRED A. KNOPF

This is a work of fiction. Names, characters, places, and incidents either are the product of the author's imagination or are used fictitiously. Any resemblance to actual persons, living or dead, events, or locales is entirely coincidental. Except for the Art Institute of Chicago and Stan's Donuts. Those are real places. They just don't (usually) have doodles causing mischief in them.

Knopf, Borzoi Books, and the colophon are registered trademarks of Penguin Random House LLC.

Visit us on the Web! rhcbooks.com

Educators and librarians, for a variety of teaching tools, visit us at RHTeachersLibrarians.com

Library of Congress Cataloging-in-Publication Data is available upon request.
ISBN 978-1-9848-9473-1 (trade) — ISBN 978-0-593-56930-6 (lib. bdg.) —
ISBN 978-1-9848-9475-5 (ebook)

The text of this book is set in Creative Block BB.
The illustrations were created using Clip Studio Paint.
Interior design by Chad Sell

MANUFACTURED IN CHINA
10 9 8 7 6 5 4 3 2 1

First Edition

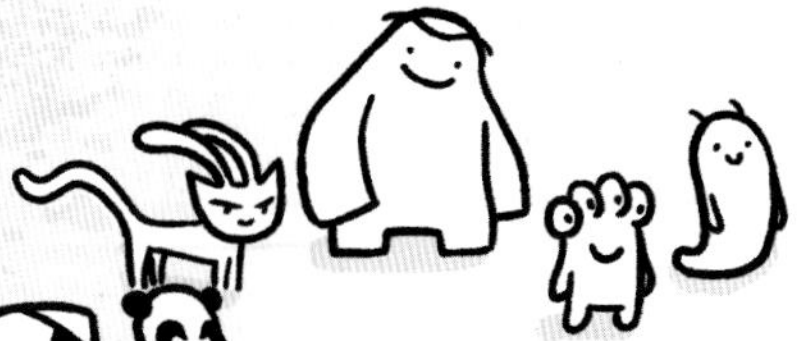

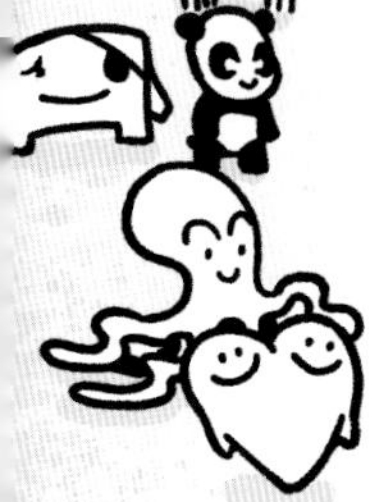

This book is dedicated to everyone at the
Art Institute of Chicago. Thank you for inspiring me
endlessly with your world-class collection of art.
Sorry for wrecking it.
—C.S.

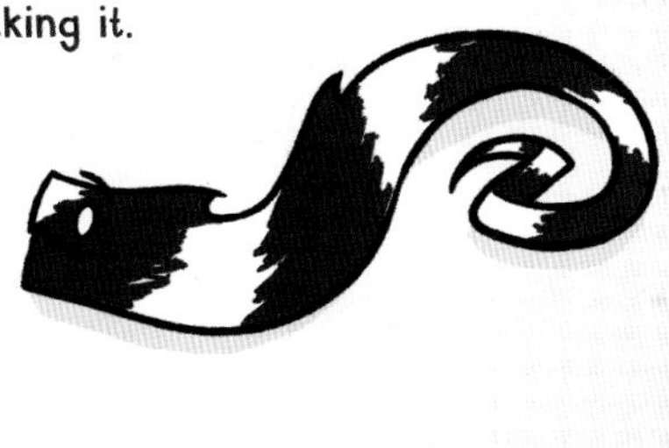

ART CLUB

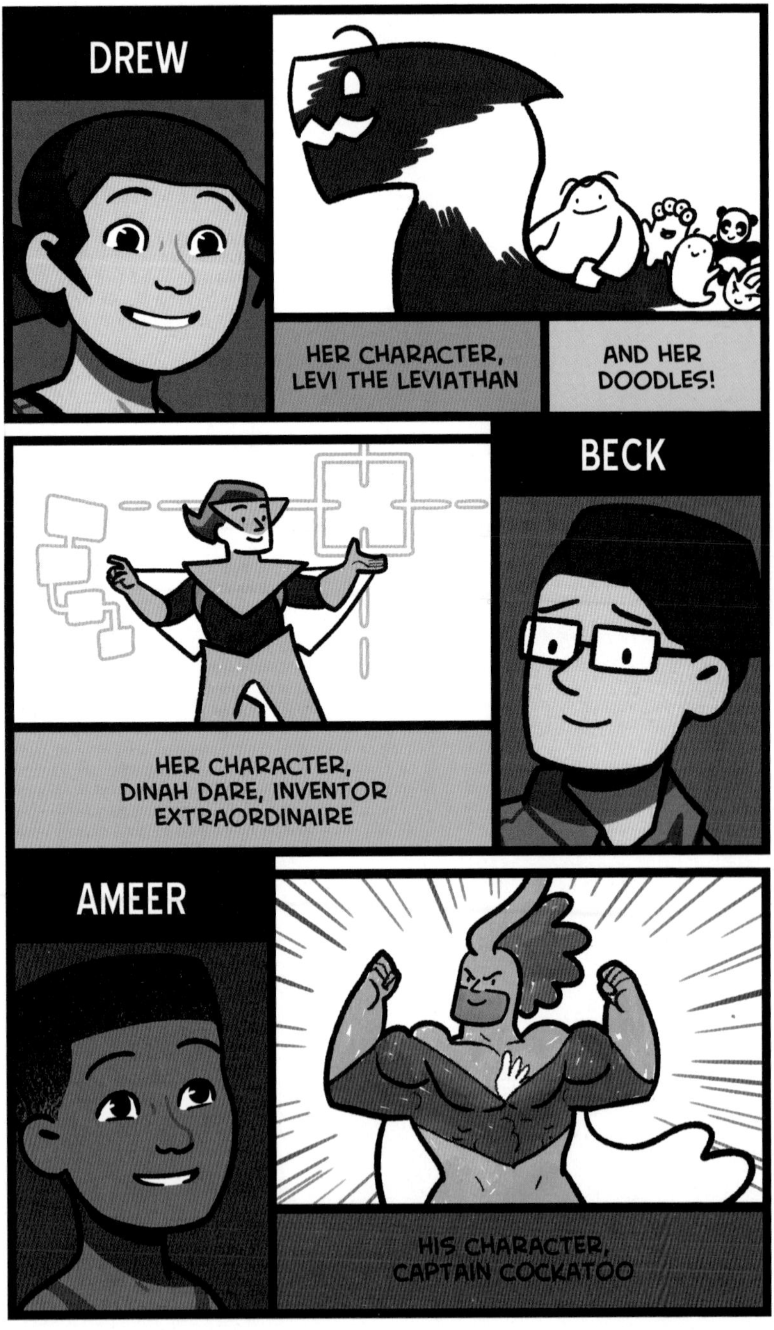
DREW
HER CHARACTER, LEVI THE LEVIATHAN
AND HER DOODLES!
BECK
HER CHARACTER, DINAH DARE, INVENTOR EXTRAORDINAIRE
AMEER
HIS CHARACTER, CAPTAIN COCKATOO

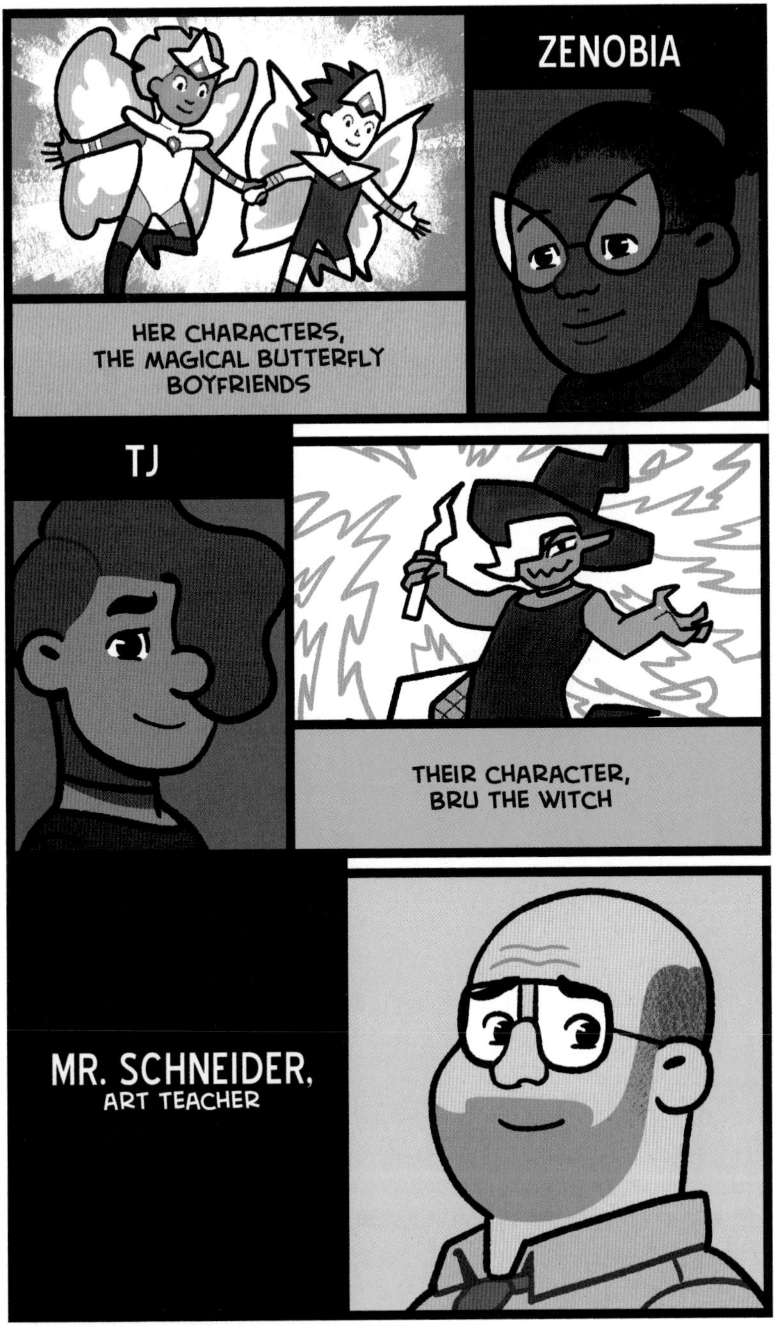
ZENOBIA
HER CHARACTERS, THE MAGICAL BUTTERFLY BOYFRIENDS
TJ
THEIR CHARACTER, BRU THE WITCH
MR. SCHNEIDER, ART TEACHER

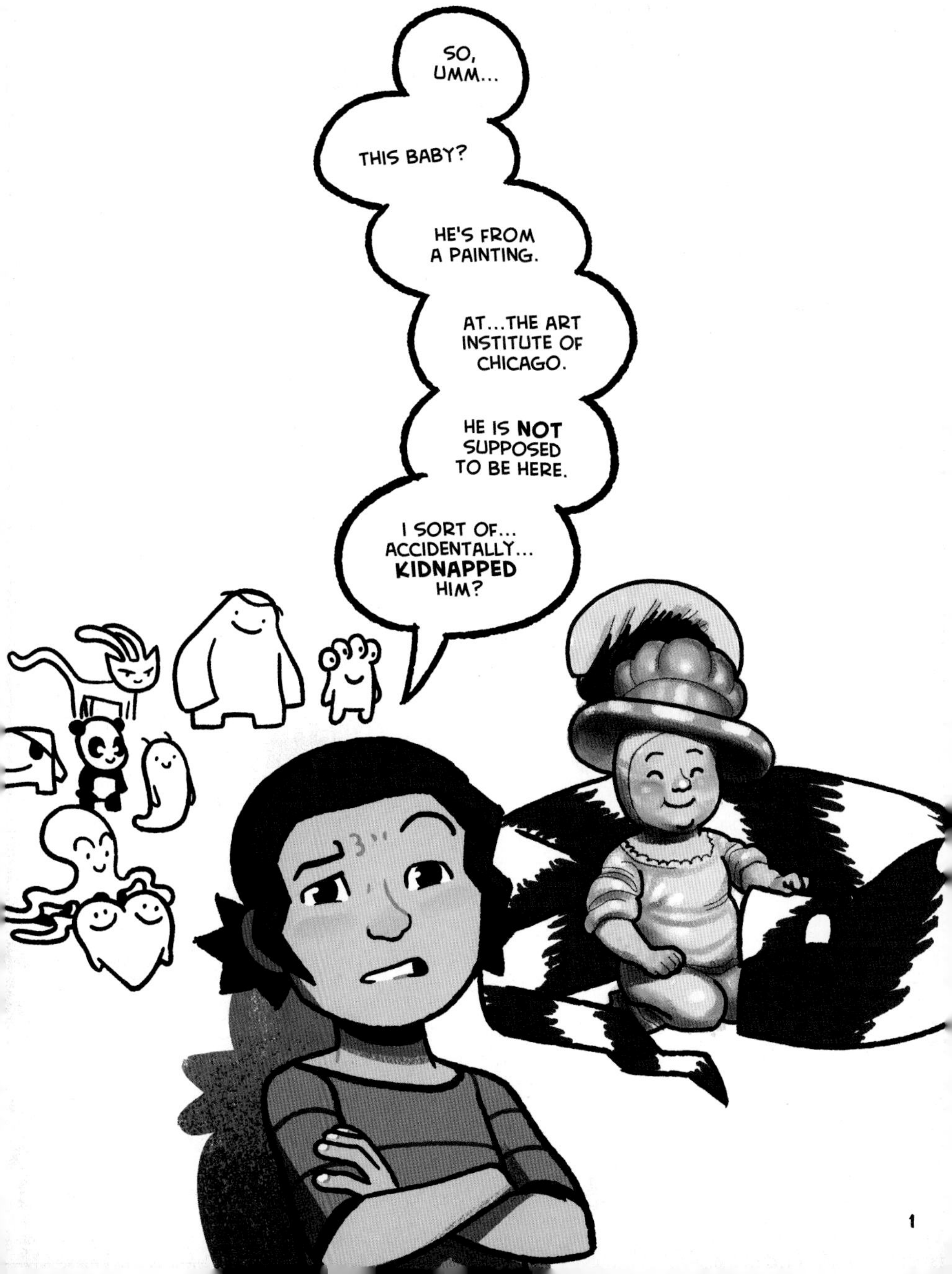
SO, UMM...
THIS BABY?
HE'S FROM A PAINTING.
AT...THE ART INSTITUTE OF CHICAGO.
HE IS NOT SUPPOSED TO BE HERE.
I SORT OF... ACCIDENTALLY... KIDNAPPED HIM?

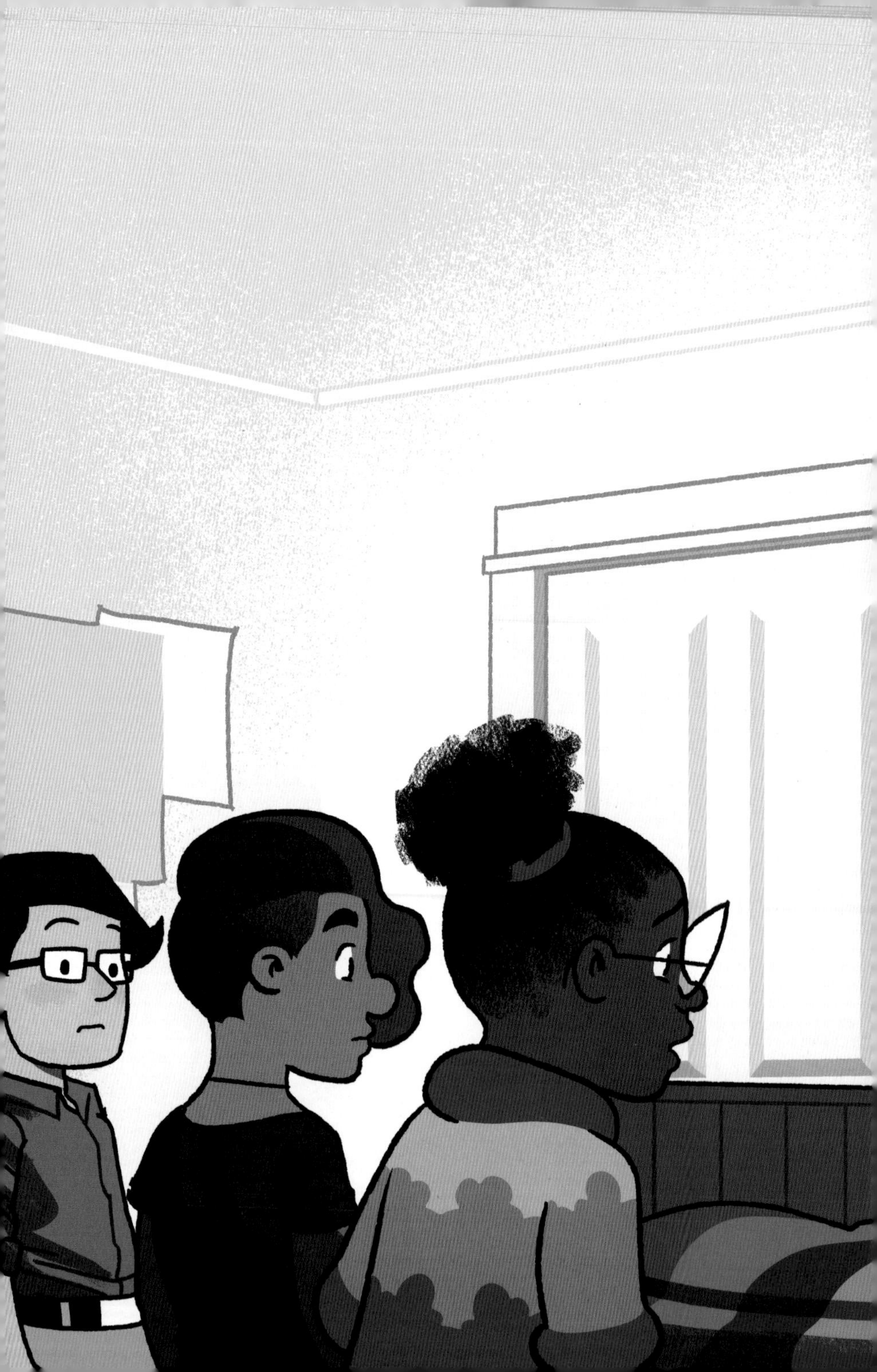

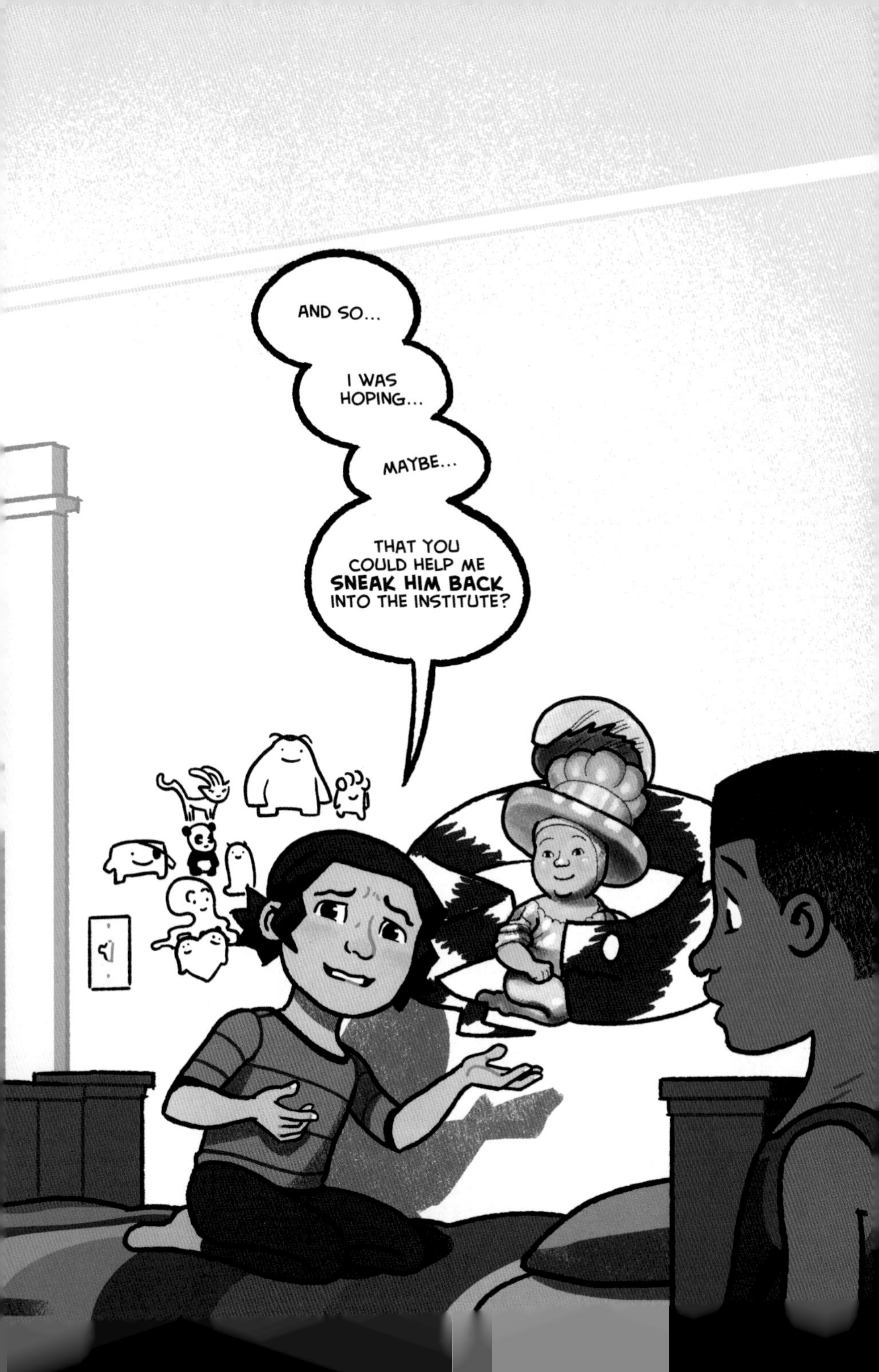
AND SO...
I WAS HOPING...
MAYBE...
THAT YOU COULD HELP ME **SNEAK HIM BACK** INTO THE INSTITUTE?

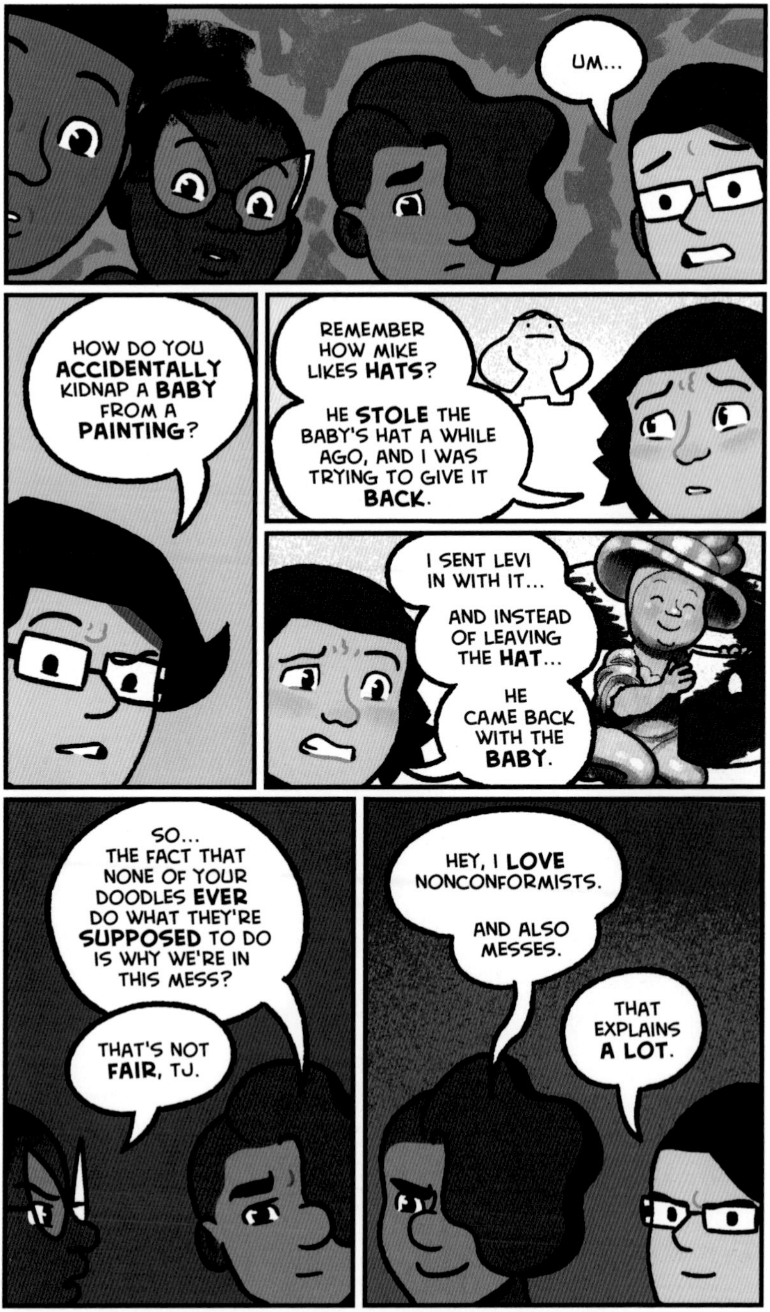
UM...
HOW DO YOU **ACCIDENTALLY** KIDNAP A **BABY** FROM A **PAINTING**?
REMEMBER HOW MIKE LIKES **HATS**?
HE **STOLE** THE BABY'S HAT A WHILE AGO, AND I WAS TRYING TO GIVE IT **BACK**.
I SENT LEVI IN WITH IT...
AND INSTEAD OF LEAVING THE **HAT**...
HE CAME BACK WITH THE **BABY**.
SO... THE FACT THAT NONE OF YOUR DOODLES **EVER** DO WHAT THEY'RE **SUPPOSED** TO DO IS WHY WE'RE IN THIS MESS?
THAT'S NOT **FAIR**, TJ.
HEY, I **LOVE** NONCONFORMISTS.
AND ALSO MESSES.
THAT EXPLAINS **A LOT**.

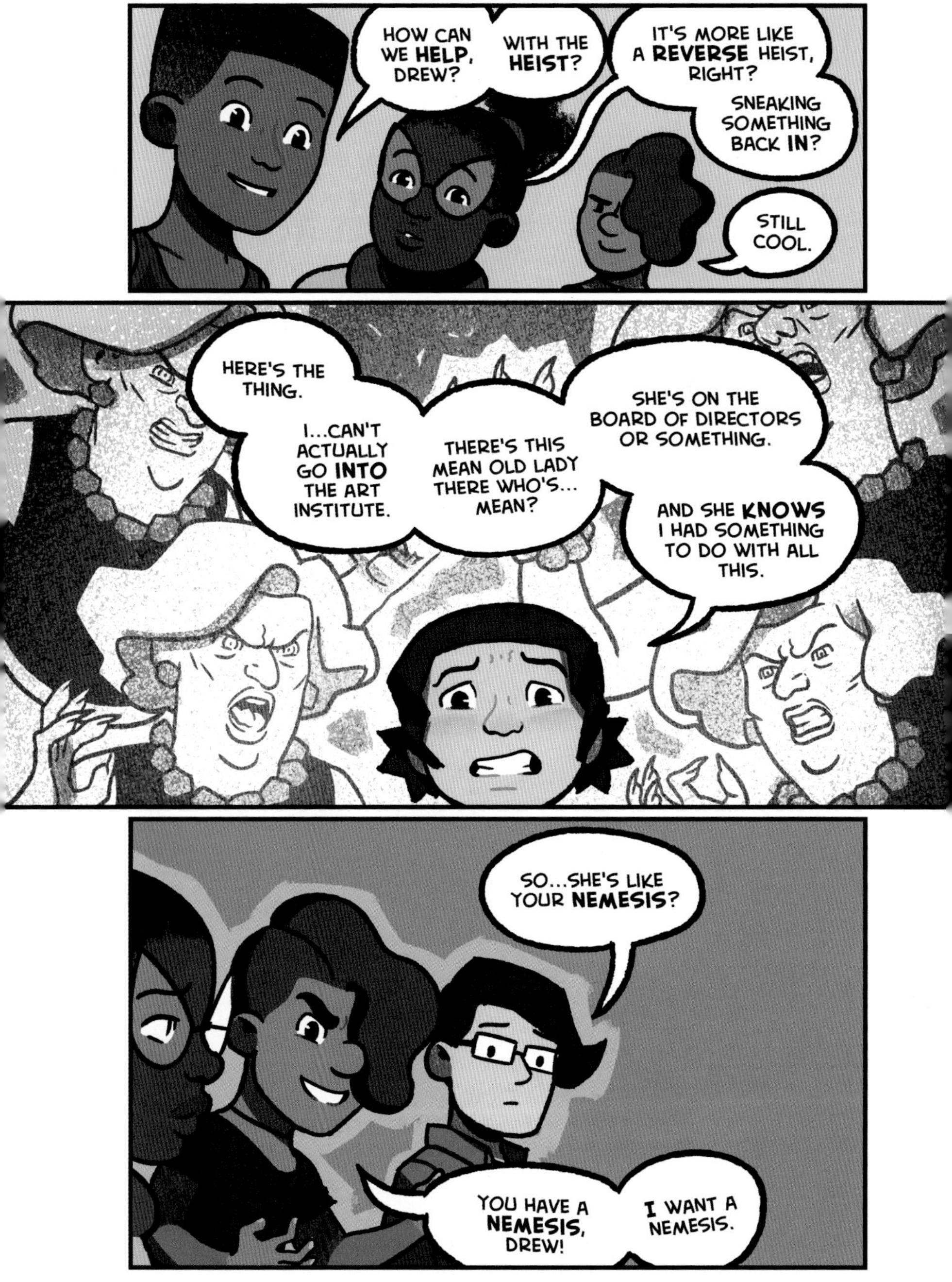
HOW CAN WE **HELP**, DREW?
WITH THE **HEIST**?
IT'S MORE LIKE A **REVERSE** HEIST, RIGHT?
SNEAKING SOMETHING BACK **IN**?
STILL COOL.
HERE'S THE THING.
I...CAN'T ACTUALLY GO **INTO** THE ART INSTITUTE.
THERE'S THIS MEAN OLD LADY THERE WHO'S... MEAN?
SHE'S ON THE BOARD OF DIRECTORS OR SOMETHING.
AND SHE **KNOWS** I HAD SOMETHING TO DO WITH ALL THIS.
SO...SHE'S LIKE YOUR **NEMESIS**?
YOU HAVE A **NEMESIS**, DREW!
I WANT A NEMESIS.

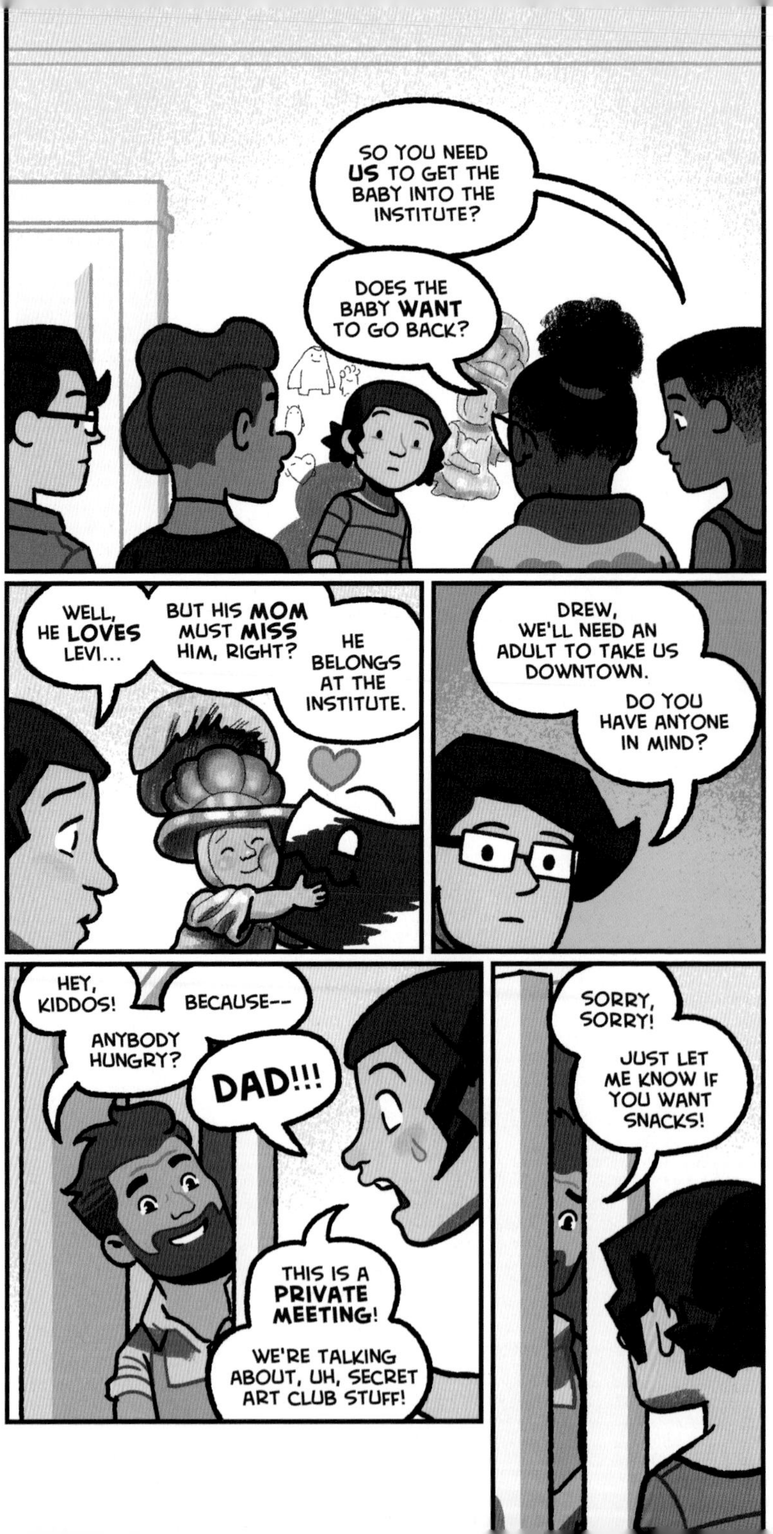
SO YOU NEED **US** TO GET THE BABY INTO THE INSTITUTE?
DOES THE BABY **WANT** TO GO BACK?
WELL, HE **LOVES** LEVI...
BUT HIS **MOM** MUST **MISS** HIM, RIGHT?
HE BELONGS AT THE INSTITUTE.
DREW, WE'LL NEED AN ADULT TO TAKE US DOWNTOWN.
DO YOU HAVE ANYONE IN MIND?
HEY, KIDDOS!
BECAUSE--
ANYBODY HUNGRY?
DAD!!!
THIS IS A **PRIVATE MEETING**!
WE'RE TALKING ABOUT, UH, SECRET ART CLUB STUFF!
SORRY, SORRY!
JUST LET ME KNOW IF YOU WANT SNACKS!

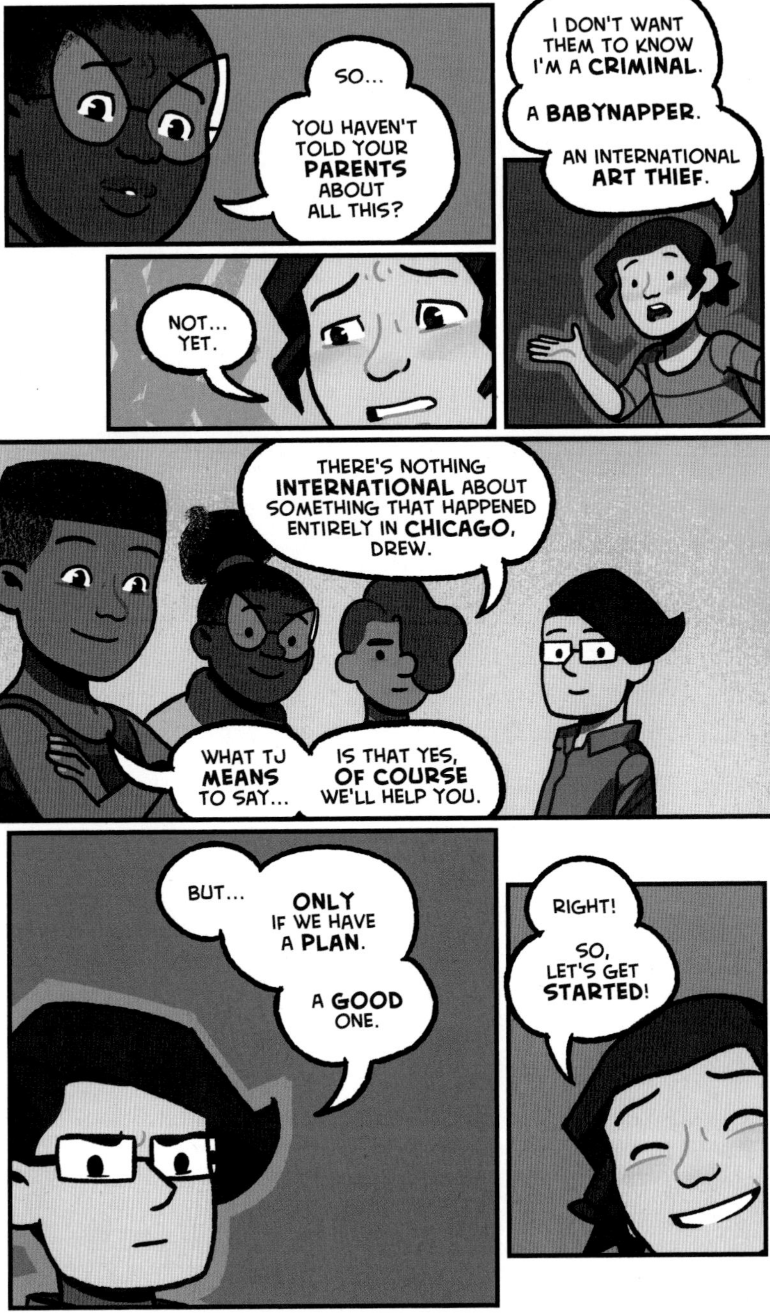
SO...
YOU HAVEN'T TOLD YOUR PARENTS ABOUT ALL THIS?
NOT... YET.
I DON'T WANT THEM TO KNOW I'M A CRIMINAL.
A BABYNAPPER.
AN INTERNATIONAL ART THIEF.
THERE'S NOTHING INTERNATIONAL ABOUT SOMETHING THAT HAPPENED ENTIRELY IN CHICAGO, DREW.
WHAT TJ MEANS TO SAY...
IS THAT YES, OF COURSE WE'LL HELP YOU.
BUT...
ONLY IF WE HAVE A PLAN.
A GOOD ONE.
RIGHT!
SO, LET'S GET STARTED!

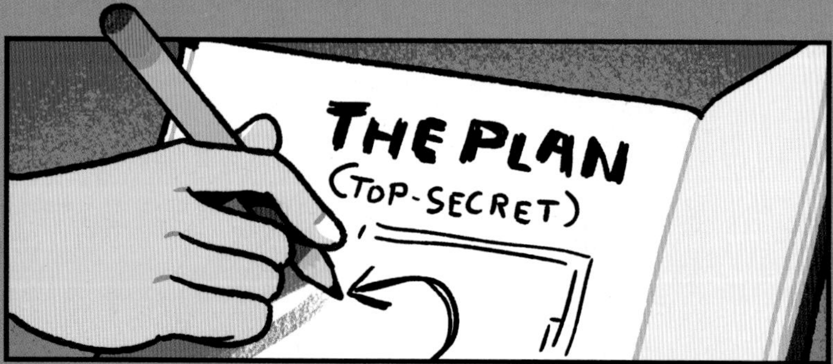
THE PLAN
(TOP-SECRET)

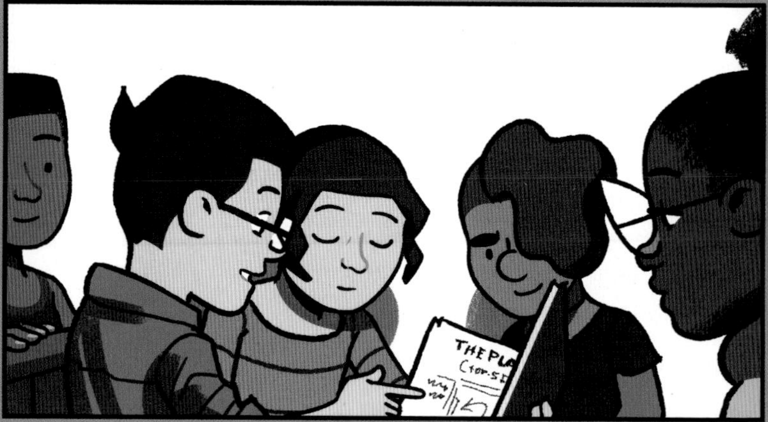
THE PLA
(TOP-SE

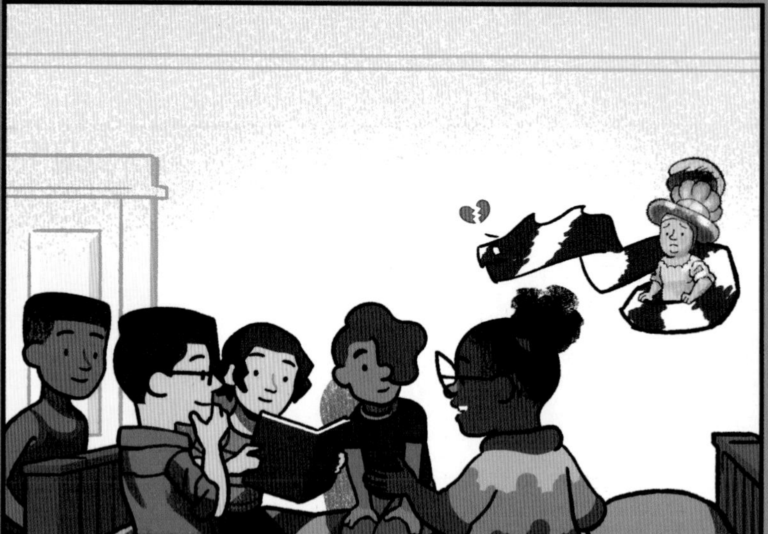

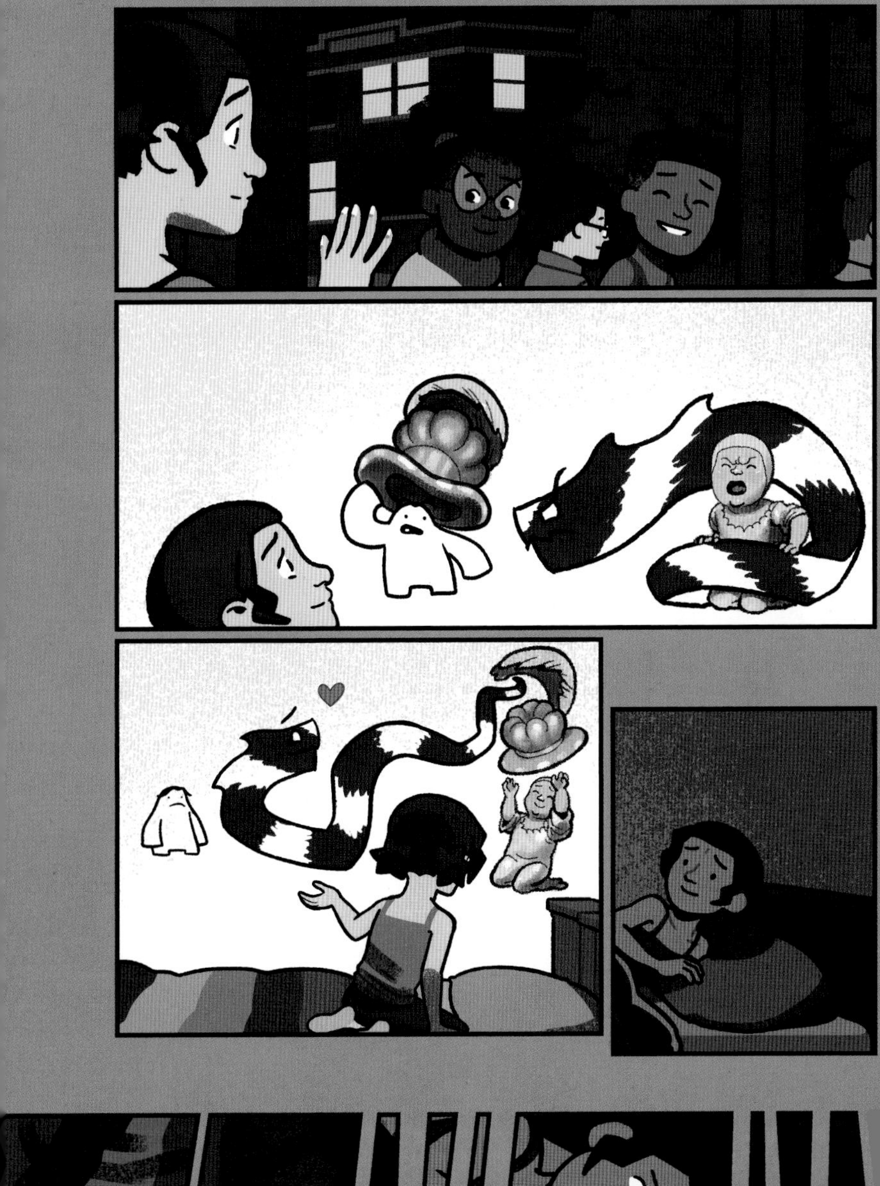

CHAPTER 1: SECRET ART CLUB STUFF

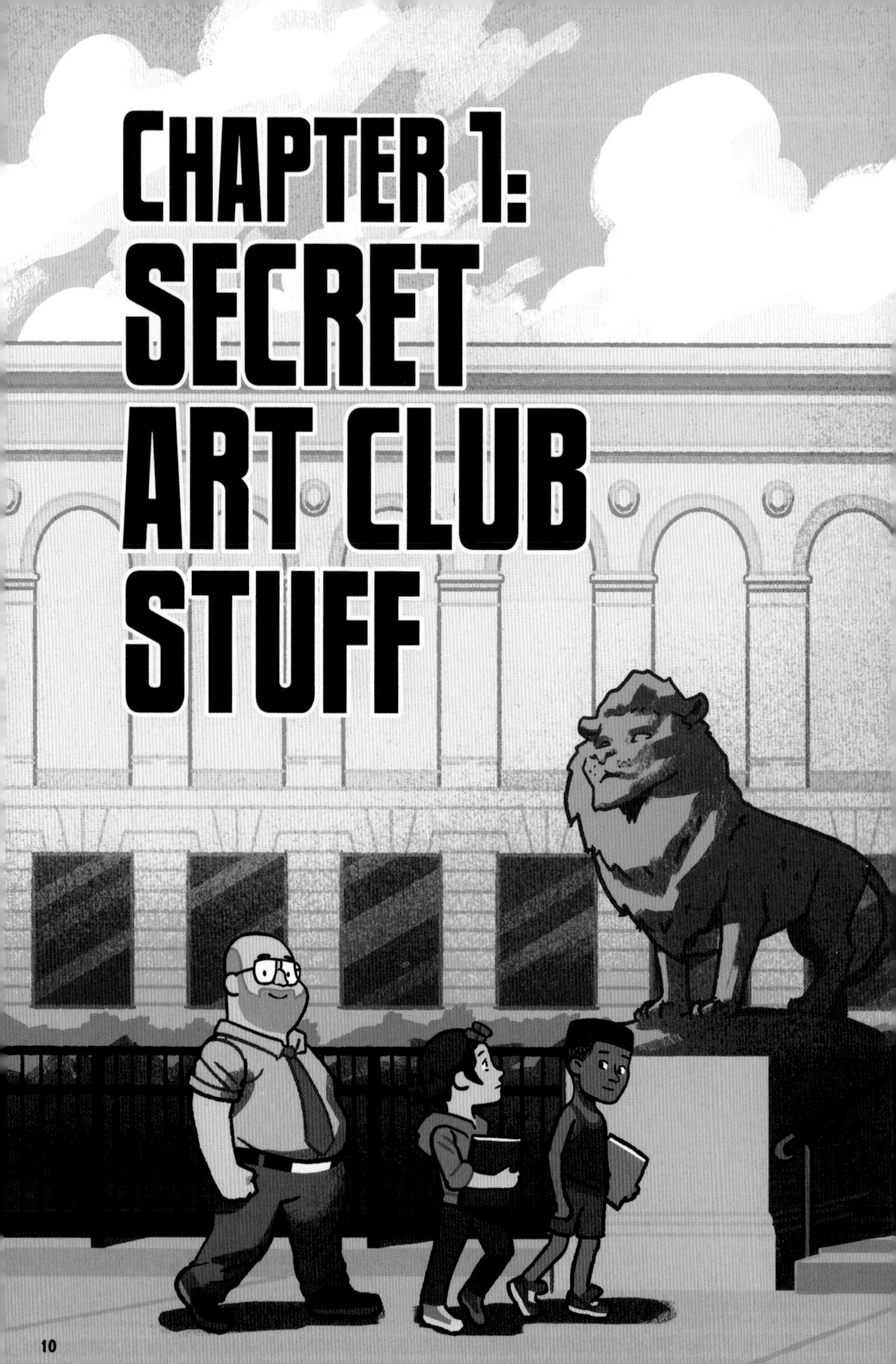

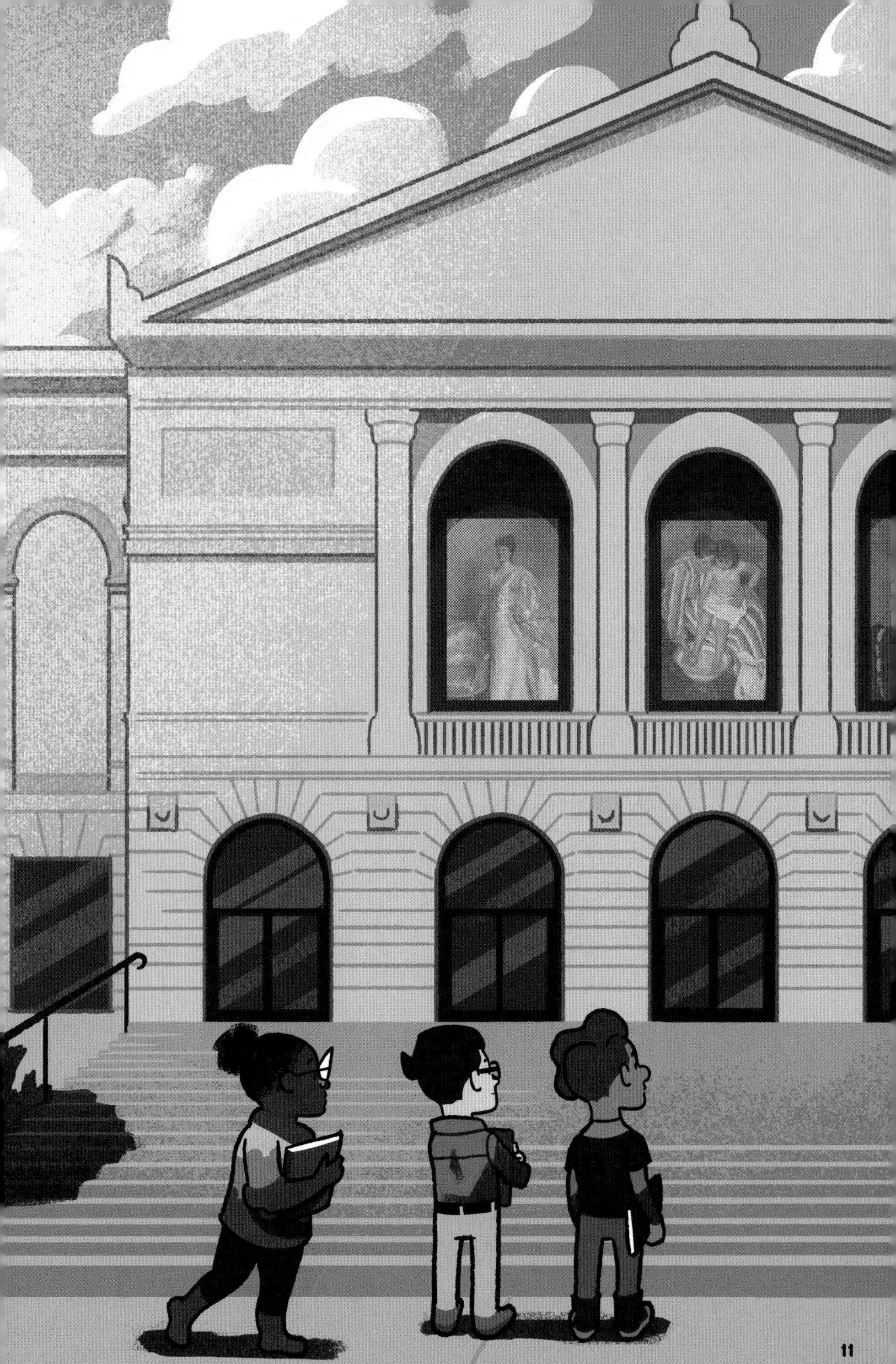

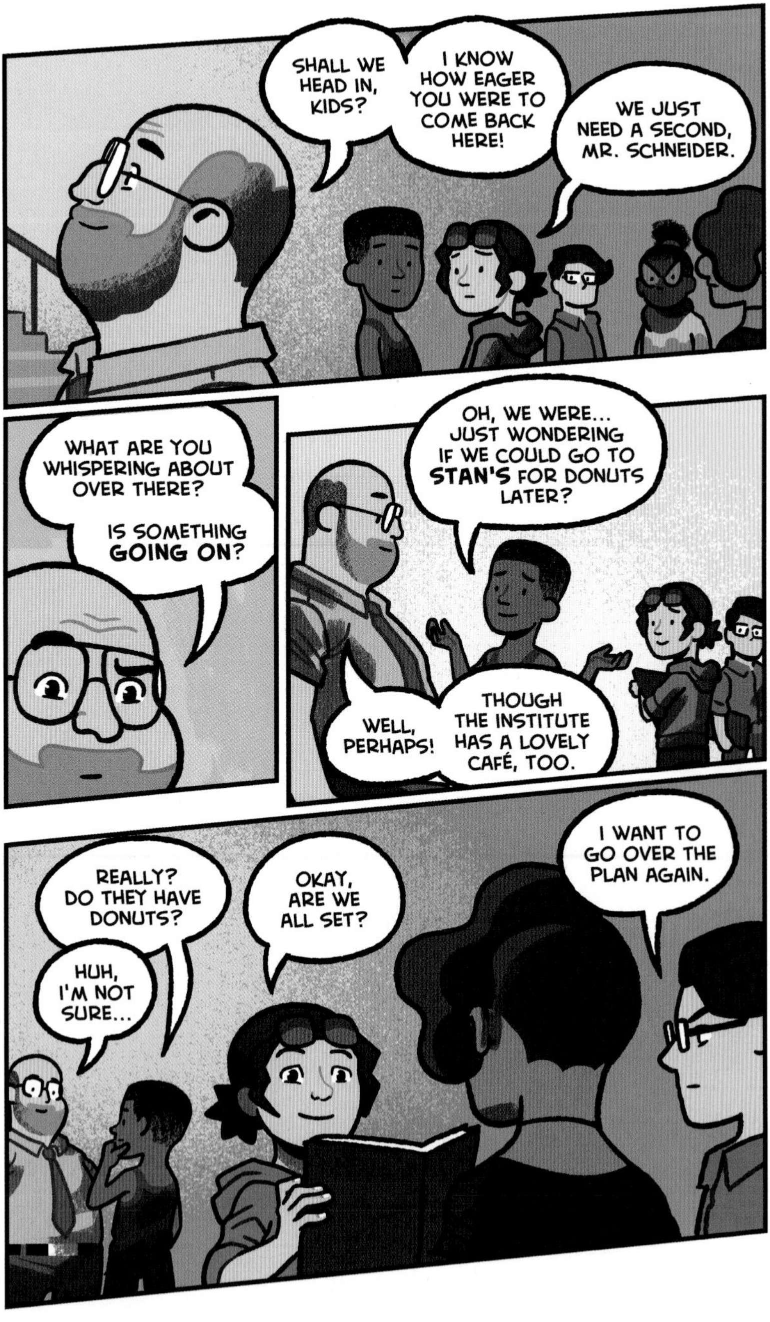
SHALL WE HEAD IN, KIDS?
I KNOW HOW EAGER YOU WERE TO COME BACK HERE!
WE JUST NEED A SECOND, MR. SCHNEIDER.
WHAT ARE YOU WHISPERING ABOUT OVER THERE?
IS SOMETHING GOING ON?
OH, WE WERE... JUST WONDERING IF WE COULD GO TO STAN'S FOR DONUTS LATER?
WELL, PERHAPS!
THOUGH THE INSTITUTE HAS A LOVELY CAFÉ, TOO.
REALLY? DO THEY HAVE DONUTS?
HUH, I'M NOT SURE...
OKAY, ARE WE ALL SET?
I WANT TO GO OVER THE PLAN AGAIN.

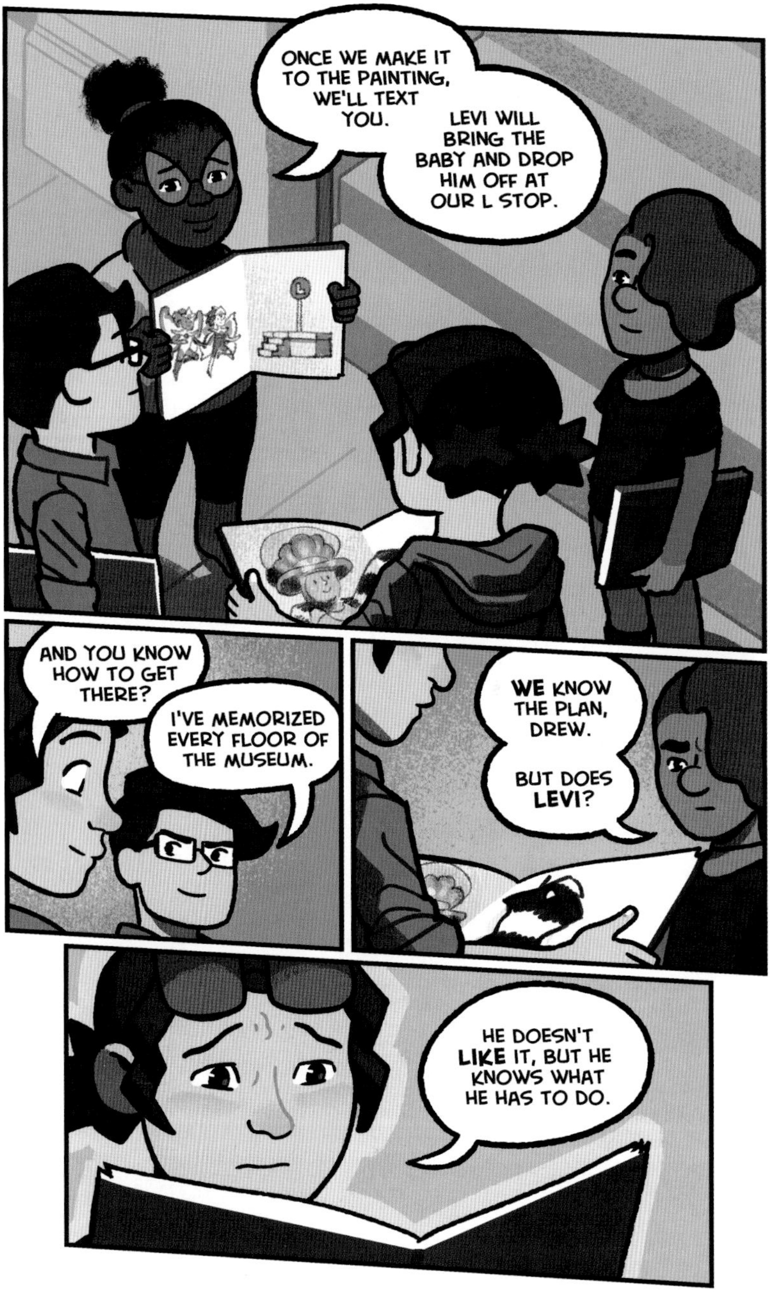
ONCE WE MAKE IT TO THE PAINTING, WE'LL TEXT YOU.
LEVI WILL BRING THE BABY AND DROP HIM OFF AT OUR L STOP.
AND YOU KNOW HOW TO GET THERE?
I'VE MEMORIZED EVERY FLOOR OF THE MUSEUM.
WE KNOW THE PLAN, DREW.
BUT DOES **LEVI**?
HE DOESN'T **LIKE** IT, BUT HE KNOWS WHAT HE HAS TO DO.

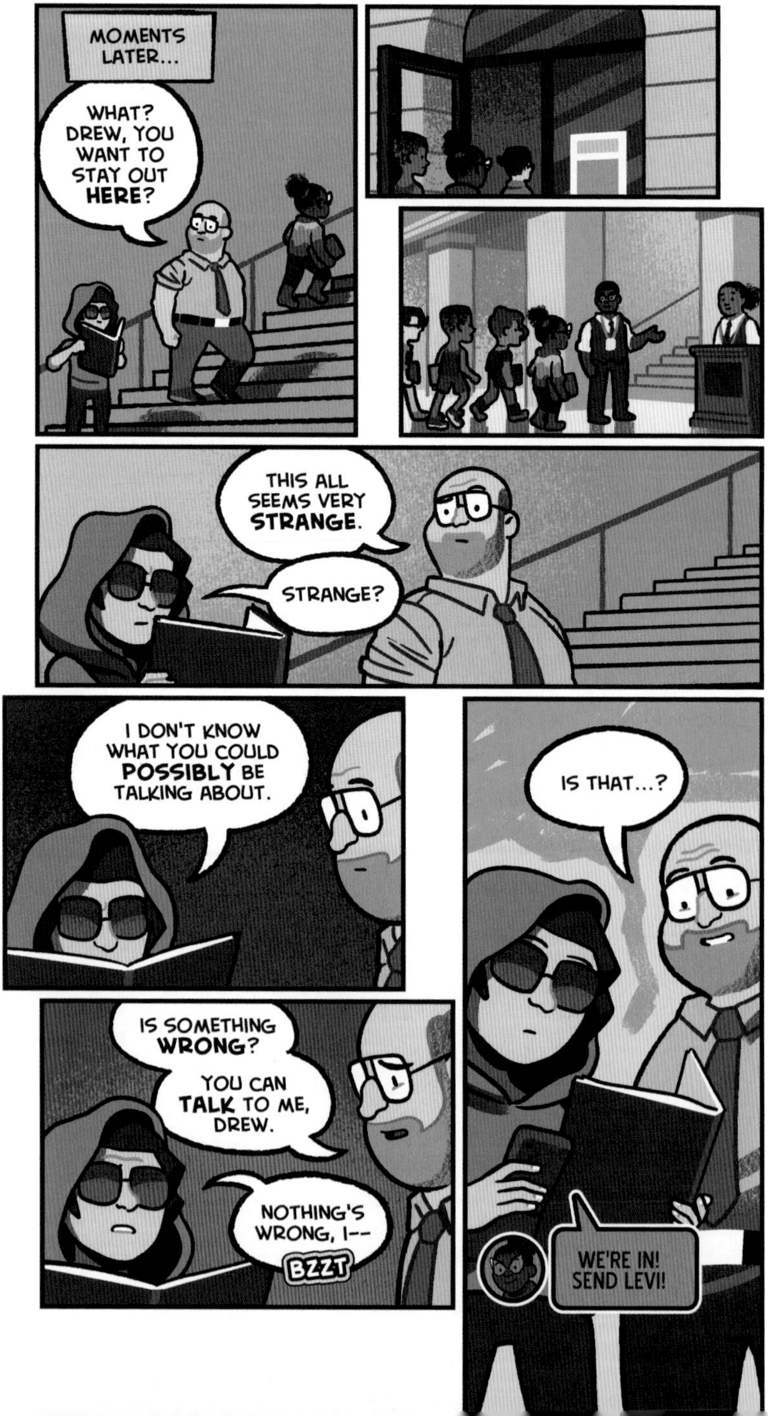
MOMENTS LATER...
WHAT? DREW, YOU WANT TO STAY OUT **HERE**?
THIS ALL SEEMS VERY **STRANGE**.
STRANGE?
I DON'T KNOW WHAT YOU COULD **POSSIBLY** BE TALKING ABOUT.
IS SOMETHING **WRONG**?
YOU CAN **TALK** TO ME, DREW.
NOTHING'S WRONG, I--
BZZT
IS THAT...?
WE'RE IN! SEND LEVI!

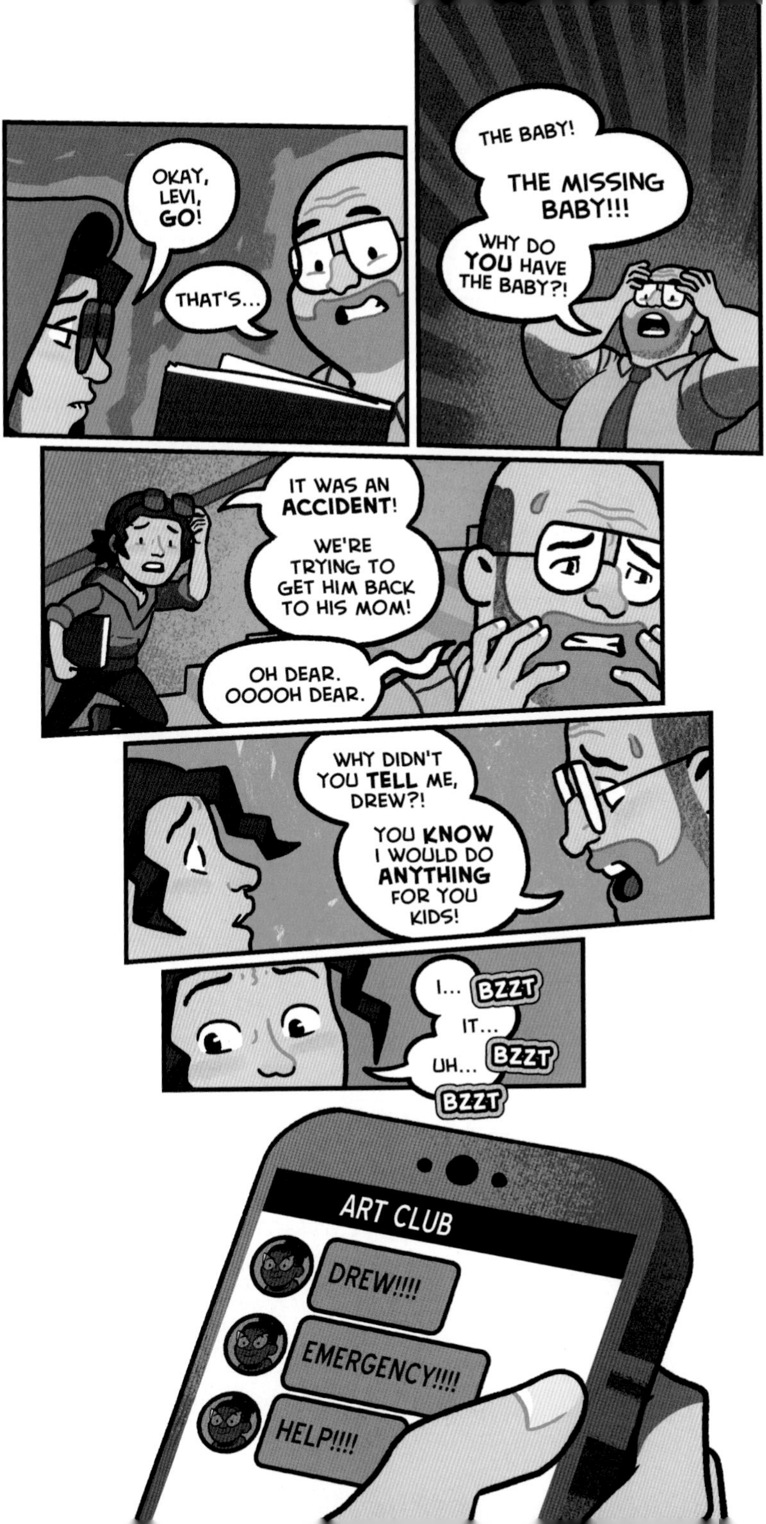
OKAY, LEVI, GO!
THAT'S...
THE BABY!
THE MISSING BABY!!!
WHY DO YOU HAVE THE BABY?!
IT WAS AN ACCIDENT!
WE'RE TRYING TO GET HIM BACK TO HIS MOM!
OH DEAR. OOOOH DEAR.
WHY DIDN'T YOU TELL ME, DREW?!
YOU KNOW I WOULD DO ANYTHING FOR YOU KIDS!
I... BZZT
IT...
UH... BZZT
BZZT
ART CLUB
DREW!!!!
EMERGENCY!!!!
HELP!!!!

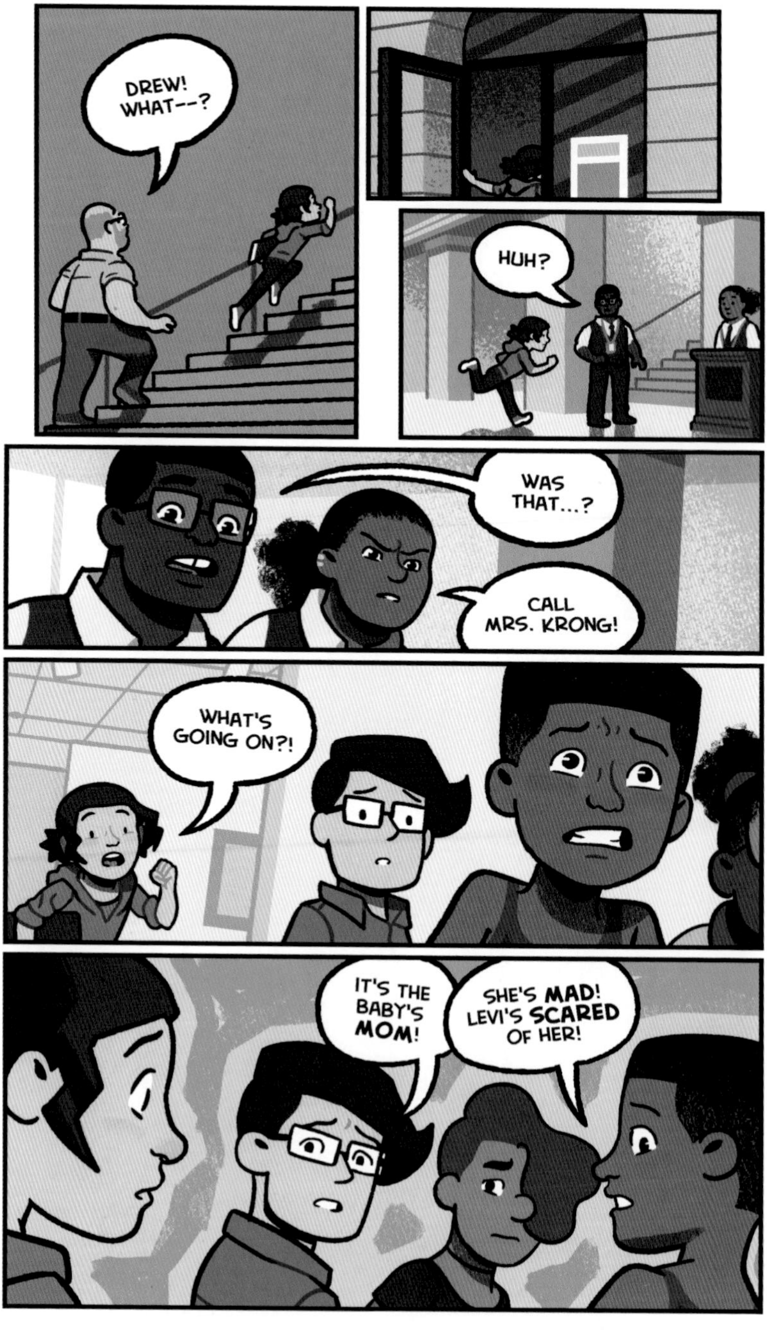
DREW! WHAT--?
HUH?
WAS THAT...?
CALL MRS. KRONG!
WHAT'S GOING ON?!
IT'S THE BABY'S **MOM**!
SHE'S **MAD**! LEVI'S **SCARED** OF HER!

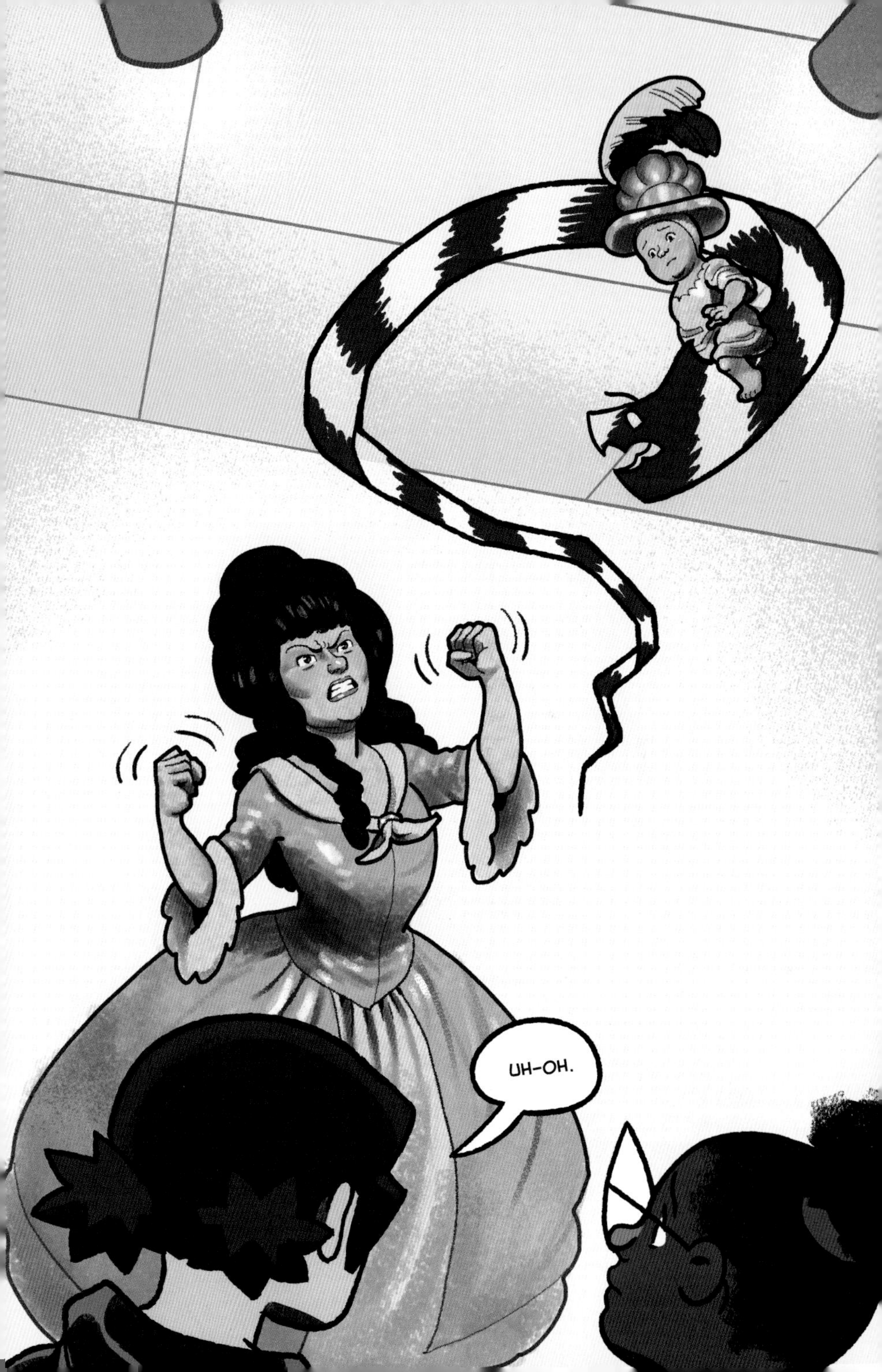
UH-OH.

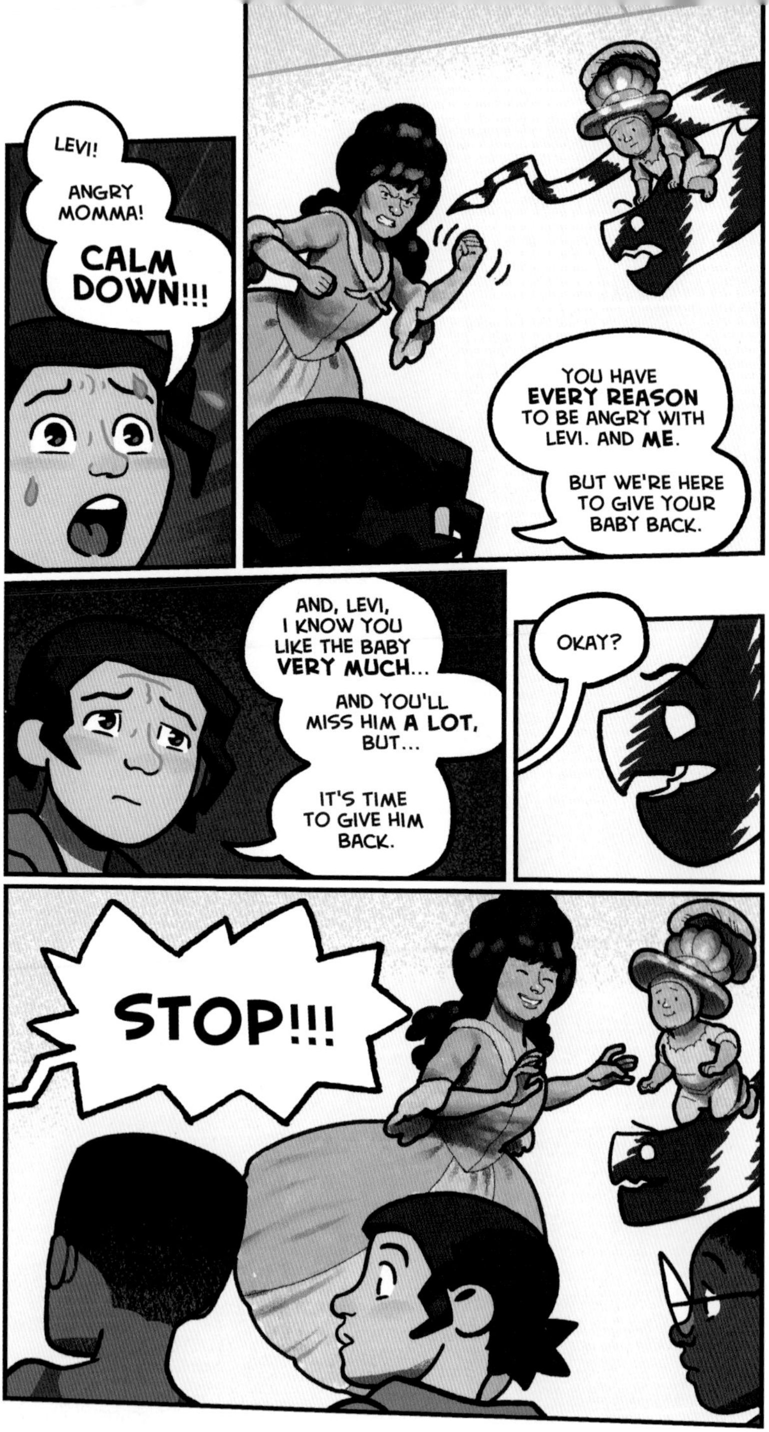
LEVI!
ANGRY MOMMA!
CALM DOWN!!!
YOU HAVE EVERY REASON TO BE ANGRY WITH LEVI. AND ME.
BUT WE'RE HERE TO GIVE YOUR BABY BACK.
AND, LEVI, I KNOW YOU LIKE THE BABY VERY MUCH...
AND YOU'LL MISS HIM A LOT, BUT...
IT'S TIME TO GIVE HIM BACK.
OKAY?
STOP!!!

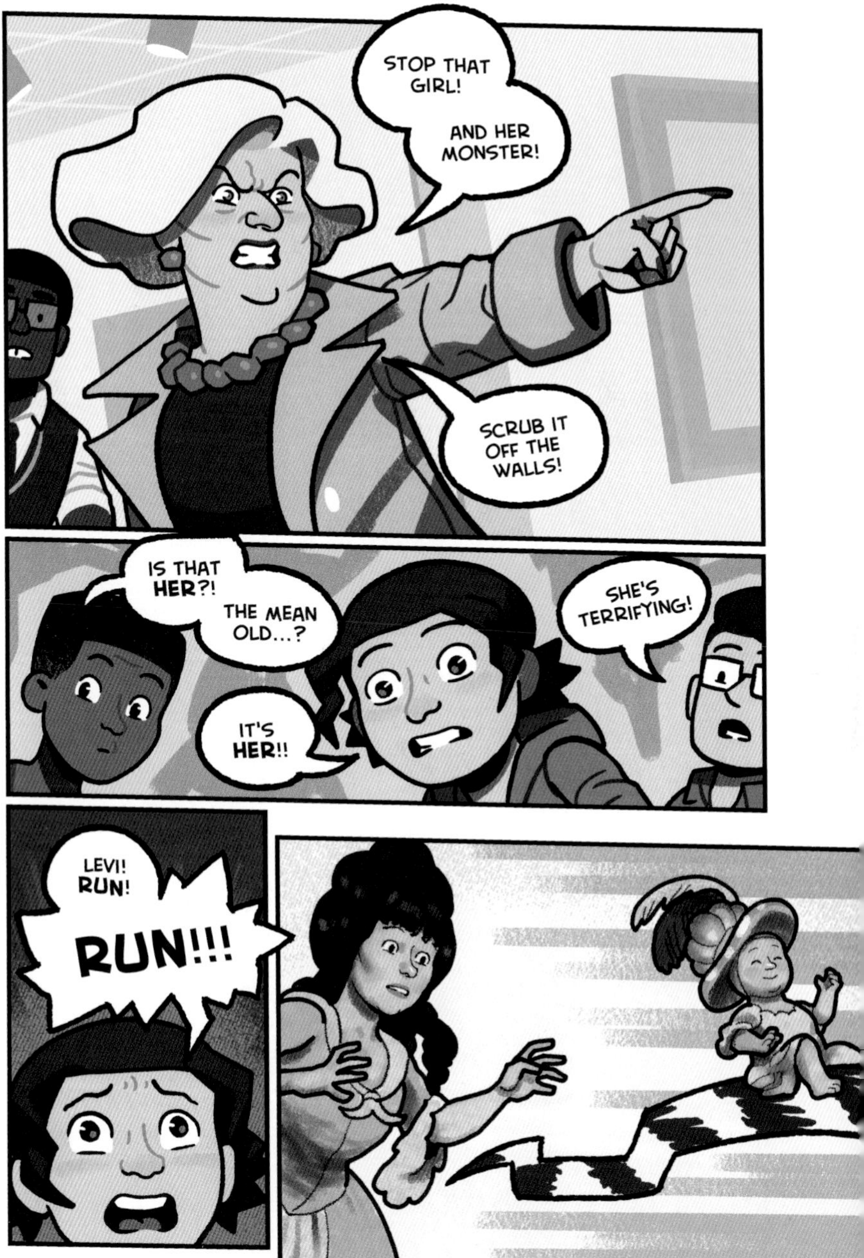
STOP THAT GIRL!
AND HER MONSTER!
SCRUB IT OFF THE WALLS!
IS THAT HER?!
THE MEAN OLD...?
IT'S HER!!
SHE'S TERRIFYING!
LEVI! RUN!
RUN!!!

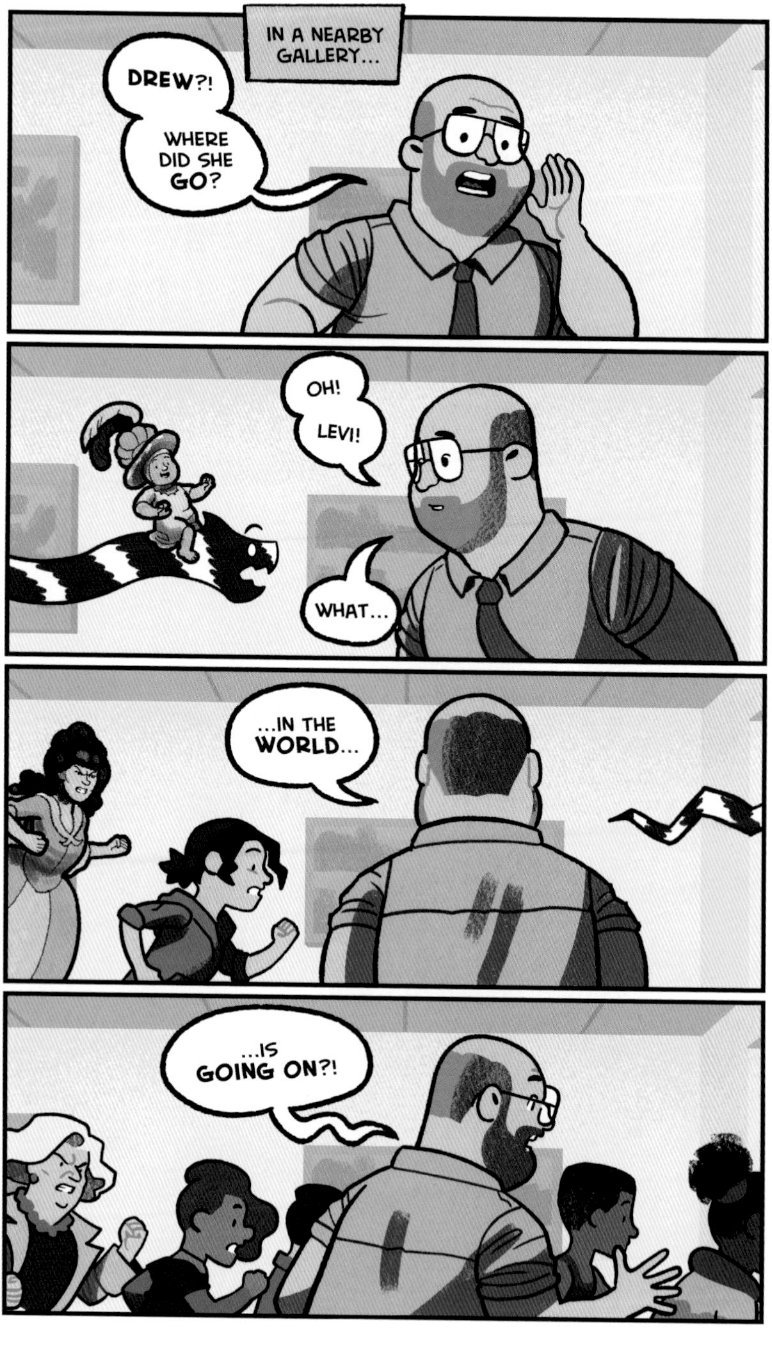
IN A NEARBY GALLERY...
DREW?!
WHERE DID SHE GO?
OH!
LEVI!
WHAT...
...IN THE WORLD...
...IS GOING ON?!

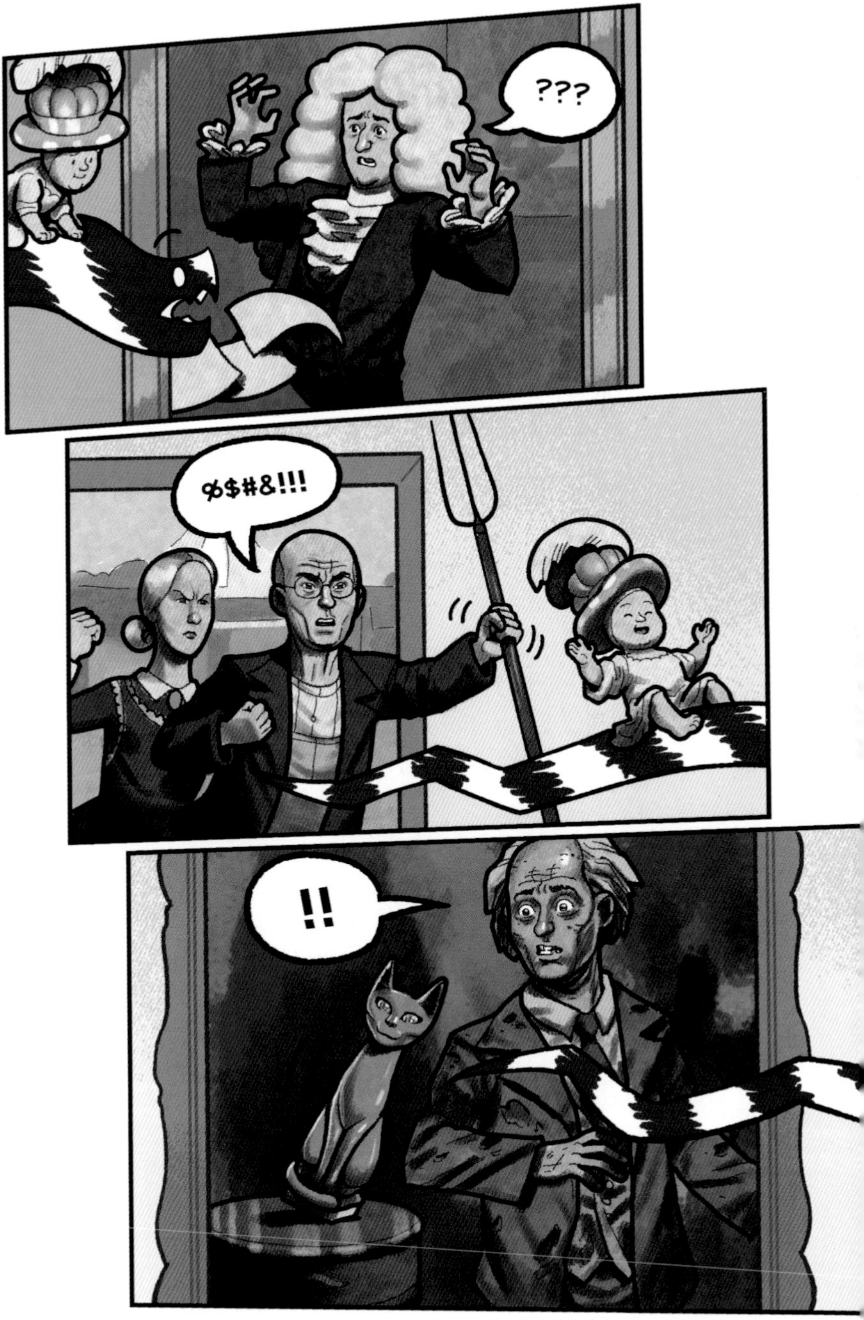
???
%$#&!!!
!!

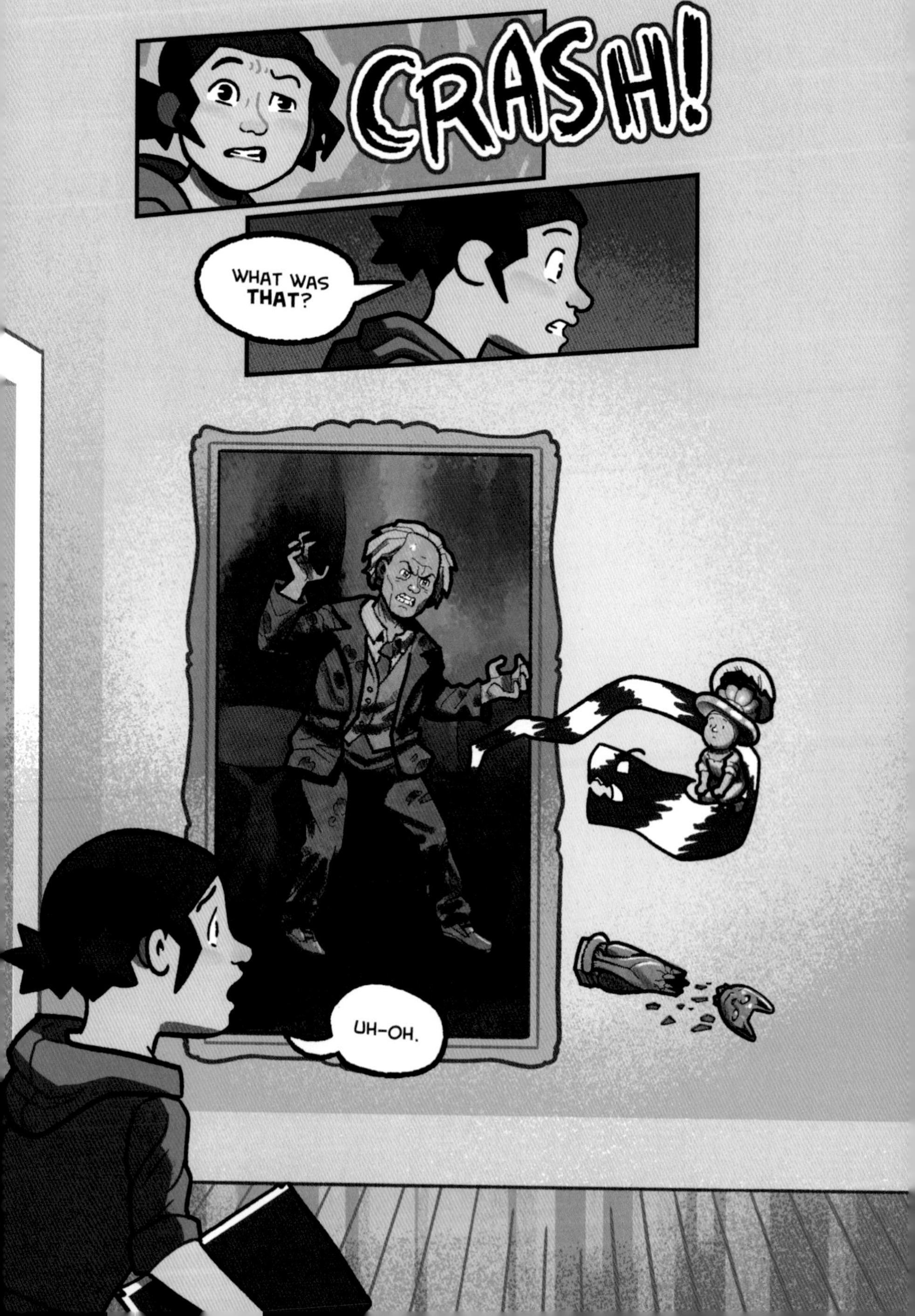

CRASH!
WHAT WAS THAT?
UH-OH.

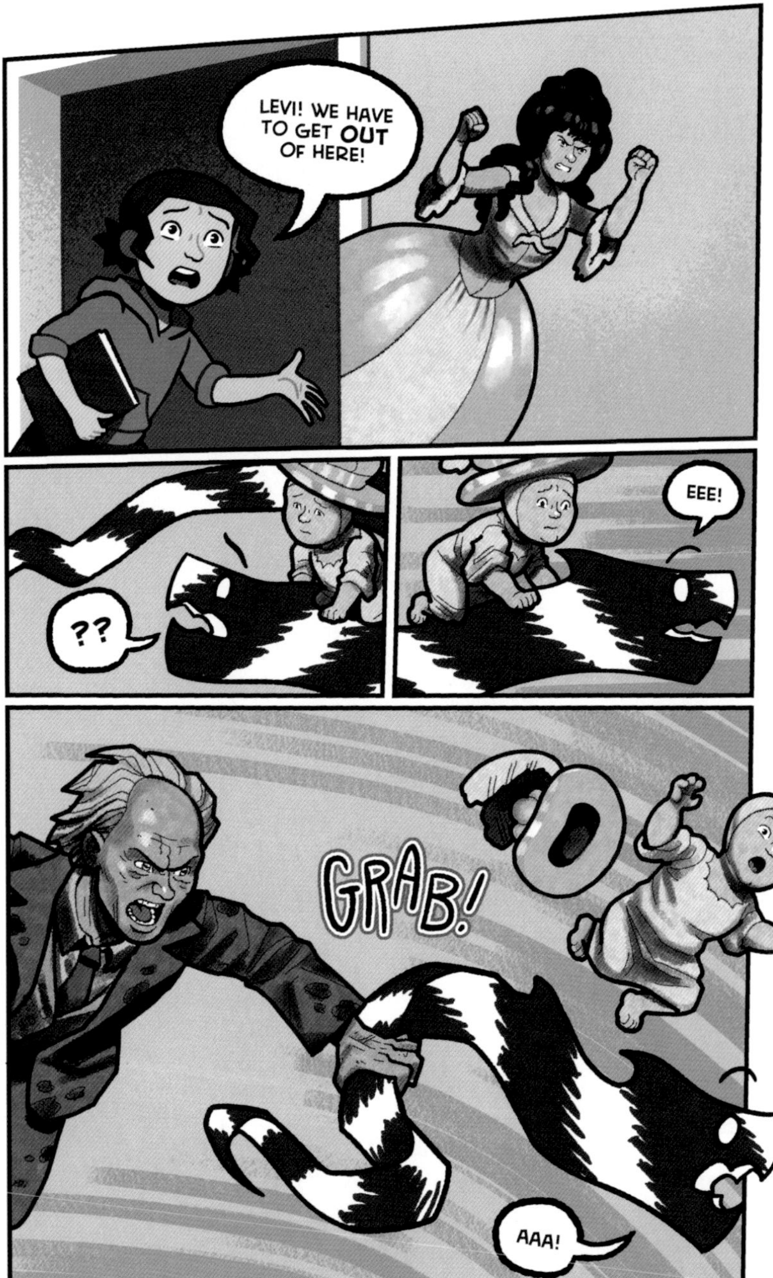
LEVI! WE HAVE TO GET OUT OF HERE!
??
EEE!
GRAB!
AAA!

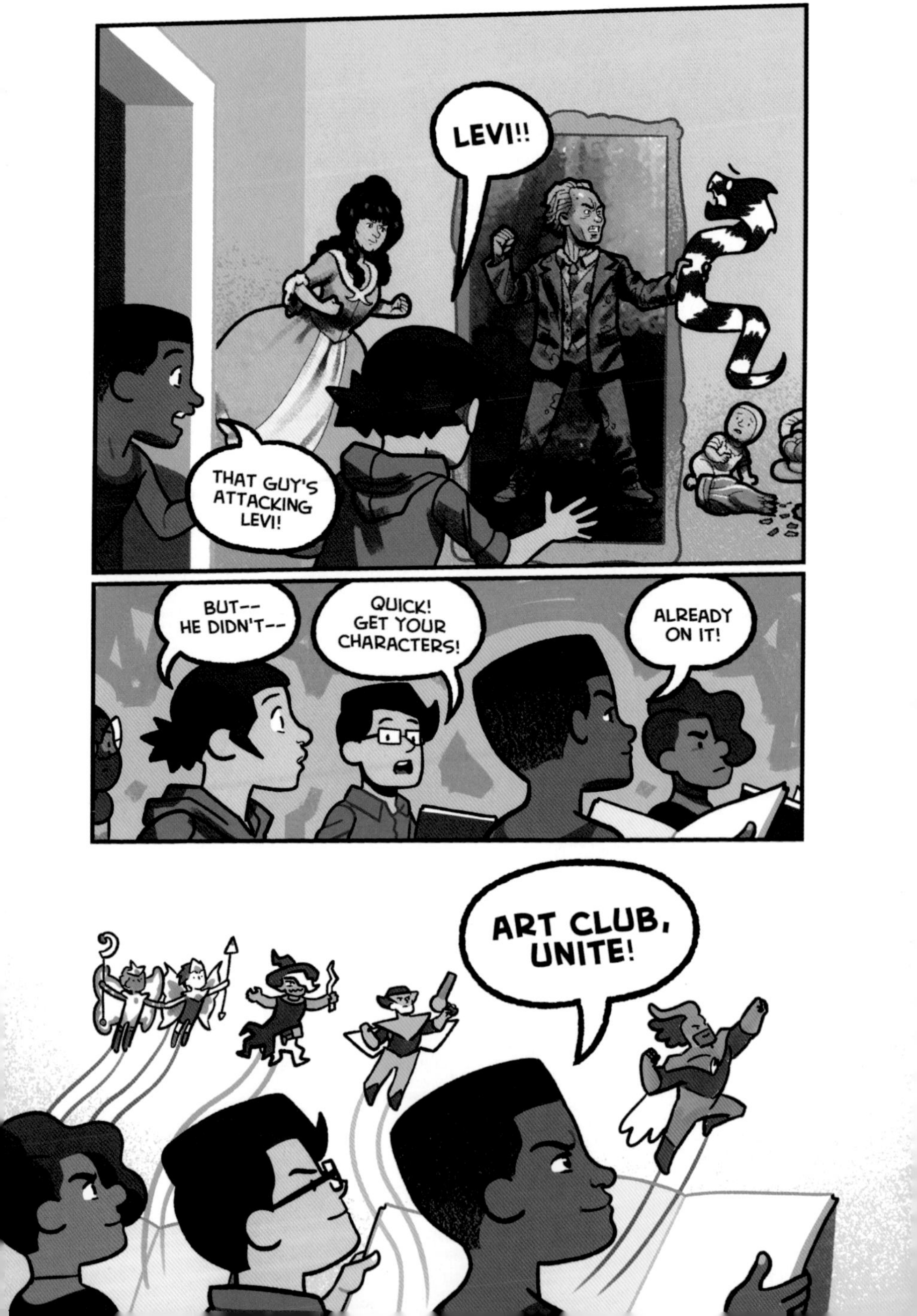
LEVI!!
THAT GUY'S ATTACKING LEVI!
BUT-- HE DIDN'T--
QUICK! GET YOUR CHARACTERS!
ALREADY ON IT!
ART CLUB, UNITE!

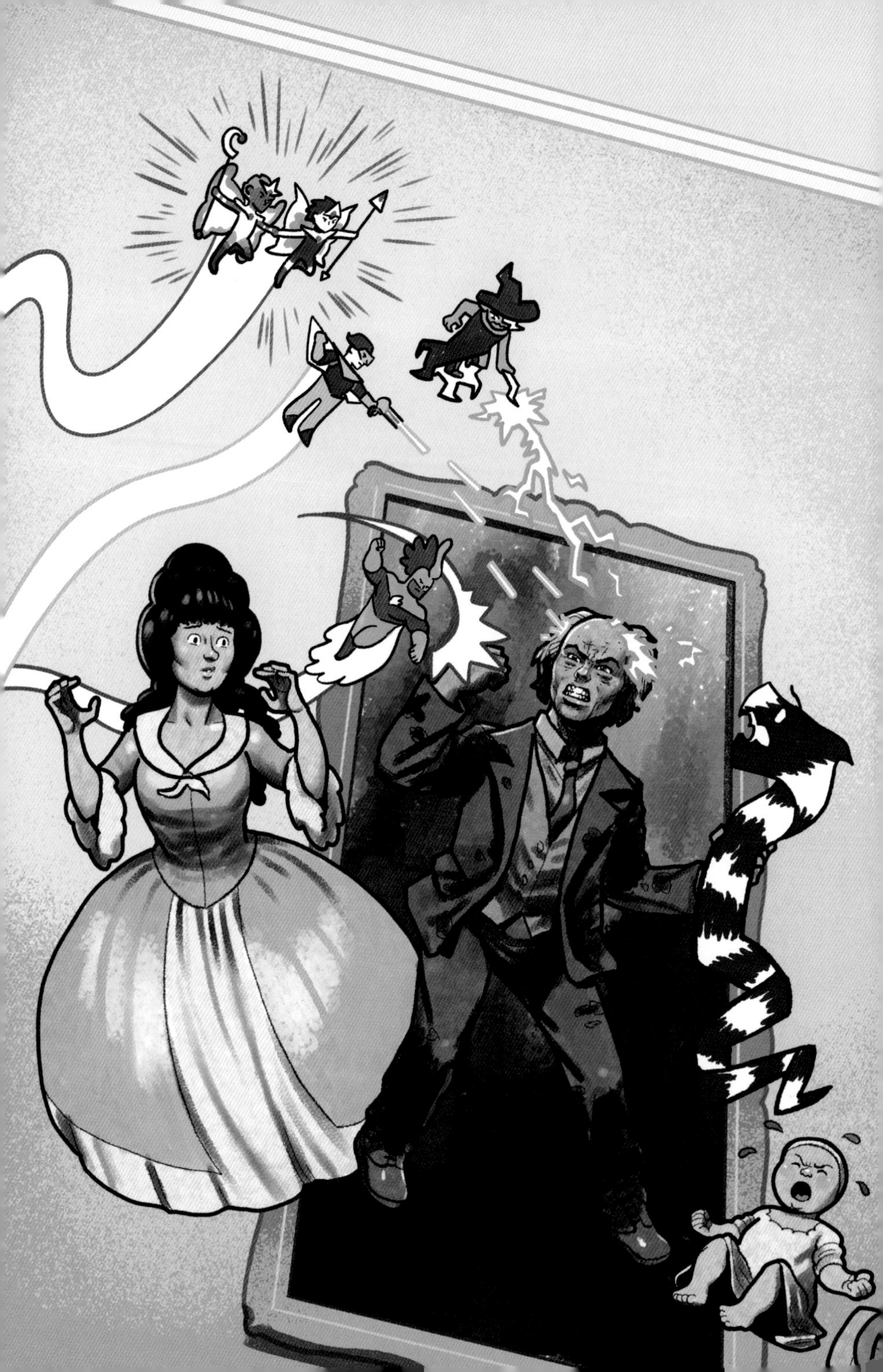

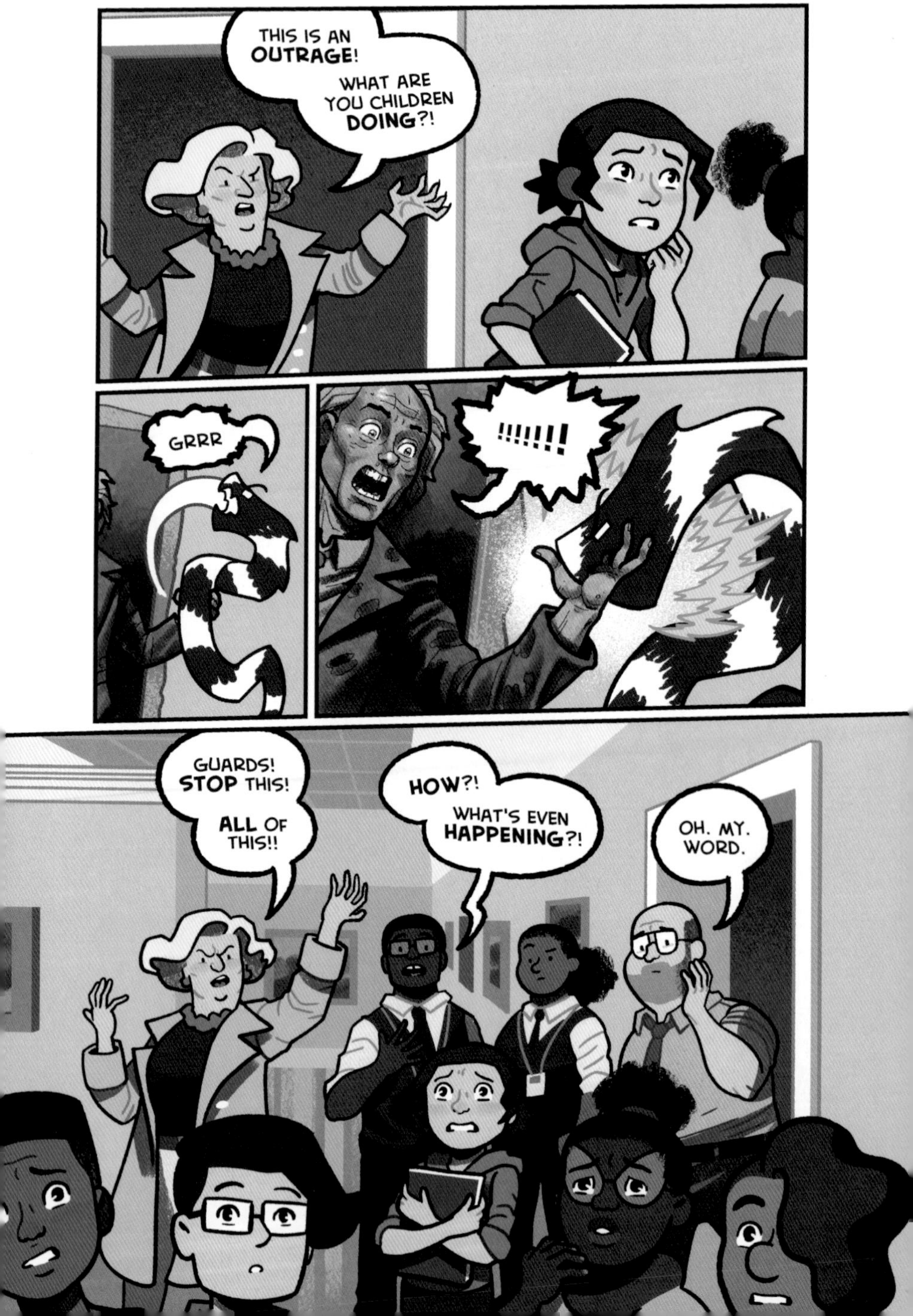
THIS IS AN **OUTRAGE**!
WHAT ARE YOU CHILDREN **DOING**?!
GRRR
!!!!!!!
GUARDS! **STOP** THIS!
ALL OF THIS!!
HOW?!
WHAT'S EVEN **HAPPENING**?!
OH. MY. WORD.

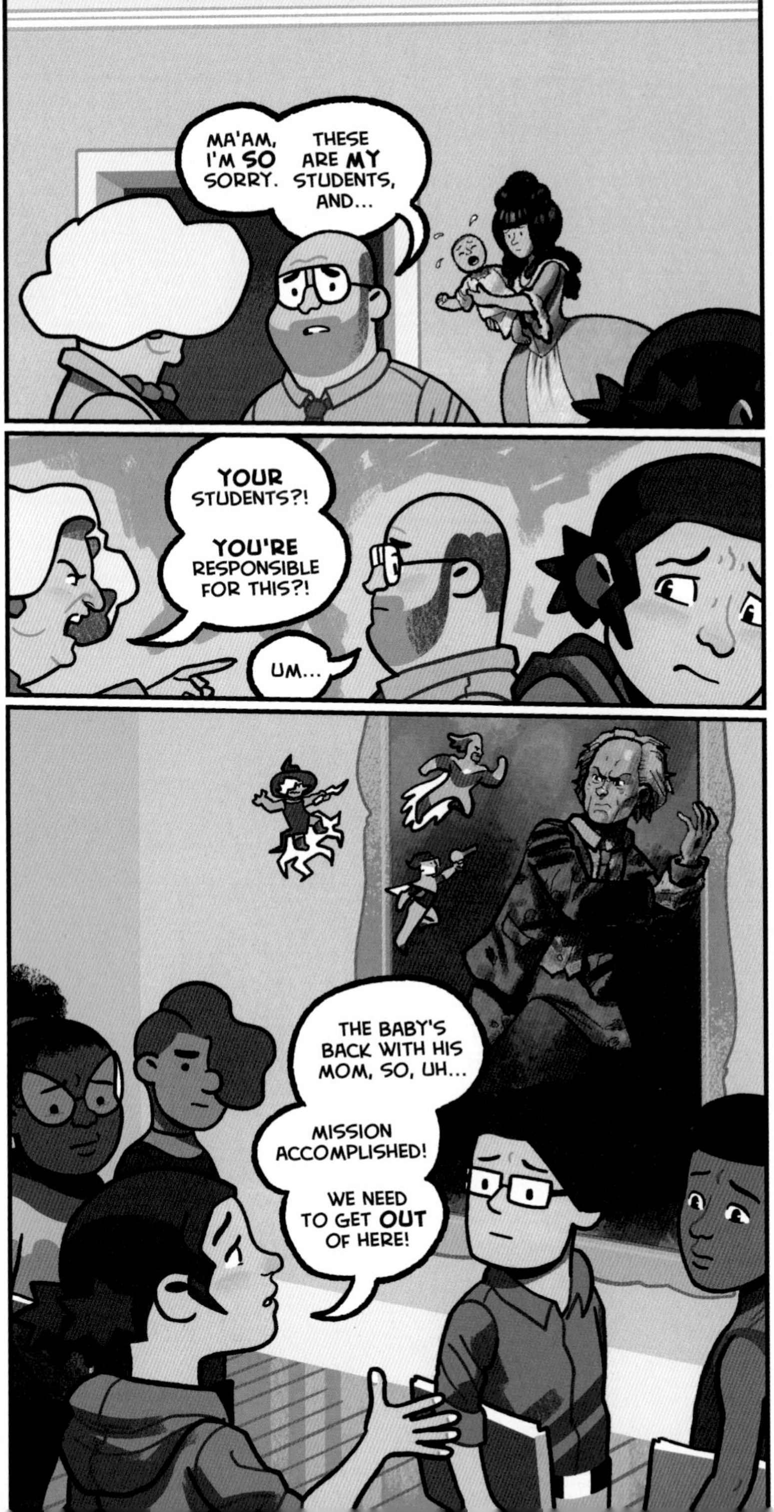
MA'AM, I'M SO SORRY.
THESE ARE MY STUDENTS, AND...
YOUR STUDENTS?!
YOU'RE RESPONSIBLE FOR THIS?!
UM...
THE BABY'S BACK WITH HIS MOM, SO, UH...
MISSION ACCOMPLISHED!
WE NEED TO GET OUT OF HERE!

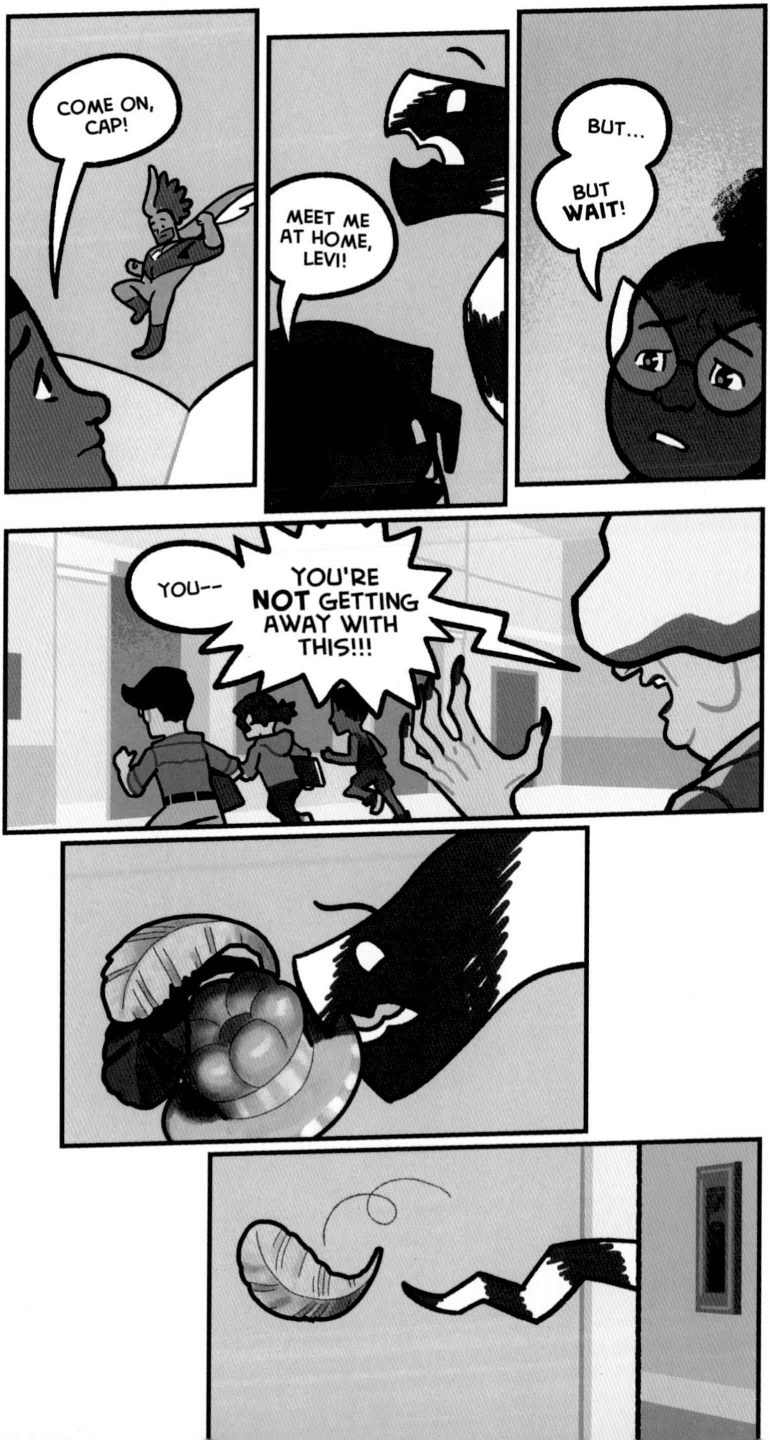
COME ON, CAP!
MEET ME AT HOME, LEVI!
BUT...
BUT WAIT!
YOU--
YOU'RE NOT GETTING AWAY WITH THIS!!!

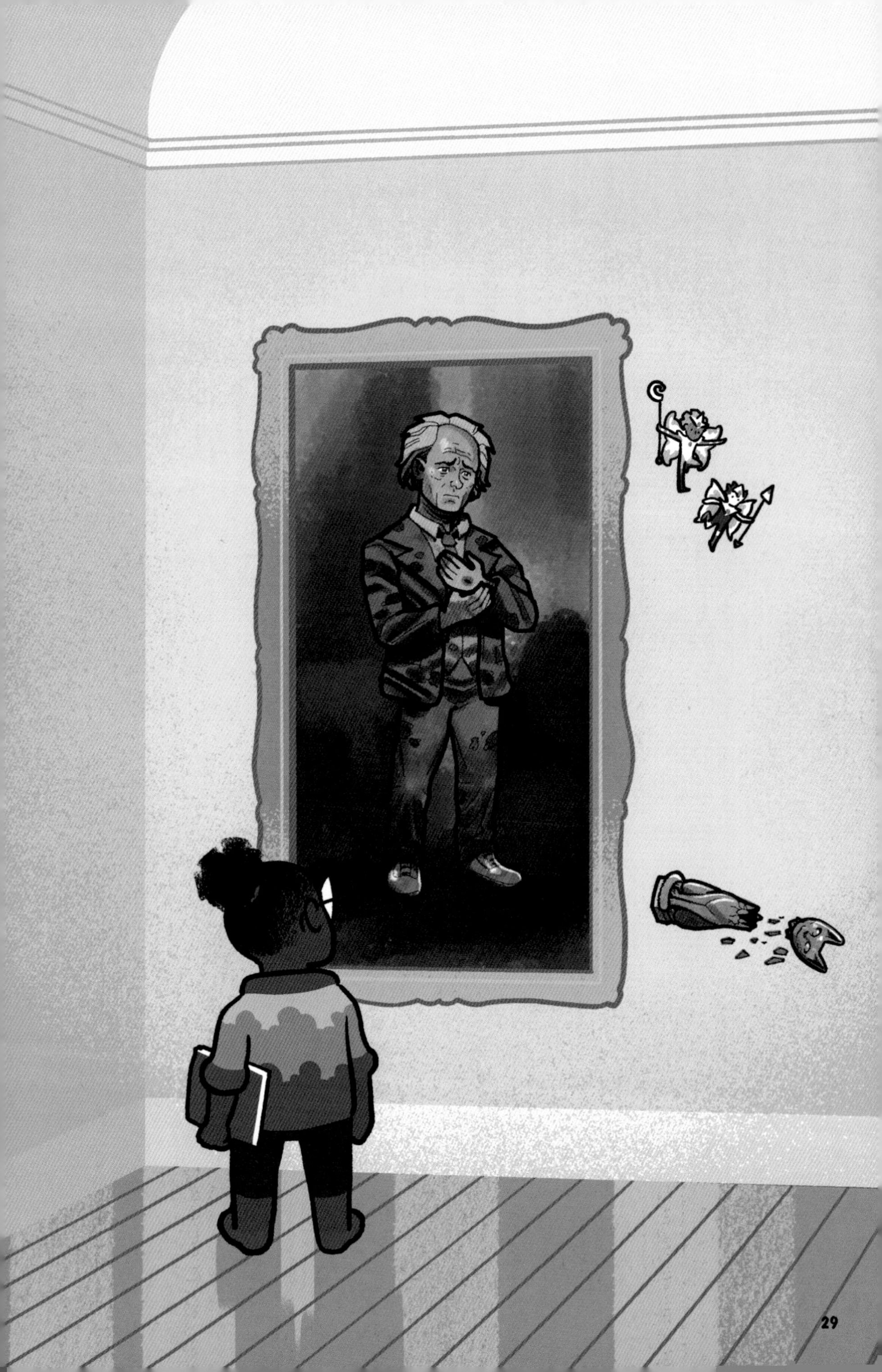

CHAPTER 2: MISSION... ACCOMPLISHED?

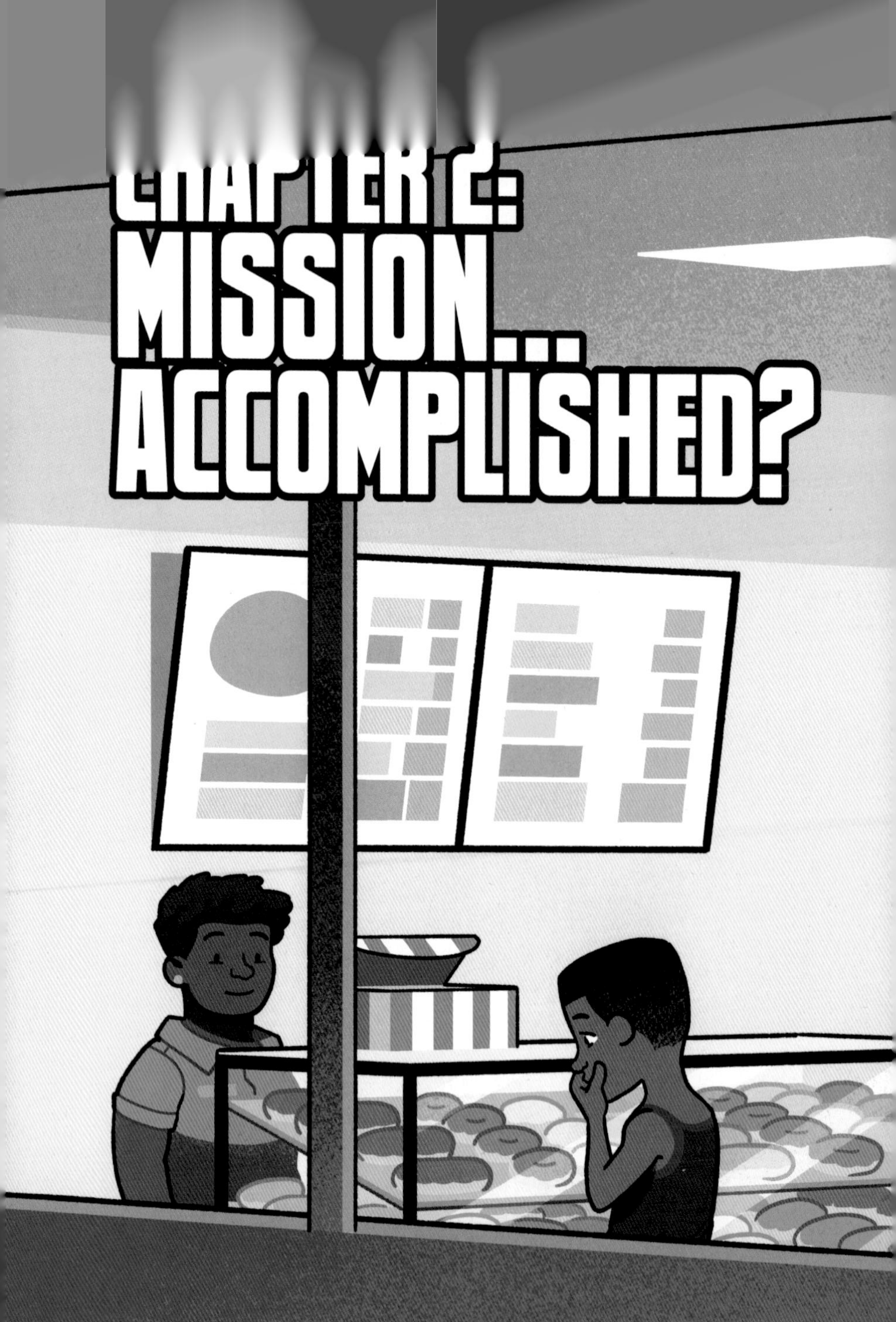

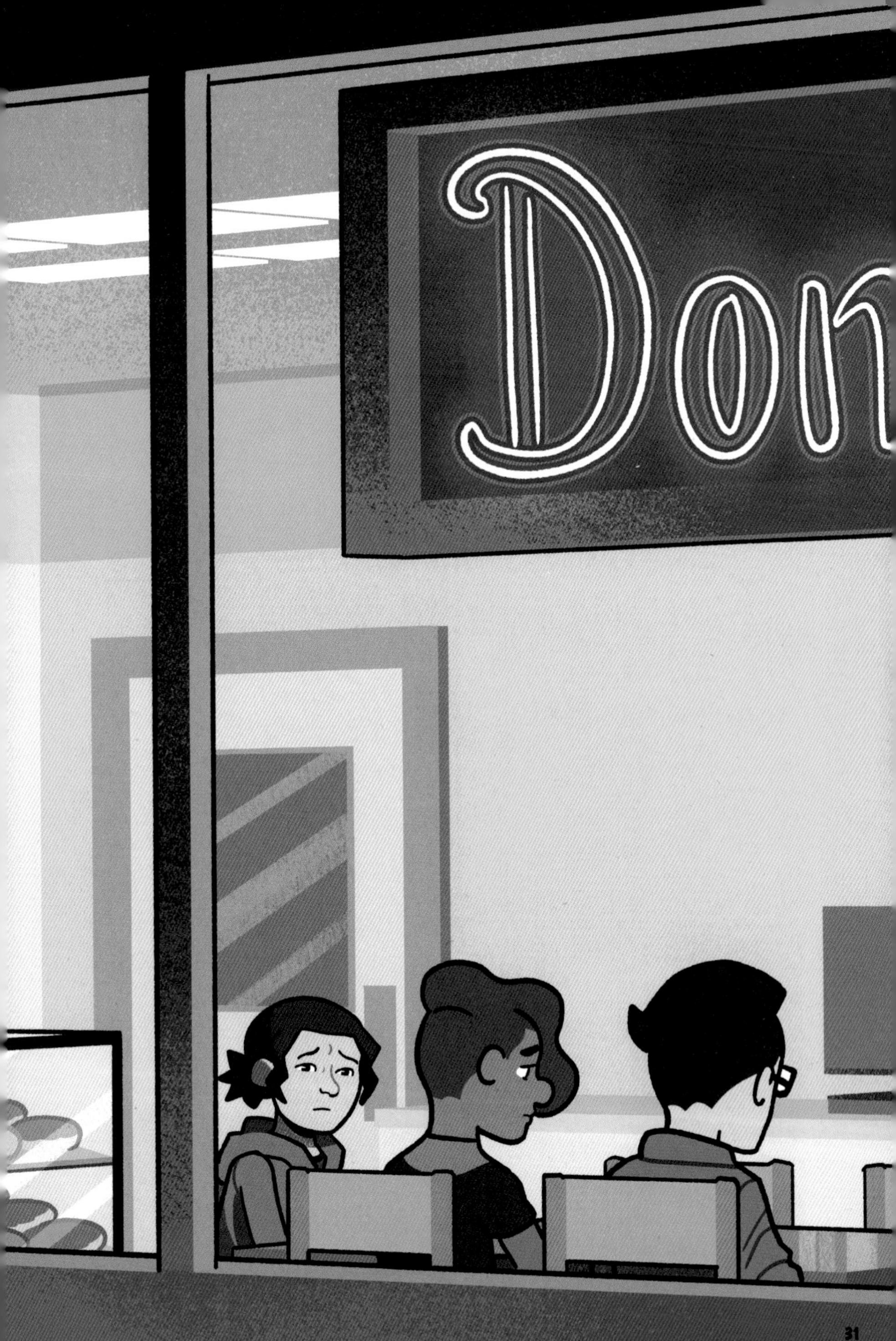
Don

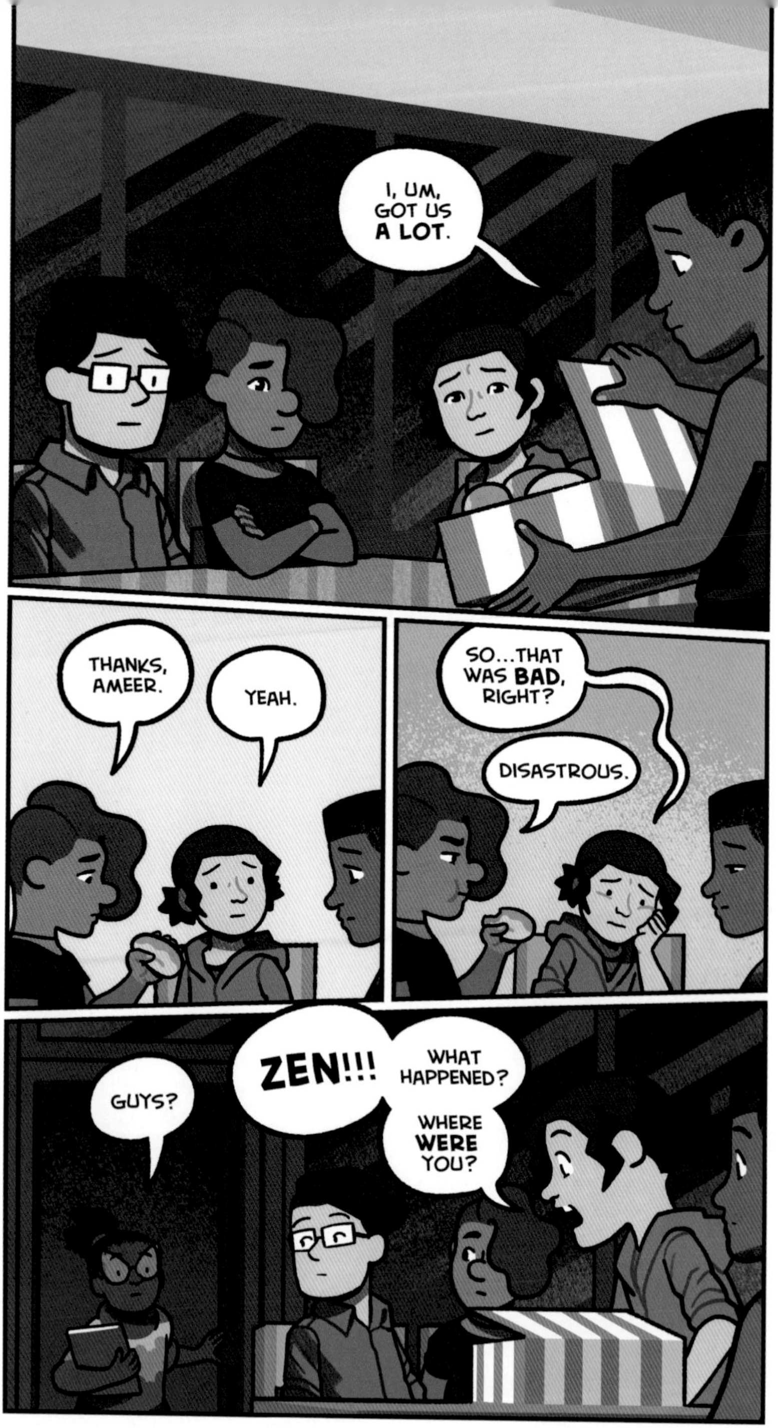
I, UM, GOT US A LOT.
THANKS, AMEER.
YEAH.
SO...THAT WAS BAD, RIGHT?
DISASTROUS.
GUYS?
ZEN!!!
WHAT HAPPENED?
WHERE WERE YOU?

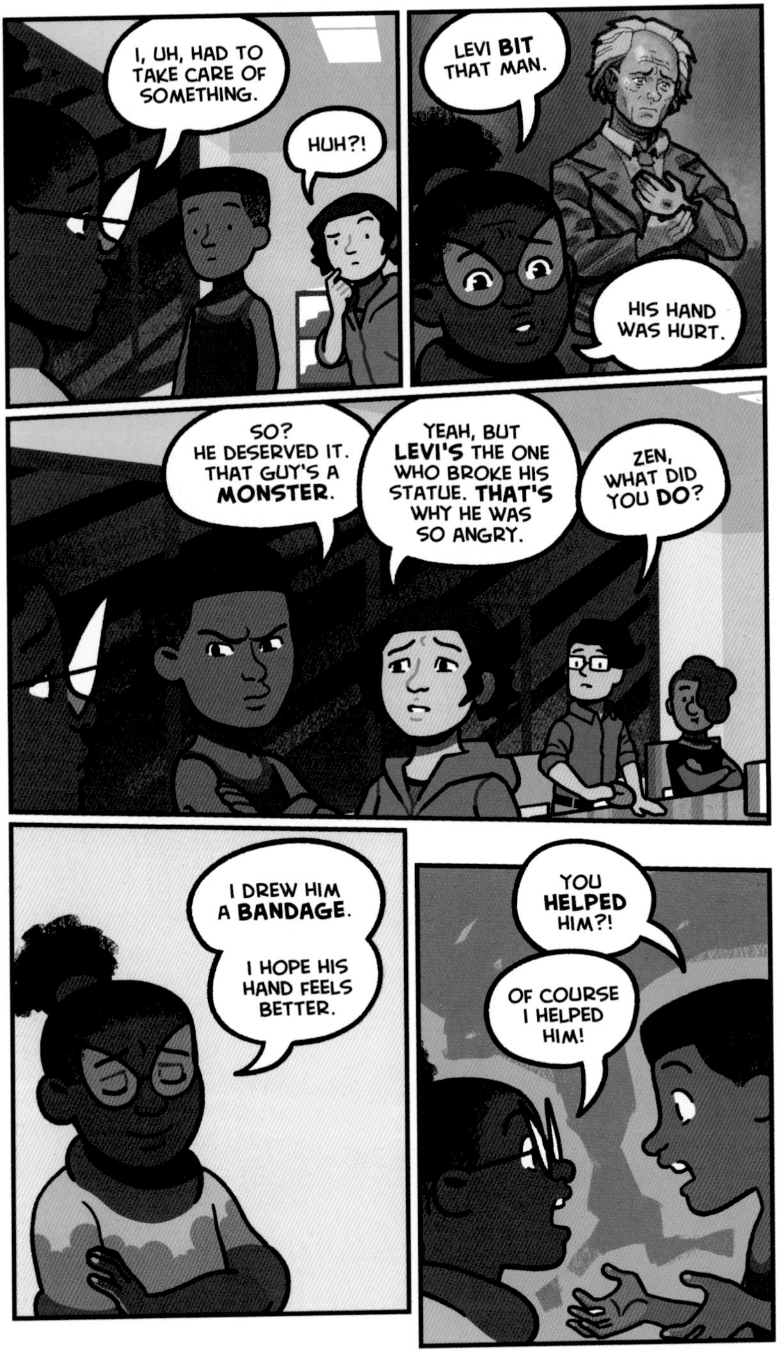
I, UH, HAD TO TAKE CARE OF SOMETHING.
HUH?!
LEVI **BIT** THAT MAN.
HIS HAND WAS HURT.
SO? HE DESERVED IT. THAT GUY'S A **MONSTER**.
YEAH, BUT **LEVI'S** THE ONE WHO BROKE HIS STATUE. **THAT'S** WHY HE WAS SO ANGRY.
ZEN, WHAT DID YOU **DO**?
I DREW HIM A **BANDAGE**.
I HOPE HIS HAND FEELS BETTER.
YOU **HELPED** HIM?!
OF COURSE I HELPED HIM!

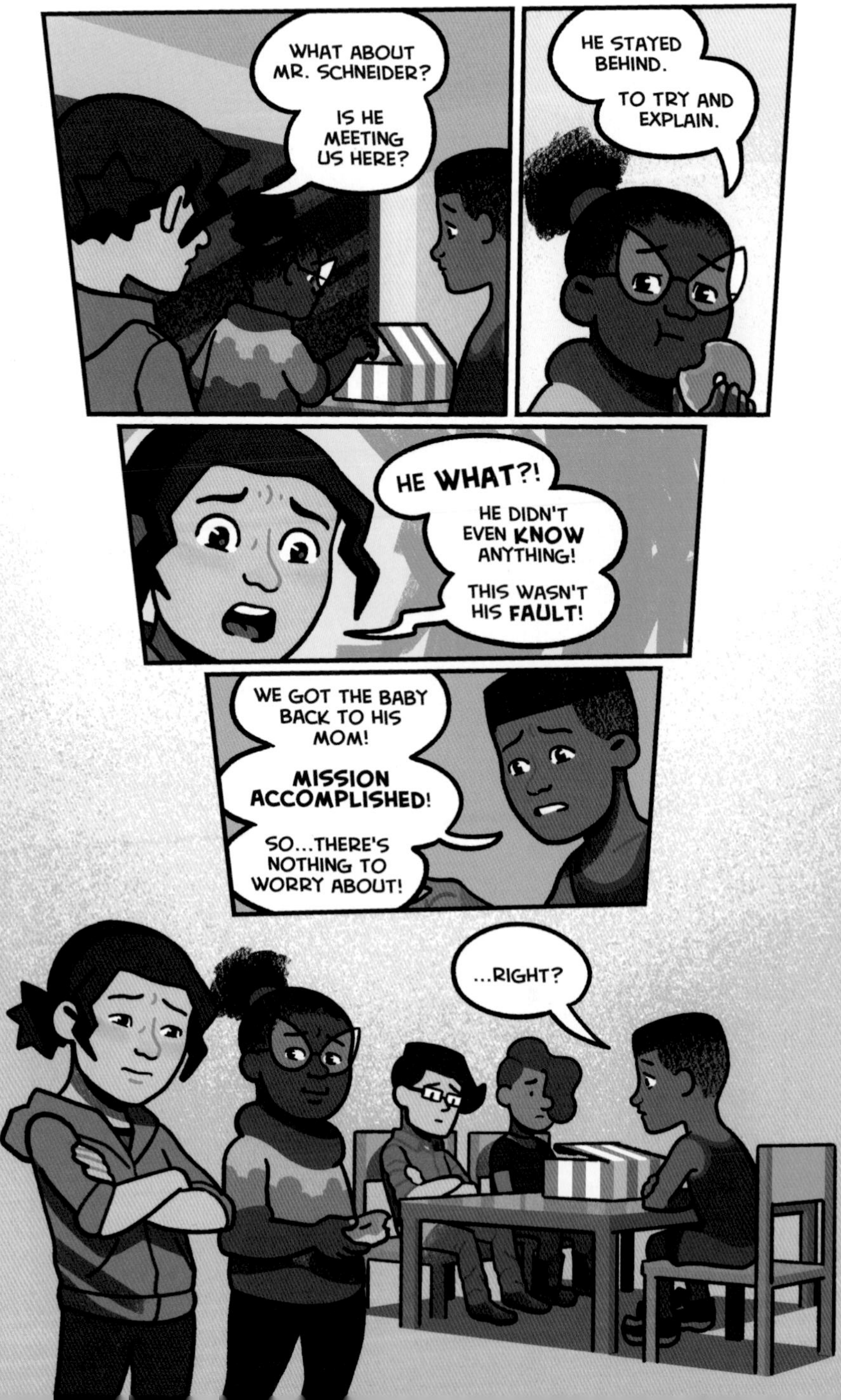
WHAT ABOUT MR. SCHNEIDER?
IS HE MEETING US HERE?
HE STAYED BEHIND.
TO TRY AND EXPLAIN.
HE WHAT?!
HE DIDN'T EVEN KNOW ANYTHING!
THIS WASN'T HIS FAULT!
WE GOT THE BABY BACK TO HIS MOM!
MISSION ACCOMPLISHED!
SO...THERE'S NOTHING TO WORRY ABOUT!
...RIGHT?

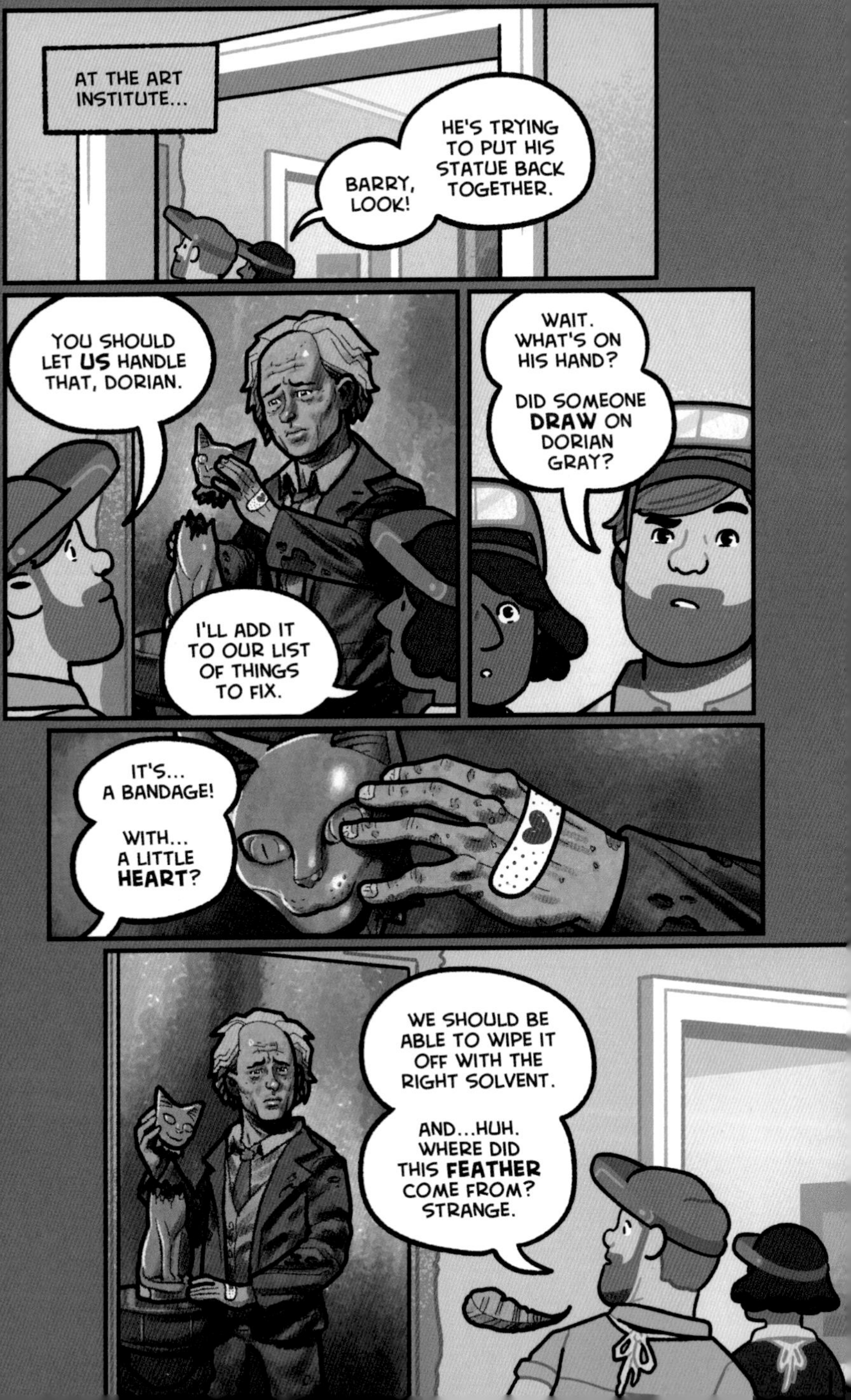
AT THE ART INSTITUTE...
BARRY, LOOK!
HE'S TRYING TO PUT HIS STATUE BACK TOGETHER.
YOU SHOULD LET **US** HANDLE THAT, DORIAN.
I'LL ADD IT TO OUR LIST OF THINGS TO FIX.
WAIT. WHAT'S ON HIS HAND?
DID SOMEONE **DRAW** ON DORIAN GRAY?
IT'S... A BANDAGE!
WITH... A LITTLE **HEART**?
WE SHOULD BE ABLE TO WIPE IT OFF WITH THE RIGHT SOLVENT.
AND...HUH. WHERE DID THIS **FEATHER** COME FROM? STRANGE.

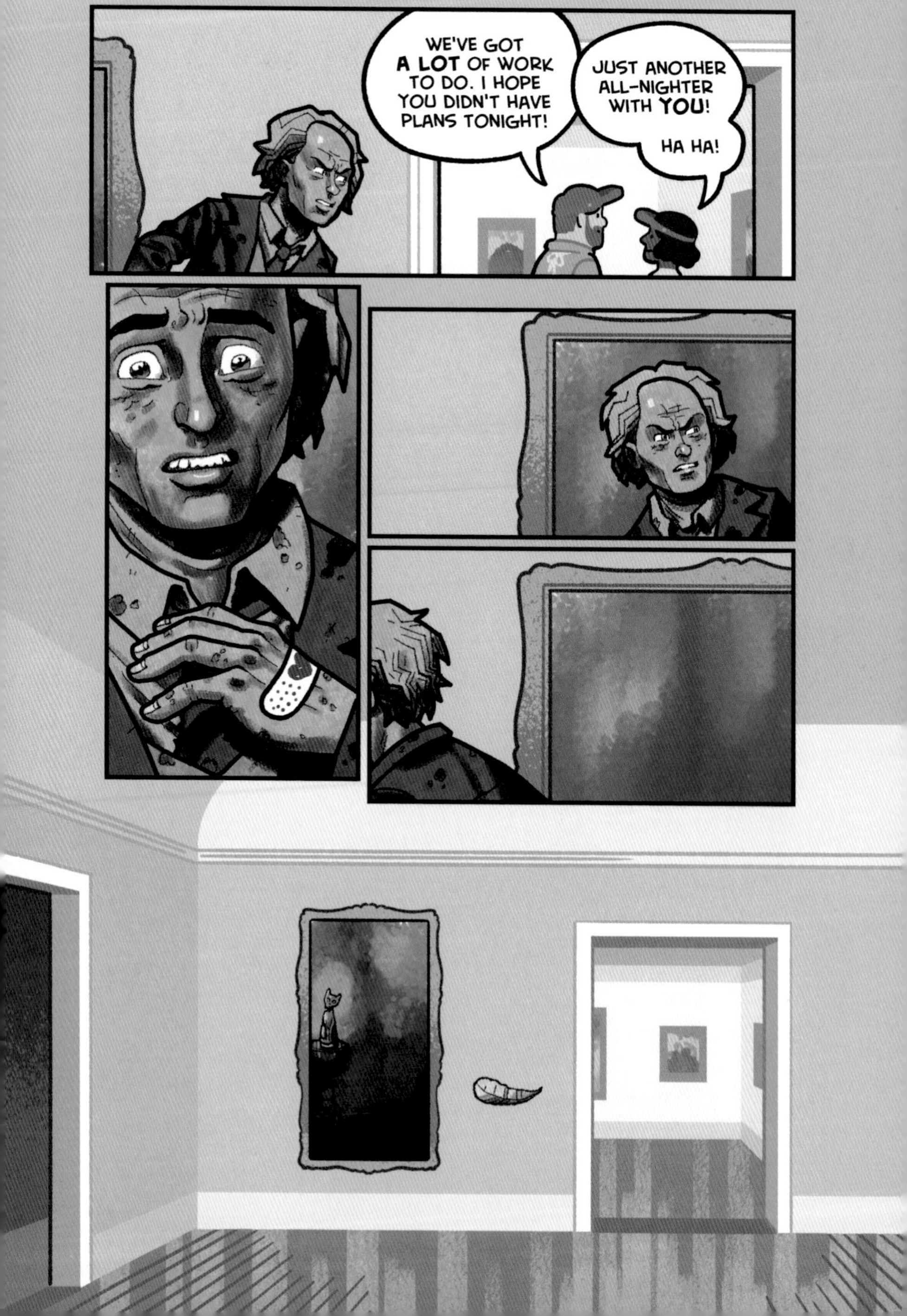
WE'VE GOT A LOT OF WORK TO DO. I HOPE YOU DIDN'T HAVE PLANS TONIGHT!
JUST ANOTHER ALL-NIGHTER WITH YOU!
HA HA!

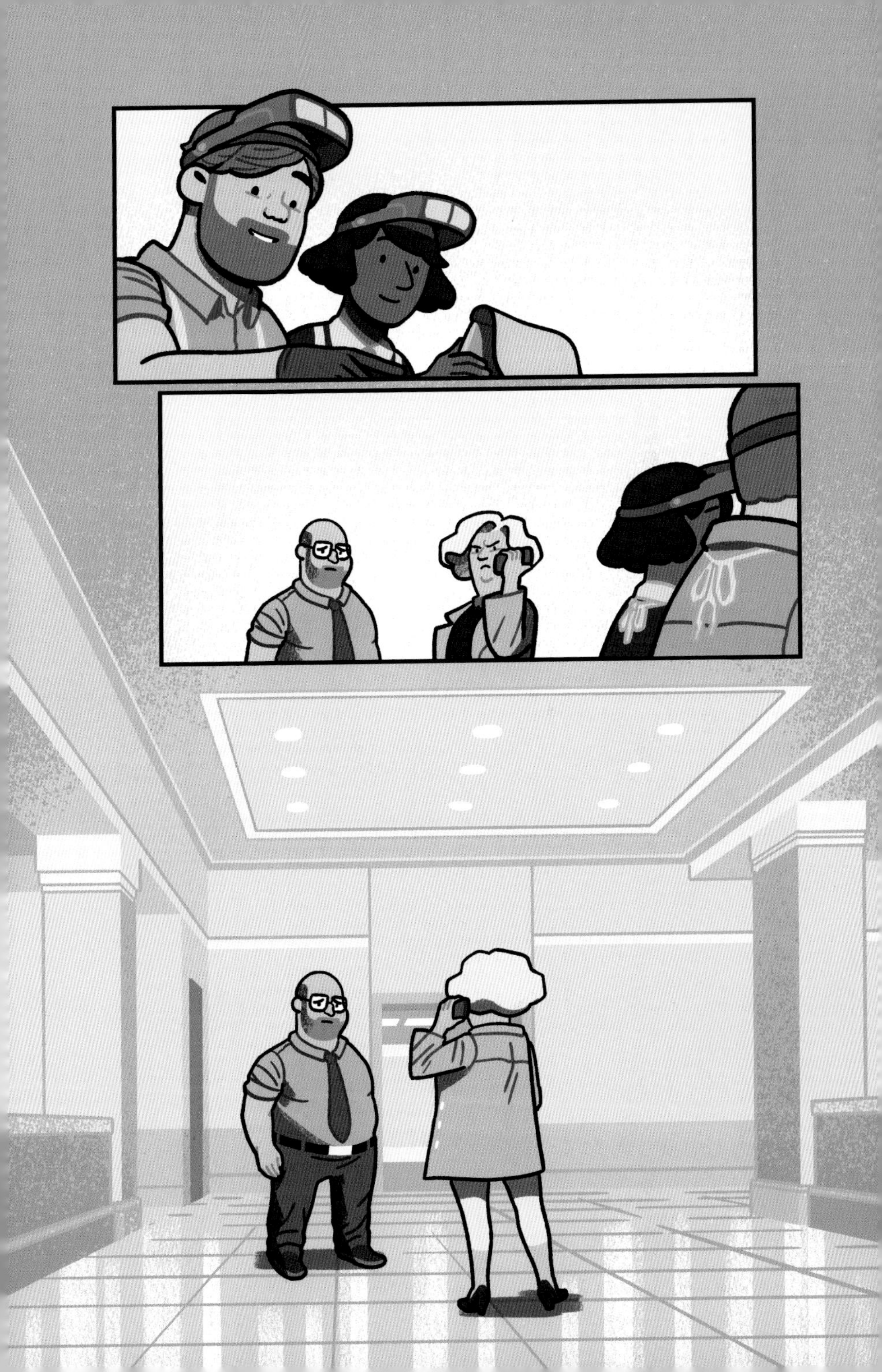

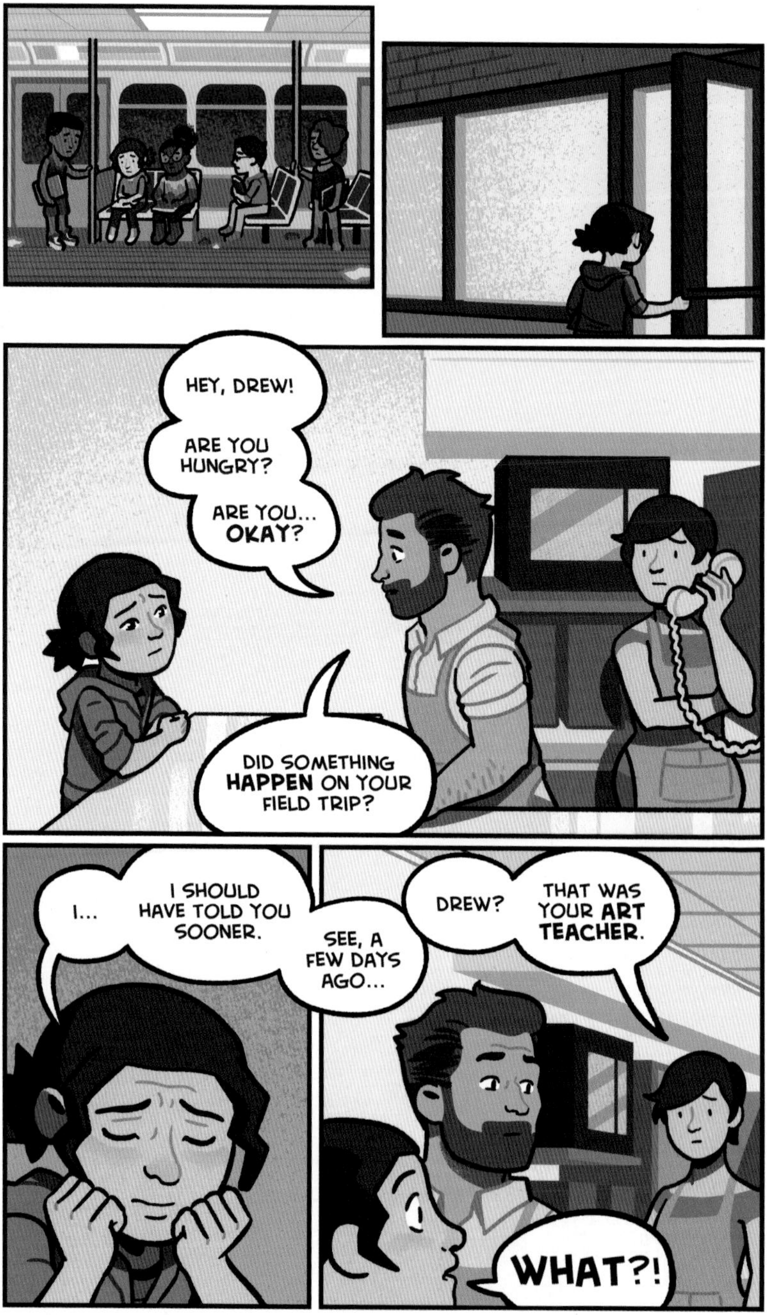
HEY, DREW!
ARE YOU HUNGRY?
ARE YOU... **OKAY**?
DID SOMETHING **HAPPEN** ON YOUR FIELD TRIP?
I...
I SHOULD HAVE TOLD YOU SOONER.
SEE, A FEW DAYS AGO...
DREW?
THAT WAS YOUR **ART TEACHER**.
WHAT?!

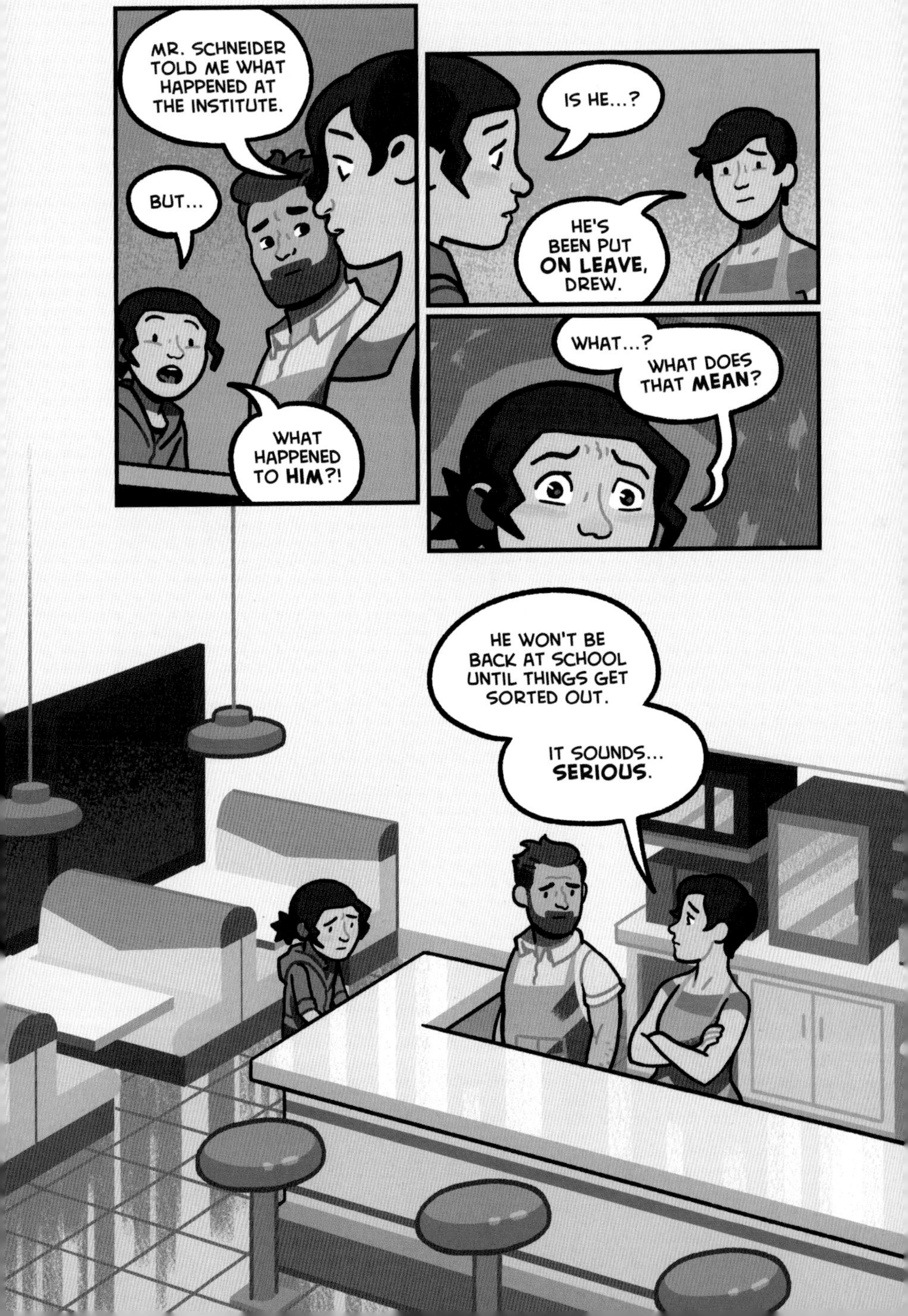
MR. SCHNEIDER TOLD ME WHAT HAPPENED AT THE INSTITUTE.
BUT...
WHAT HAPPENED TO HIM?!
IS HE...?
HE'S BEEN PUT ON LEAVE, DREW.
WHAT...?
WHAT DOES THAT MEAN?
HE WON'T BE BACK AT SCHOOL UNTIL THINGS GET SORTED OUT.
IT SOUNDS... SERIOUS.

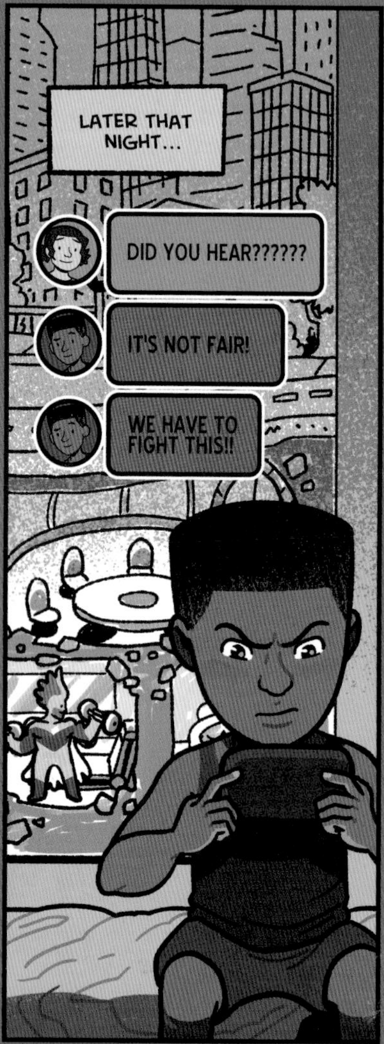
LATER THAT NIGHT...
DID YOU HEAR??????
IT'S NOT FAIR!
WE HAVE TO FIGHT THIS!!

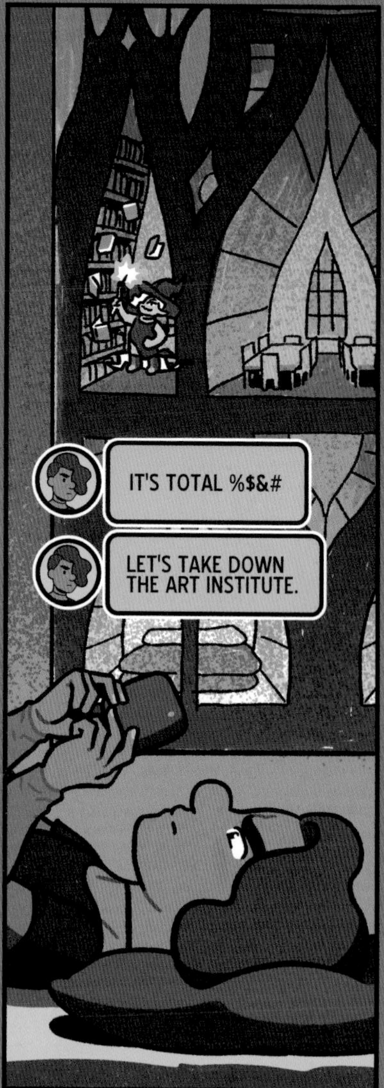
IT'S TOTAL %$&#
LET'S TAKE DOWN THE ART INSTITUTE.

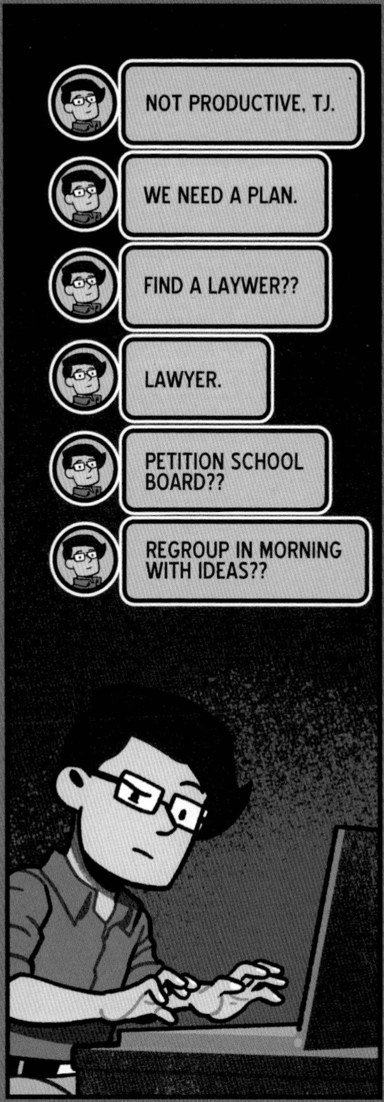
NOT PRODUCTIVE, TJ.
WE NEED A PLAN.
FIND A LAYWER??
LAWYER.
PETITION SCHOOL BOARD??
REGROUP IN MORNING WITH IDEAS??
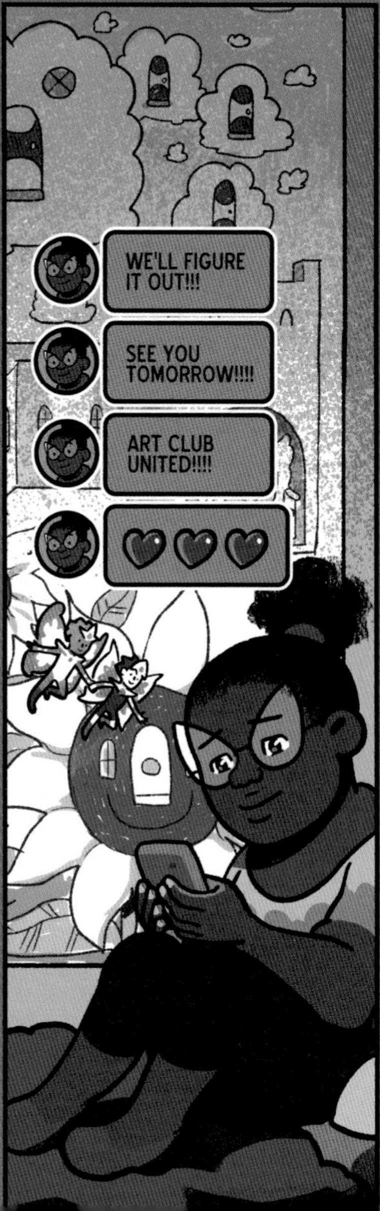
WE'LL FIGURE IT OUT!!!
SEE YOU TOMORROW!!!!
ART CLUB UNITED!!!!

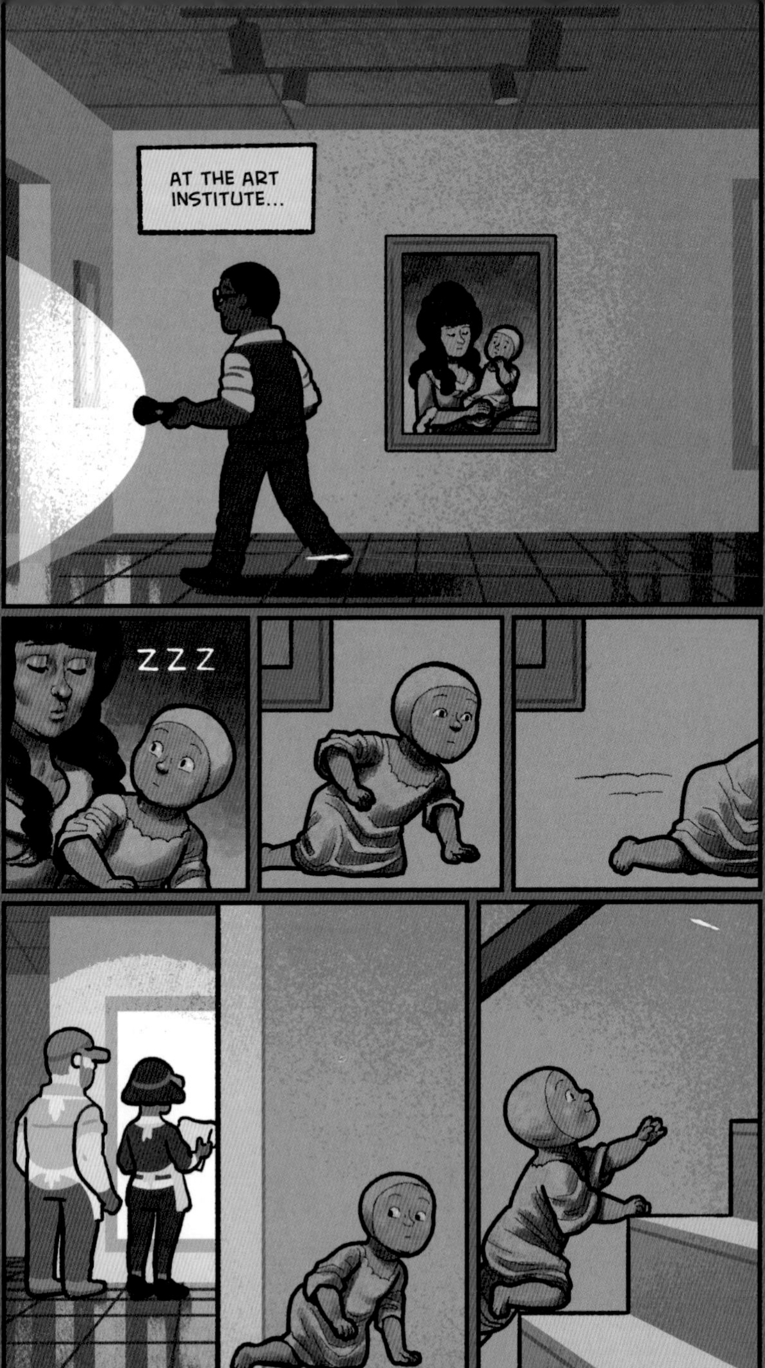
AT THE ART INSTITUTE...
ZZZ

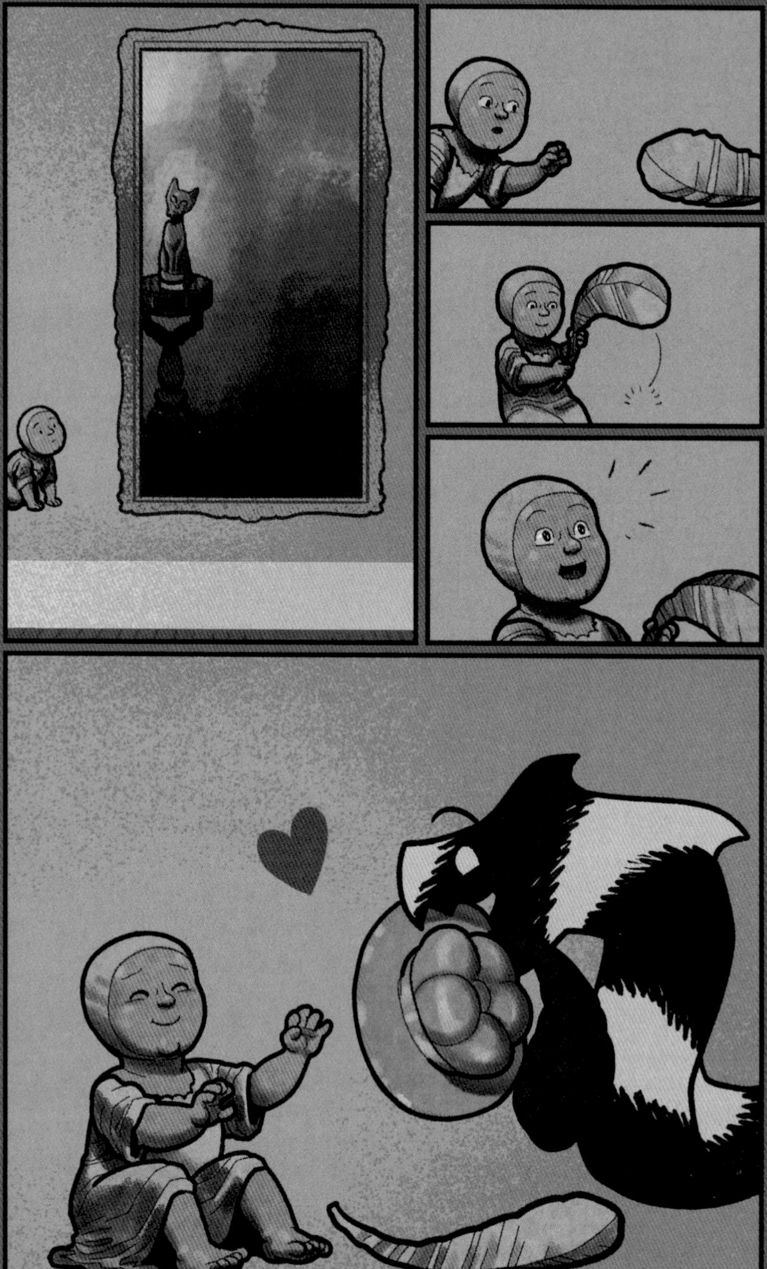

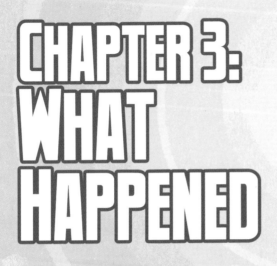

CHAPTER 3: WHAT HAPPENED

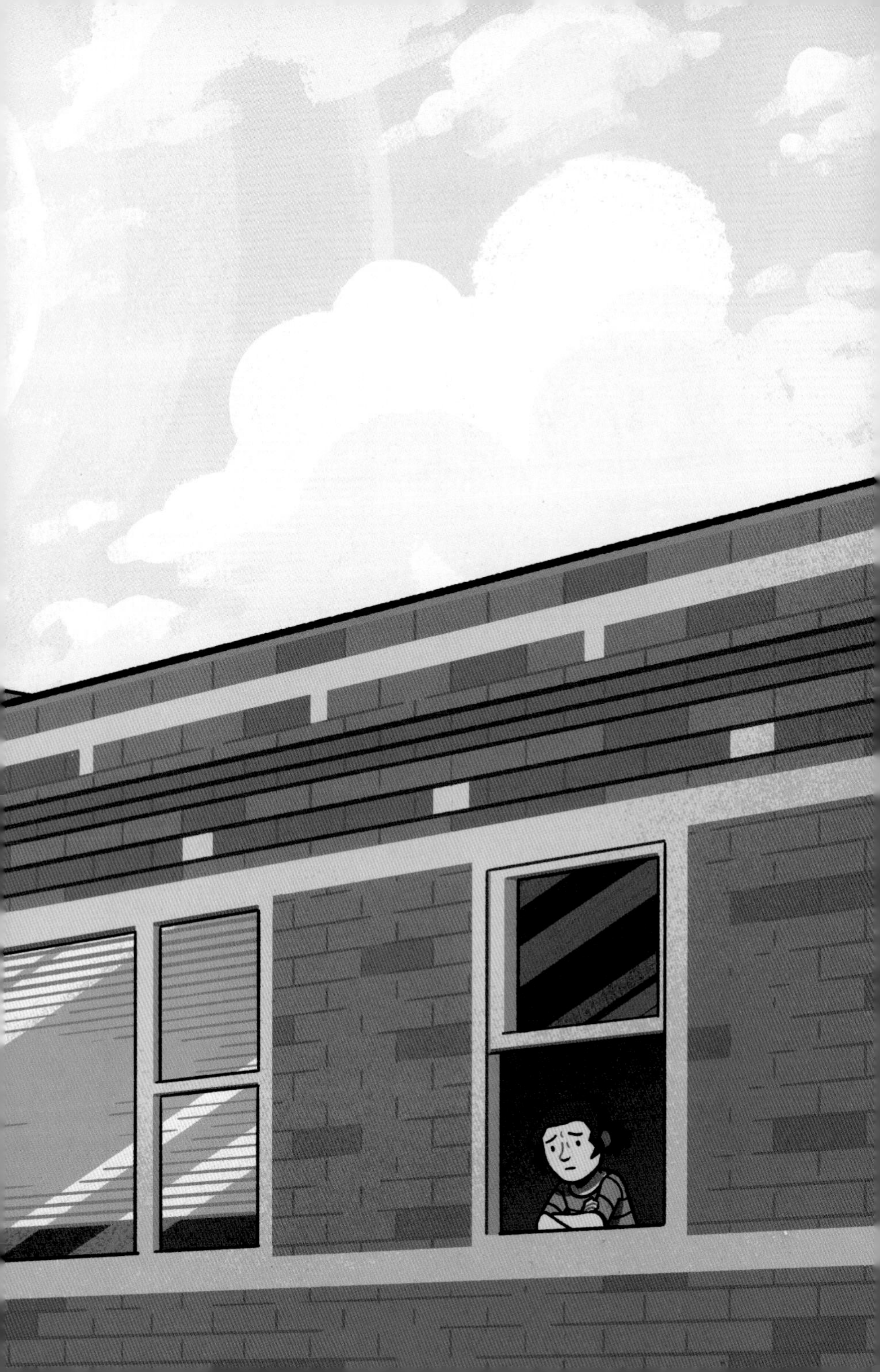

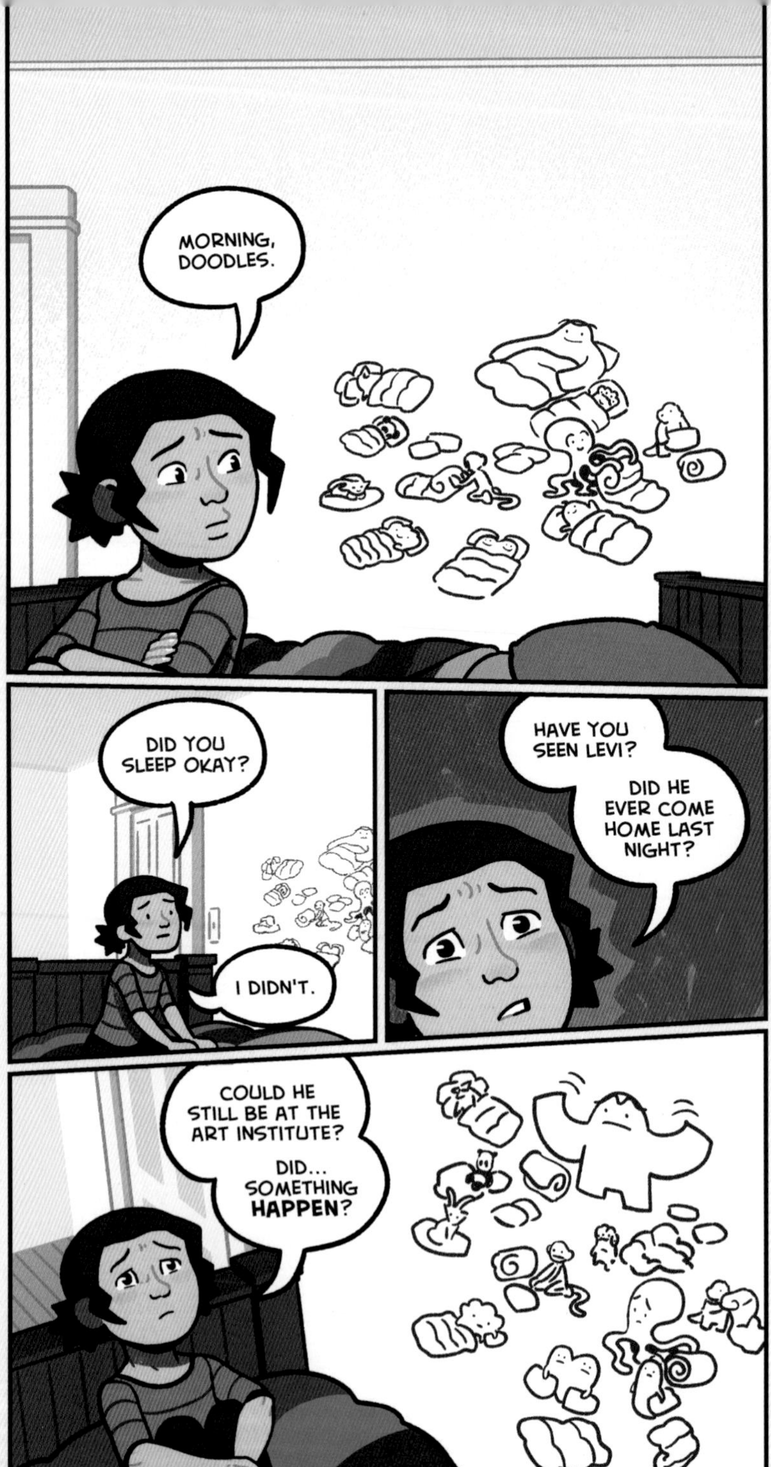
MORNING, DOODLES.
DID YOU SLEEP OKAY?
I DIDN'T.
HAVE YOU SEEN LEVI?
DID HE EVER COME HOME LAST NIGHT?
COULD HE STILL BE AT THE ART INSTITUTE?
DID... SOMETHING **HAPPEN**?

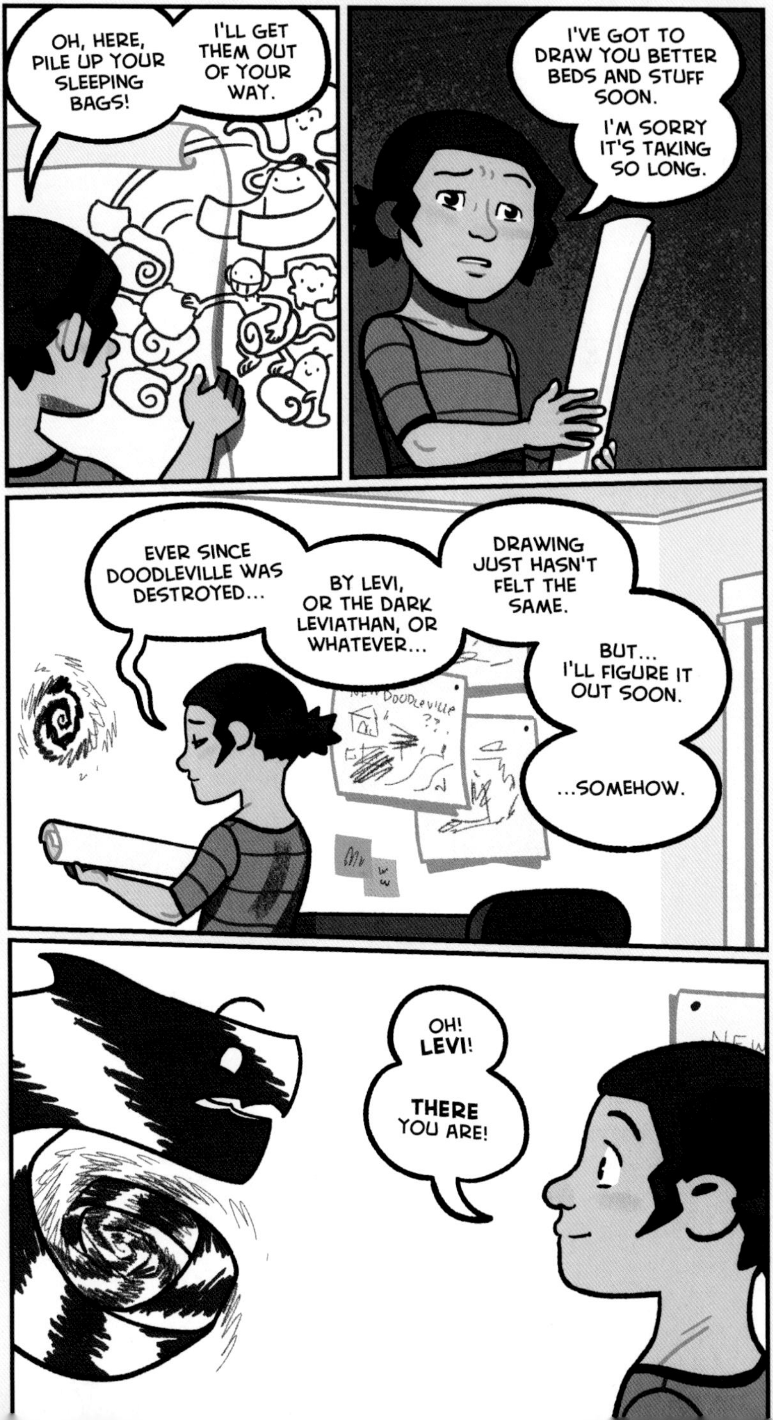
OH, HERE, PILE UP YOUR SLEEPING BAGS!
I'LL GET THEM OUT OF YOUR WAY.
I'VE GOT TO DRAW YOU BETTER BEDS AND STUFF SOON.
I'M SORRY IT'S TAKING SO LONG.
EVER SINCE DOODLEVILLE WAS DESTROYED...
BY LEVI, OR THE DARK LEVIATHAN, OR WHATEVER...
DRAWING JUST HASN'T FELT THE SAME.
BUT... I'LL FIGURE IT OUT SOON.
...SOMEHOW.
NEW DOODLEVILLE ??
OH! LEVI!
THERE YOU ARE!

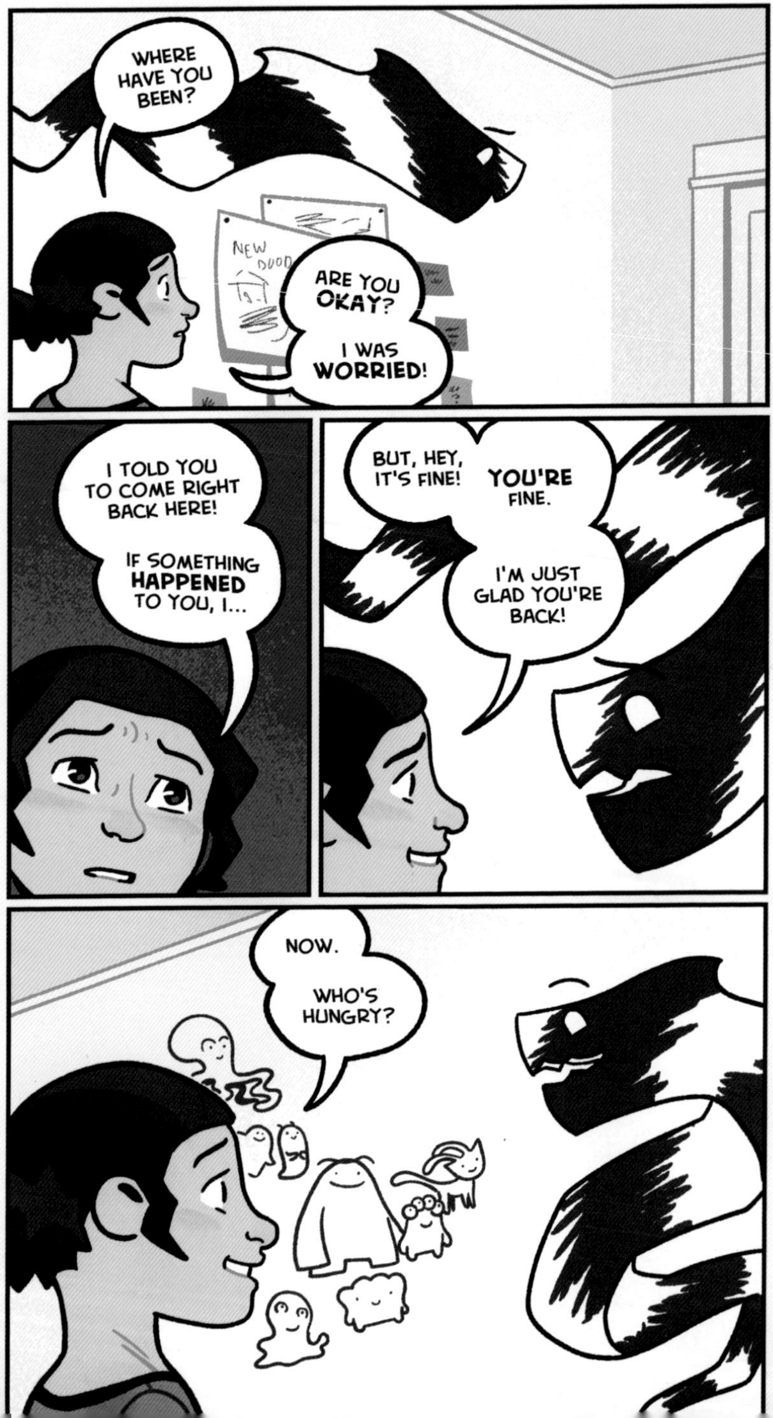
WHERE HAVE YOU BEEN?
NEW DUOD
ARE YOU OKAY?
I WAS WORRIED!
I TOLD YOU TO COME RIGHT BACK HERE!
IF SOMETHING HAPPENED TO YOU, I...
BUT, HEY, IT'S FINE!
YOU'RE FINE.
I'M JUST GLAD YOU'RE BACK!
NOW.
WHO'S HUNGRY?

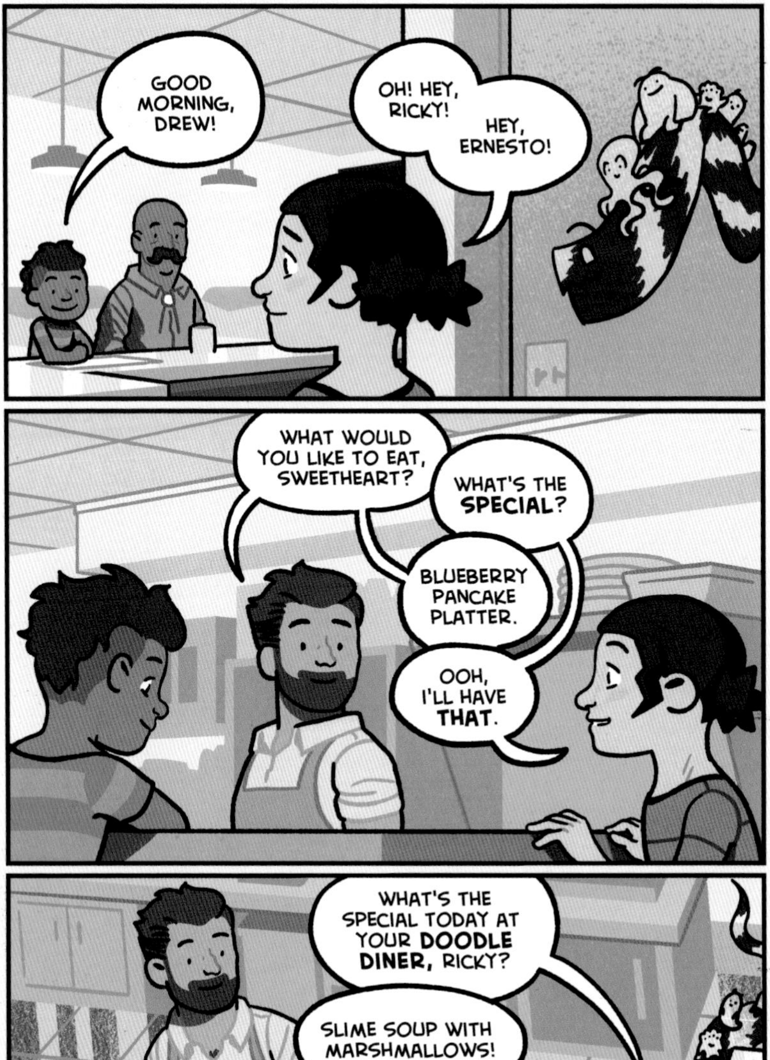
GOOD MORNING, DREW!
OH! HEY, RICKY!
HEY, ERNESTO!
WHAT WOULD YOU LIKE TO EAT, SWEETHEART?
WHAT'S THE **SPECIAL**?
BLUEBERRY PANCAKE PLATTER.
OOH, I'LL HAVE **THAT**.
WHAT'S THE SPECIAL TODAY AT YOUR **DOODLE DINER,** RICKY?
SLIME SOUP WITH MARSHMALLOWS!

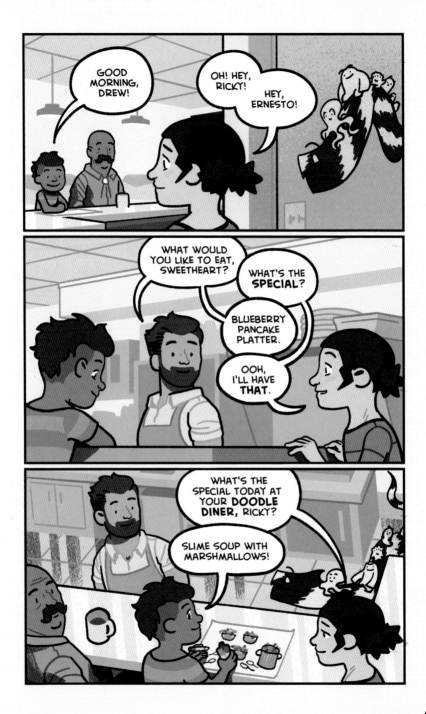

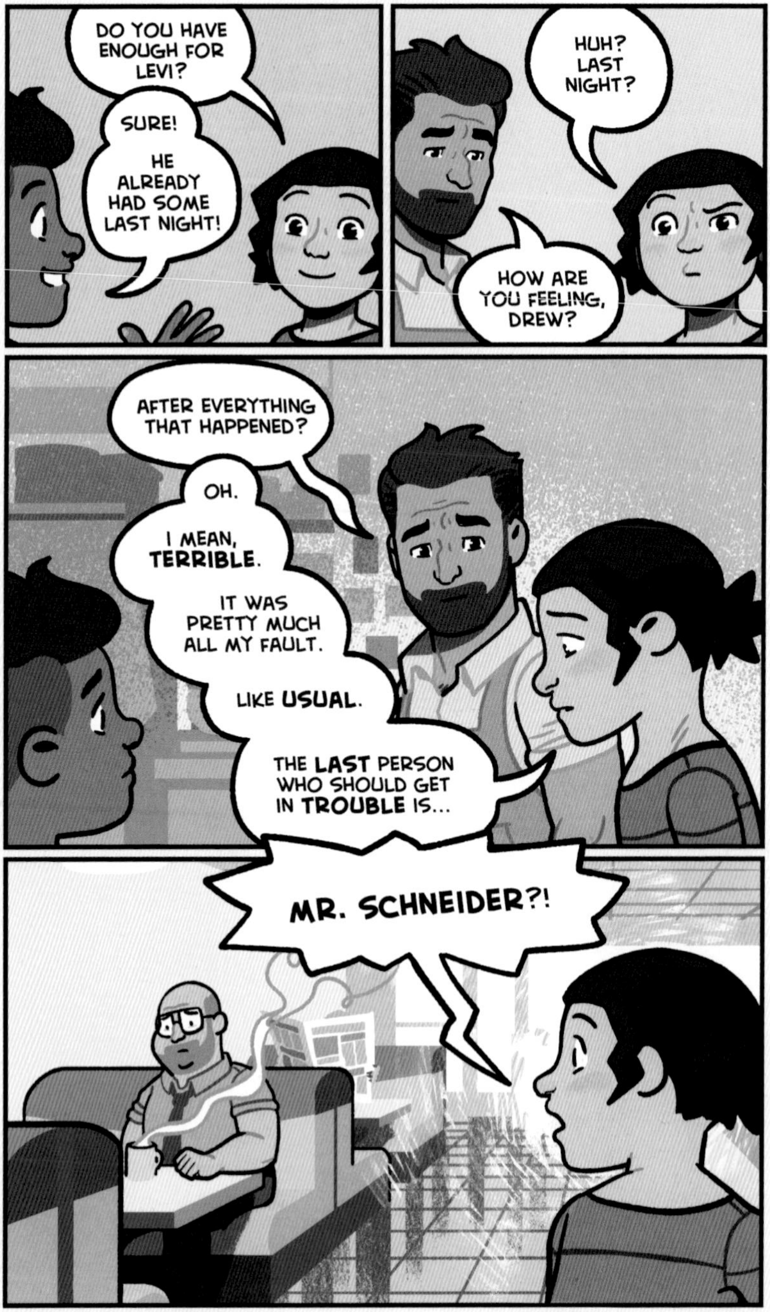
DO YOU HAVE ENOUGH FOR LEVI?
SURE!
HE ALREADY HAD SOME LAST NIGHT!
HUH? LAST NIGHT?
HOW ARE YOU FEELING, DREW?
AFTER EVERYTHING THAT HAPPENED?
OH.
I MEAN, **TERRIBLE**.
IT WAS PRETTY MUCH ALL MY FAULT.
LIKE **USUAL**.
THE **LAST** PERSON WHO SHOULD GET IN **TROUBLE** IS...
MR. SCHNEIDER?!

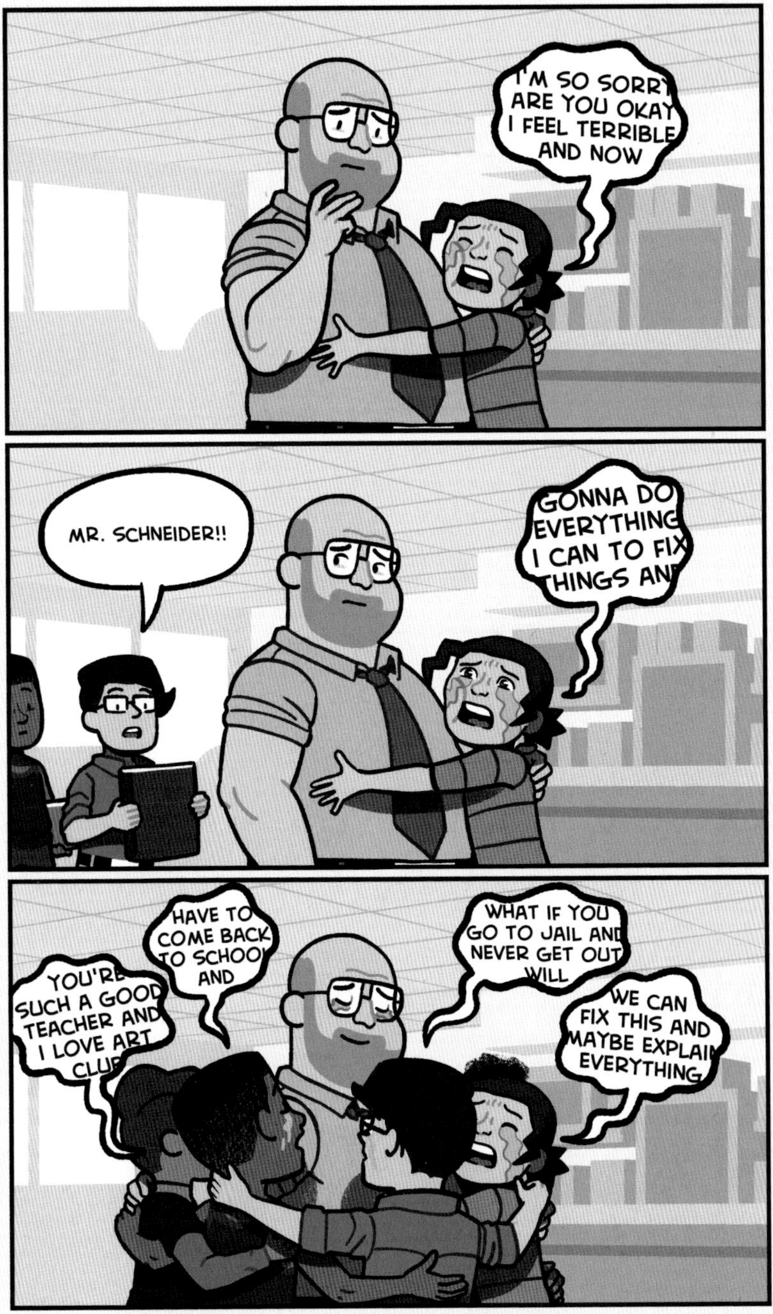
I'M SO SORRY
ARE YOU OKAY
I FEEL TERRIBLE
AND NOW
MR. SCHNEIDER!!
GONNA DO
EVERYTHING
I CAN TO FIX
THINGS AN
YOU'RE
SUCH A GOOD
TEACHER AND
I LOVE ART
CLUB
HAVE TO
COME BACK
TO SCHOOL
AND
WHAT IF YOU
GO TO JAIL AND
NEVER GET OUT
WILL
WE CAN
FIX THIS AND
MAYBE EXPLAIN
EVERYTHING

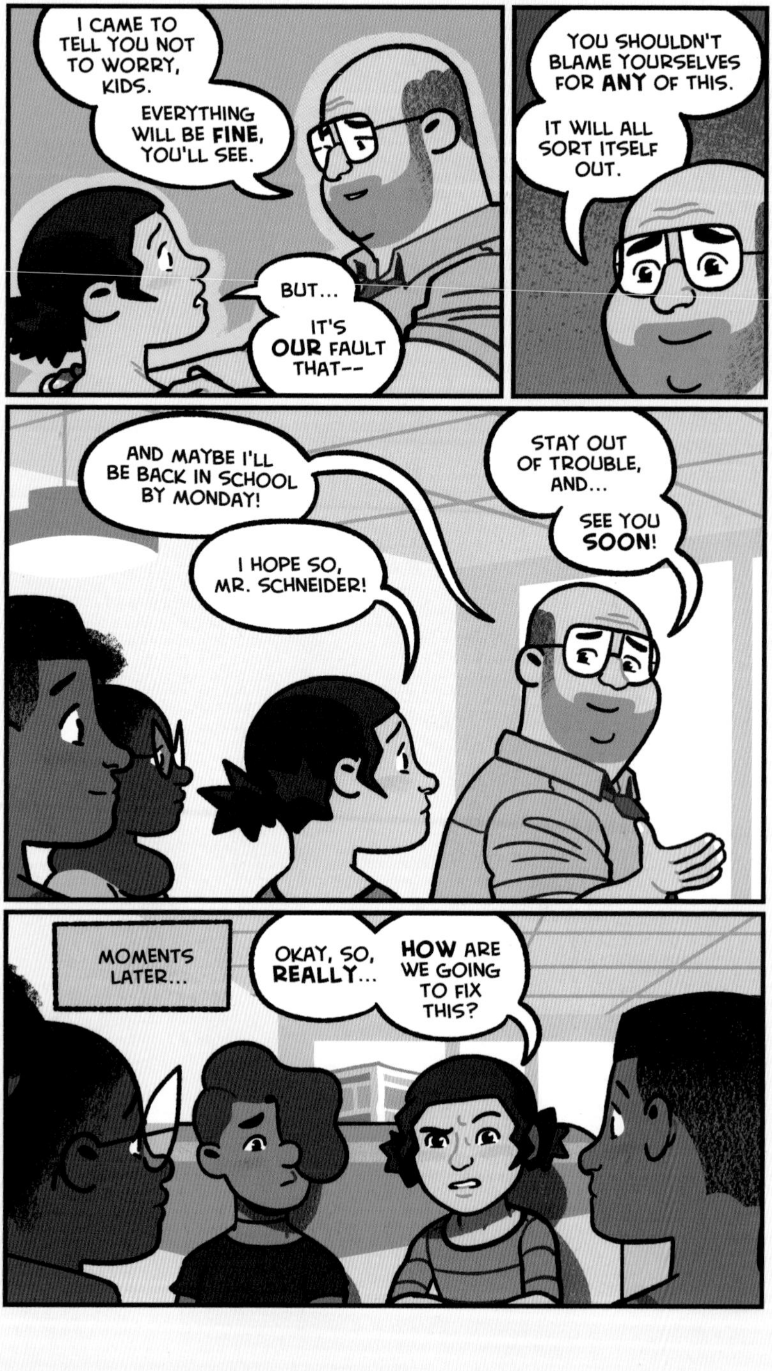
I CAME TO TELL YOU NOT TO WORRY, KIDS.
EVERYTHING WILL BE FINE, YOU'LL SEE.
BUT...
IT'S OUR FAULT THAT--
YOU SHOULDN'T BLAME YOURSELVES FOR ANY OF THIS.
IT WILL ALL SORT ITSELF OUT.
AND MAYBE I'LL BE BACK IN SCHOOL BY MONDAY!
STAY OUT OF TROUBLE, AND...
SEE YOU SOON!
I HOPE SO, MR. SCHNEIDER!
MOMENTS LATER...
OKAY, SO, REALLY...
HOW ARE WE GOING TO FIX THIS?

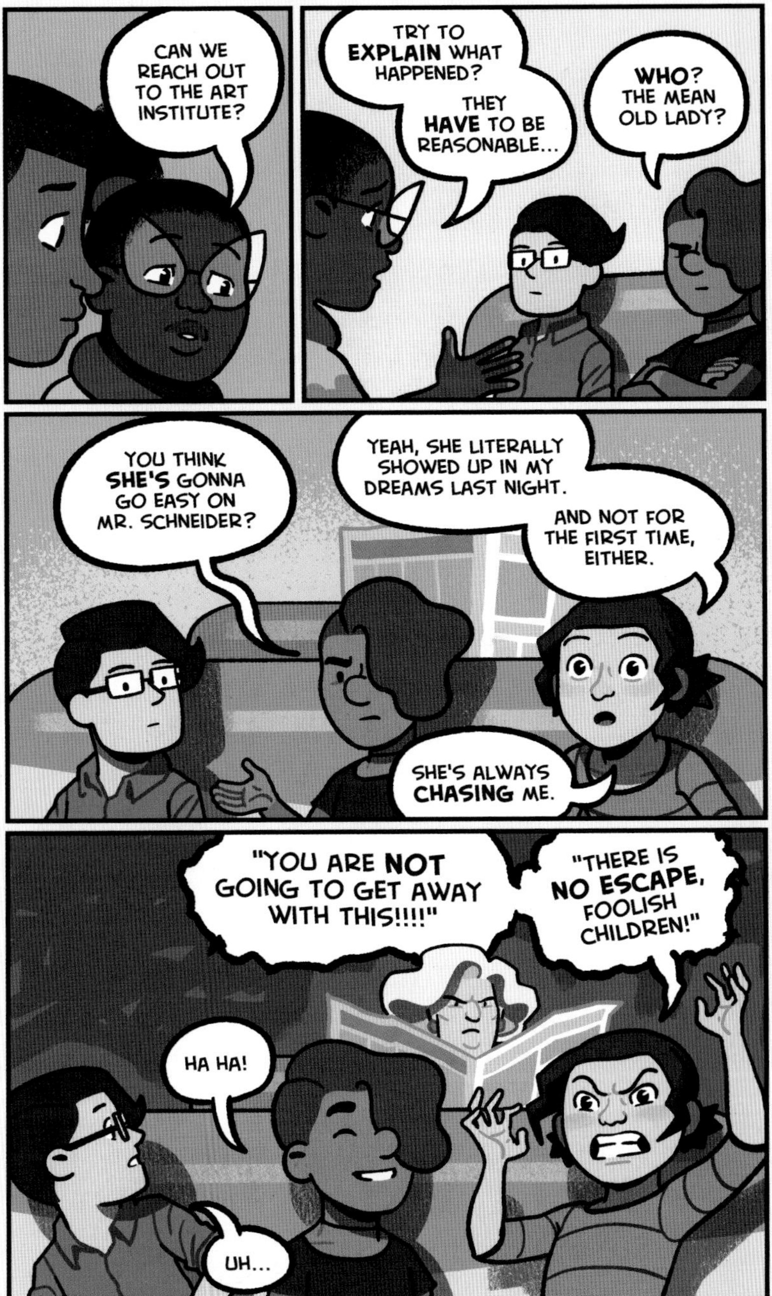
CAN WE REACH OUT TO THE ART INSTITUTE?
TRY TO **EXPLAIN** WHAT HAPPENED?
THEY **HAVE** TO BE REASONABLE...
WHO? THE MEAN OLD LADY?
YOU THINK **SHE'S** GONNA GO EASY ON MR. SCHNEIDER?
YEAH, SHE LITERALLY SHOWED UP IN MY DREAMS LAST NIGHT.
AND NOT FOR THE FIRST TIME, EITHER.
SHE'S ALWAYS **CHASING** ME.
"YOU ARE **NOT** GOING TO GET AWAY WITH THIS!!!!"
"THERE IS **NO ESCAPE**, FOOLISH CHILDREN!"
HA HA!
UH...

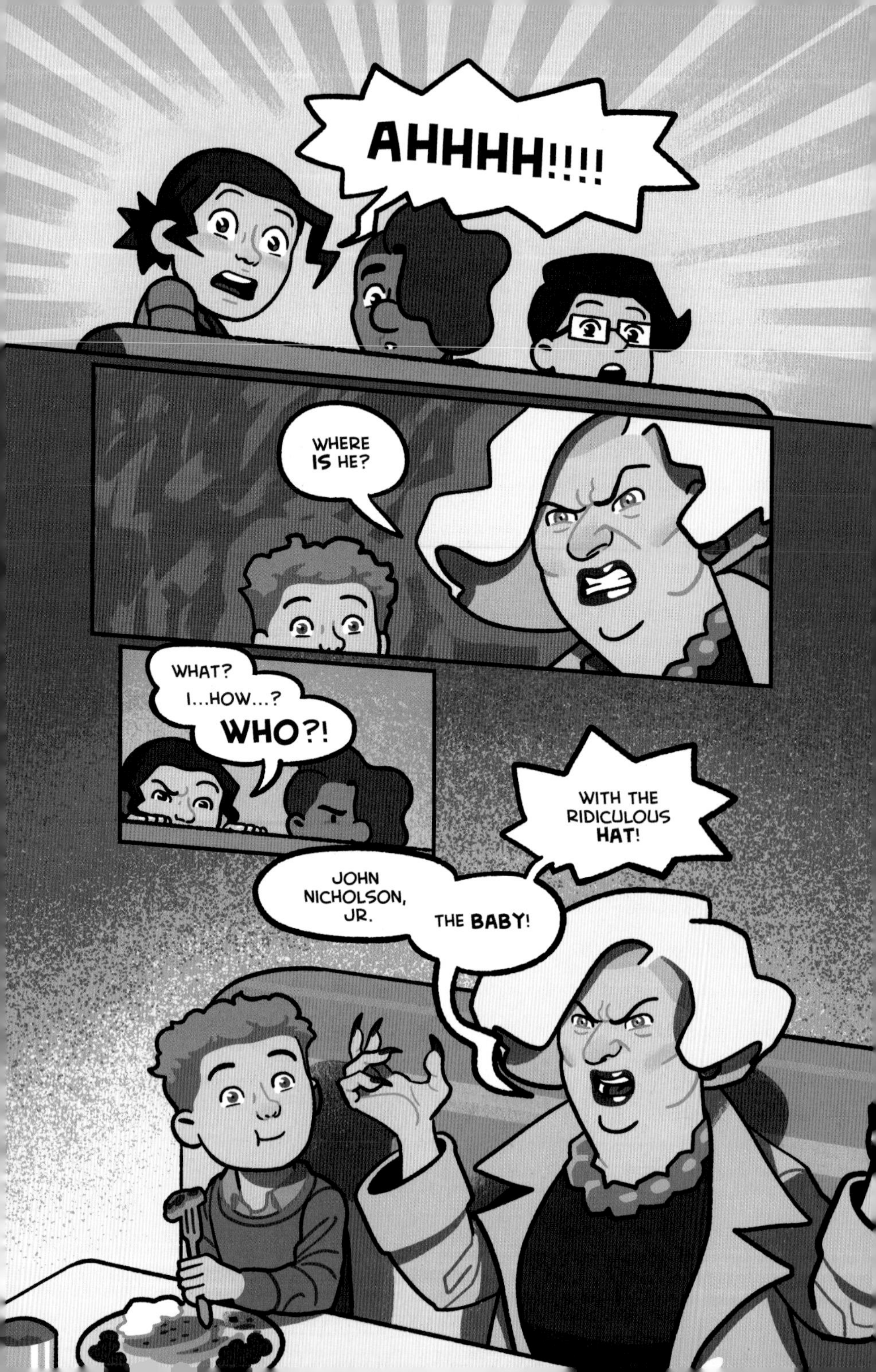
AHHHH!!!!
WHERE IS HE?
WHAT?
I...HOW...?
WHO?!
WITH THE RIDICULOUS HAT!
JOHN NICHOLSON, JR.
THE BABY!

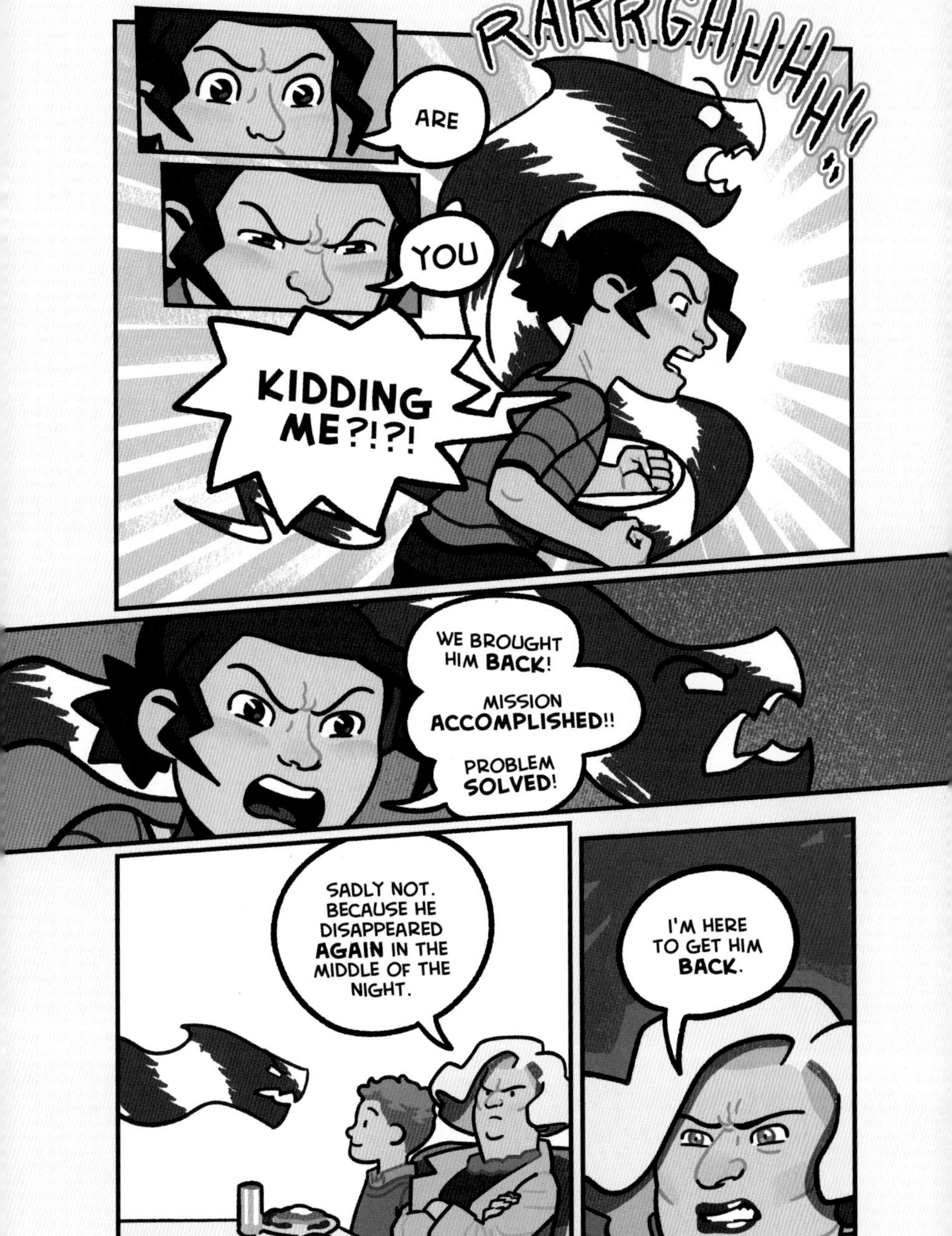
RARRGHHHH!!!
ARE
YOU
KIDDING ME?!?!
WE BROUGHT HIM BACK!
MISSION ACCOMPLISHED!!
PROBLEM SOLVED!
SADLY NOT. BECAUSE HE DISAPPEARED AGAIN IN THE MIDDLE OF THE NIGHT.
I'M HERE TO GET HIM BACK.

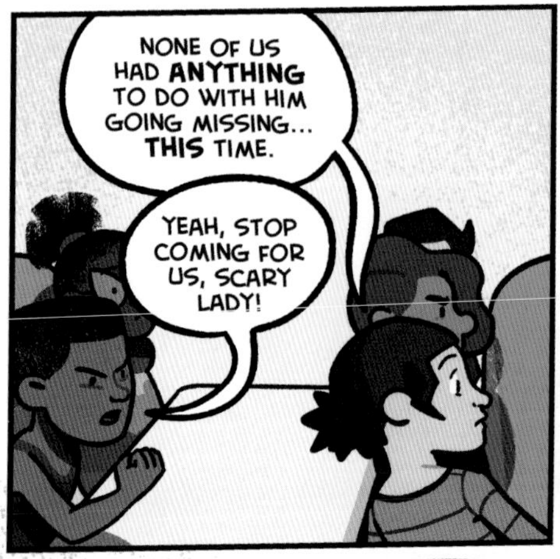
NONE OF US HAD **ANYTHING** TO DO WITH HIM GOING MISSING... **THIS** TIME.
YEAH, STOP COMING FOR US, SCARY LADY!

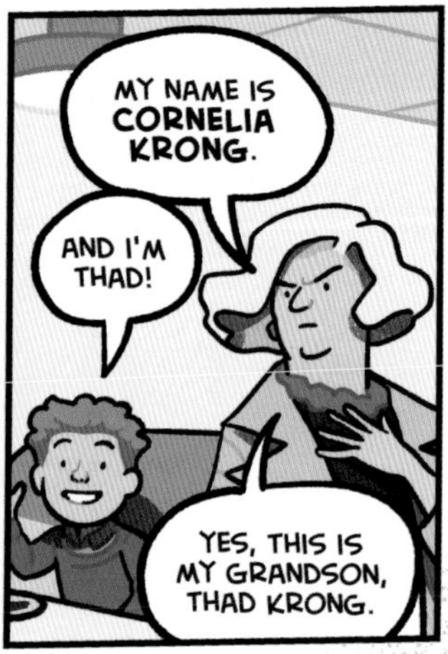
MY NAME IS **CORNELIA KRONG**.
AND I'M THAD!
YES, THIS IS MY GRANDSON, THAD KRONG.

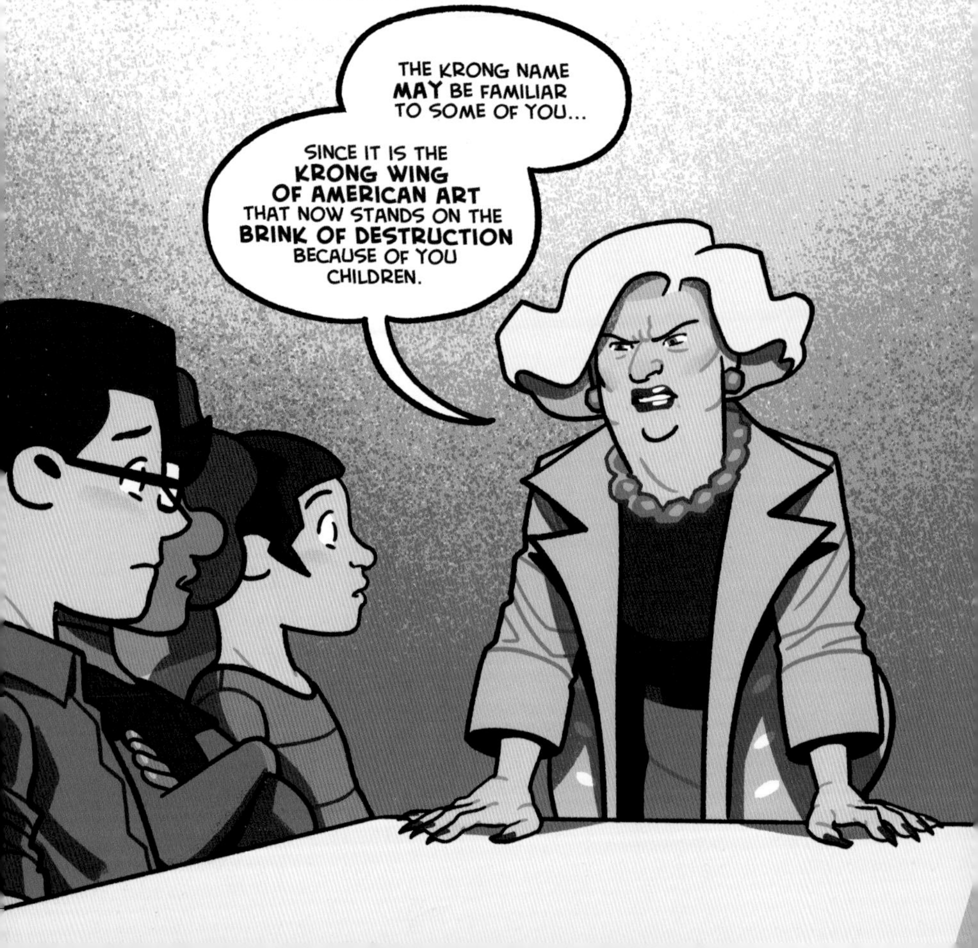
THE KRONG NAME **MAY** BE FAMILIAR TO SOME OF YOU...
SINCE IT IS THE **KRONG WING OF AMERICAN ART** THAT NOW STANDS ON THE **BRINK OF DESTRUCTION** BECAUSE OF YOU CHILDREN.

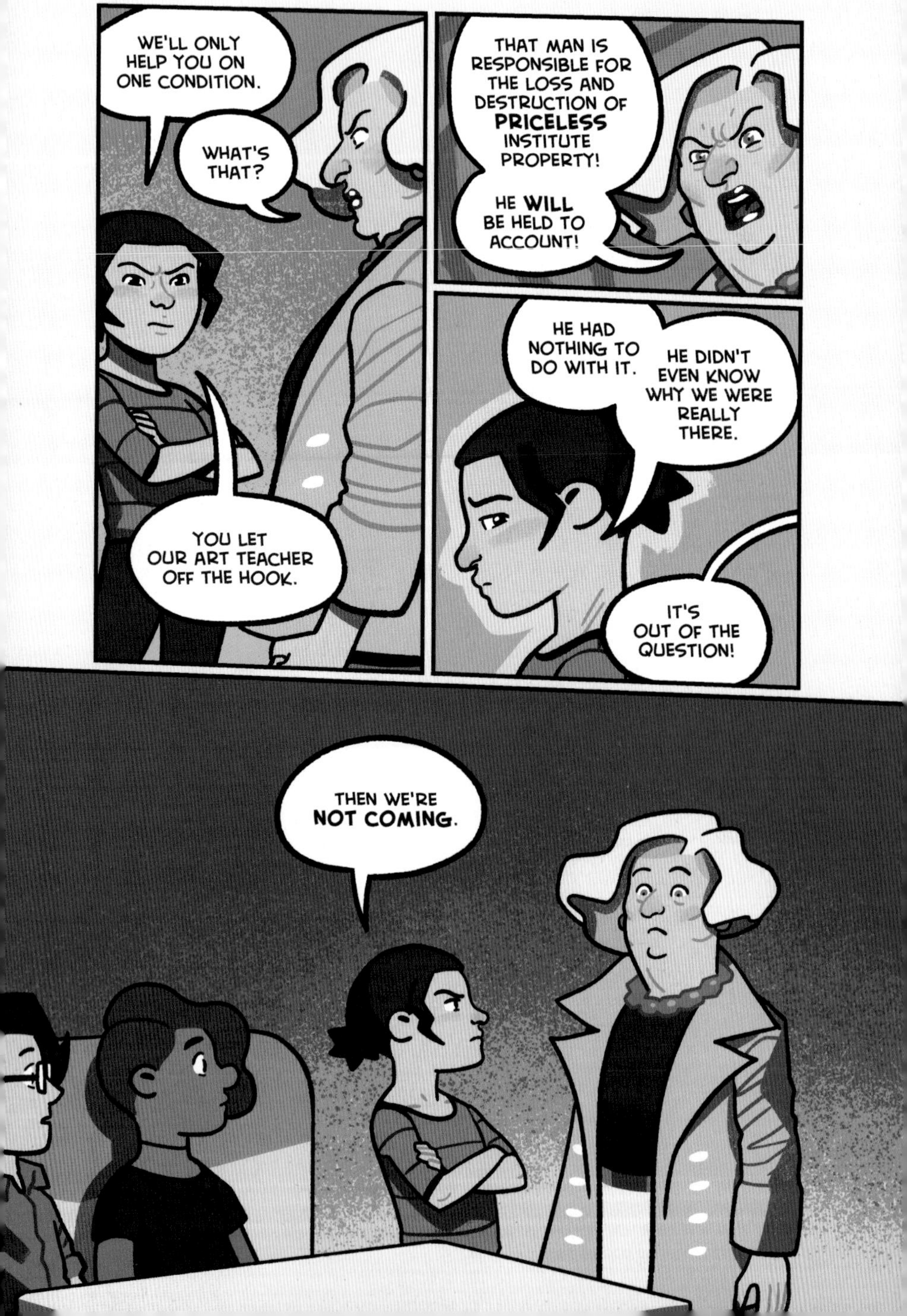
WE'LL ONLY HELP YOU ON ONE CONDITION.
WHAT'S THAT?
YOU LET OUR ART TEACHER OFF THE HOOK.
THAT MAN IS RESPONSIBLE FOR THE LOSS AND DESTRUCTION OF **PRICELESS** INSTITUTE PROPERTY!
HE **WILL** BE HELD TO ACCOUNT!
HE HAD NOTHING TO DO WITH IT.
HE DIDN'T EVEN KNOW WHY WE WERE REALLY THERE.
IT'S OUT OF THE QUESTION!
THEN WE'RE **NOT COMING**.

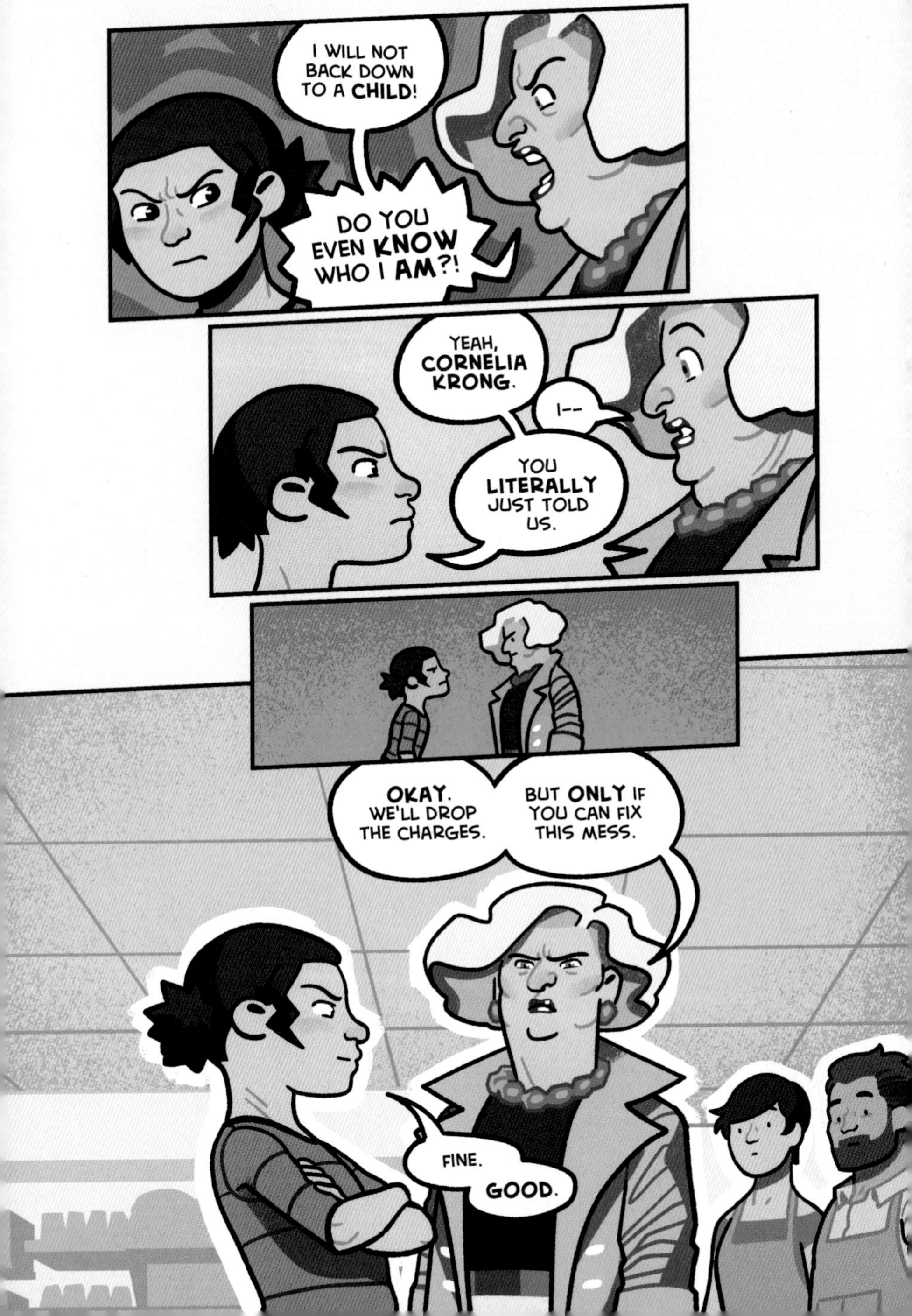
I WILL NOT BACK DOWN TO A CHILD!
DO YOU EVEN KNOW WHO I AM?!
YEAH, CORNELIA KRONG.
I--
YOU LITERALLY JUST TOLD US.
OKAY. WE'LL DROP THE CHARGES.
BUT ONLY IF YOU CAN FIX THIS MESS.
FINE.
GOOD.

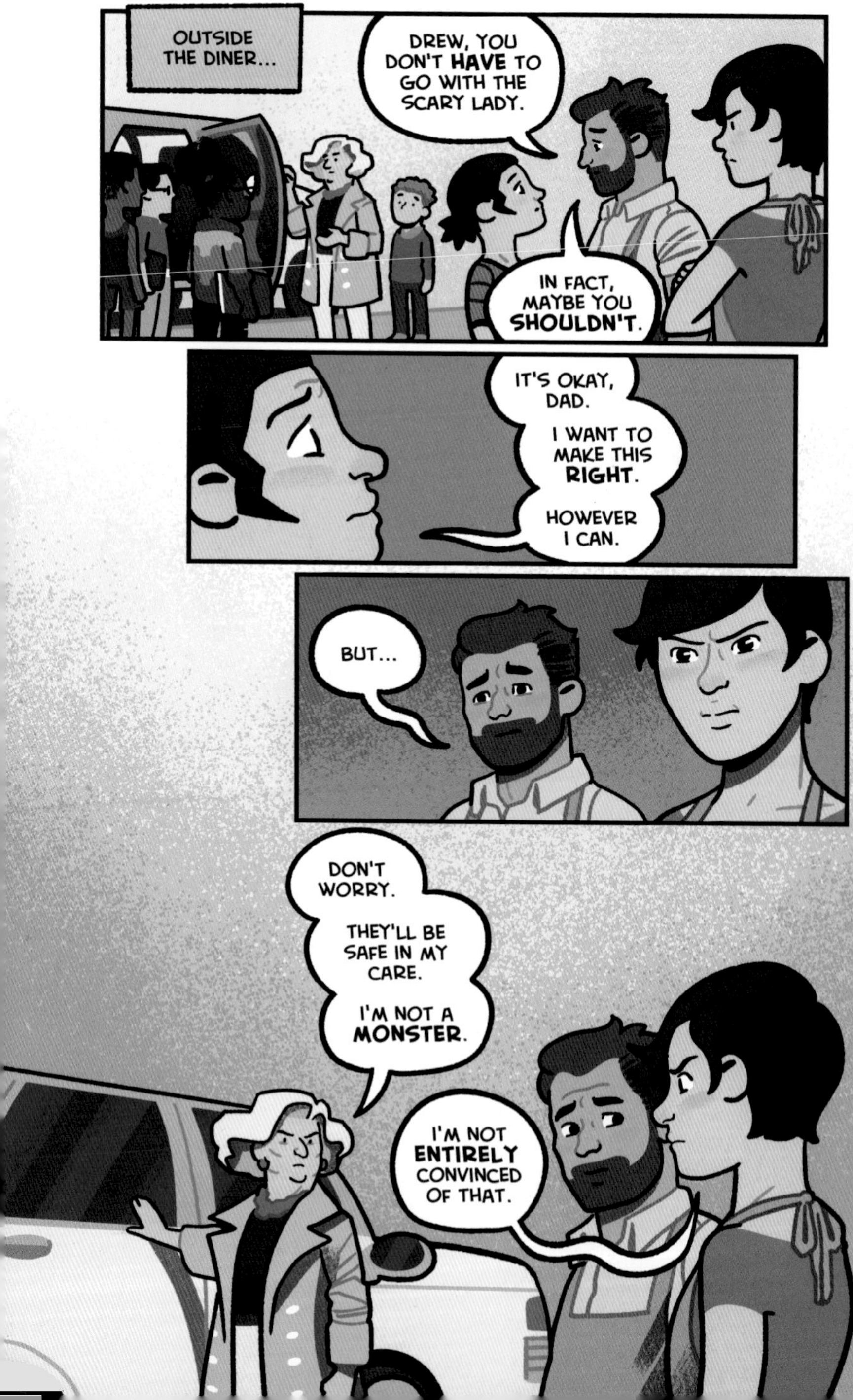
OUTSIDE THE DINER...
DREW, YOU DON'T **HAVE** TO GO WITH THE SCARY LADY.
IN FACT, MAYBE YOU **SHOULDN'T**.
IT'S OKAY, DAD.
I WANT TO MAKE THIS **RIGHT**.
HOWEVER I CAN.
BUT...
DON'T WORRY.
THEY'LL BE SAFE IN MY CARE.
I'M NOT A **MONSTER**.
I'M NOT **ENTIRELY** CONVINCED OF THAT.

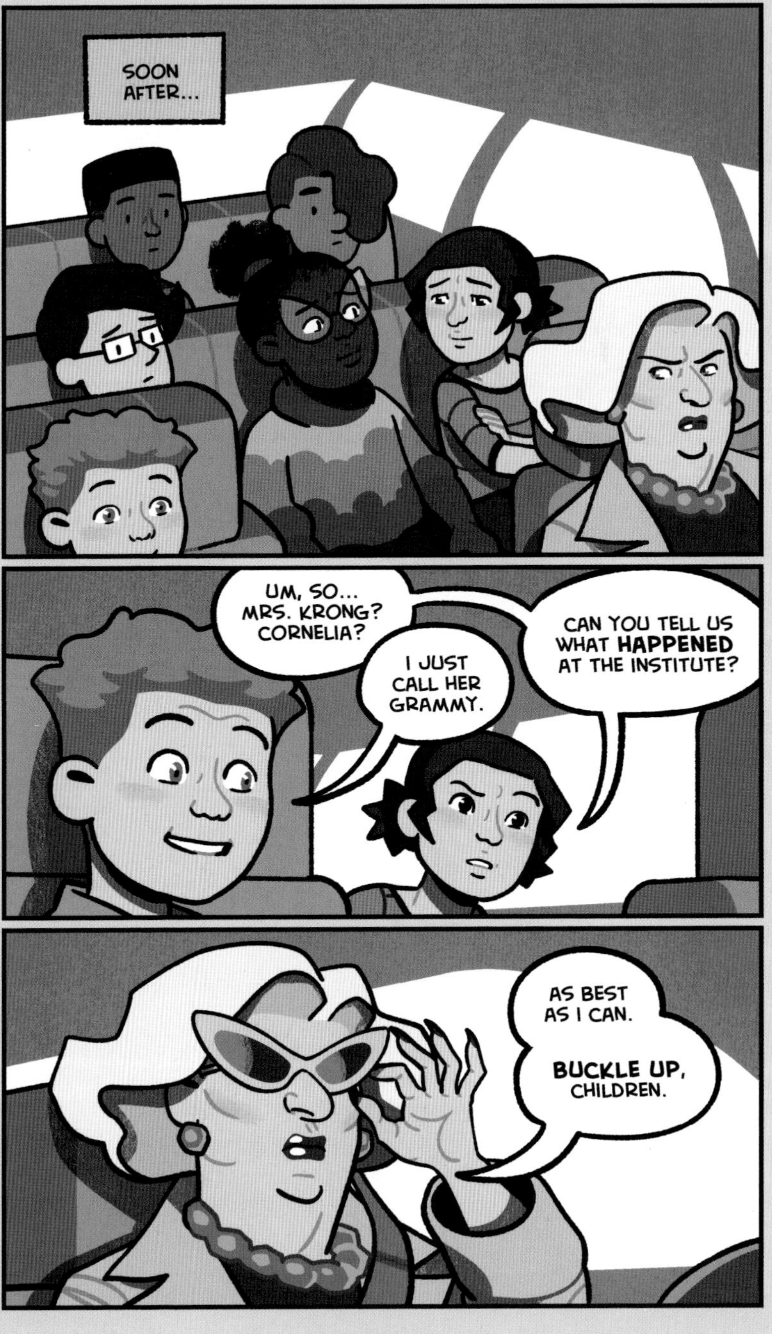
SOON AFTER...
UM, SO... MRS. KRONG? CORNELIA?
I JUST CALL HER GRAMMY.
CAN YOU TELL US WHAT **HAPPENED** AT THE INSTITUTE?
AS BEST AS I CAN.
BUCKLE UP, CHILDREN.

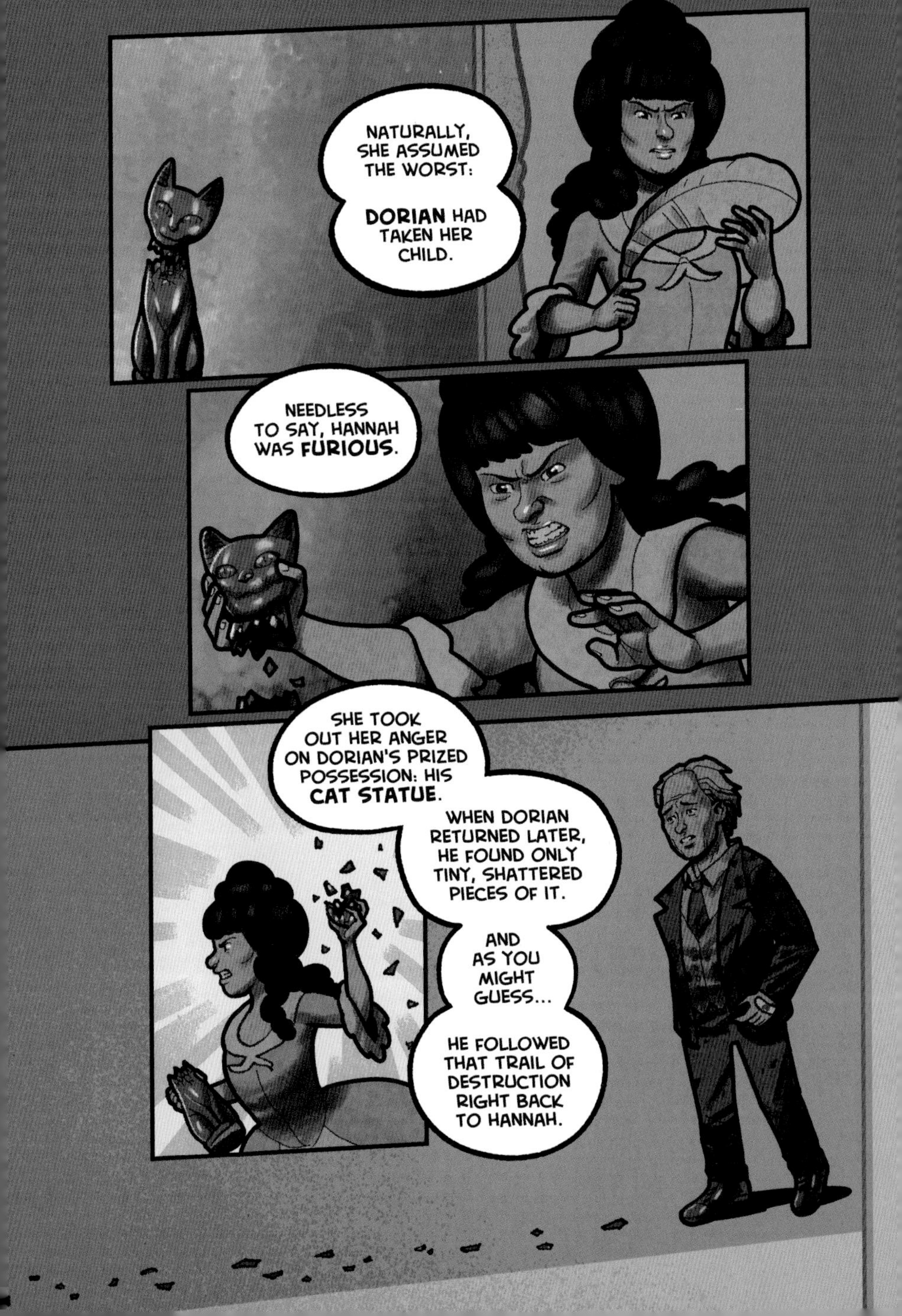
NATURALLY, SHE ASSUMED THE WORST:
DORIAN HAD TAKEN HER CHILD.
NEEDLESS TO SAY, HANNAH WAS FURIOUS.
SHE TOOK OUT HER ANGER ON DORIAN'S PRIZED POSSESSION: HIS CAT STATUE.
WHEN DORIAN RETURNED LATER, HE FOUND ONLY TINY, SHATTERED PIECES OF IT.
AND AS YOU MIGHT GUESS...
HE FOLLOWED THAT TRAIL OF DESTRUCTION RIGHT BACK TO HANNAH.

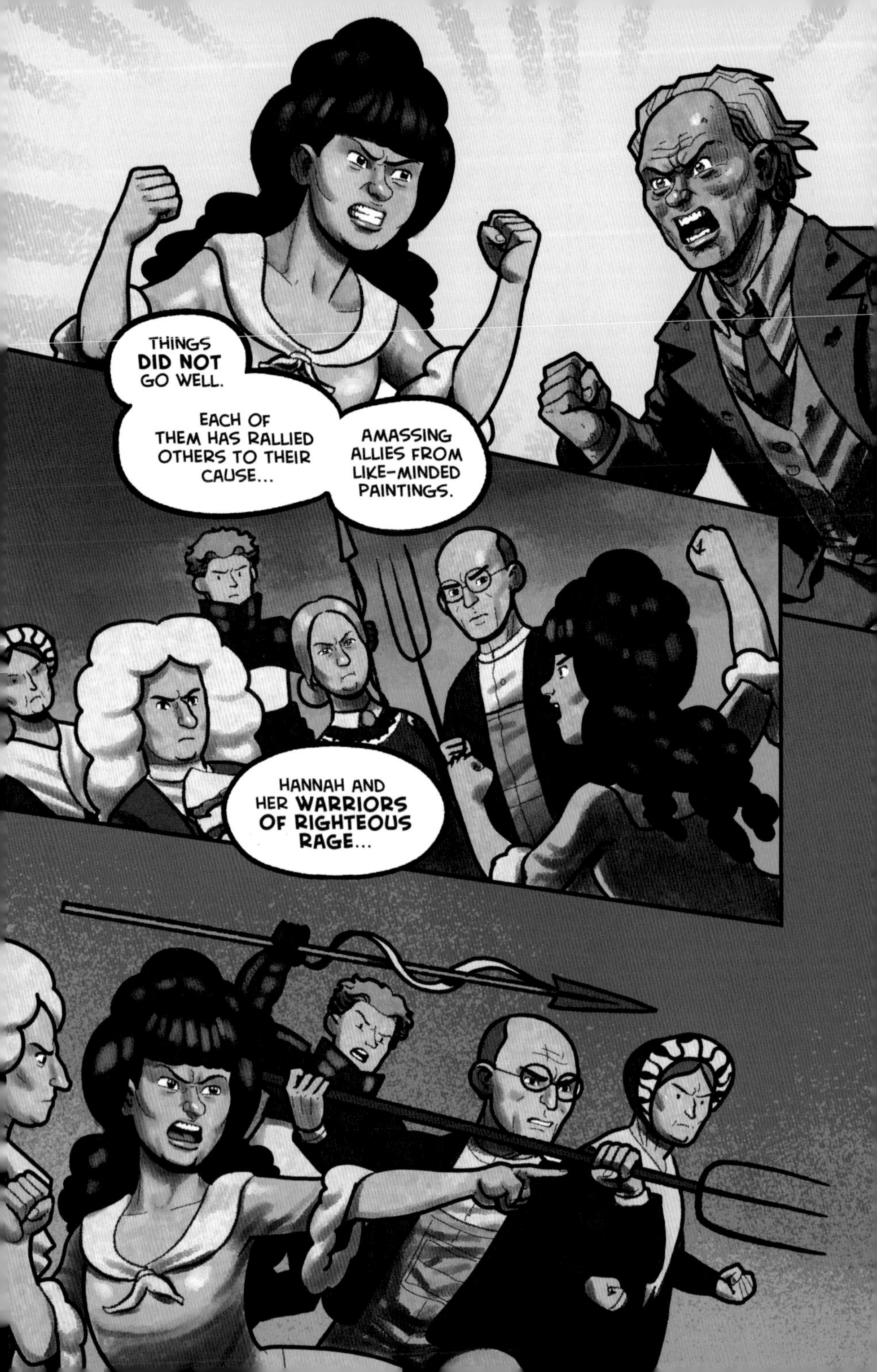
THINGS DID NOT GO WELL.
EACH OF THEM HAS RALLIED OTHERS TO THEIR CAUSE...
AMASSING ALLIES FROM LIKE-MINDED PAINTINGS.
HANNAH AND HER WARRIORS OF RIGHTEOUS RAGE...

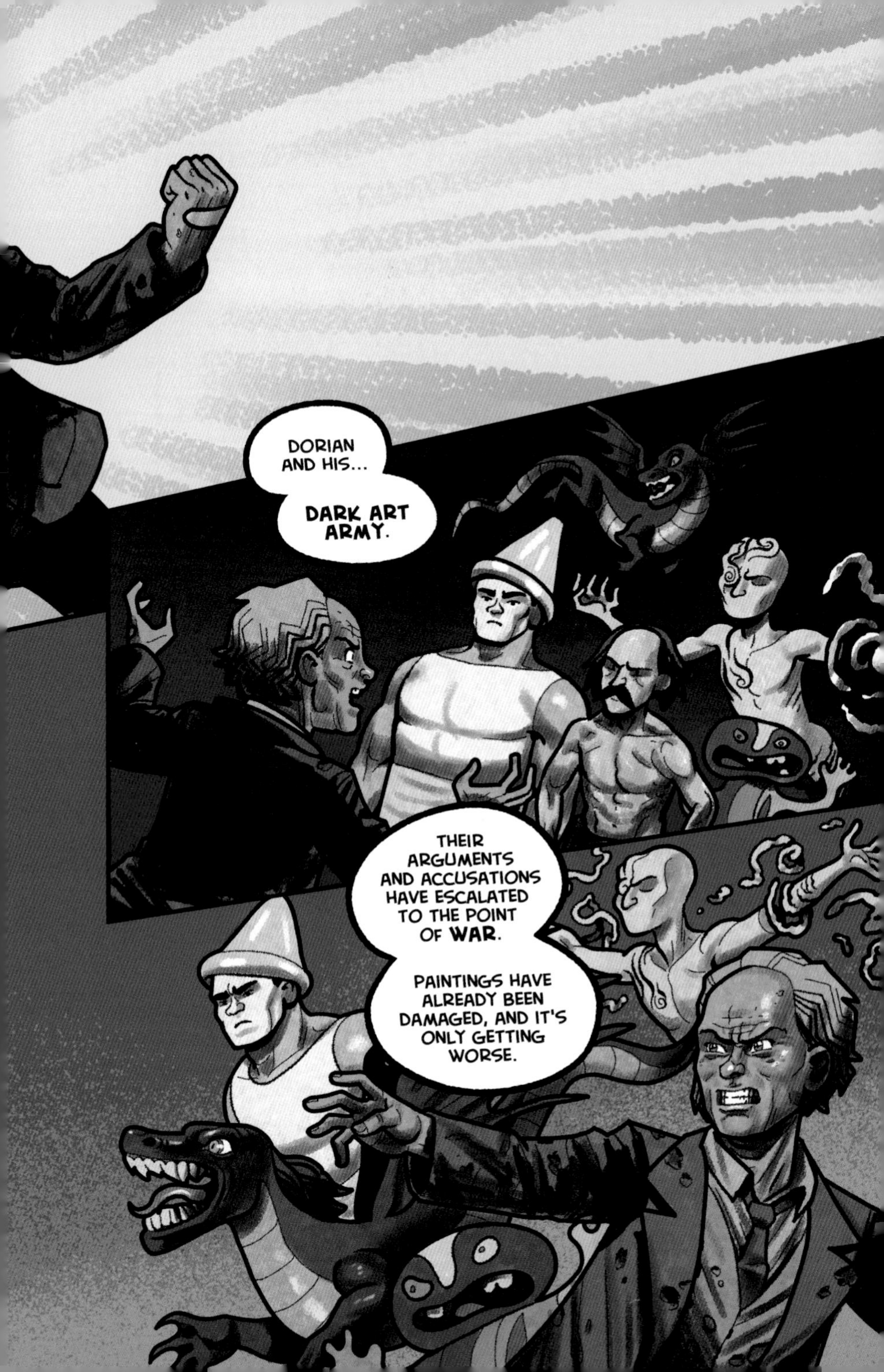
DORIAN AND HIS...
DARK ART ARMY.
THEIR ARGUMENTS AND ACCUSATIONS HAVE ESCALATED TO THE POINT OF WAR.
PAINTINGS HAVE ALREADY BEEN DAMAGED, AND IT'S ONLY GETTING WORSE.

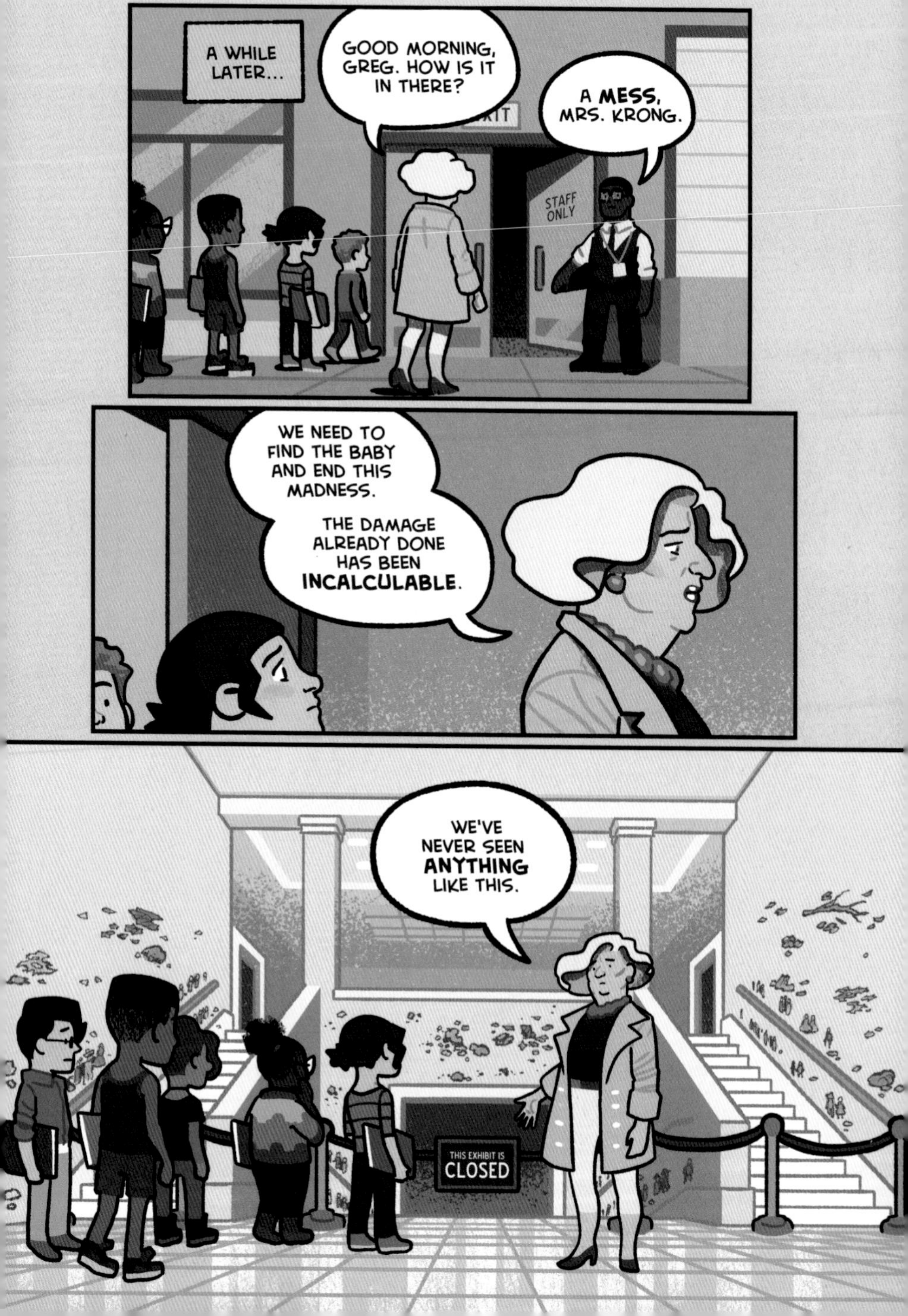
A WHILE LATER...
GOOD MORNING, GREG. HOW IS IT IN THERE?
A MESS, MRS. KRONG.
EXIT
STAFF ONLY
WE NEED TO FIND THE BABY AND END THIS MADNESS.
THE DAMAGE ALREADY DONE HAS BEEN INCALCULABLE.
WE'VE NEVER SEEN ANYTHING LIKE THIS.
THIS EXHIBIT IS CLOSED

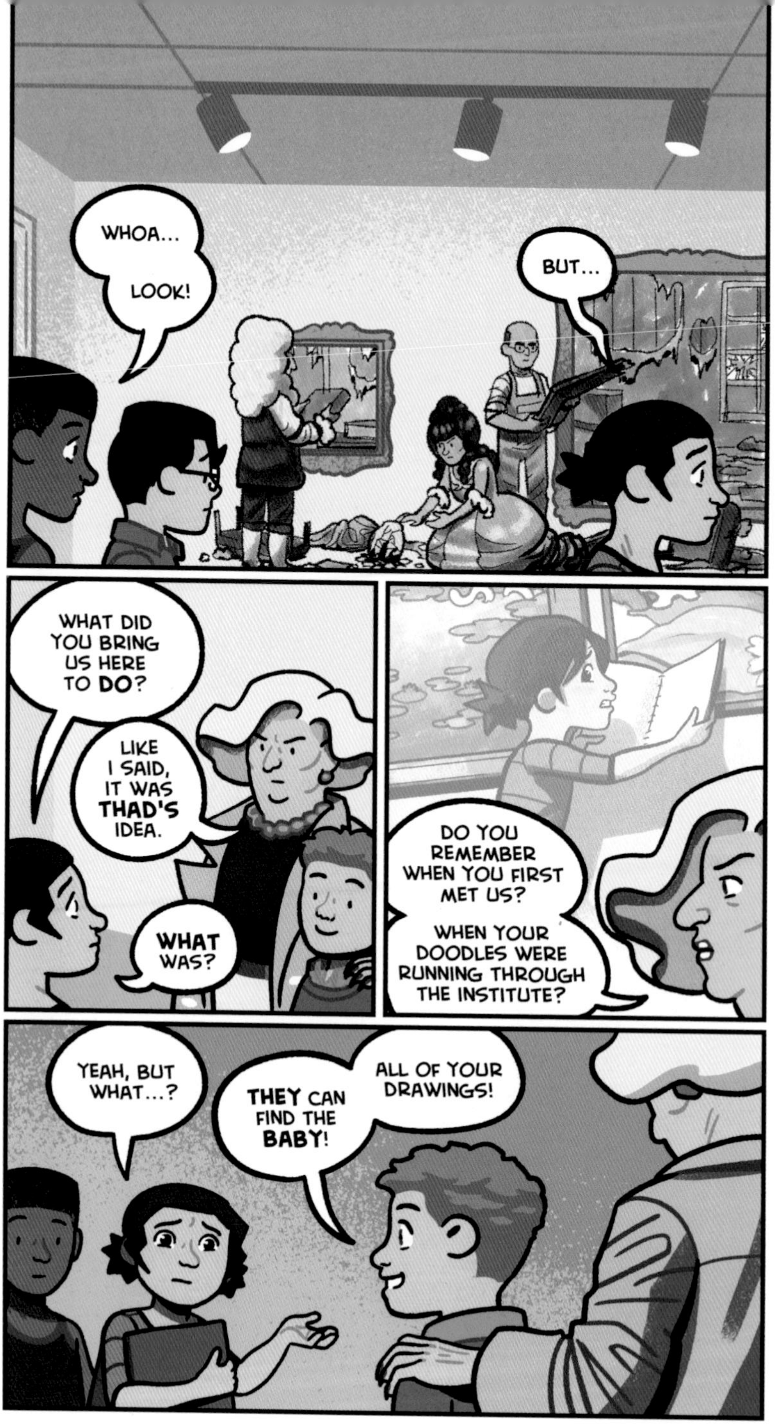
WHOA...
LOOK!
BUT...
WHAT DID YOU BRING US HERE TO **DO**?
LIKE I SAID, IT WAS **THAD'S** IDEA.
WHAT WAS?
DO YOU REMEMBER WHEN YOU FIRST MET US?
WHEN YOUR DOODLES WERE RUNNING THROUGH THE INSTITUTE?
YEAH, BUT WHAT...?
ALL OF YOUR DRAWINGS!
THEY CAN FIND THE **BABY**!

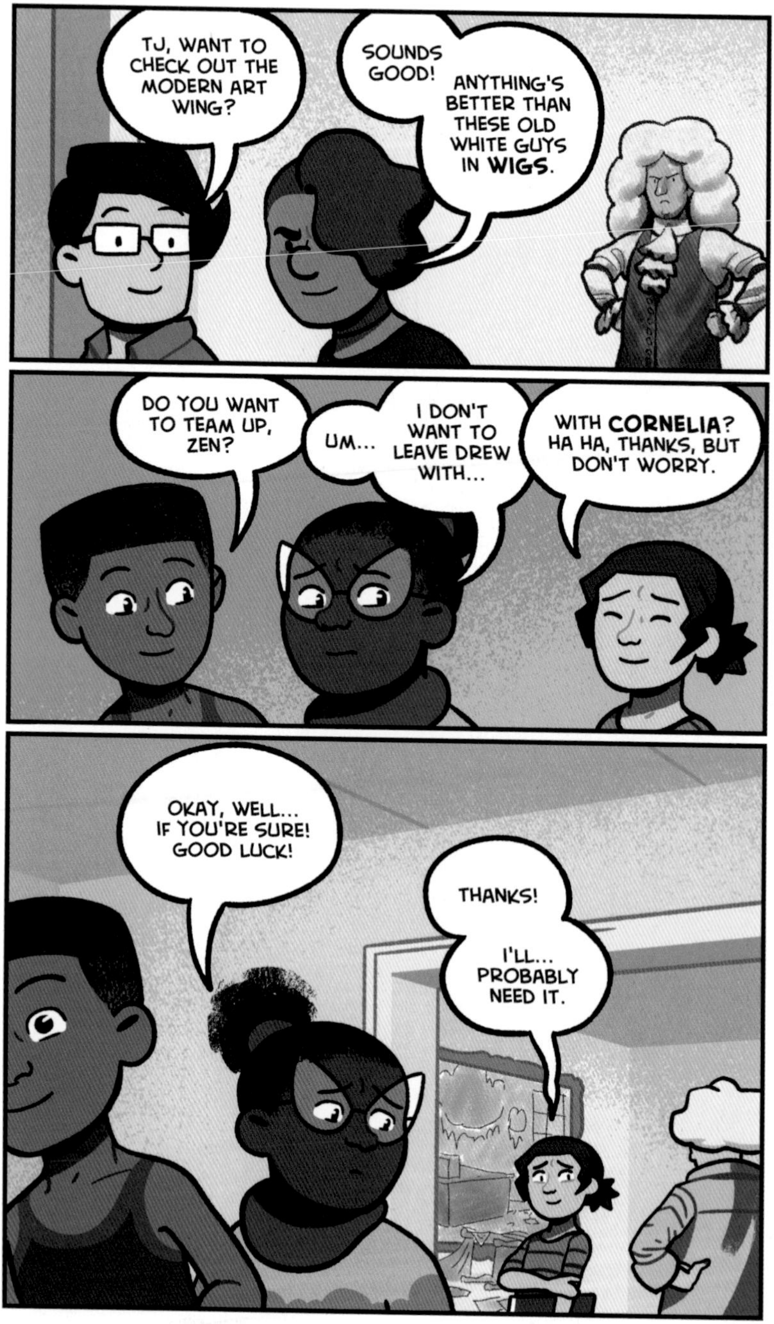
TJ, WANT TO CHECK OUT THE MODERN ART WING?
SOUNDS GOOD!
ANYTHING'S BETTER THAN THESE OLD WHITE GUYS IN **WIGS**.
DO YOU WANT TO TEAM UP, ZEN?
UM...
I DON'T WANT TO LEAVE DREW WITH...
WITH **CORNELIA**? HA HA, THANKS, BUT DON'T WORRY.
OKAY, WELL... IF YOU'RE SURE! GOOD LUCK!
THANKS!
I'LL... PROBABLY NEED IT.

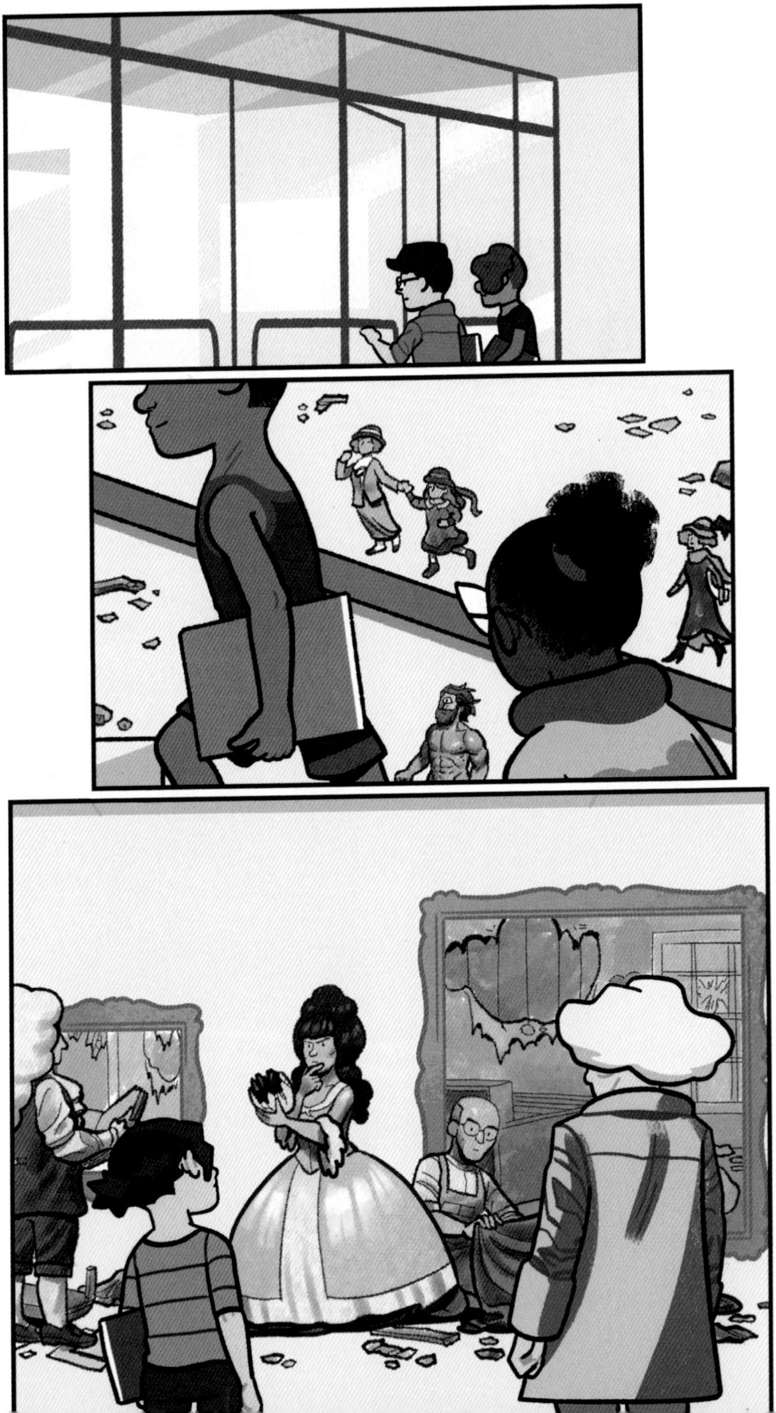

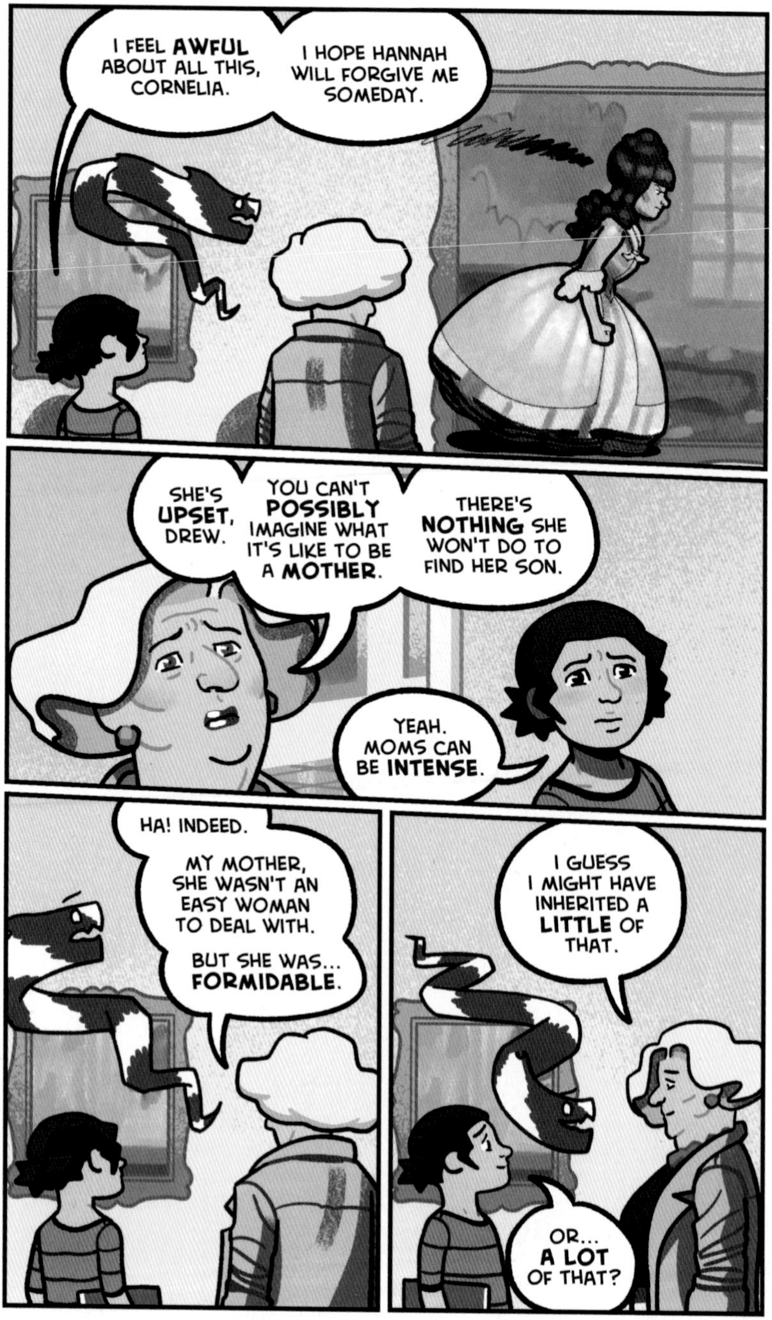
I FEEL AWFUL ABOUT ALL THIS, CORNELIA.
I HOPE HANNAH WILL FORGIVE ME SOMEDAY.
SHE'S UPSET, DREW.
YOU CAN'T POSSIBLY IMAGINE WHAT IT'S LIKE TO BE A MOTHER.
THERE'S NOTHING SHE WON'T DO TO FIND HER SON.
YEAH. MOMS CAN BE INTENSE.
HA! INDEED.
MY MOTHER, SHE WASN'T AN EASY WOMAN TO DEAL WITH.
BUT SHE WAS... FORMIDABLE.
I GUESS I MIGHT HAVE INHERITED A LITTLE OF THAT.
OR... A LOT OF THAT?

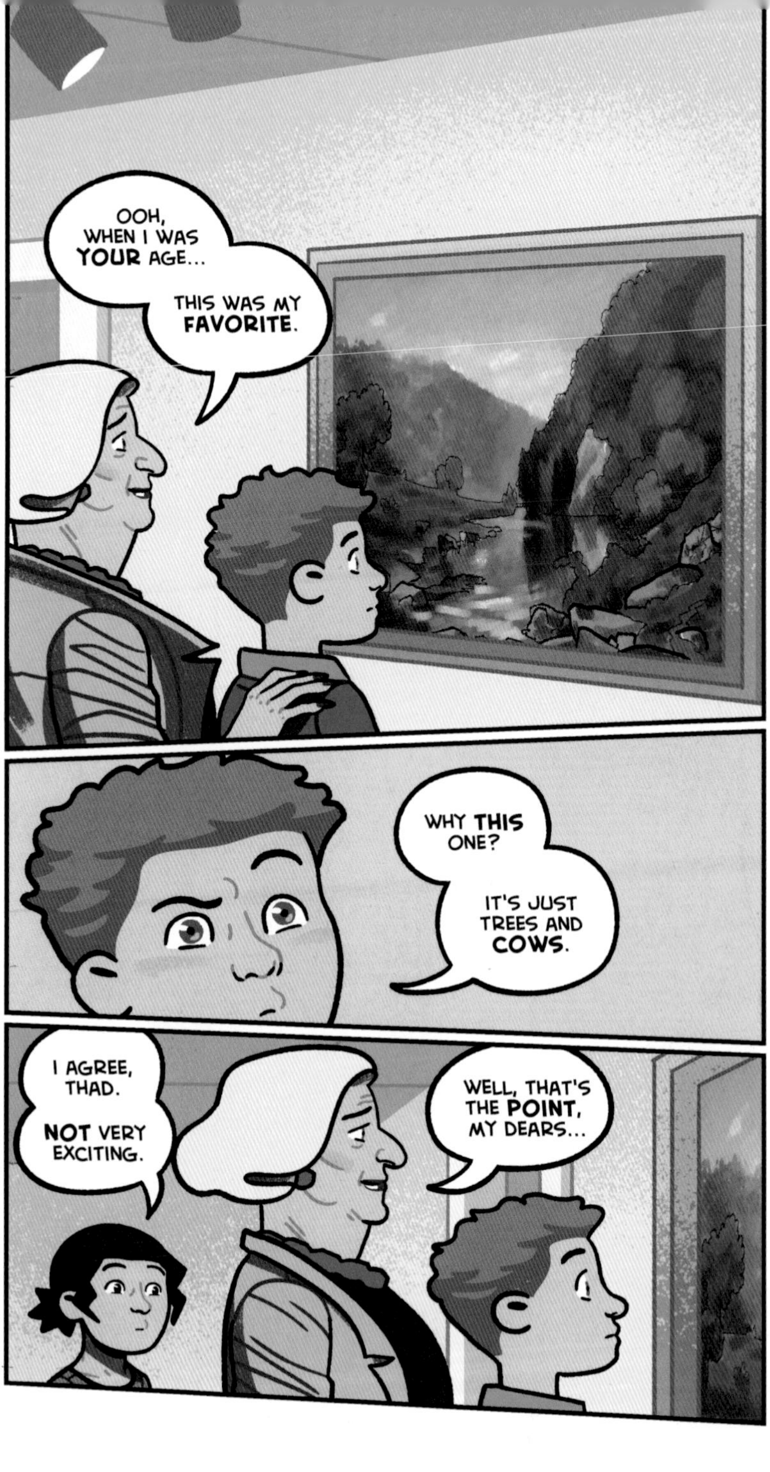
OOH, WHEN I WAS YOUR AGE...
THIS WAS MY FAVORITE.
WHY THIS ONE?
IT'S JUST TREES AND COWS.
I AGREE, THAD.
NOT VERY EXCITING.
WELL, THAT'S THE POINT, MY DEARS...

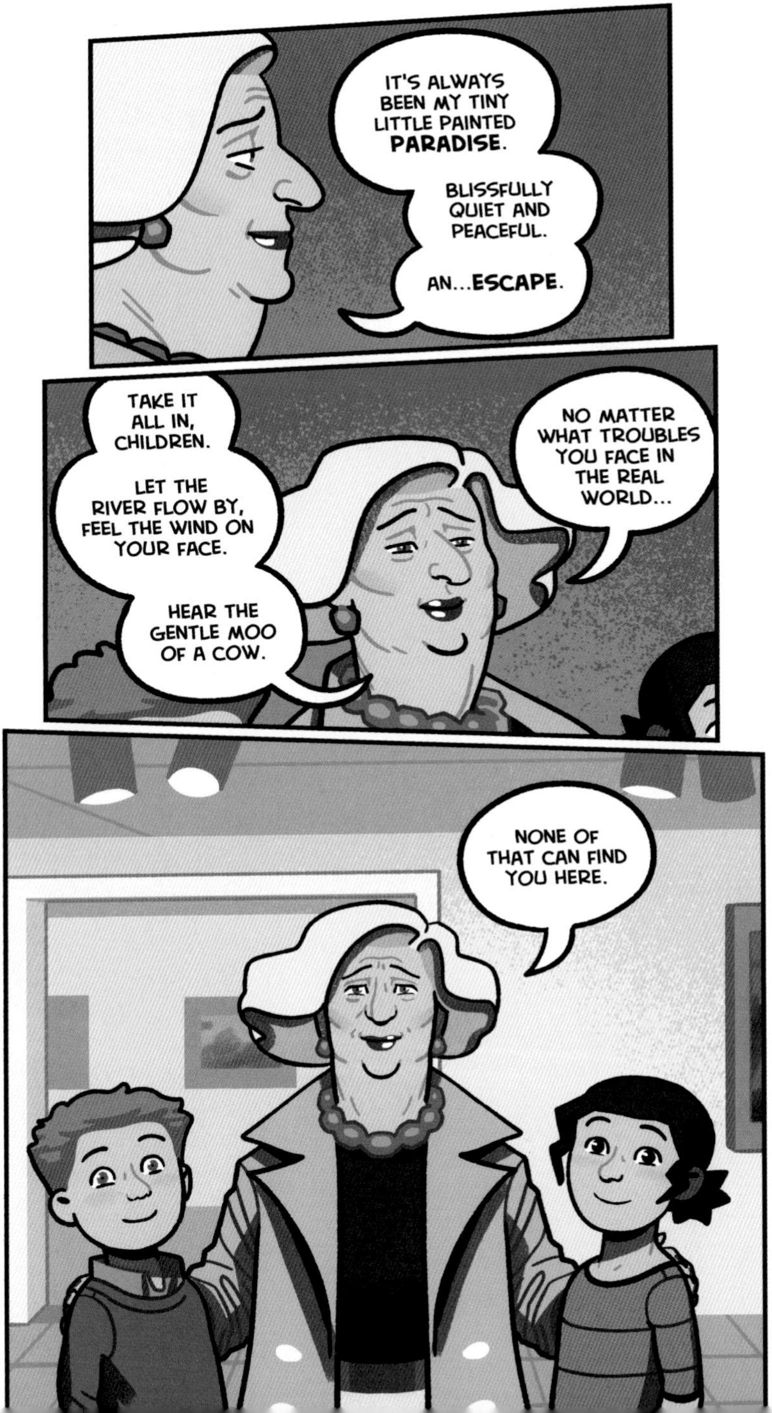
IT'S ALWAYS BEEN MY TINY LITTLE PAINTED **PARADISE**.
BLISSFULLY QUIET AND PEACEFUL.
AN...**ESCAPE**.
TAKE IT ALL IN, CHILDREN.
LET THE RIVER FLOW BY, FEEL THE WIND ON YOUR FACE.
HEAR THE GENTLE MOO OF A COW.
NO MATTER WHAT TROUBLES YOU FACE IN THE REAL WORLD...
NONE OF THAT CAN FIND YOU HERE.

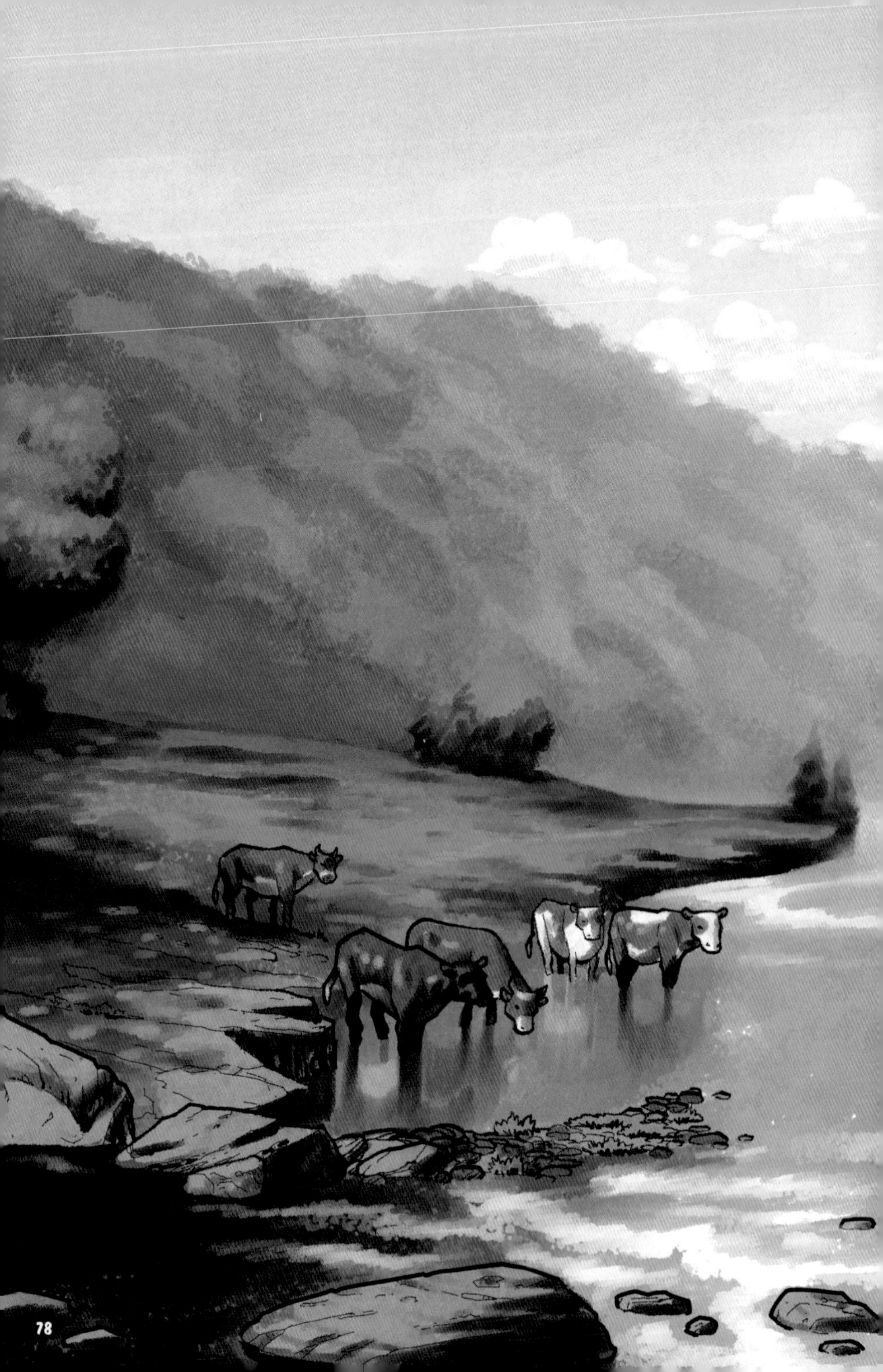

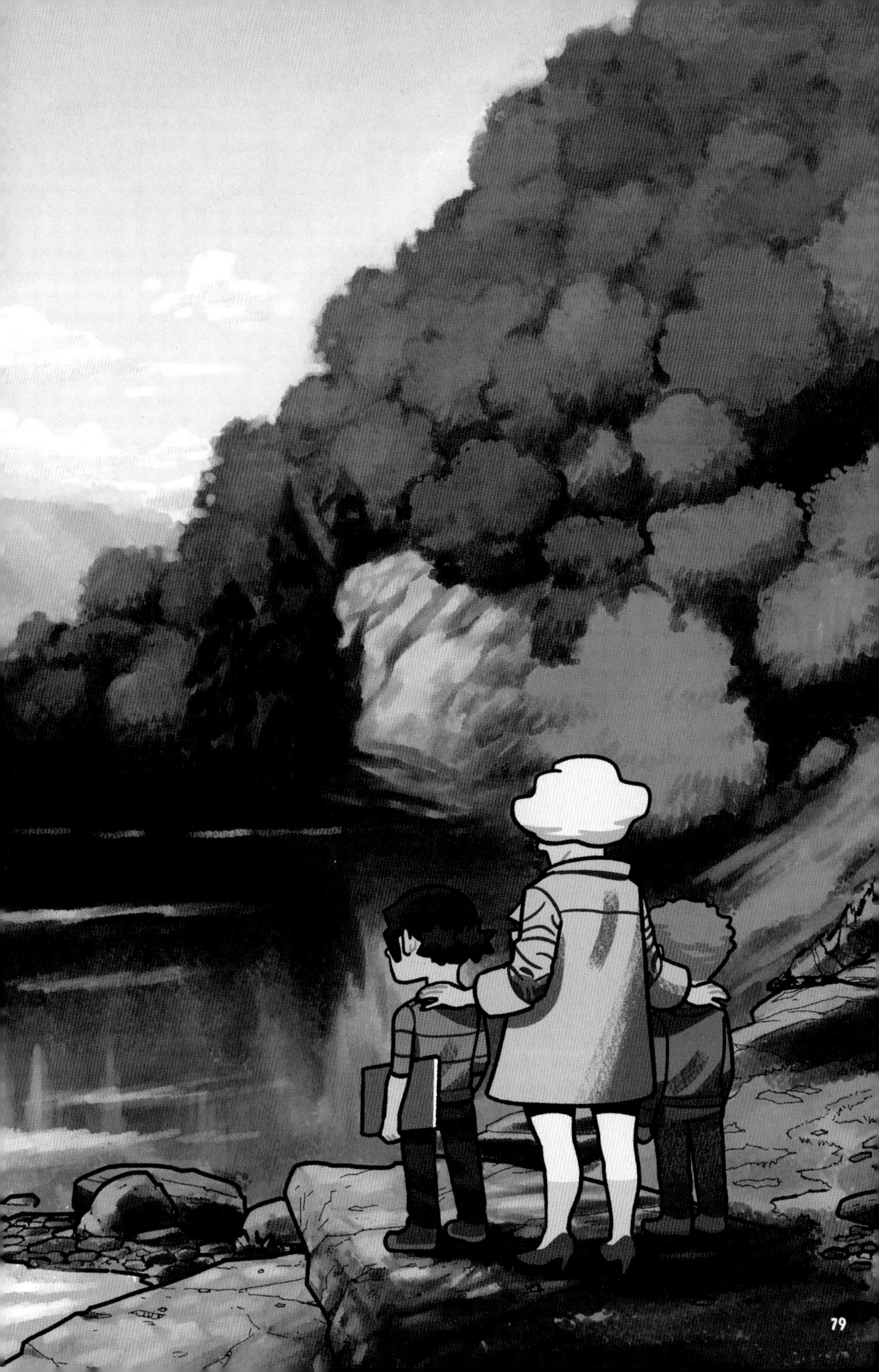

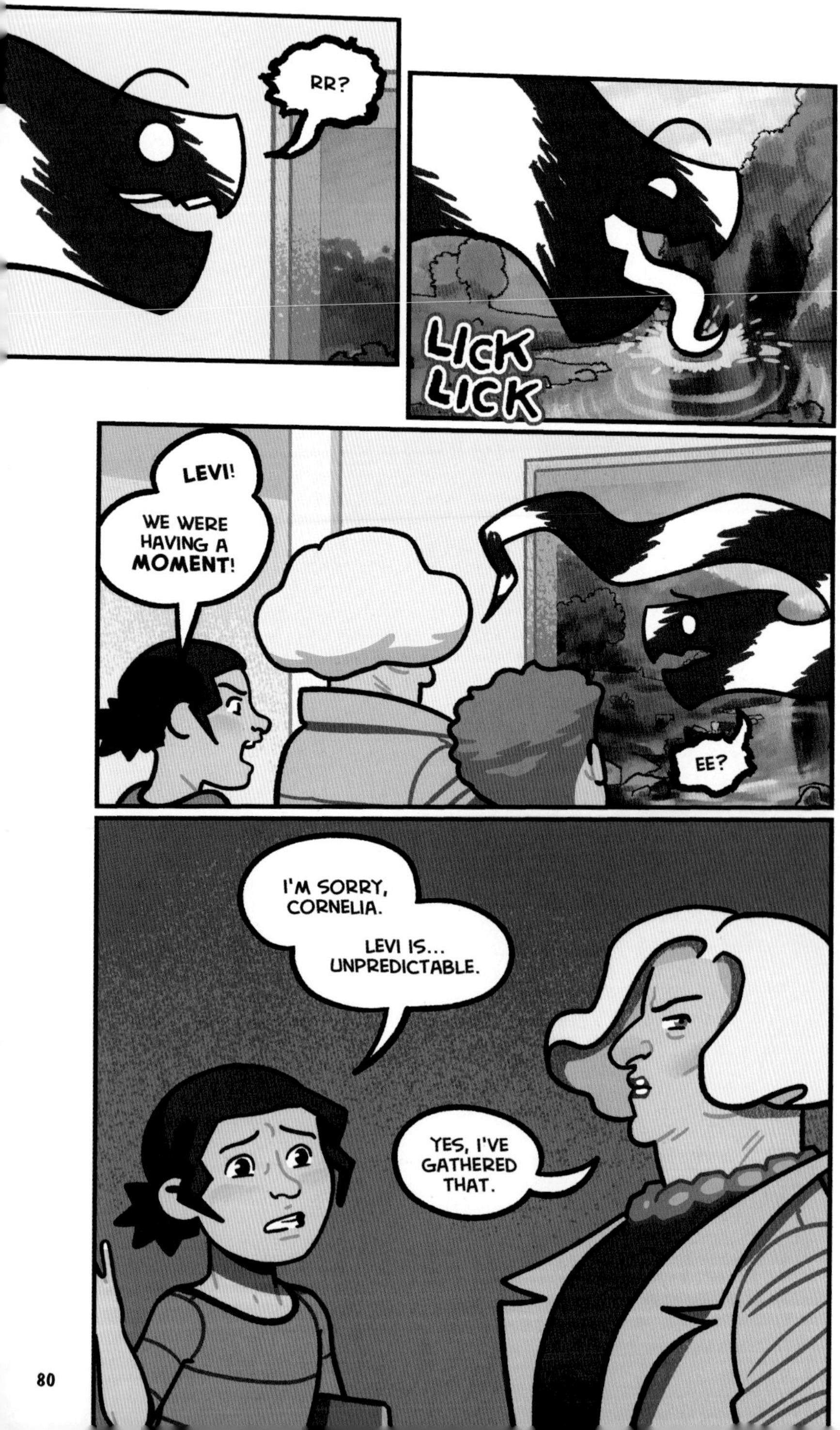
RR?
LICK LICK
LEVI!
WE WERE HAVING A MOMENT!
EE?
I'M SORRY, CORNELIA.
LEVI IS... UNPREDICTABLE.
YES, I'VE GATHERED THAT.

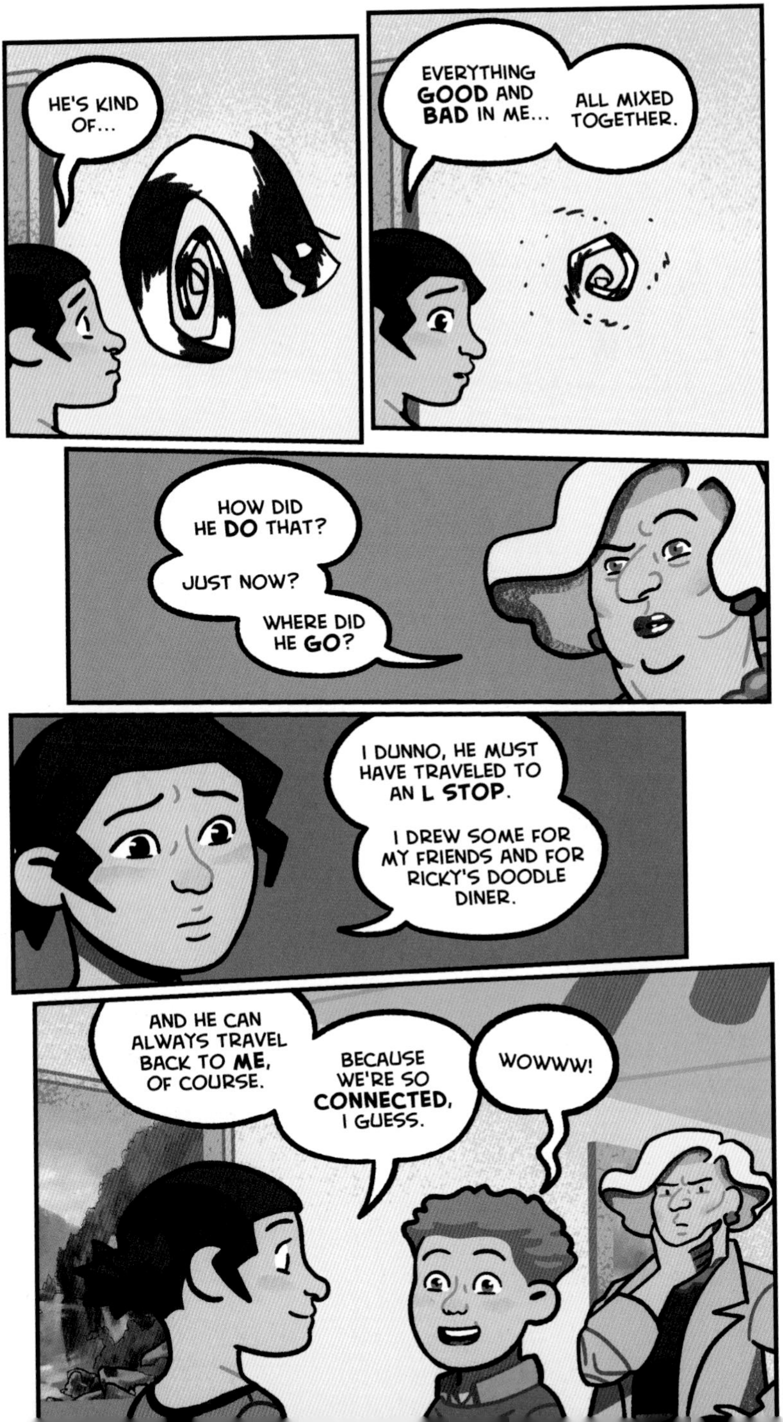
HE'S KIND OF...
EVERYTHING GOOD AND BAD IN ME...
ALL MIXED TOGETHER.
HOW DID HE DO THAT?
JUST NOW?
WHERE DID HE GO?
I DUNNO, HE MUST HAVE TRAVELED TO AN L STOP.
I DREW SOME FOR MY FRIENDS AND FOR RICKY'S DOODLE DINER.
AND HE CAN ALWAYS TRAVEL BACK TO ME, OF COURSE.
BECAUSE WE'RE SO CONNECTED, I GUESS.
WOWWW!

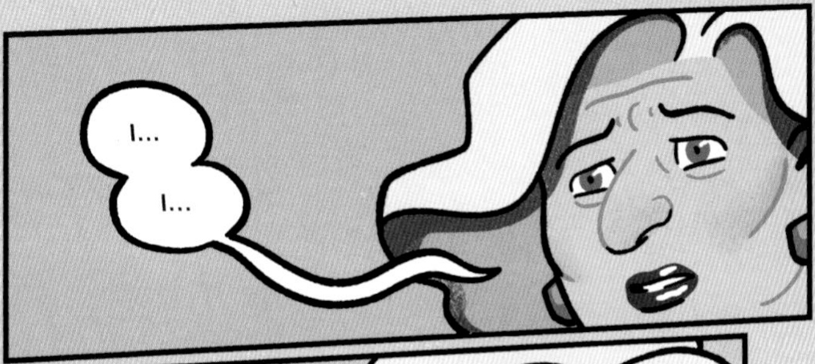
I...
I...

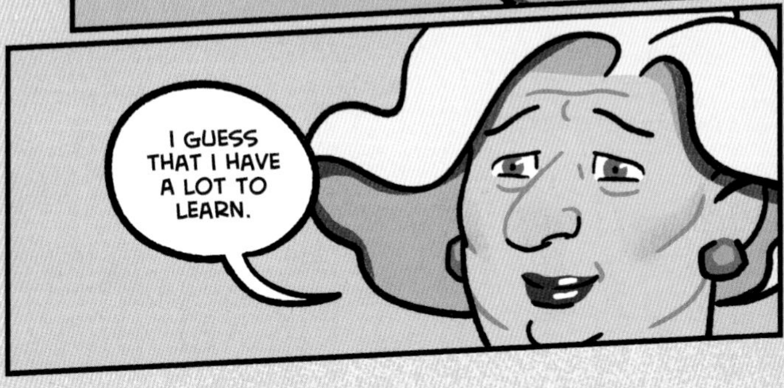
I GUESS THAT I HAVE A LOT TO LEARN.

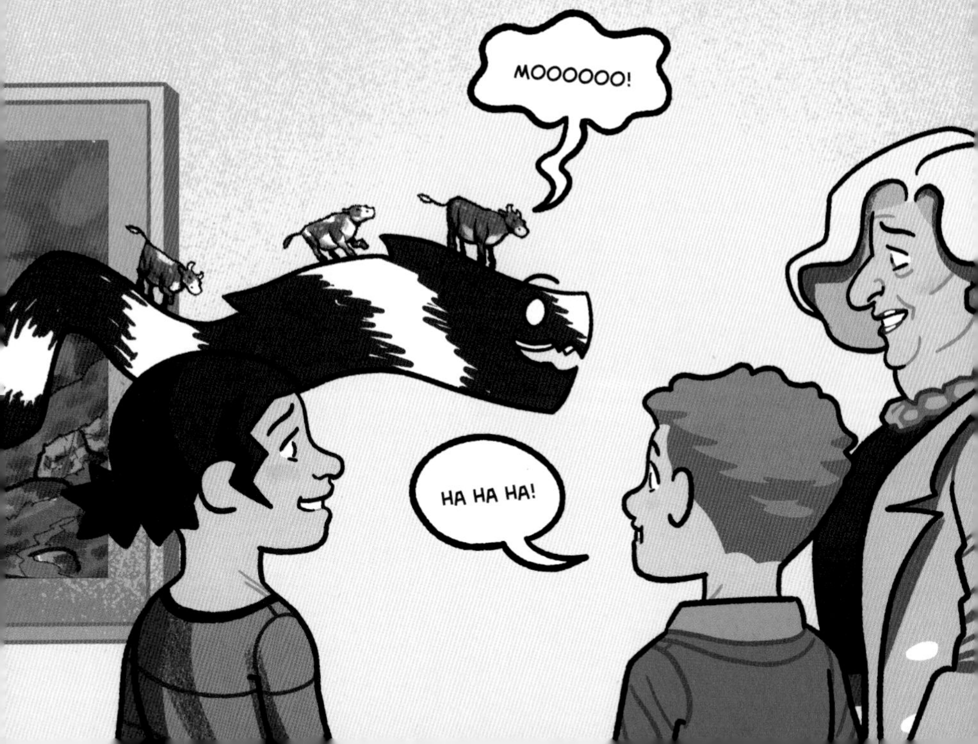
MOOOOOO!
HA HA HA!

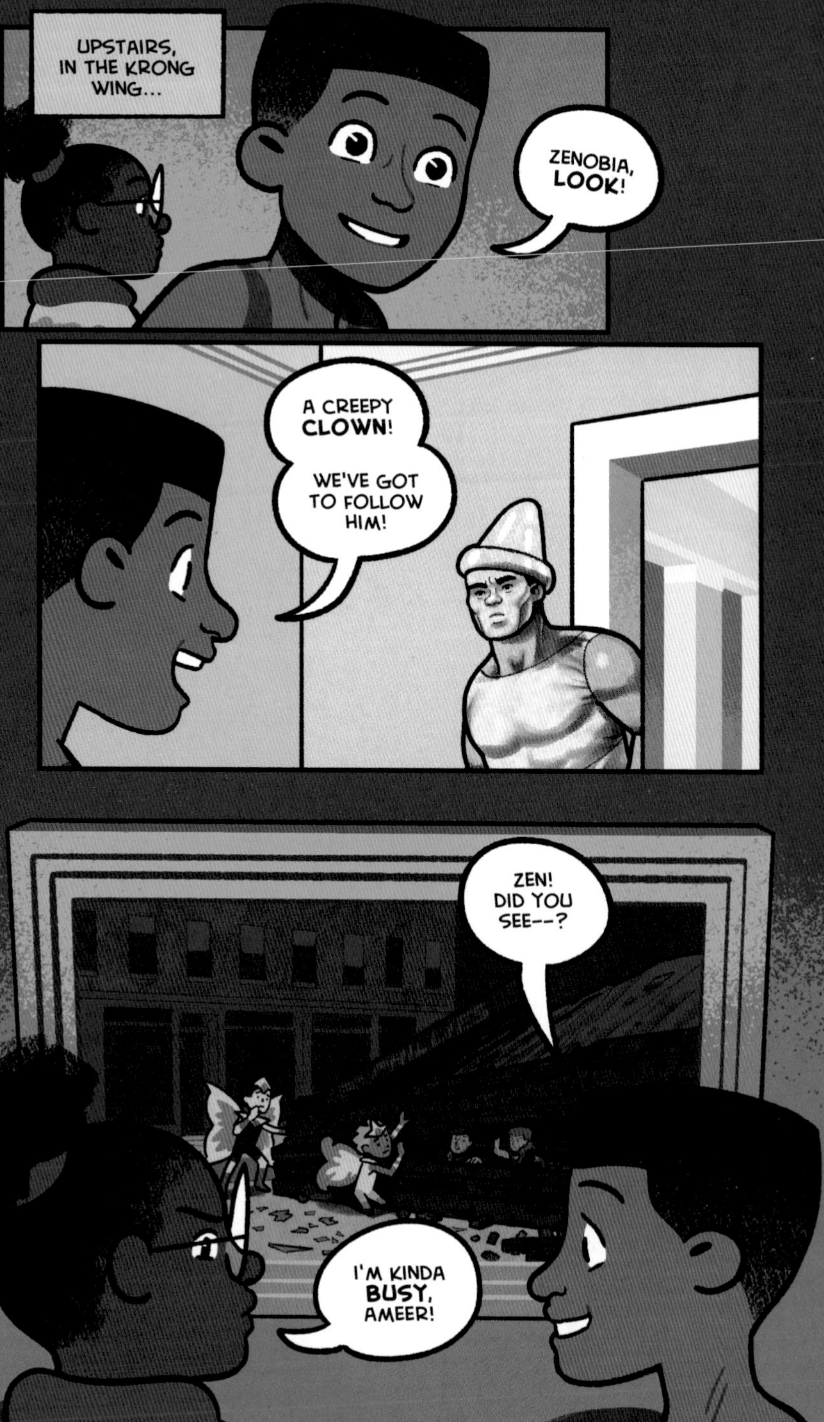
UPSTAIRS, IN THE KRONG WING...
ZENOBIA, LOOK!
A CREEPY CLOWN!
WE'VE GOT TO FOLLOW HIM!
ZEN! DID YOU SEE--?
I'M KINDA BUSY, AMEER!

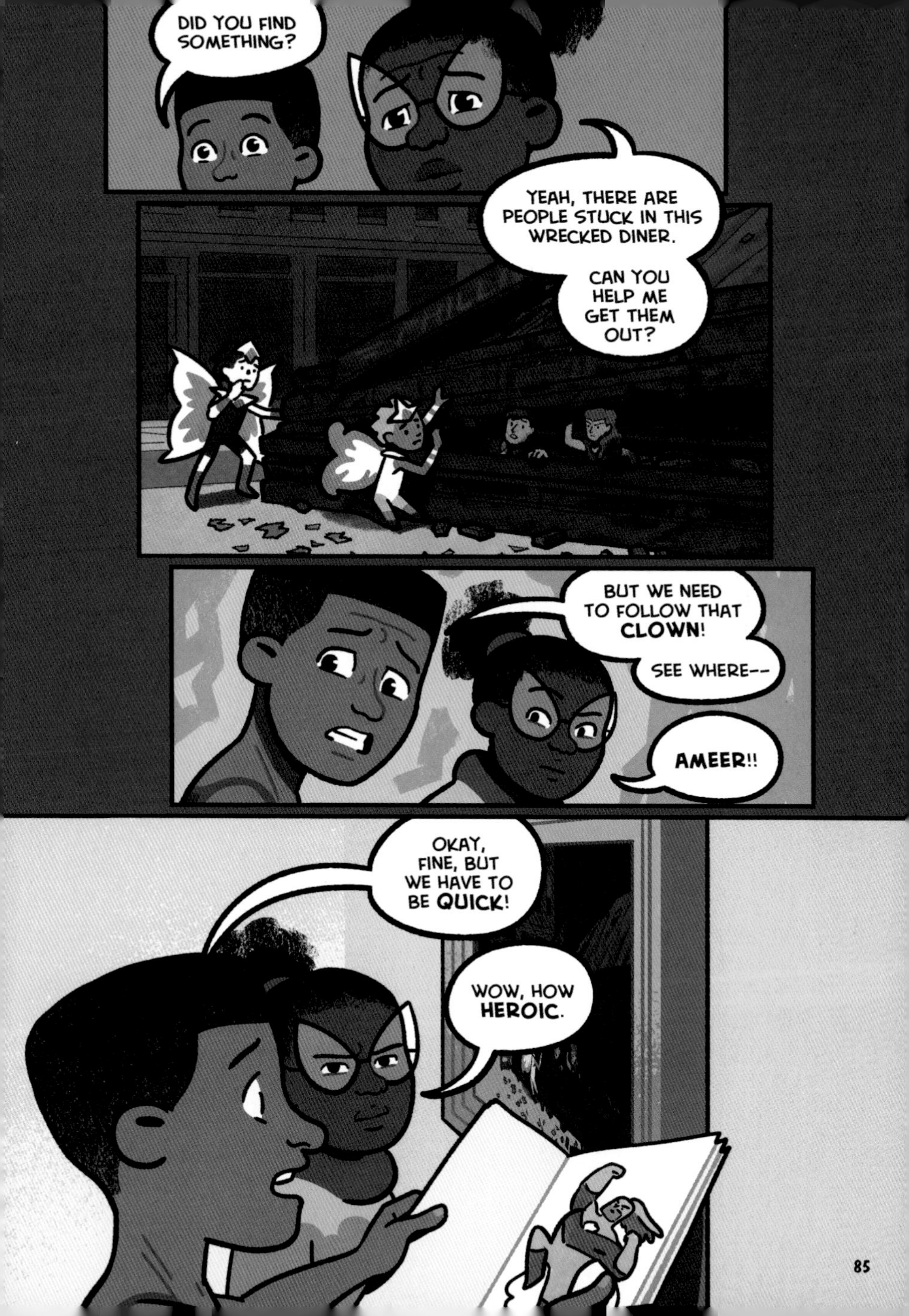

DID YOU FIND SOMETHING?
YEAH, THERE ARE PEOPLE STUCK IN THIS WRECKED DINER.
CAN YOU HELP ME GET THEM OUT?
BUT WE NEED TO FOLLOW THAT **CLOWN**!
SEE WHERE--
AMEER!!
OKAY, FINE, BUT WE HAVE TO BE **QUICK**!
WOW, HOW **HEROIC**.

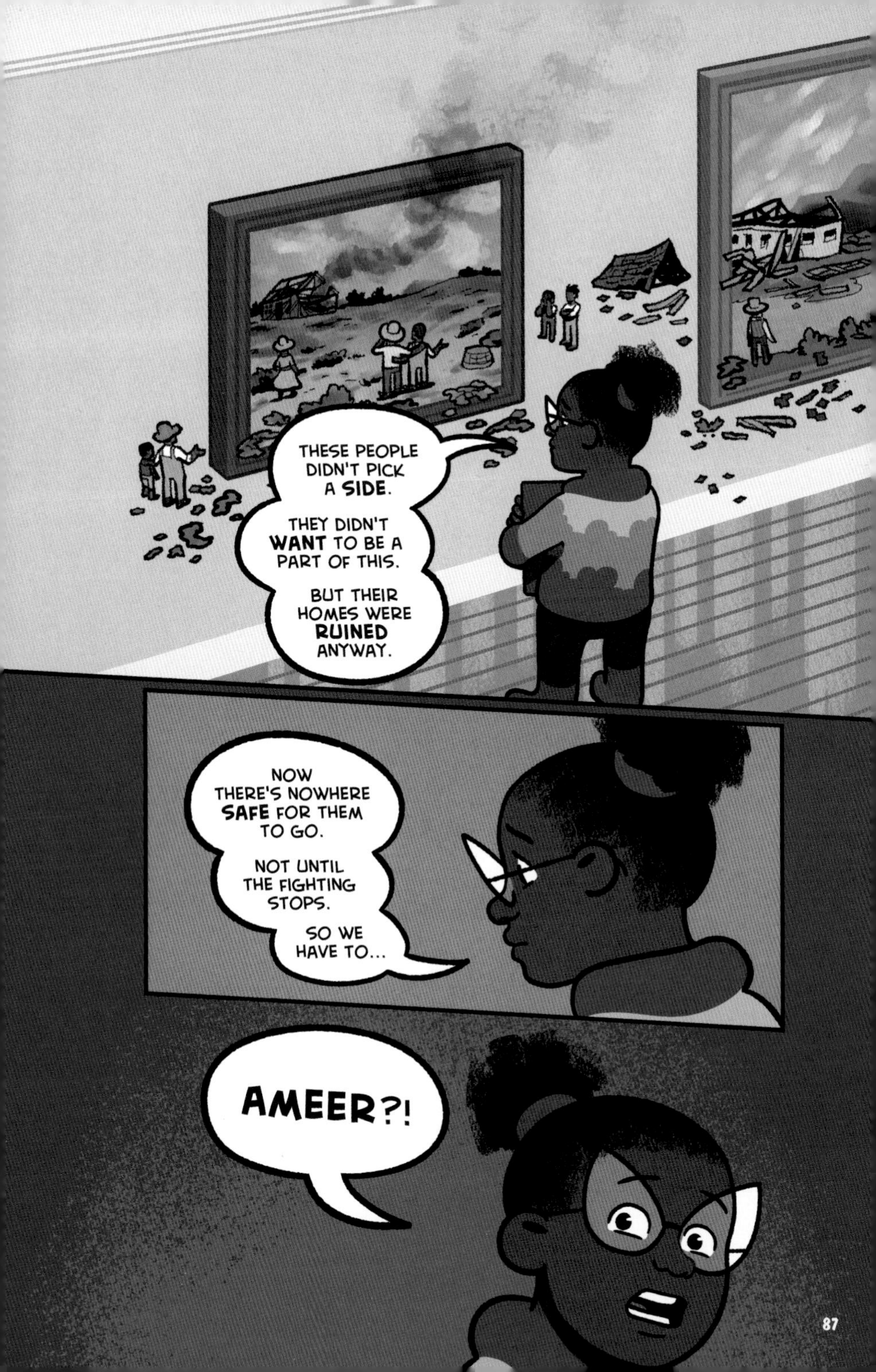

THESE PEOPLE DIDN'T PICK A **SIDE**.
THEY DIDN'T **WANT** TO BE A PART OF THIS.
BUT THEIR HOMES WERE **RUINED** ANYWAY.
NOW THERE'S NOWHERE **SAFE** FOR THEM TO GO.
NOT UNTIL THE FIGHTING STOPS.
SO WE HAVE TO...
AMEER?!

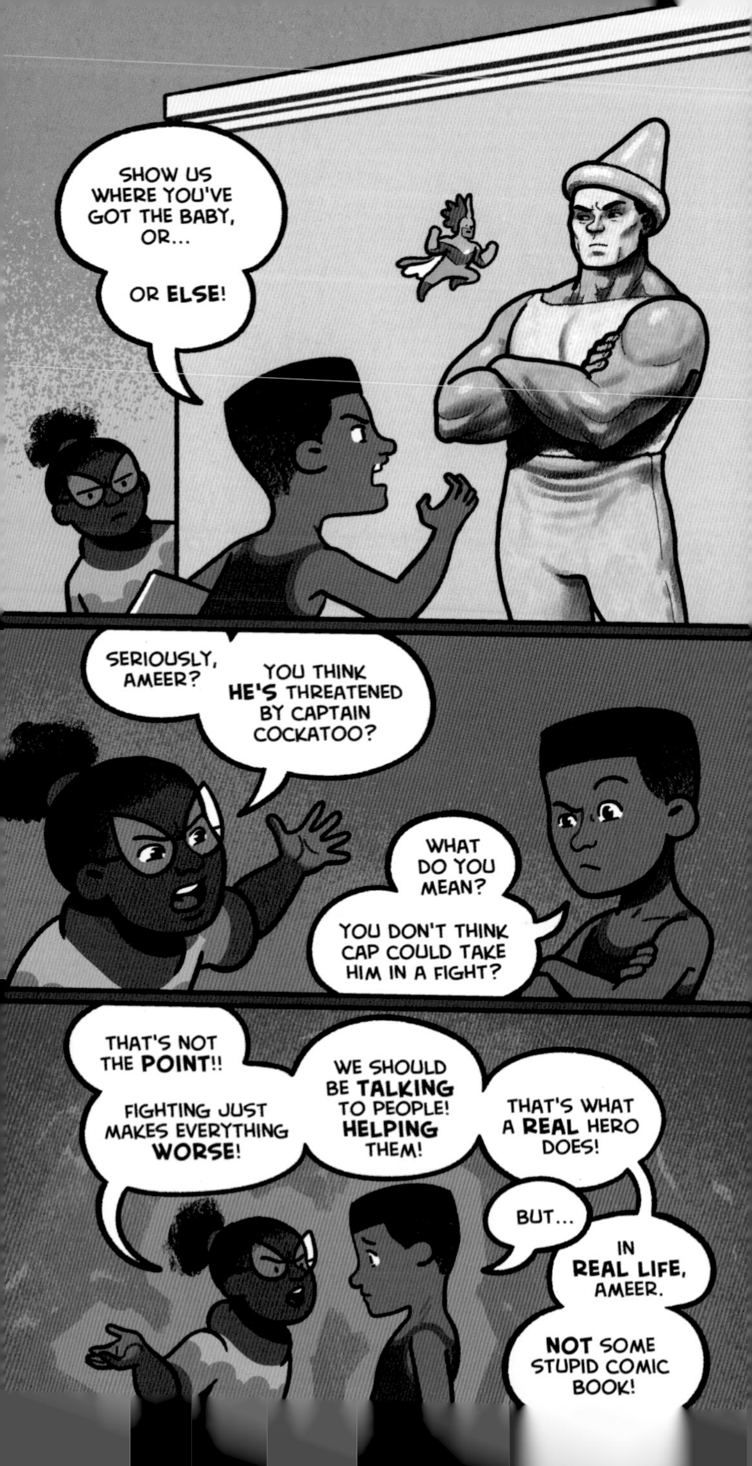
SHOW US WHERE YOU'VE GOT THE BABY, OR...
OR **ELSE**!
SERIOUSLY, AMEER?
YOU THINK **HE'S** THREATENED BY CAPTAIN COCKATOO?
WHAT DO YOU MEAN?
YOU DON'T THINK CAP COULD TAKE HIM IN A FIGHT?
THAT'S NOT THE **POINT**!!
FIGHTING JUST MAKES EVERYTHING **WORSE**!
WE SHOULD BE **TALKING** TO PEOPLE! **HELPING** THEM!
THAT'S WHAT A **REAL** HERO DOES!
BUT...
IN **REAL LIFE,** AMEER.
NOT SOME STUPID COMIC BOOK!

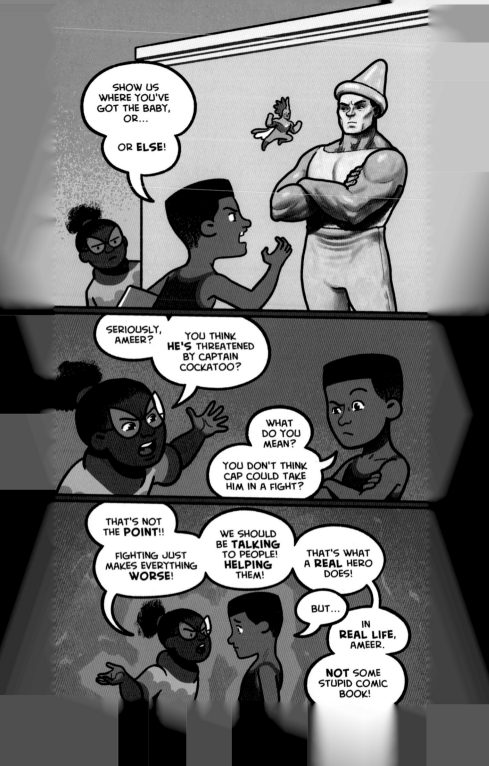

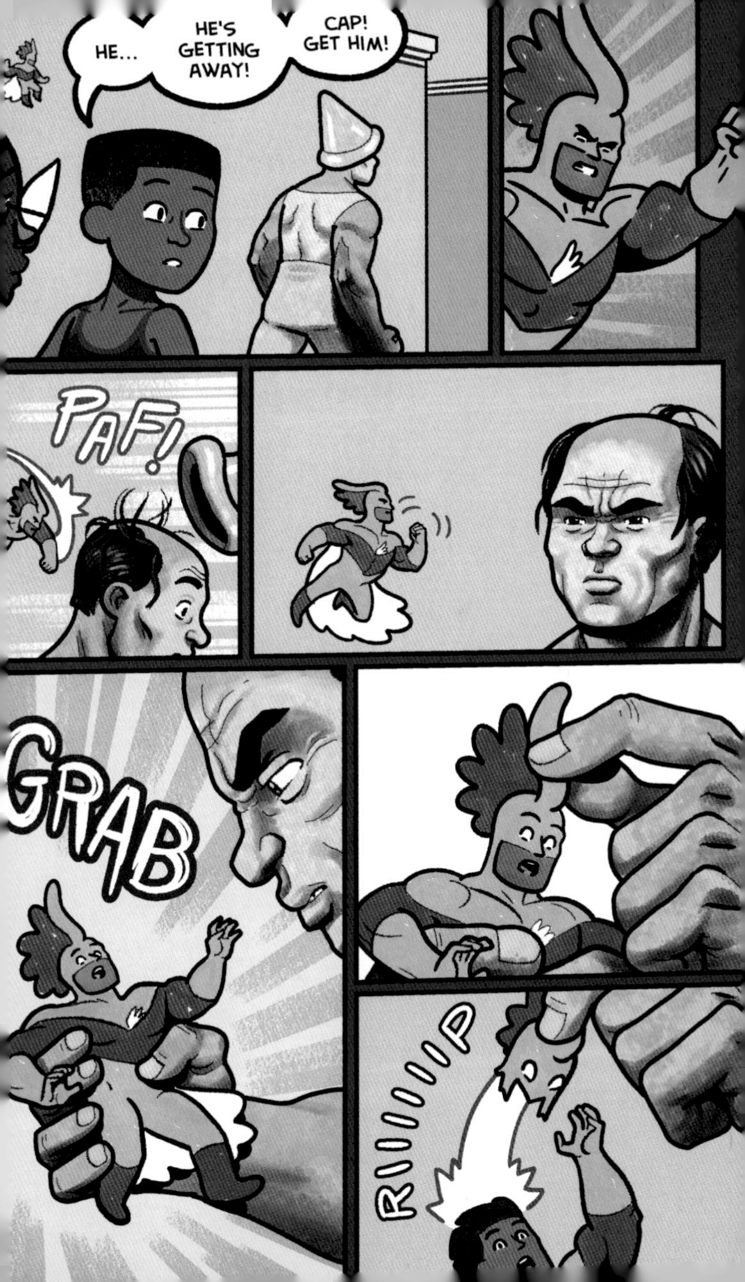
HE...
HE'S GETTING AWAY!
CAP! GET HIM!
PAF!
GRAB
RIIIIIIP

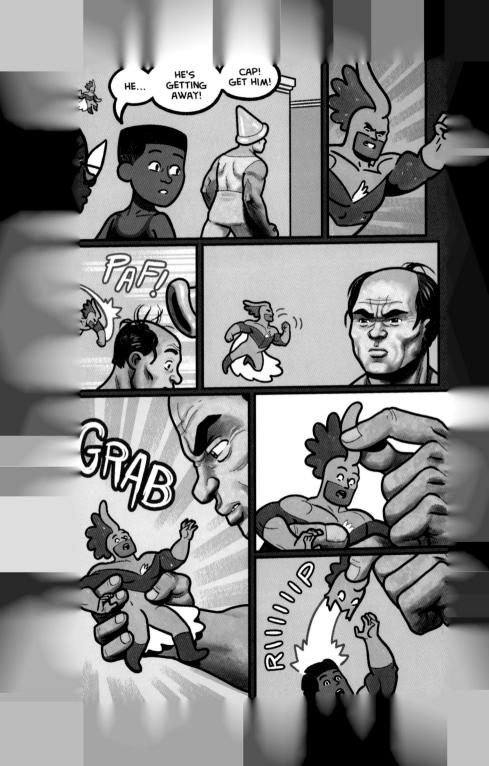

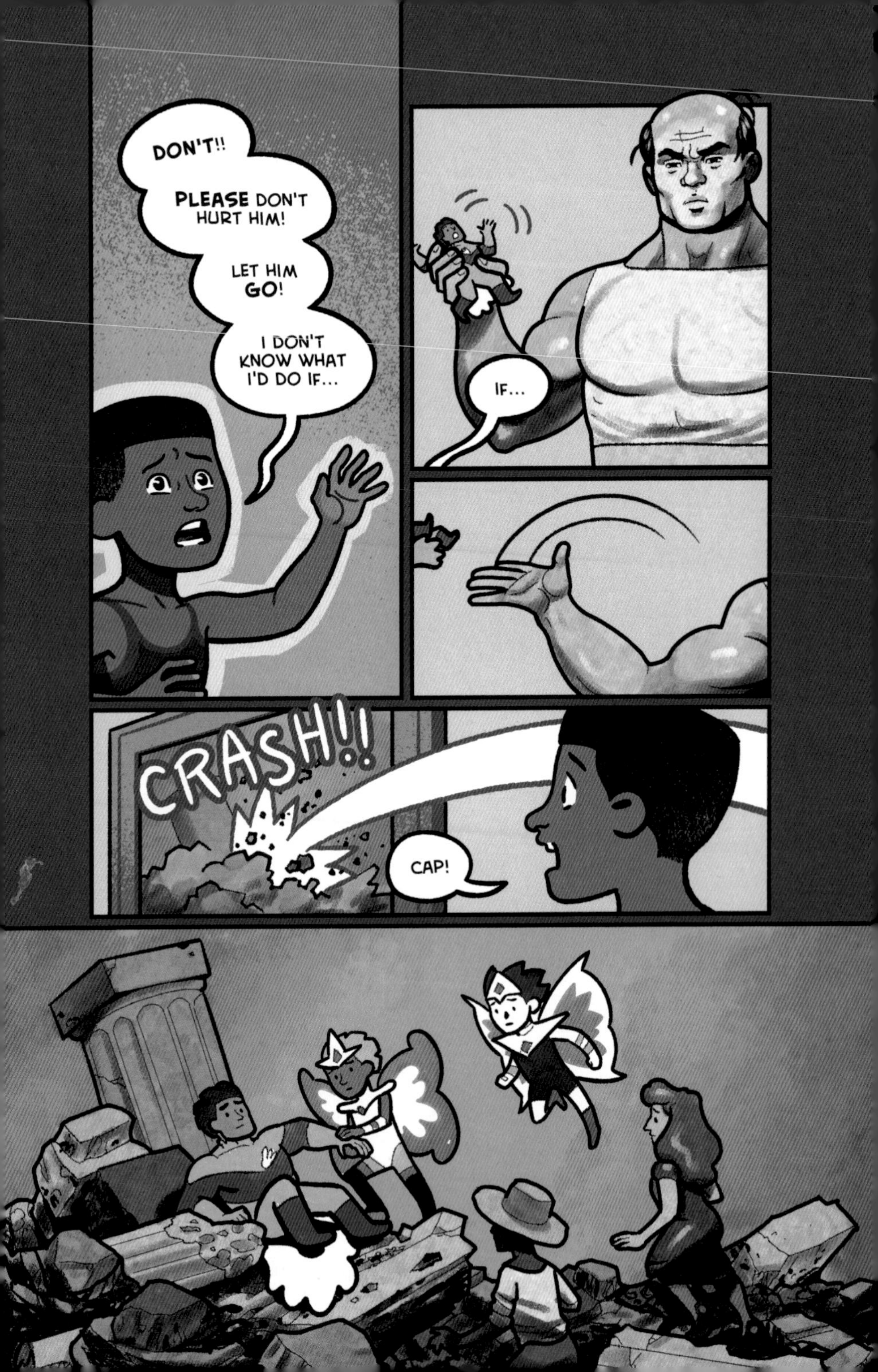
DON'T!!
PLEASE DON'T HURT HIM!
LET HIM GO!
I DON'T KNOW WHAT I'D DO IF...
IF...
CRASH!!
CAP!

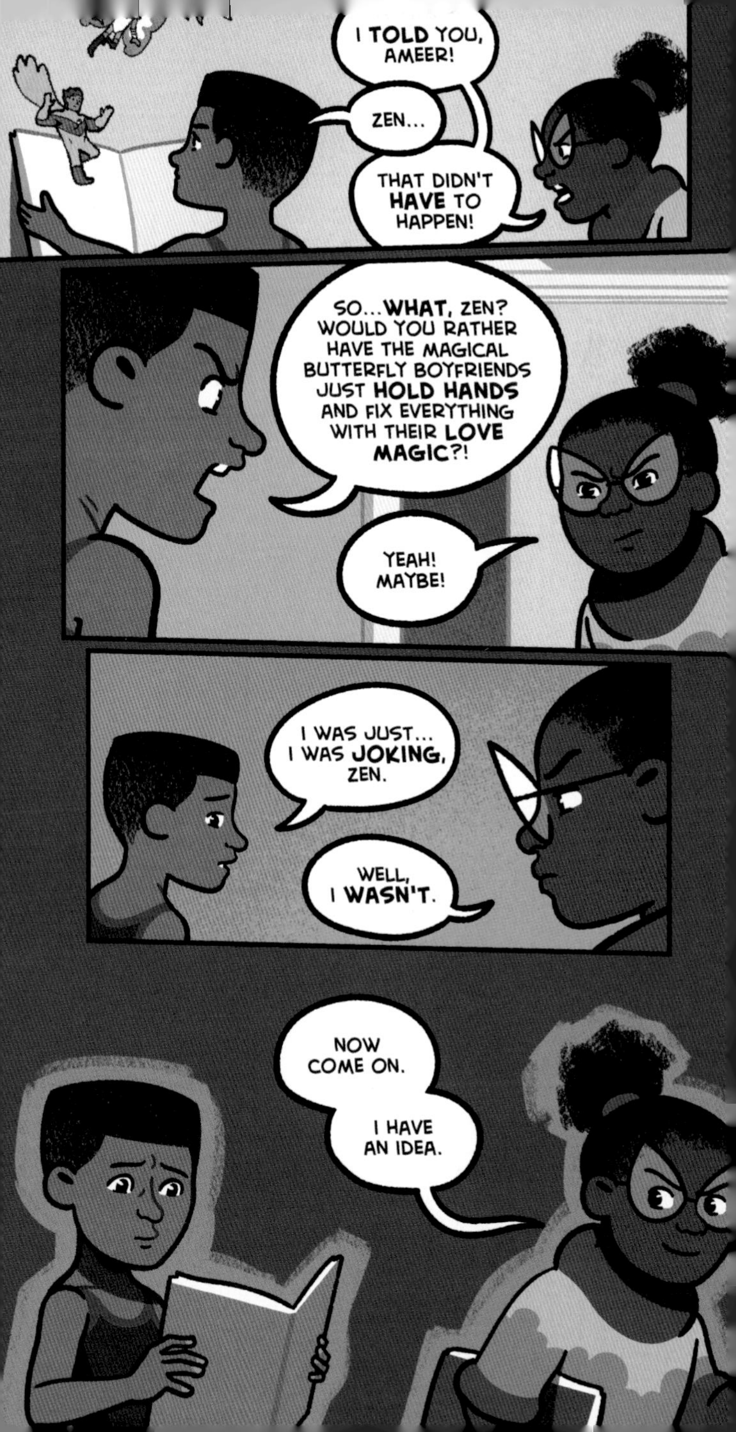
I **TOLD** YOU, AMEER!
ZEN...
THAT DIDN'T **HAVE** TO HAPPEN!
SO...**WHAT,** ZEN? WOULD YOU RATHER HAVE THE MAGICAL BUTTERFLY BOYFRIENDS JUST **HOLD HANDS** AND FIX EVERYTHING WITH THEIR **LOVE MAGIC**?!
YEAH! MAYBE!
I WAS JUST... I WAS **JOKING,** ZEN.
WELL, I **WASN'T**.
NOW COME ON.
I HAVE AN IDEA.

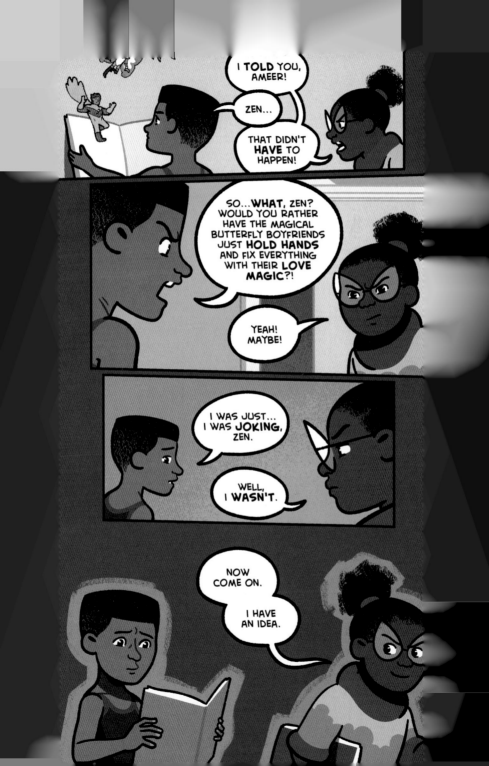

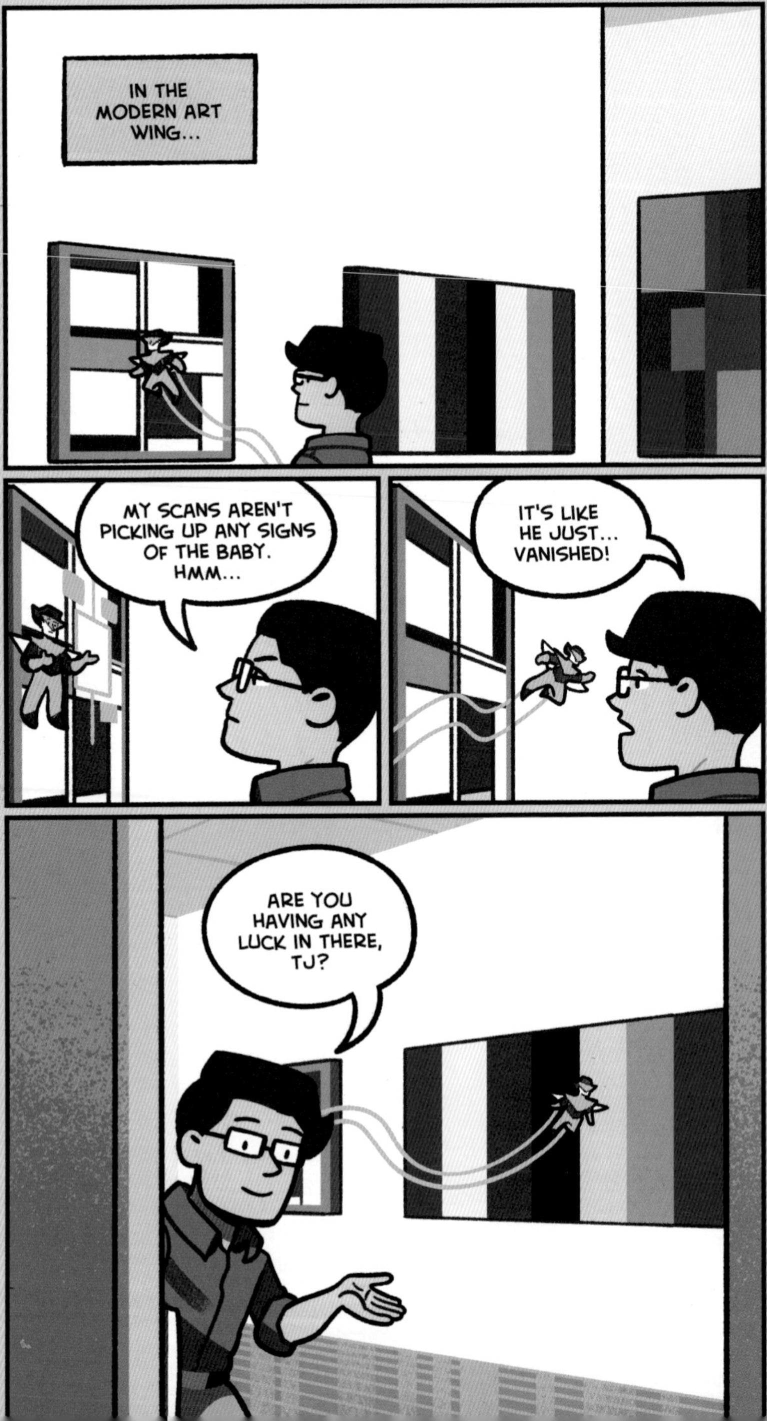
IN THE MODERN ART WING...
MY SCANS AREN'T PICKING UP ANY SIGNS OF THE BABY. HMM...
IT'S LIKE HE JUST... VANISHED!
ARE YOU HAVING ANY LUCK IN THERE, TJ?

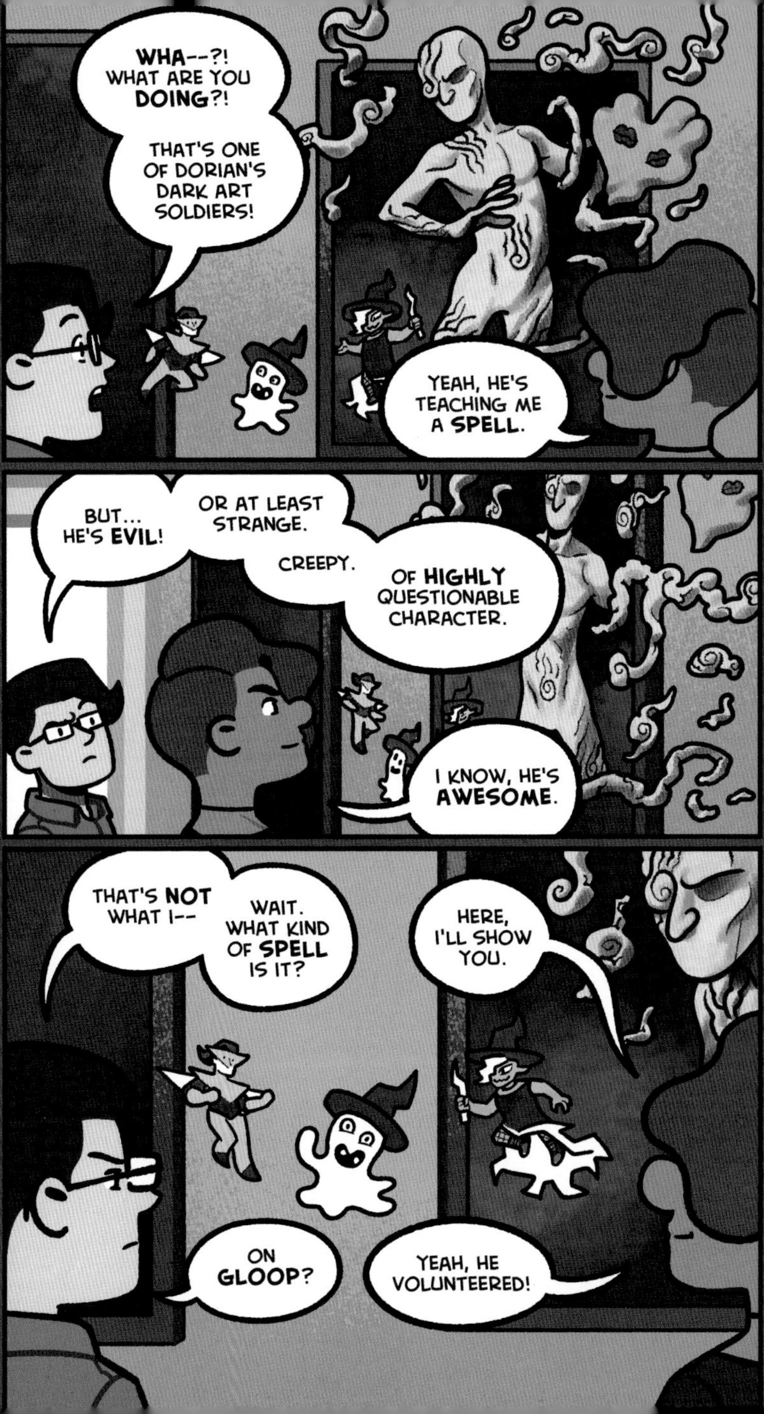
WHA--?! WHAT ARE YOU DOING?!
THAT'S ONE OF DORIAN'S DARK ART SOLDIERS!
YEAH, HE'S TEACHING ME A SPELL.
BUT... HE'S EVIL!
OR AT LEAST STRANGE.
CREEPY.
OF HIGHLY QUESTIONABLE CHARACTER.
I KNOW, HE'S AWESOME.
THAT'S NOT WHAT I--
WAIT. WHAT KIND OF SPELL IS IT?
HERE, I'LL SHOW YOU.
ON GLOOP?
YEAH, HE VOLUNTEERED!

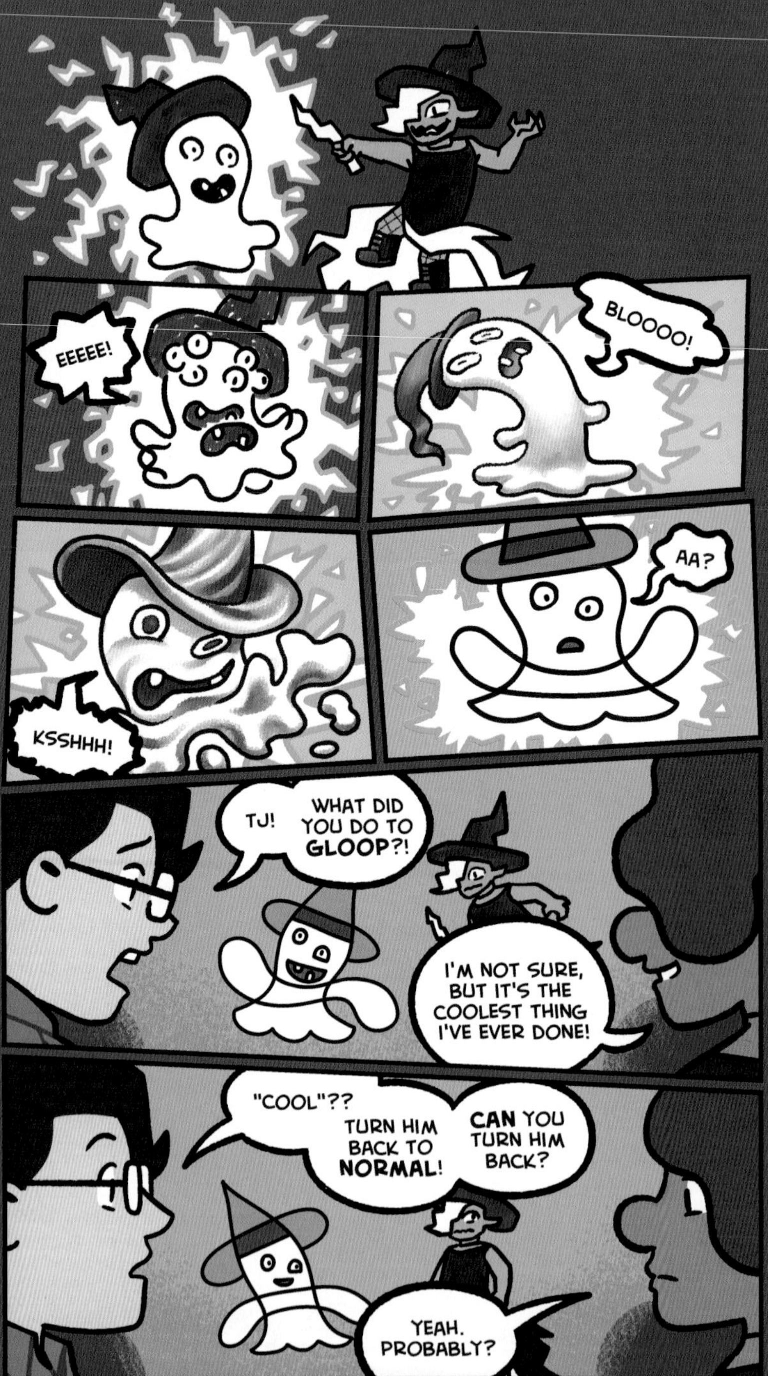
EEEEE!
BLOOOO!
KSSHHH!
AA?
TJ!
WHAT DID YOU DO TO GLOOP?!
I'M NOT SURE, BUT IT'S THE COOLEST THING I'VE EVER DONE!
"COOL"?? TURN HIM BACK TO NORMAL!
CAN YOU TURN HIM BACK?
YEAH. PROBABLY?

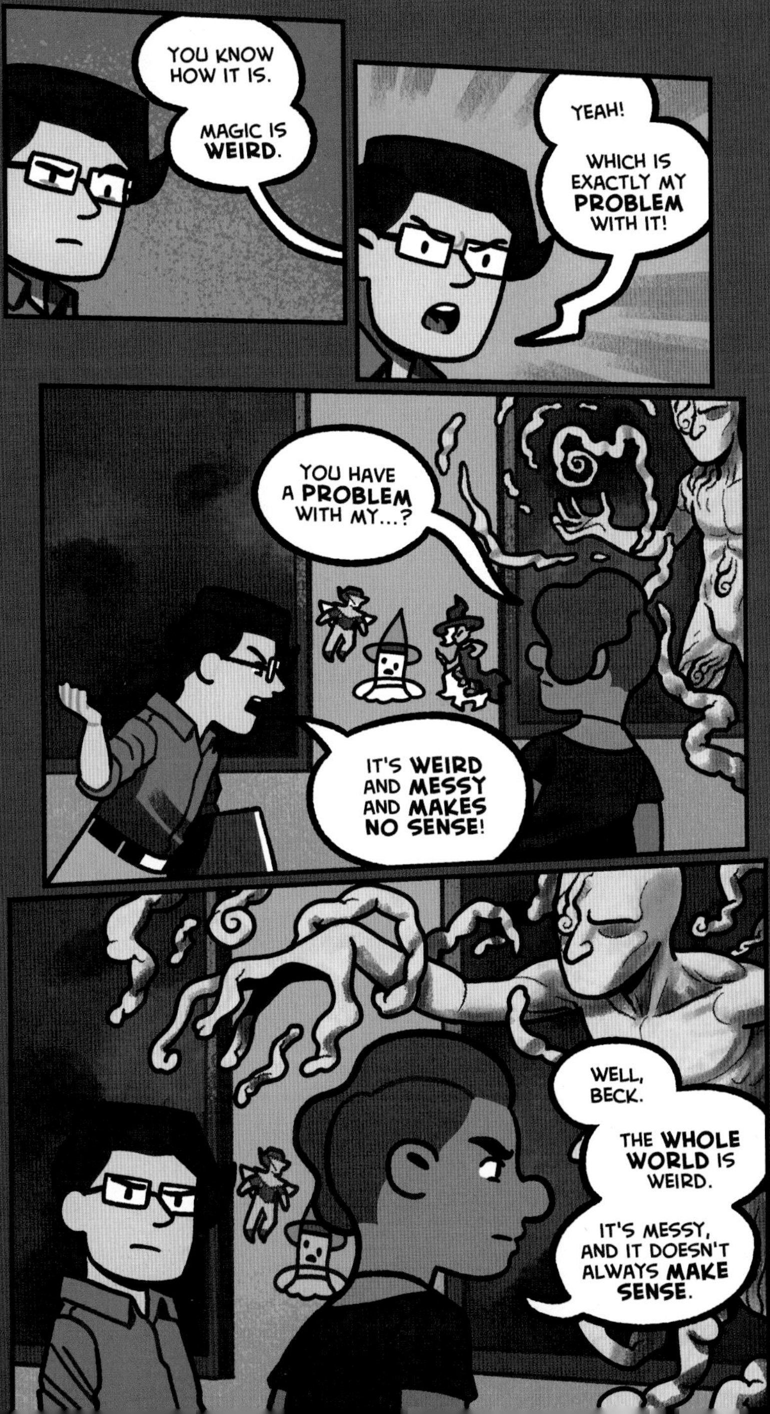
YOU KNOW HOW IT IS.
MAGIC IS **WEIRD**.
YEAH!
WHICH IS EXACTLY MY **PROBLEM** WITH IT!
YOU HAVE A **PROBLEM** WITH MY...?
IT'S **WEIRD** AND **MESSY** AND **MAKES NO SENSE**!
WELL, BECK.
THE **WHOLE WORLD** IS WEIRD.
IT'S MESSY, AND IT DOESN'T ALWAYS **MAKE SENSE**.

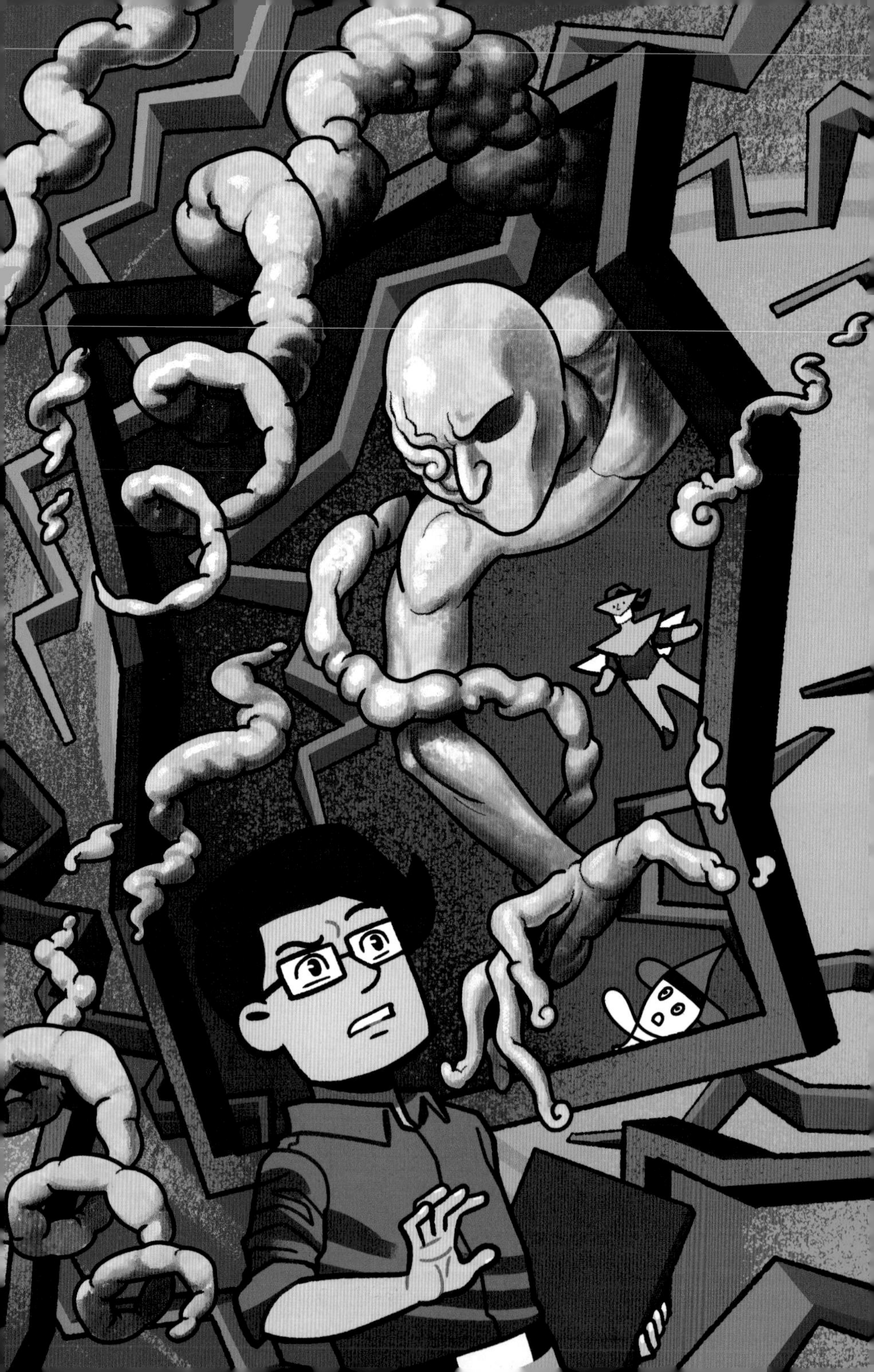

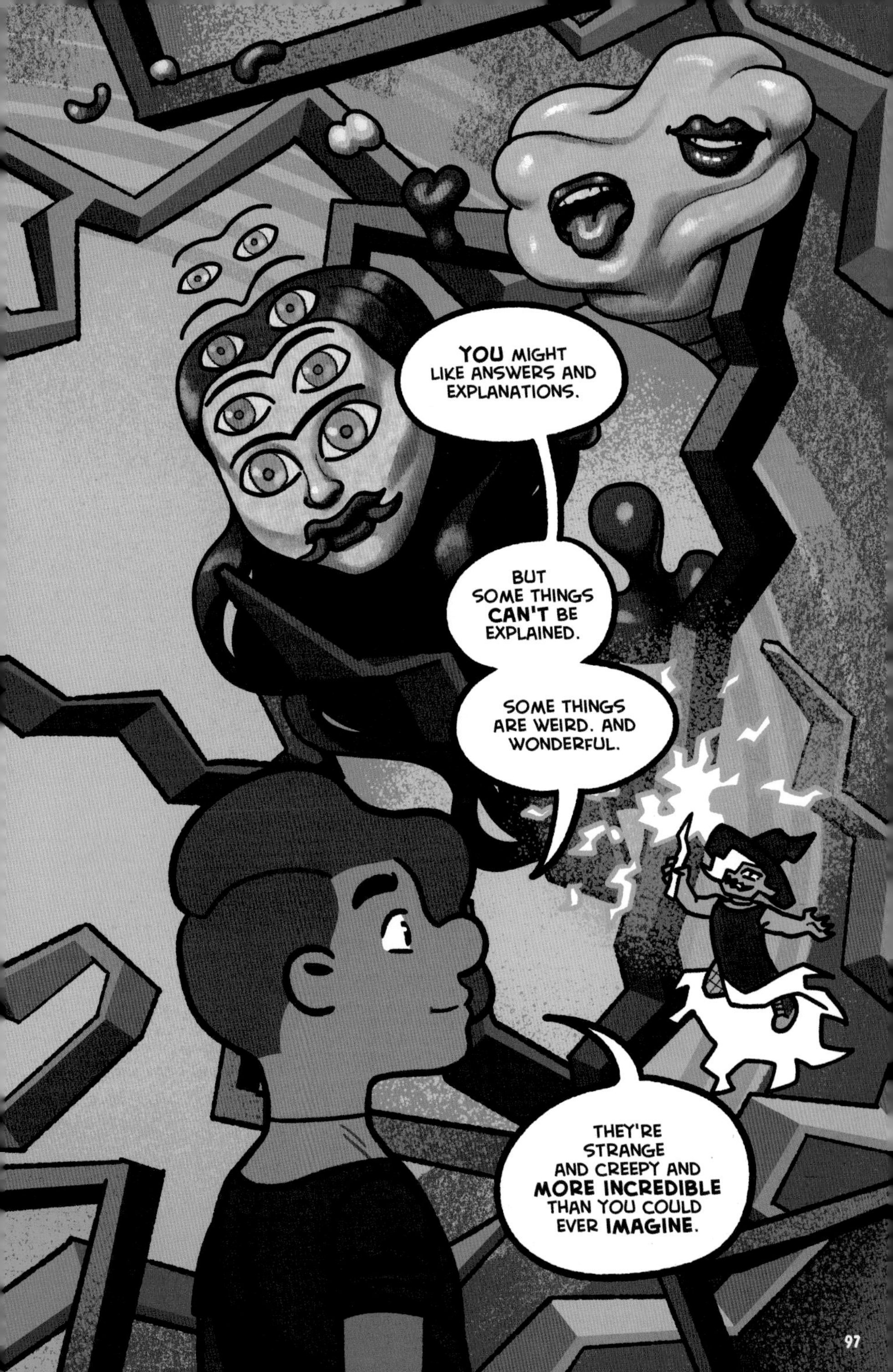
YOU MIGHT LIKE ANSWERS AND EXPLANATIONS.
BUT SOME THINGS CAN'T BE EXPLAINED.
SOME THINGS ARE WEIRD. AND WONDERFUL.
THEY'RE STRANGE AND CREEPY AND MORE INCREDIBLE THAN YOU COULD EVER IMAGINE.

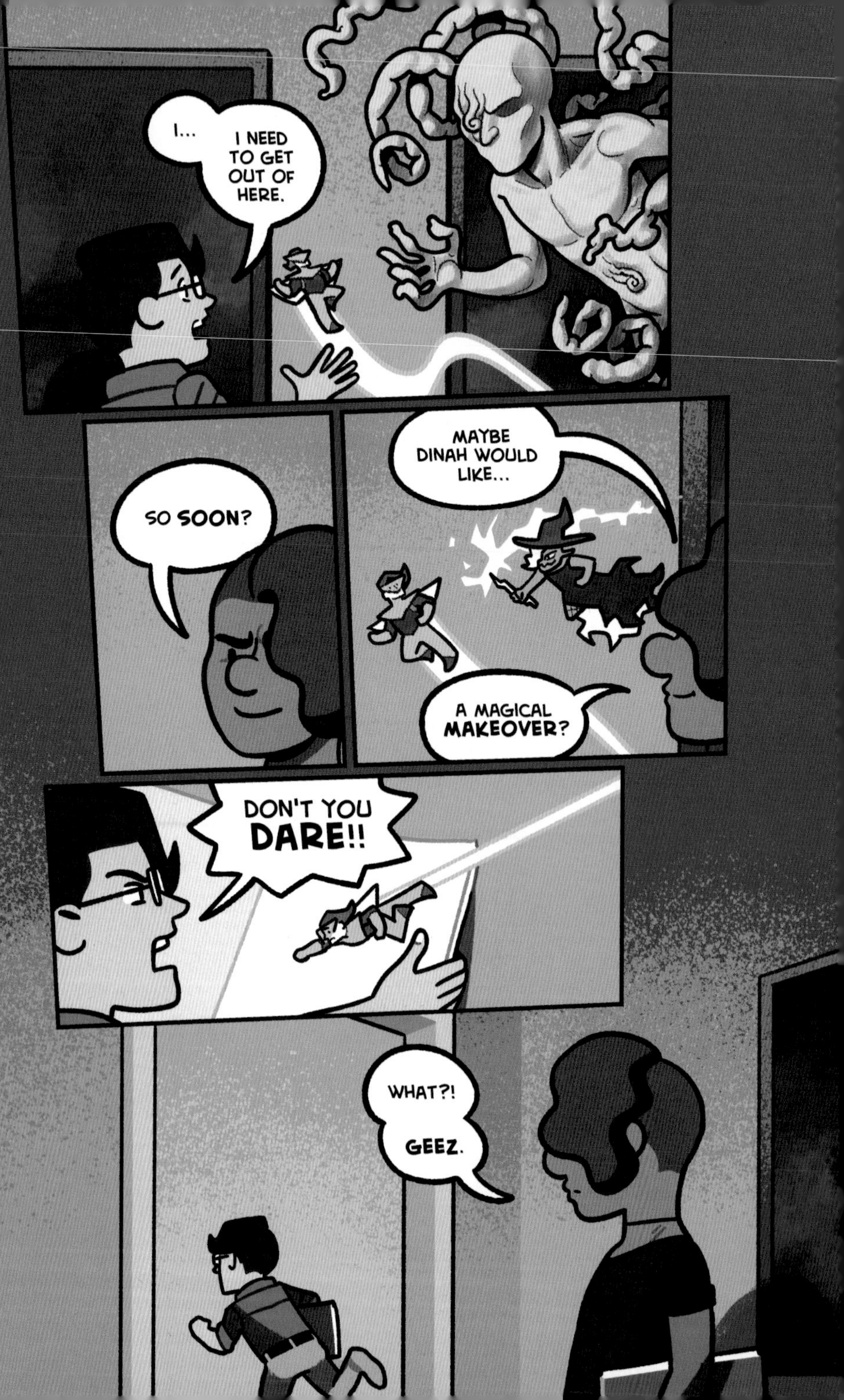
I...
I NEED TO GET OUT OF HERE.
SO SOON?
MAYBE DINAH WOULD LIKE...
A MAGICAL MAKEOVER?
DON'T YOU DARE!!
WHAT?!
GEEZ.

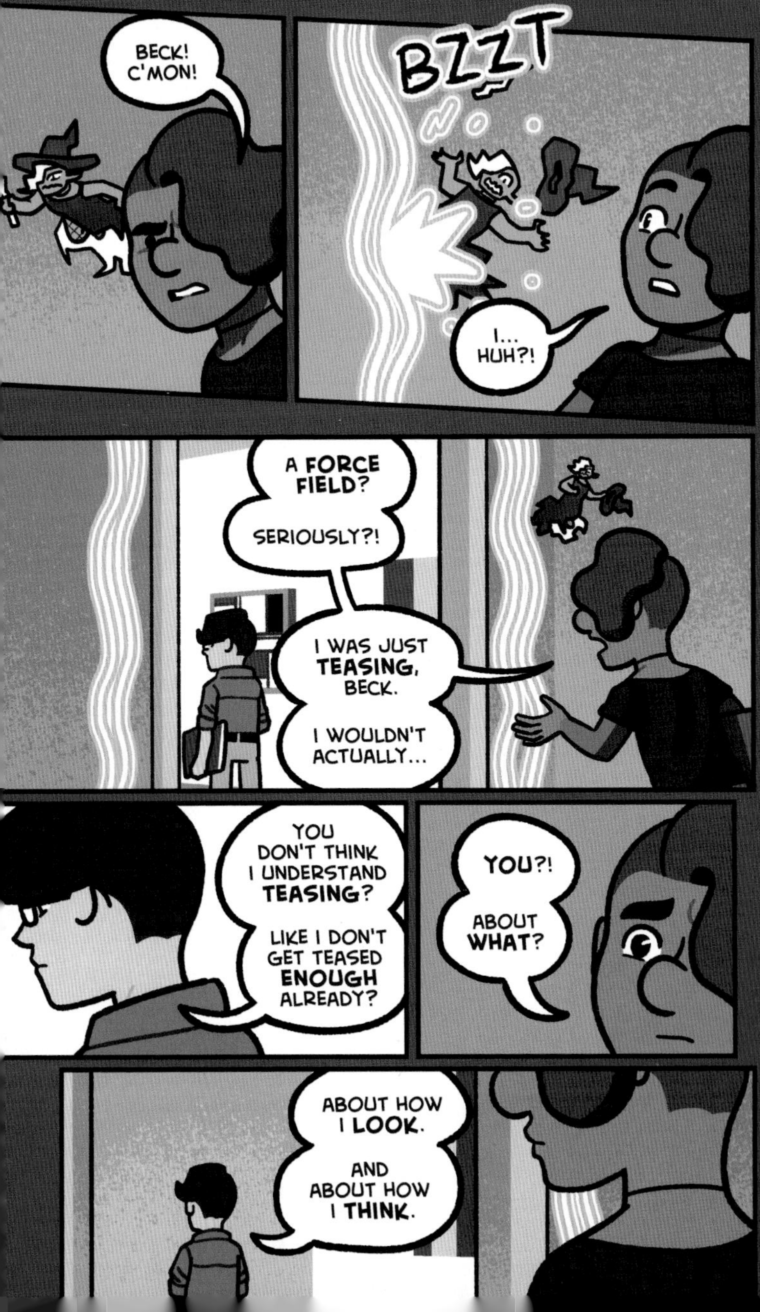
BECK! C'MON!
BZZT
I... HUH?!
A **FORCE FIELD**?
SERIOUSLY?!
I WAS JUST **TEASING**, BECK.
I WOULDN'T ACTUALLY...
YOU DON'T THINK I UNDERSTAND **TEASING**?
LIKE I DON'T GET TEASED **ENOUGH** ALREADY?
YOU?!
ABOUT **WHAT**?
ABOUT HOW I **LOOK**.
AND ABOUT HOW I **THINK**.

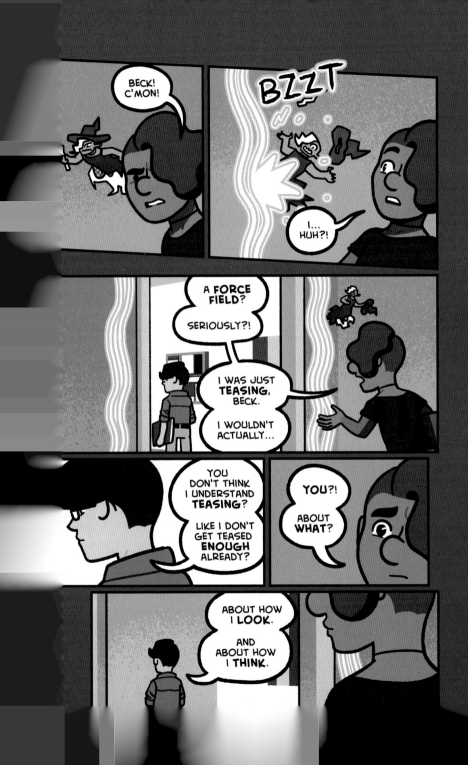

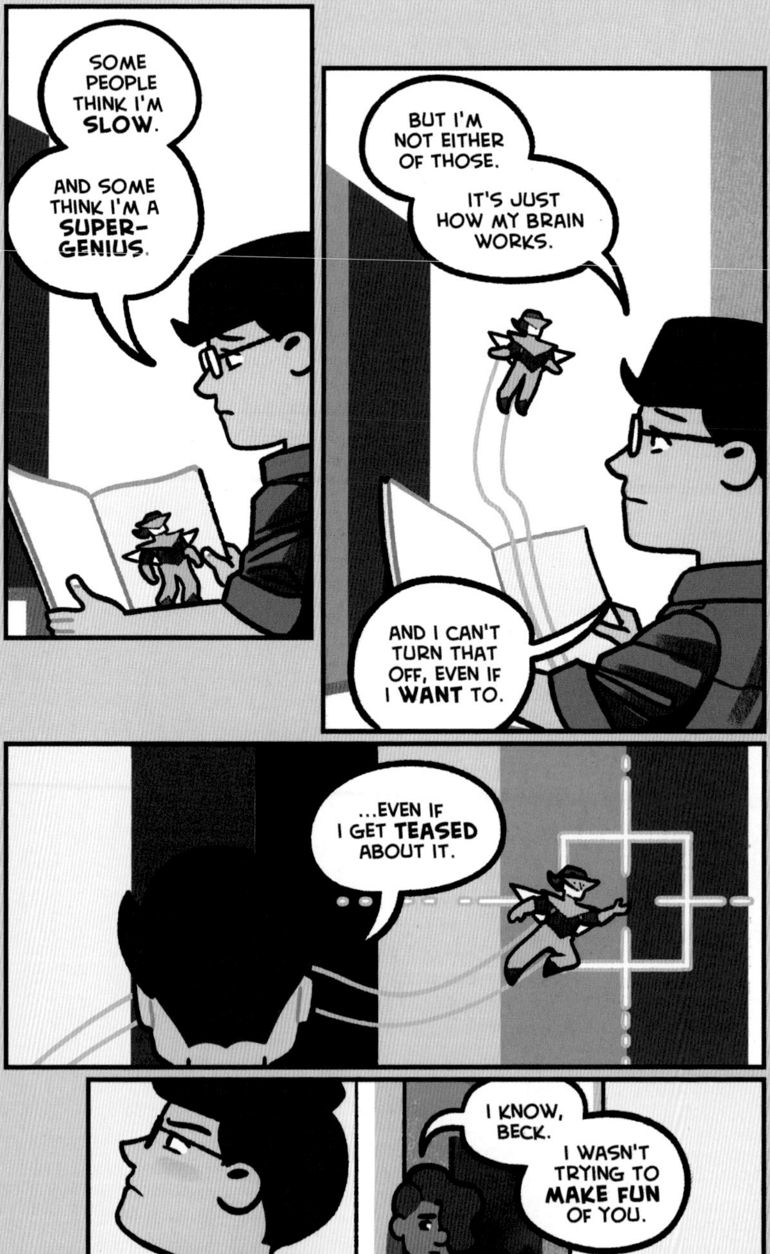
SOME PEOPLE THINK I'M **SLOW**.
AND SOME THINK I'M A **SUPER-GENIUS**.
BUT I'M NOT EITHER OF THOSE.
IT'S JUST HOW MY BRAIN WORKS.
AND I CAN'T TURN THAT OFF, EVEN IF I **WANT** TO.
...EVEN IF I GET **TEASED** ABOUT IT.
I KNOW, BECK.
I WASN'T TRYING TO **MAKE FUN** OF YOU.

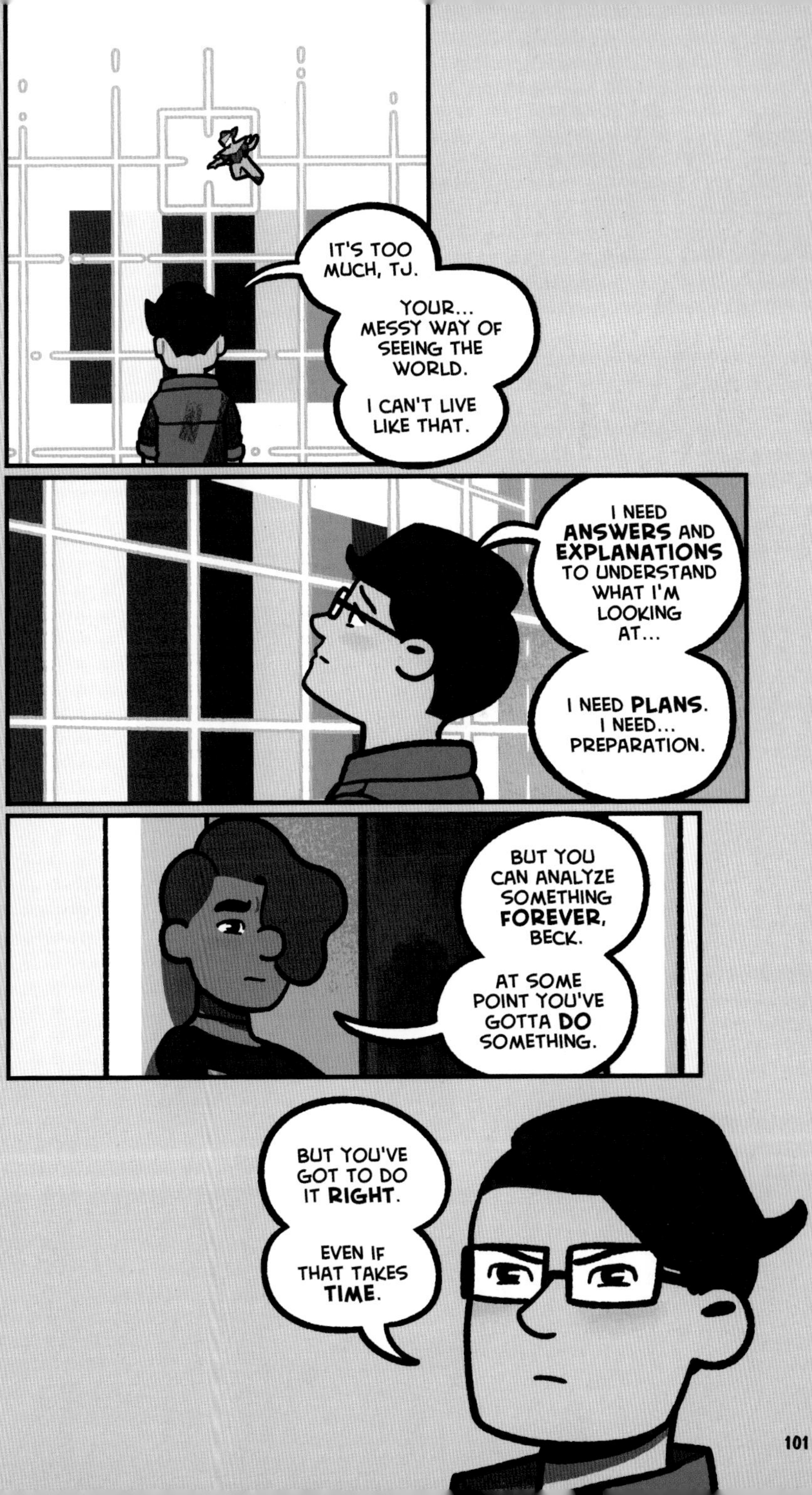
IT'S TOO MUCH, TJ.
YOUR... MESSY WAY OF SEEING THE WORLD.
I CAN'T LIVE LIKE THAT.
I NEED **ANSWERS** AND **EXPLANATIONS** TO UNDERSTAND WHAT I'M LOOKING AT...
I NEED **PLANS**. I NEED... PREPARATION.
BUT YOU CAN ANALYZE SOMETHING **FOREVER**, BECK.
AT SOME POINT YOU'VE GOTTA **DO** SOMETHING.
BUT YOU'VE GOT TO DO IT **RIGHT**.
EVEN IF THAT TAKES **TIME**.

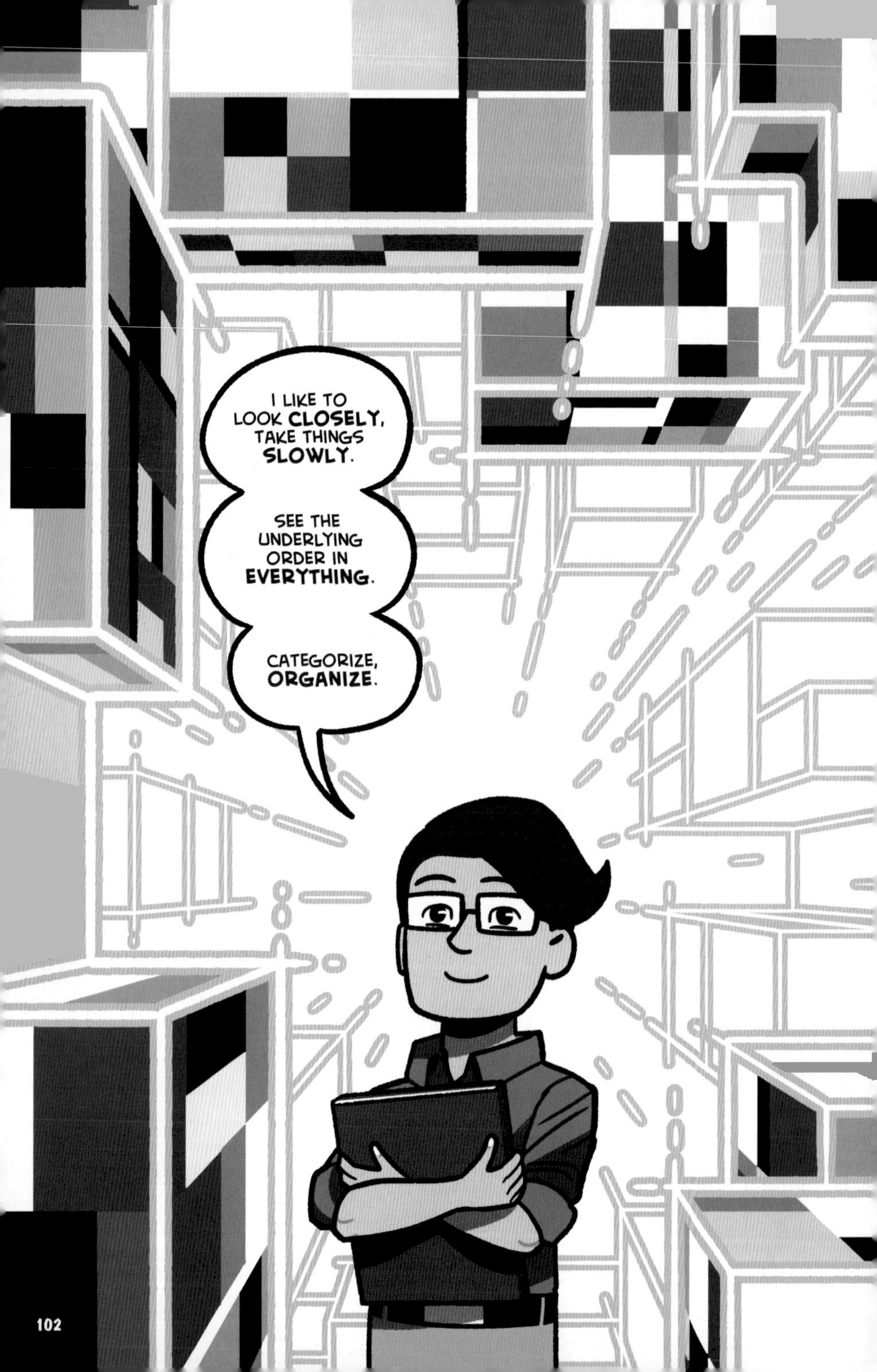
I LIKE TO LOOK CLOSELY, TAKE THINGS SLOWLY.
SEE THE UNDERLYING ORDER IN EVERYTHING.
CATEGORIZE, ORGANIZE.

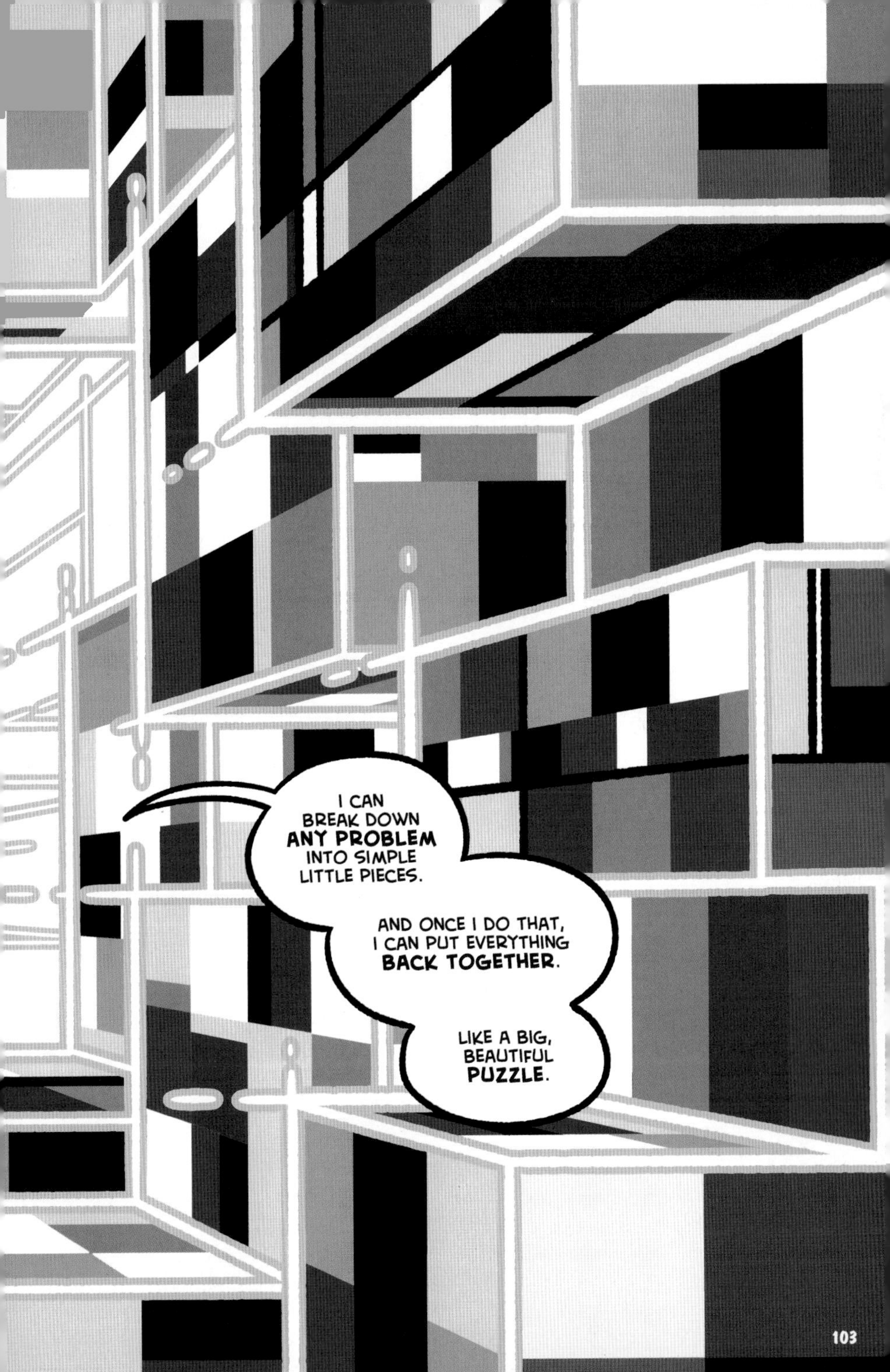
I CAN BREAK DOWN ANY PROBLEM INTO SIMPLE LITTLE PIECES.
AND ONCE I DO THAT, I CAN PUT EVERYTHING BACK TOGETHER.
LIKE A BIG, BEAUTIFUL PUZZLE.

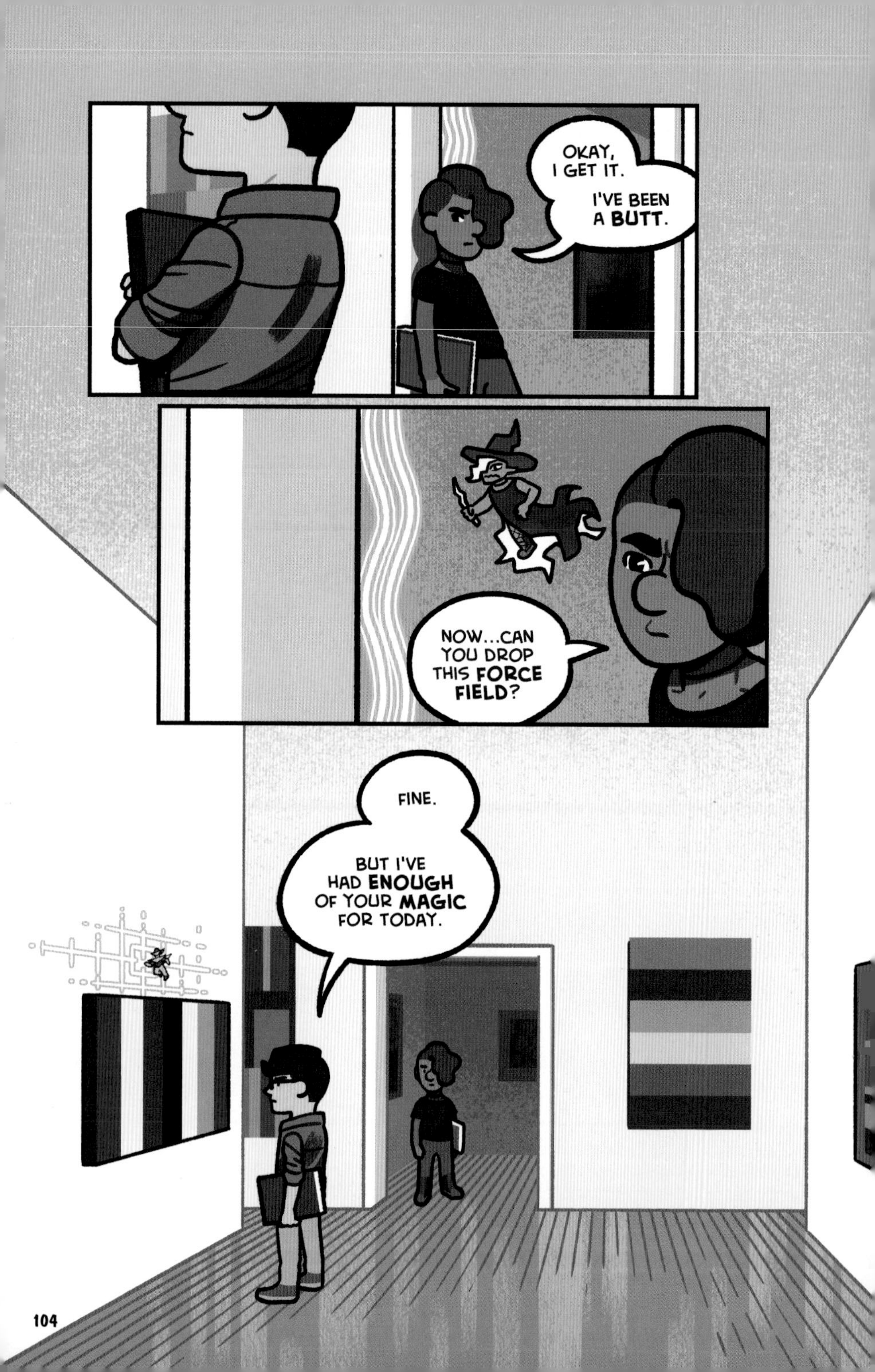
OKAY, I GET IT.
I'VE BEEN A BUTT.
NOW...CAN YOU DROP THIS FORCE FIELD?
FINE.
BUT I'VE HAD ENOUGH OF YOUR MAGIC FOR TODAY.

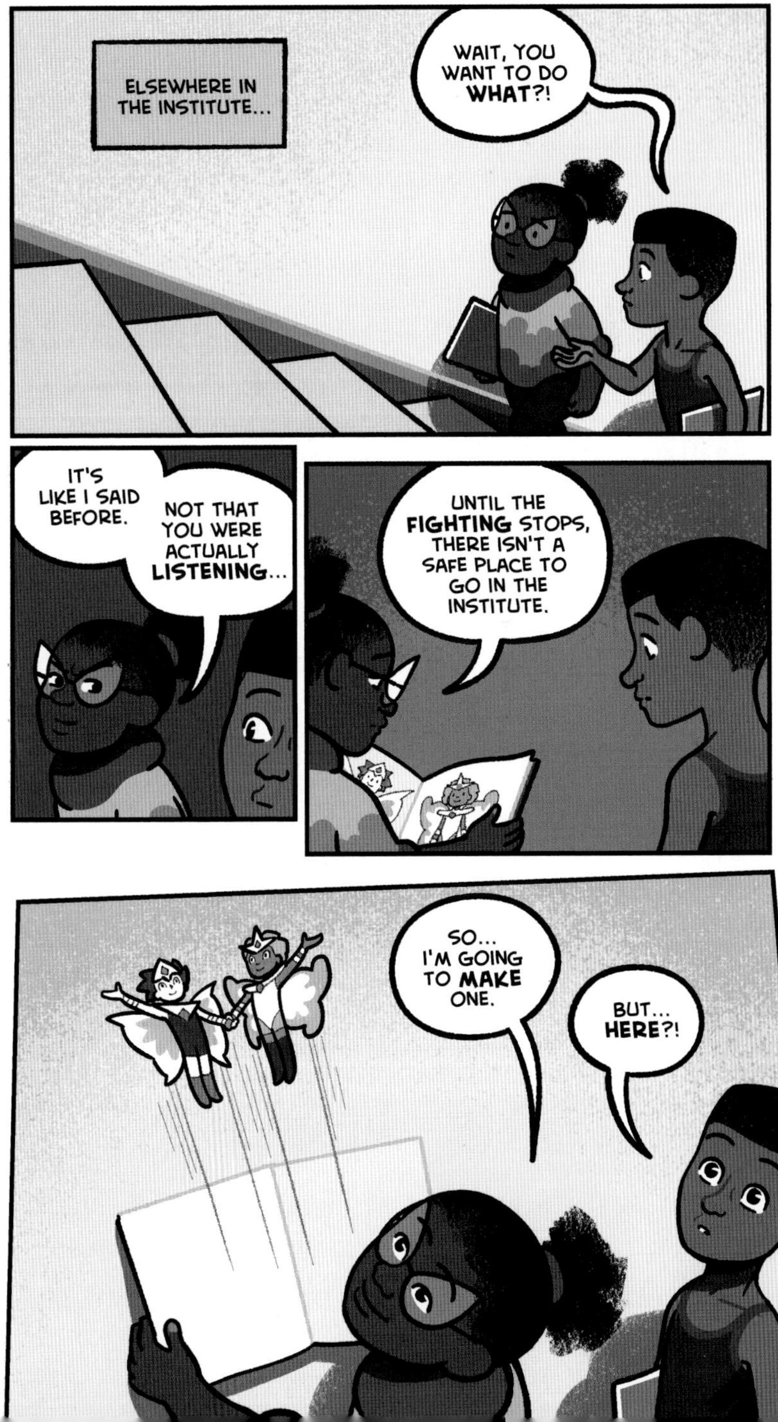
ELSEWHERE IN THE INSTITUTE...
WAIT, YOU WANT TO DO **WHAT**?!
IT'S LIKE I SAID BEFORE.
NOT THAT YOU WERE ACTUALLY **LISTENING**...
UNTIL THE **FIGHTING** STOPS, THERE ISN'T A SAFE PLACE TO GO IN THE INSTITUTE.
SO... I'M GOING TO **MAKE** ONE.
BUT... **HERE**?!

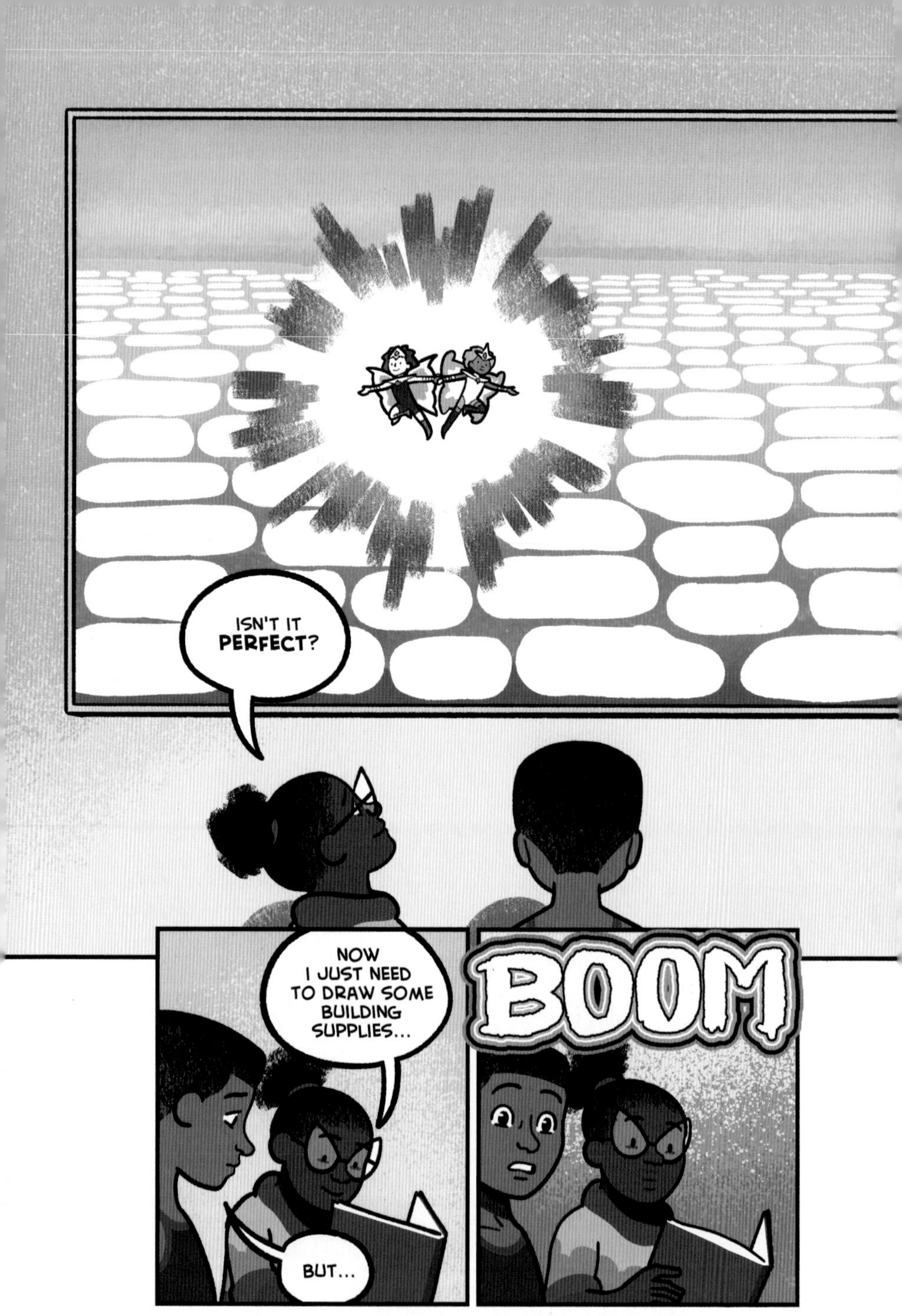
ISN'T IT PERFECT?
NOW I JUST NEED TO DRAW SOME BUILDING SUPPLIES...
BUT...
BOOM

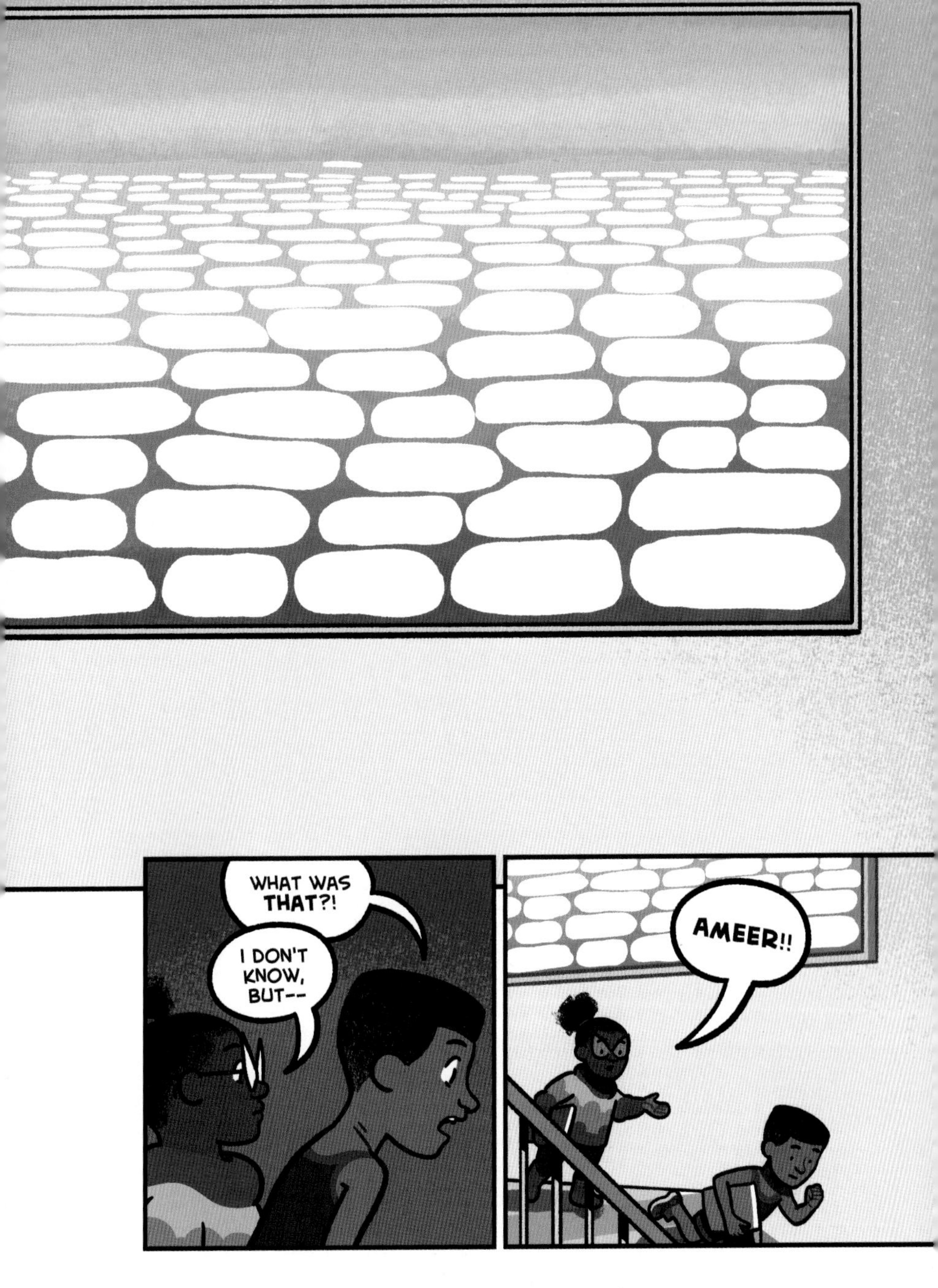
WHAT WAS THAT?!
I DON'T KNOW, BUT--
AMEER!!

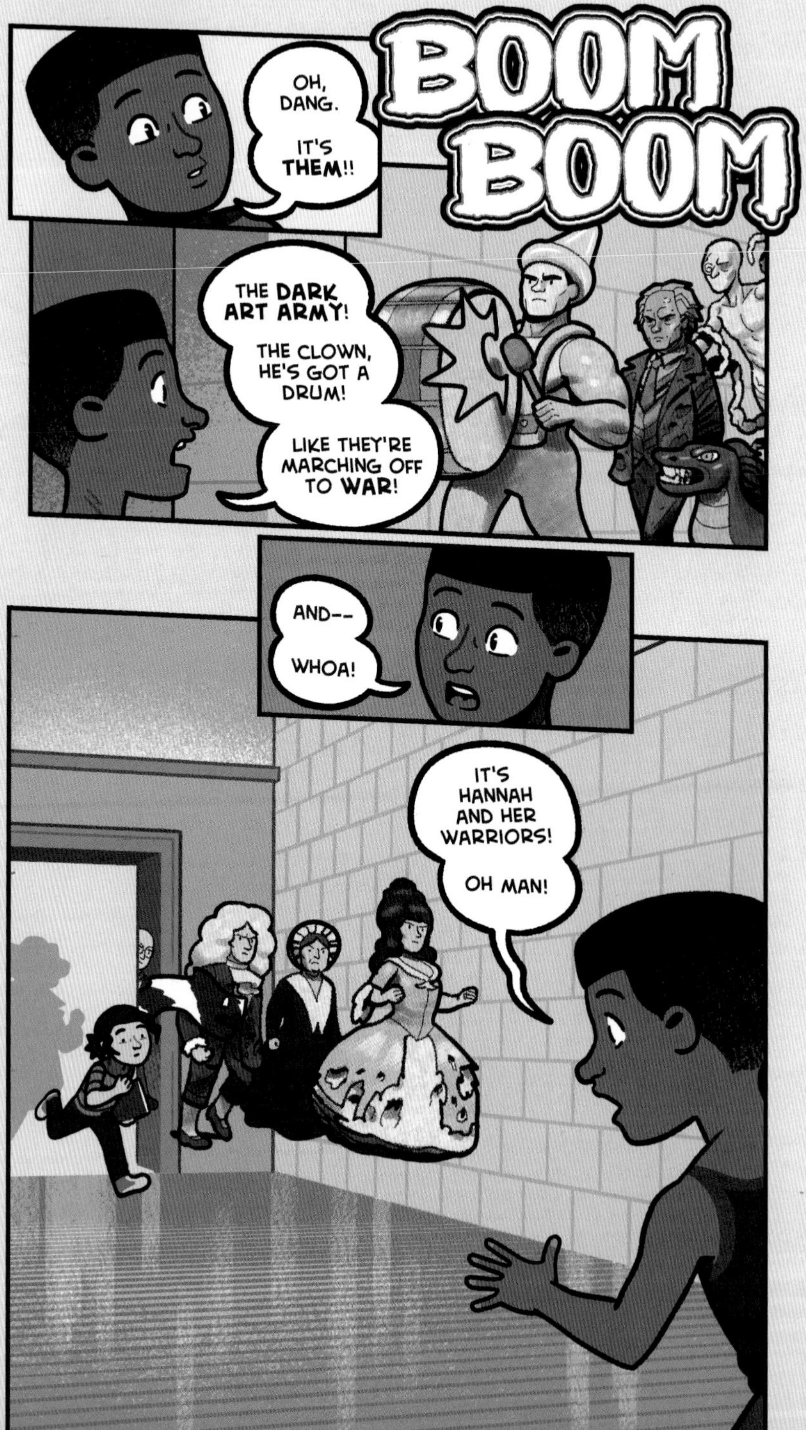
OH, DANG.
IT'S THEM!!
BOOM BOOM
THE DARK ART ARMY!
THE CLOWN, HE'S GOT A DRUM!
LIKE THEY'RE MARCHING OFF TO WAR!
AND--
WHOA!
IT'S HANNAH AND HER WARRIORS!
OH MAN!

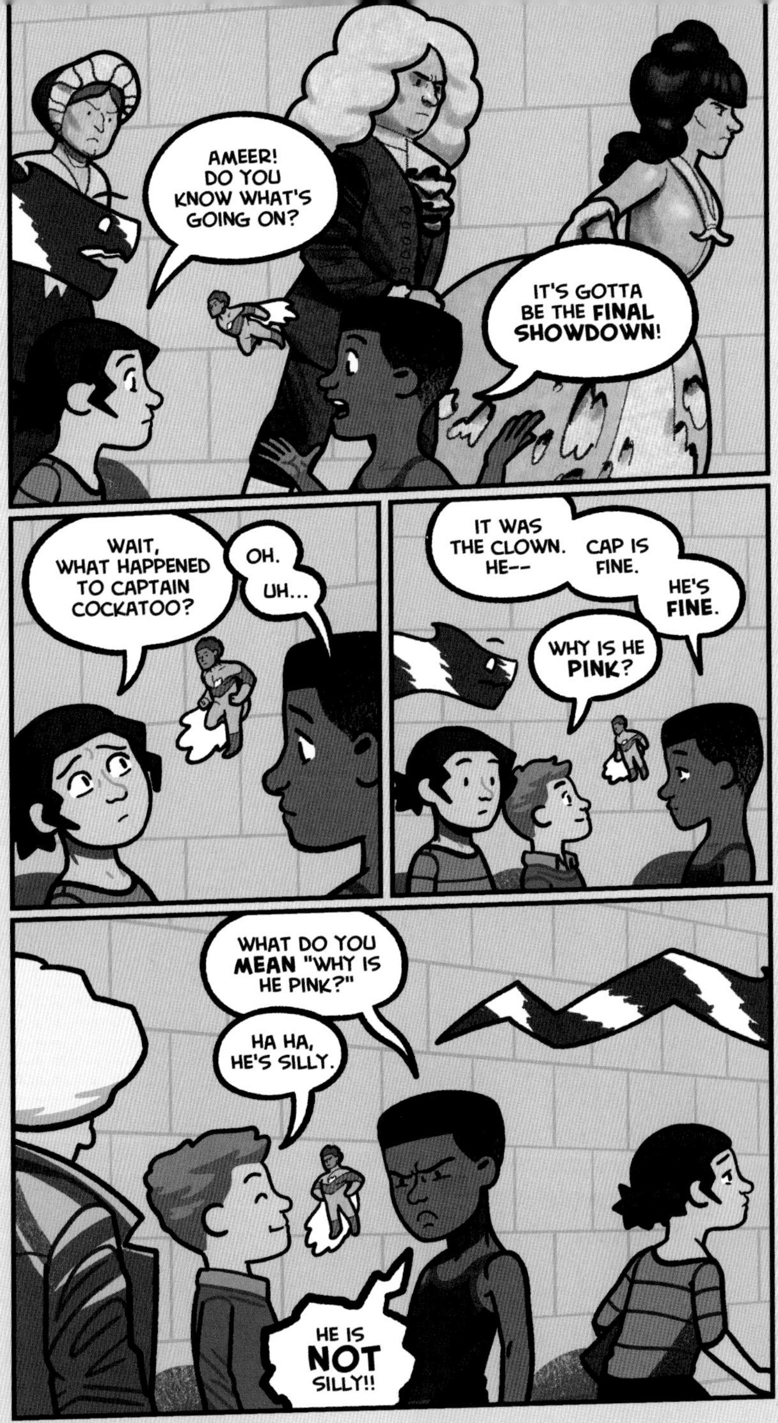
AMEER! DO YOU KNOW WHAT'S GOING ON?
IT'S GOTTA BE THE **FINAL SHOWDOWN**!
WAIT, WHAT HAPPENED TO CAPTAIN COCKATOO?
OH.
UH...
IT WAS THE CLOWN. HE--
CAP IS FINE.
HE'S **FINE**.
WHY IS HE **PINK**?
WHAT DO YOU **MEAN** "WHY IS HE PINK?"
HA HA, HE'S SILLY.
HE IS **NOT** SILLY!!

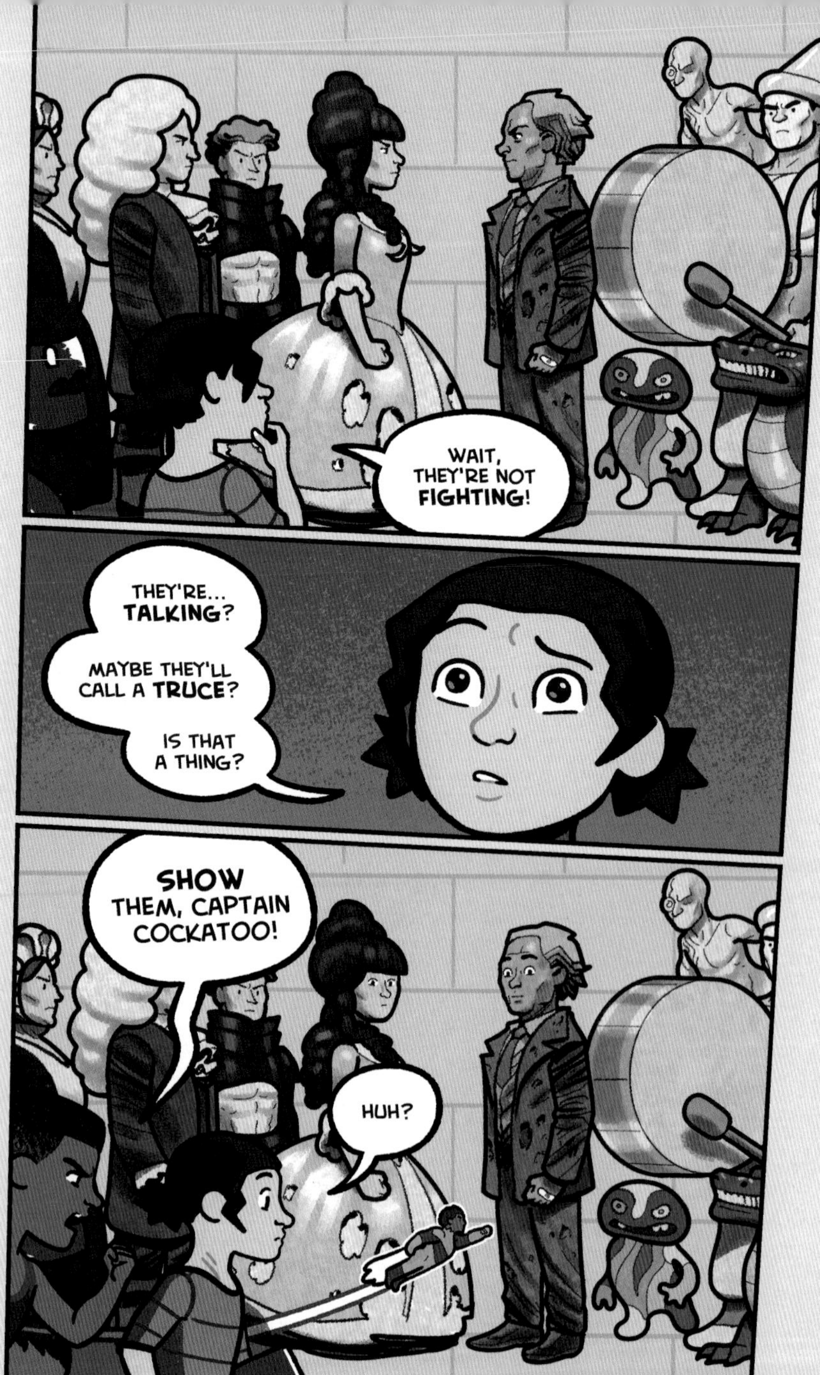
WAIT, THEY'RE NOT FIGHTING!
THEY'RE... TALKING?
MAYBE THEY'LL CALL A TRUCE?
IS THAT A THING?
SHOW THEM, CAPTAIN COCKATOO!
HUH?

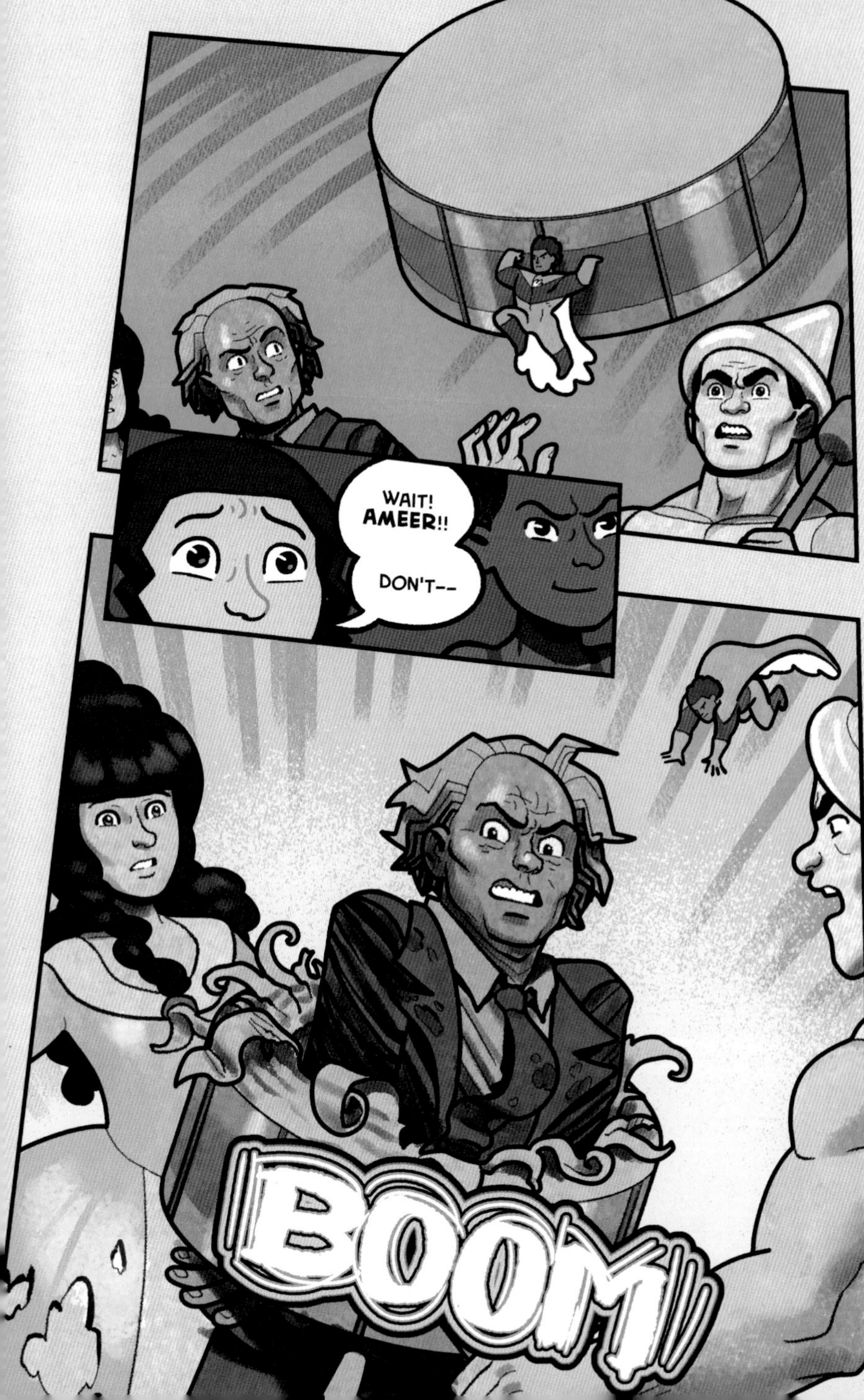
WAIT! AMEER!!
DON'T--
BOOM

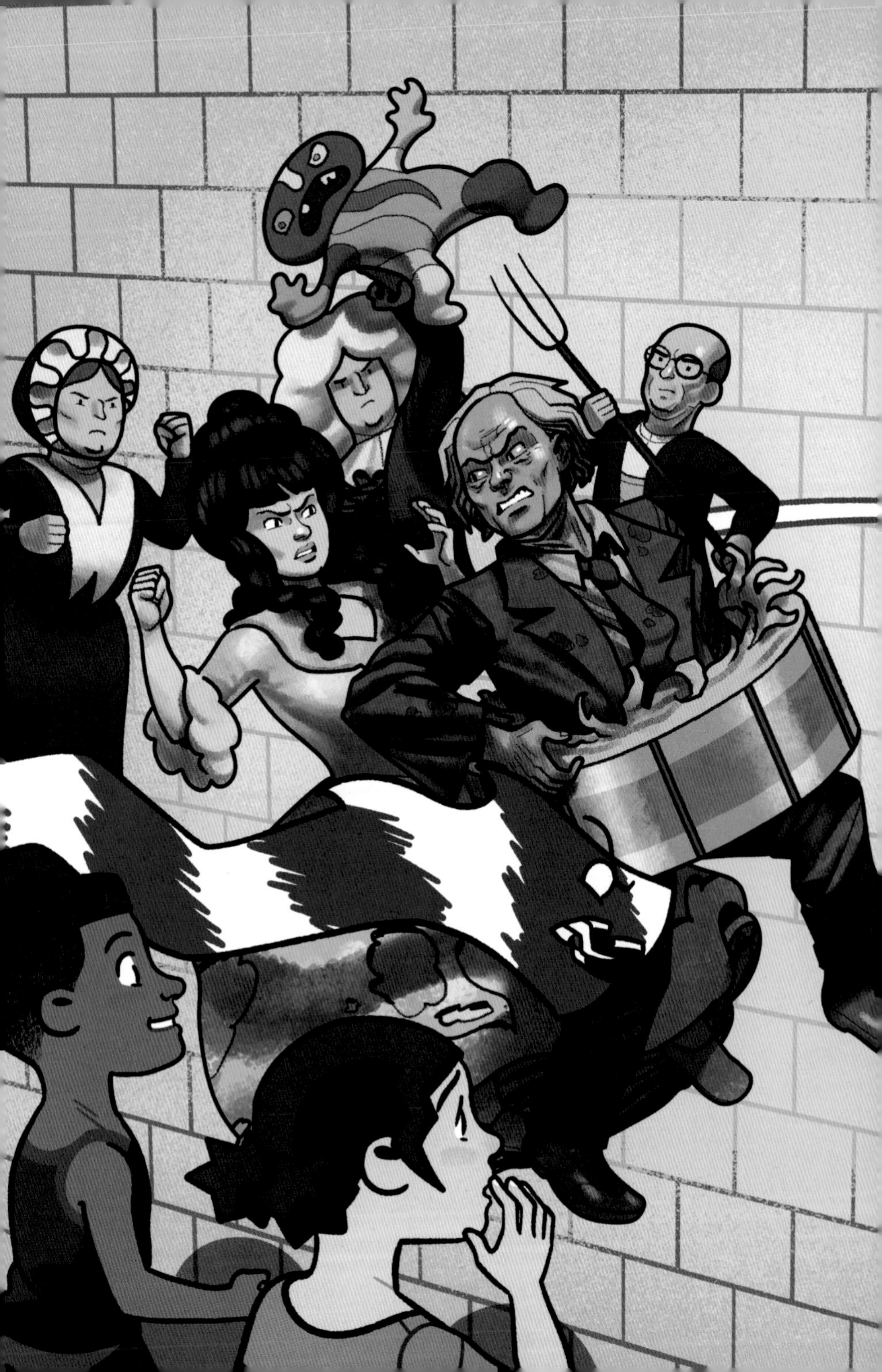

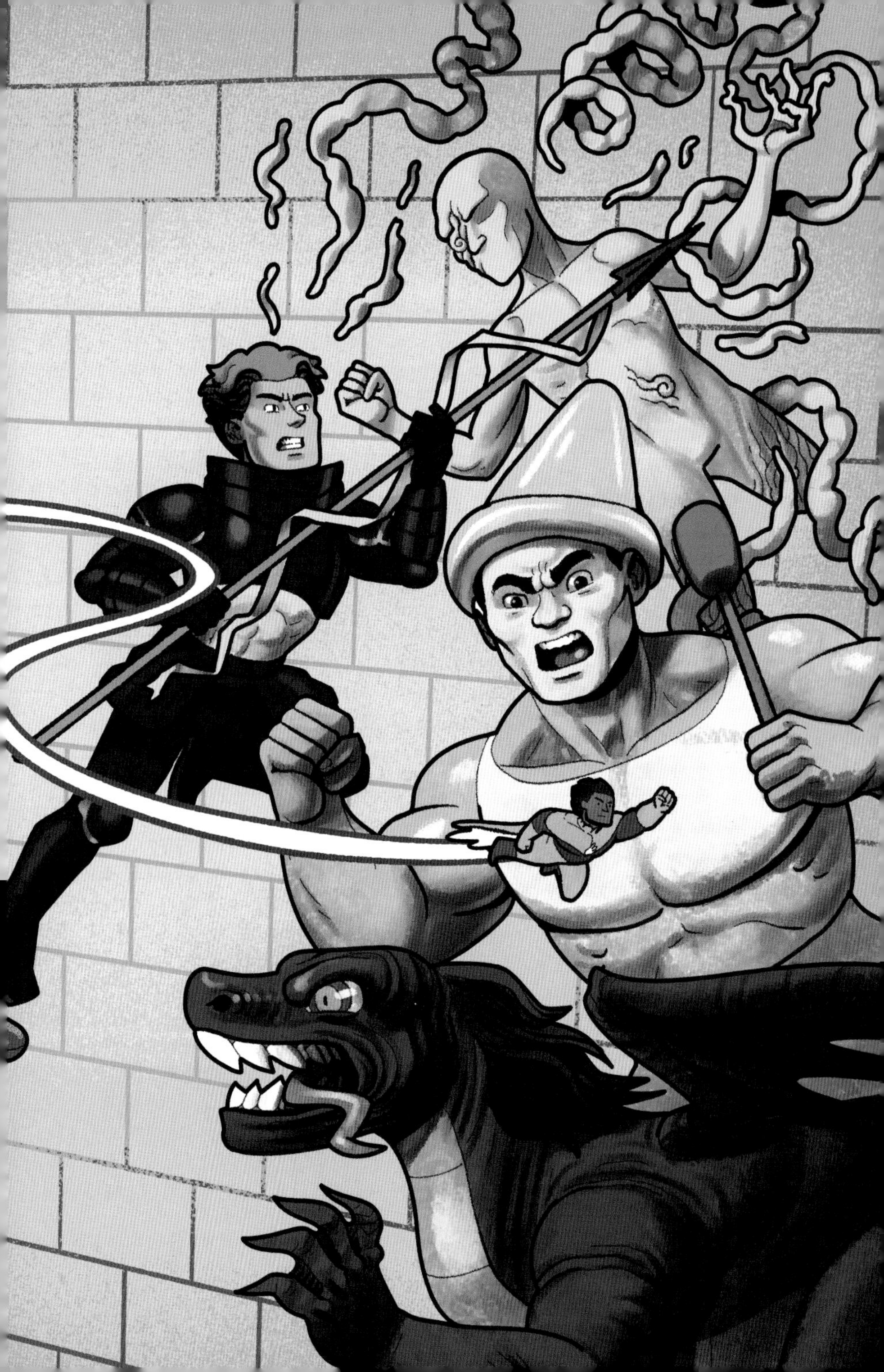

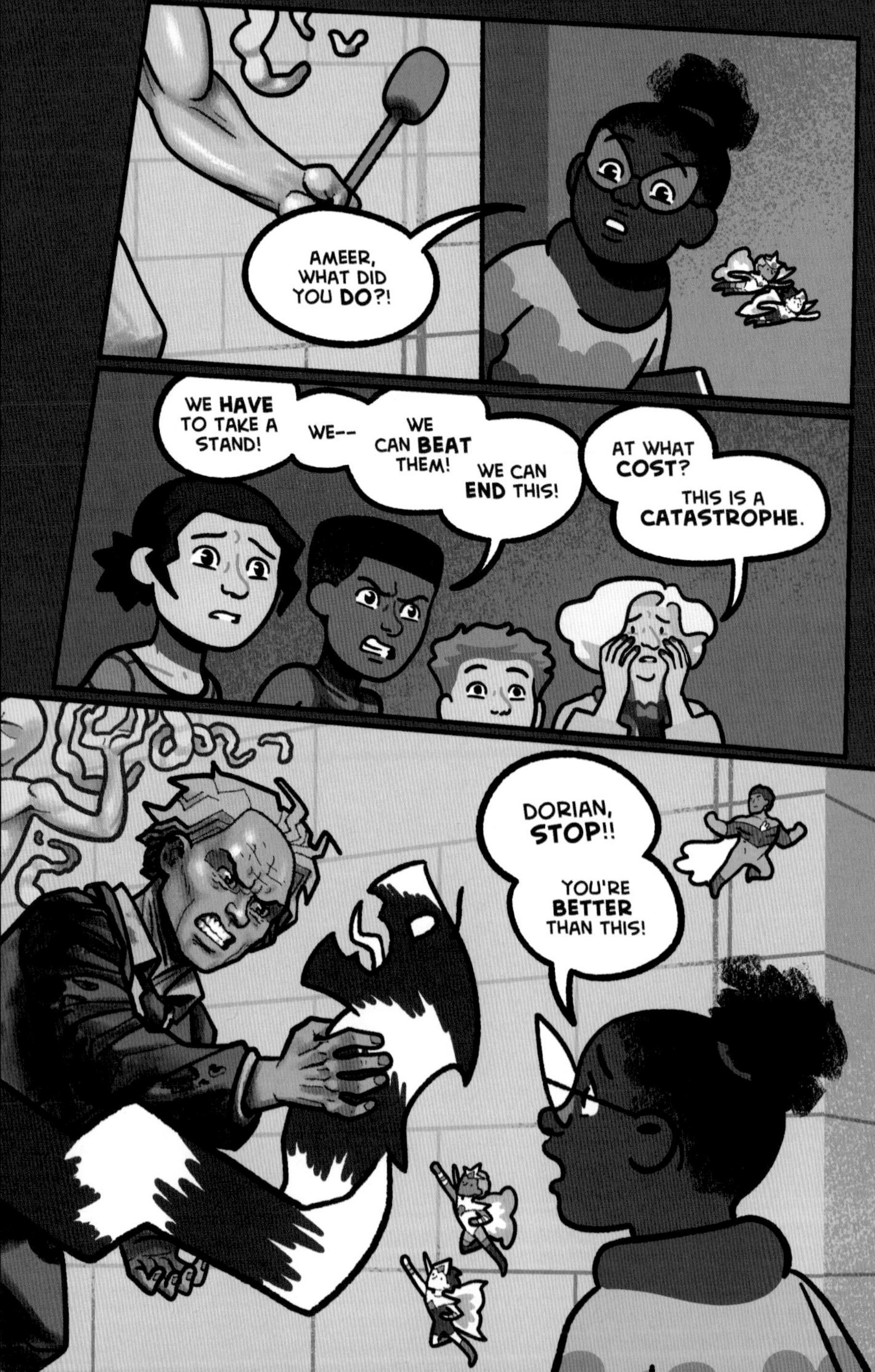
AMEER, WHAT DID YOU DO?!
WE HAVE TO TAKE A STAND!
WE--
WE CAN BEAT THEM!
WE CAN END THIS!
AT WHAT COST?
THIS IS A CATASTROPHE.
DORIAN, STOP!!
YOU'RE BETTER THAN THIS!

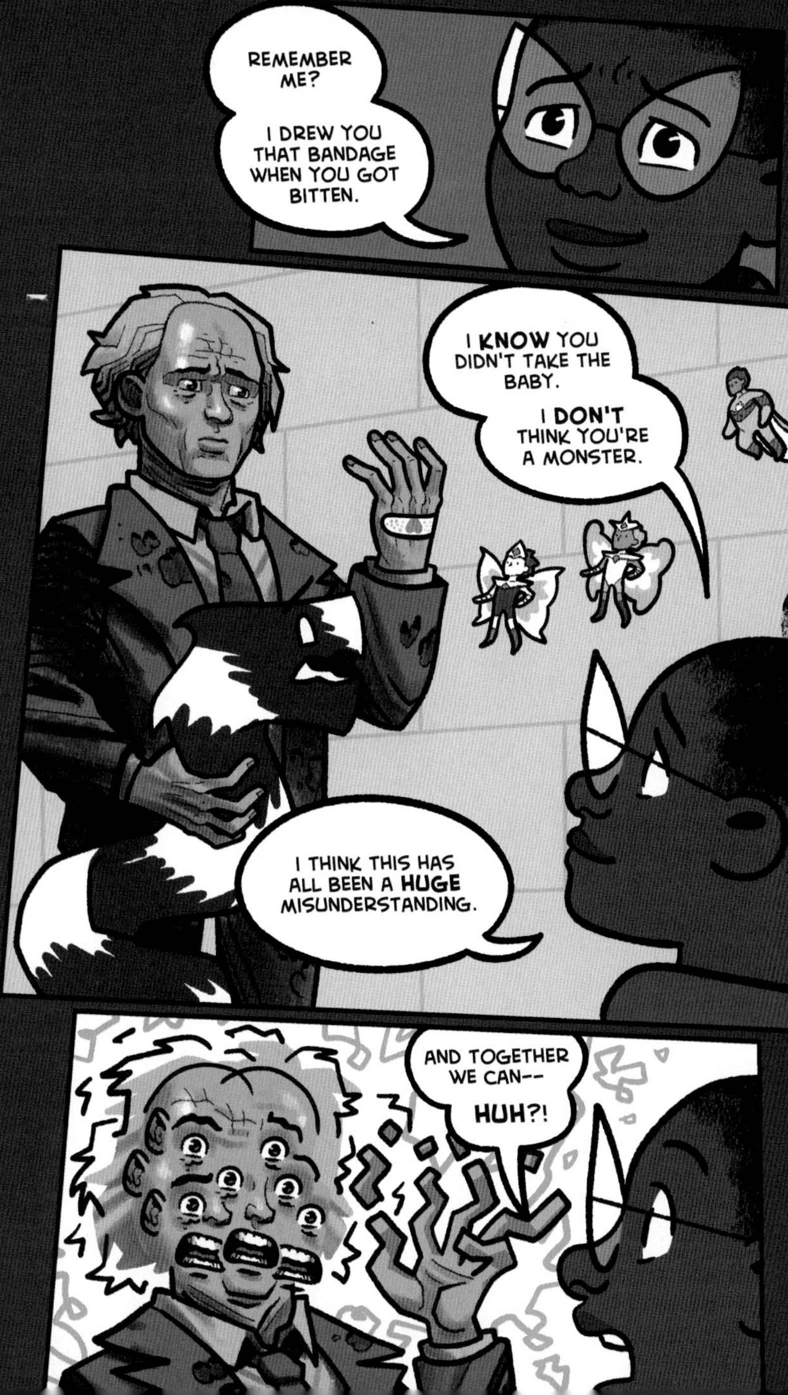
REMEMBER ME?
I DREW YOU THAT BANDAGE WHEN YOU GOT BITTEN.
I **KNOW** YOU DIDN'T TAKE THE BABY.
I **DON'T** THINK YOU'RE A MONSTER.
I THINK THIS HAS ALL BEEN A **HUGE** MISUNDERSTANDING.
AND TOGETHER WE CAN--
HUH?!

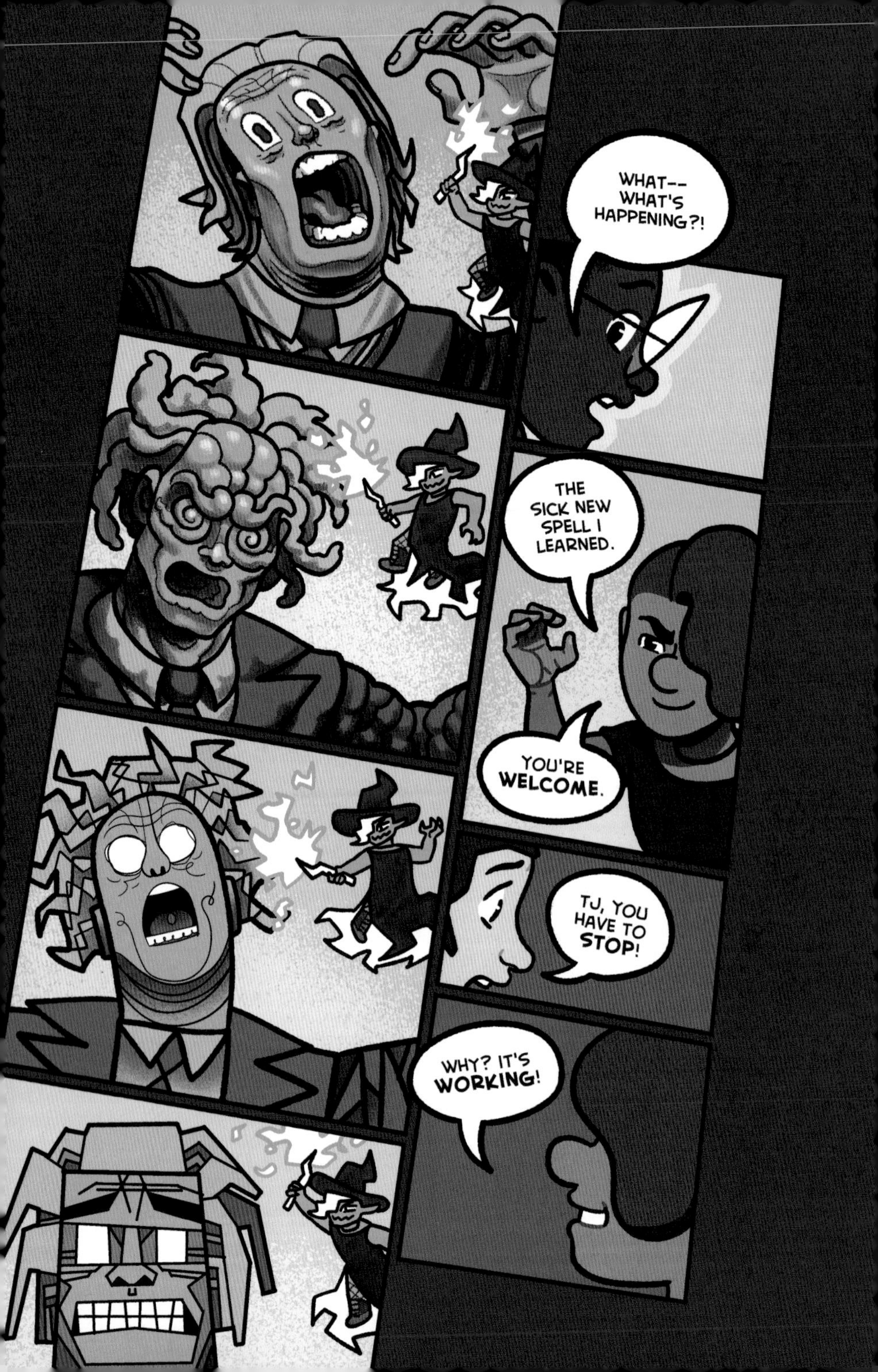
WHAT--
WHAT'S
HAPPENING?!
THE
SICK NEW
SPELL I
LEARNED.
YOU'RE
WELCOME.
TJ, YOU
HAVE TO
STOP!
WHY? IT'S
WORKING!

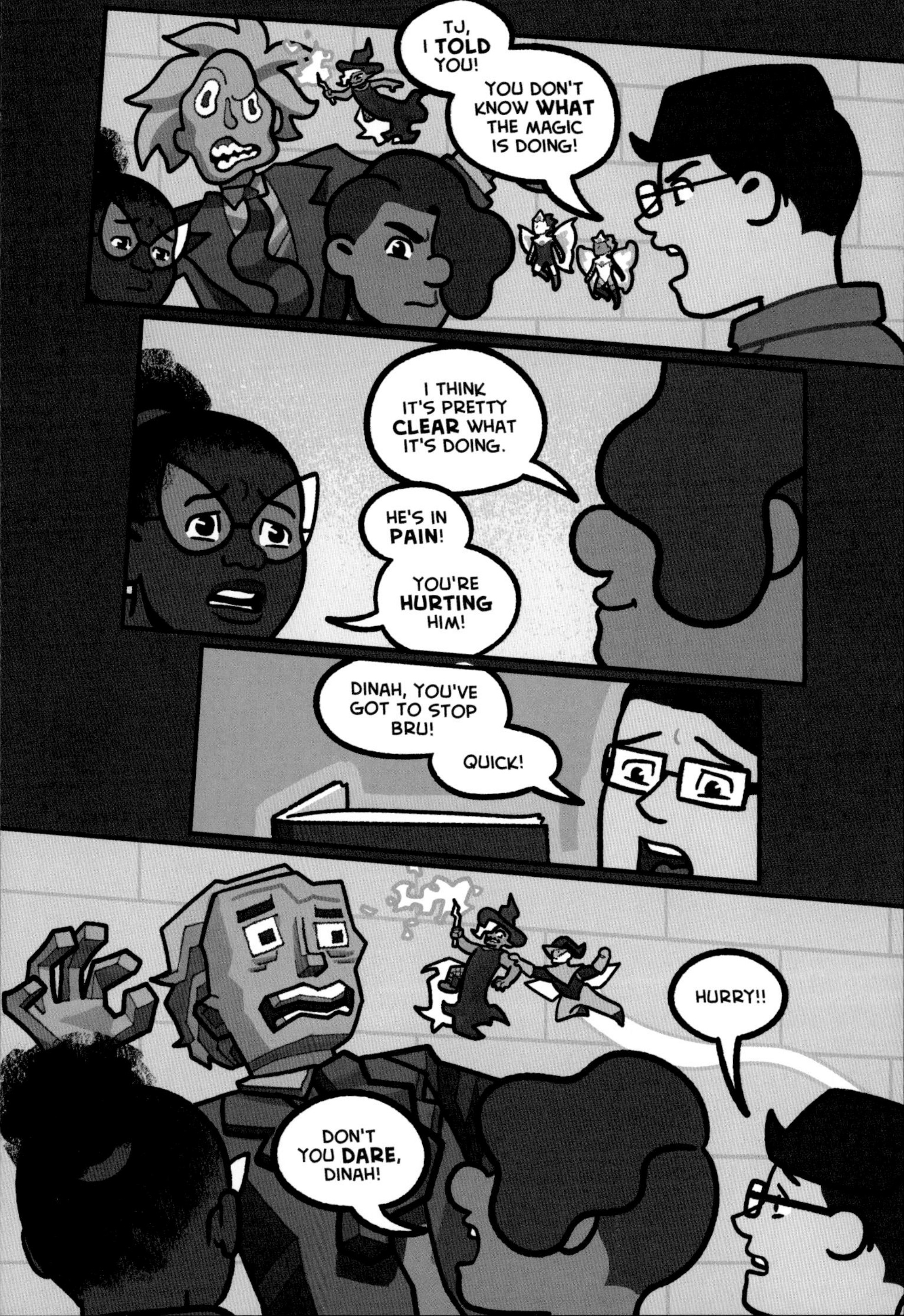
TJ, I **TOLD** YOU!
YOU DON'T KNOW **WHAT** THE MAGIC IS DOING!
I THINK IT'S PRETTY **CLEAR** WHAT IT'S DOING.
HE'S IN **PAIN**!
YOU'RE **HURTING** HIM!
DINAH, YOU'VE GOT TO STOP BRU!
QUICK!
HURRY!!
DON'T YOU **DARE**, DINAH!

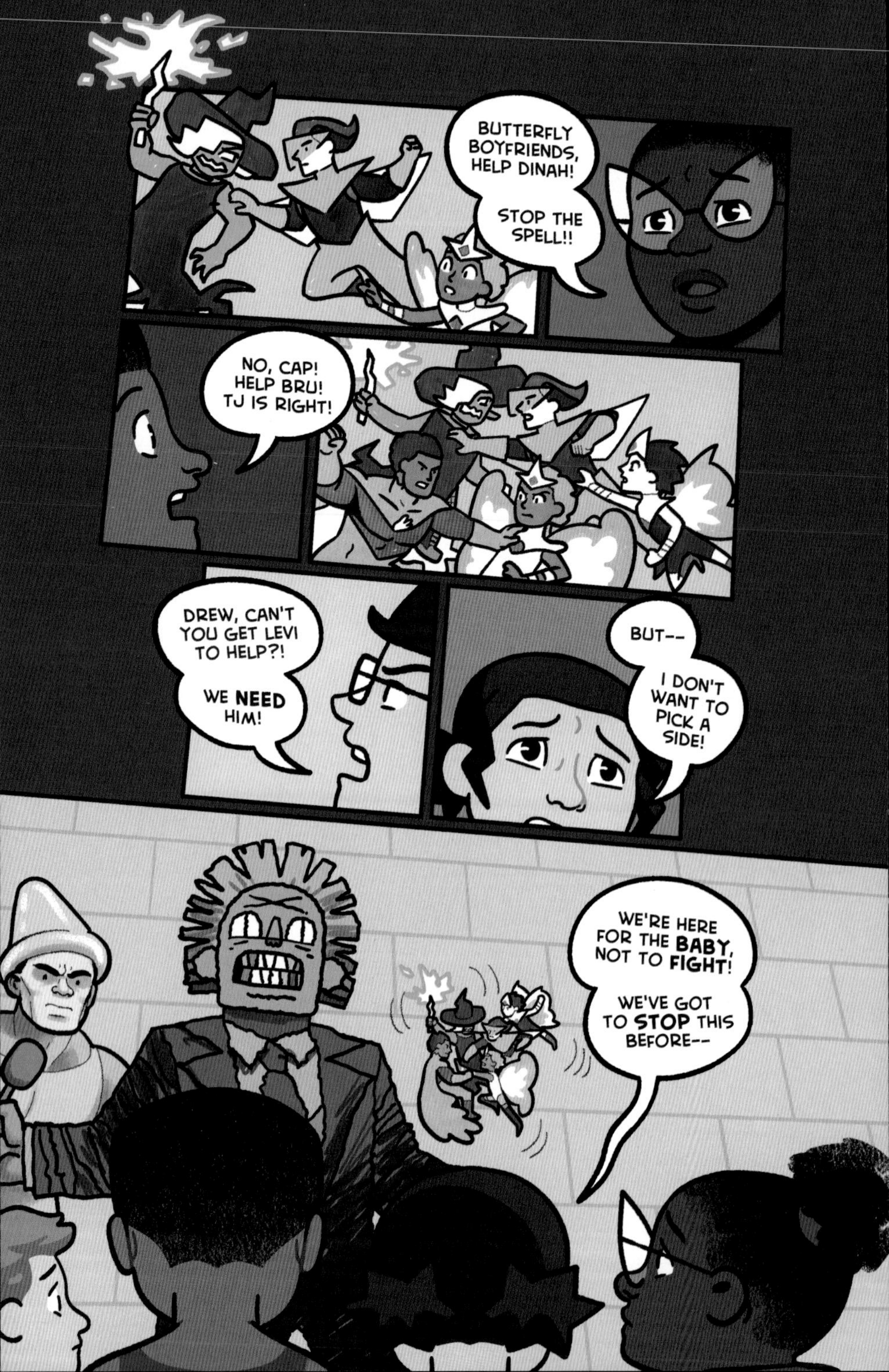
BUTTERFLY BOYFRIENDS, HELP DINAH!
STOP THE SPELL!!
NO, CAP! HELP BRU! TJ IS RIGHT!
DREW, CAN'T YOU GET LEVI TO HELP?!
WE NEED HIM!
BUT--
I DON'T WANT TO PICK A SIDE!
WE'RE HERE FOR THE BABY, NOT TO FIGHT!
WE'VE GOT TO STOP THIS BEFORE--

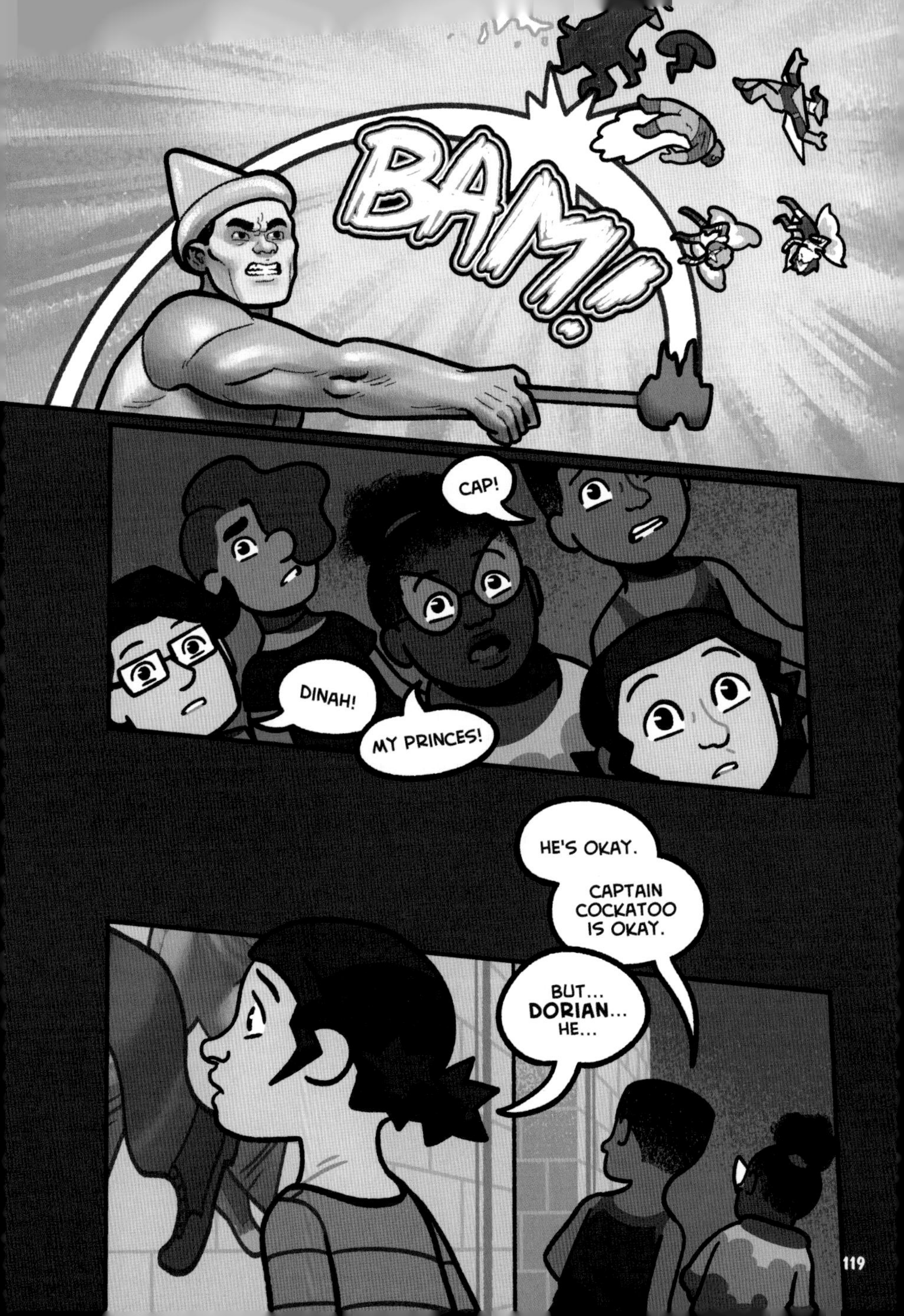
BAM!!
CAP!
DINAH!
MY PRINCES!
HE'S OKAY.
CAPTAIN COCKATOO IS OKAY.
BUT... **DORIAN**... HE...

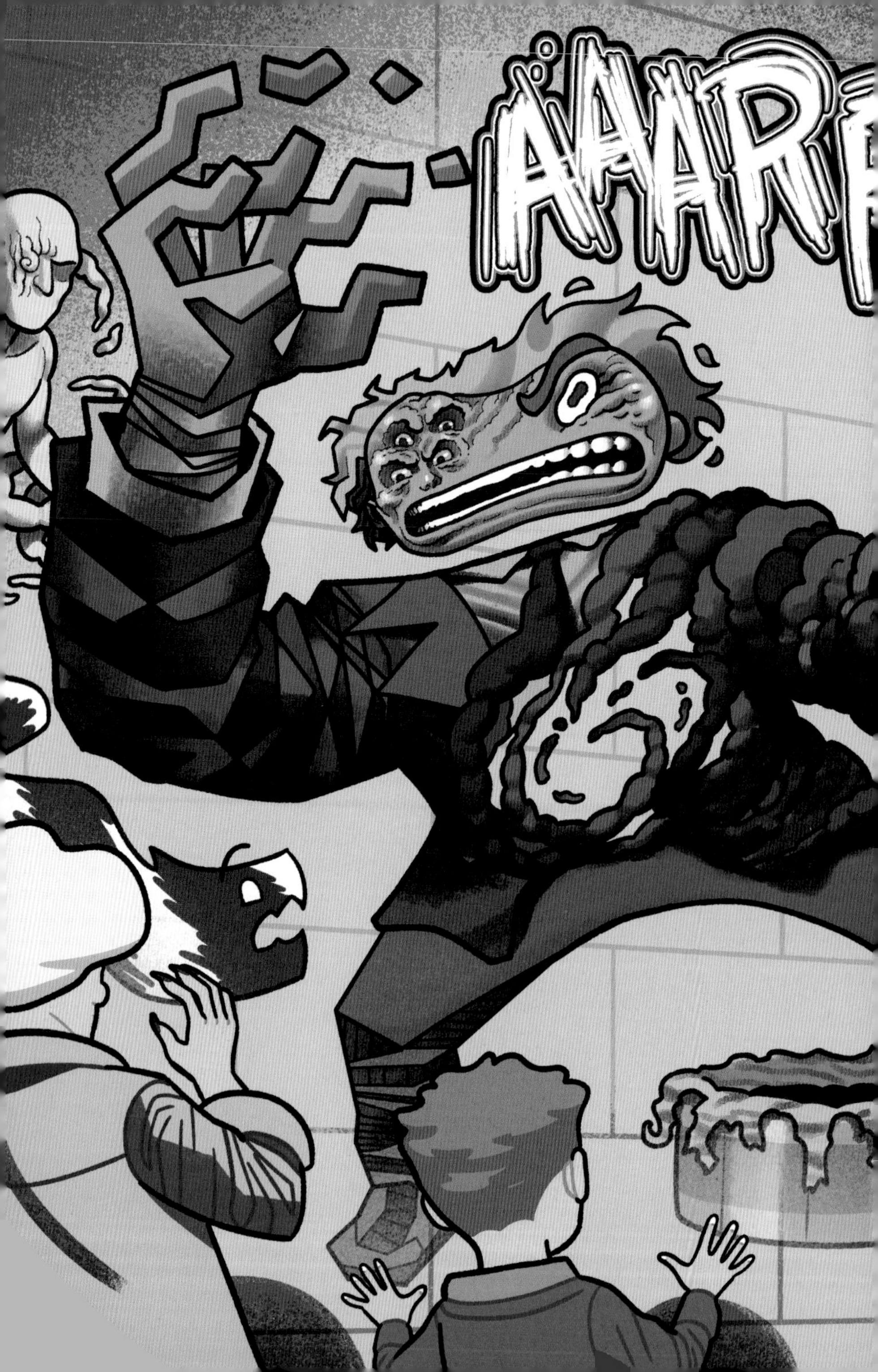
AAAR

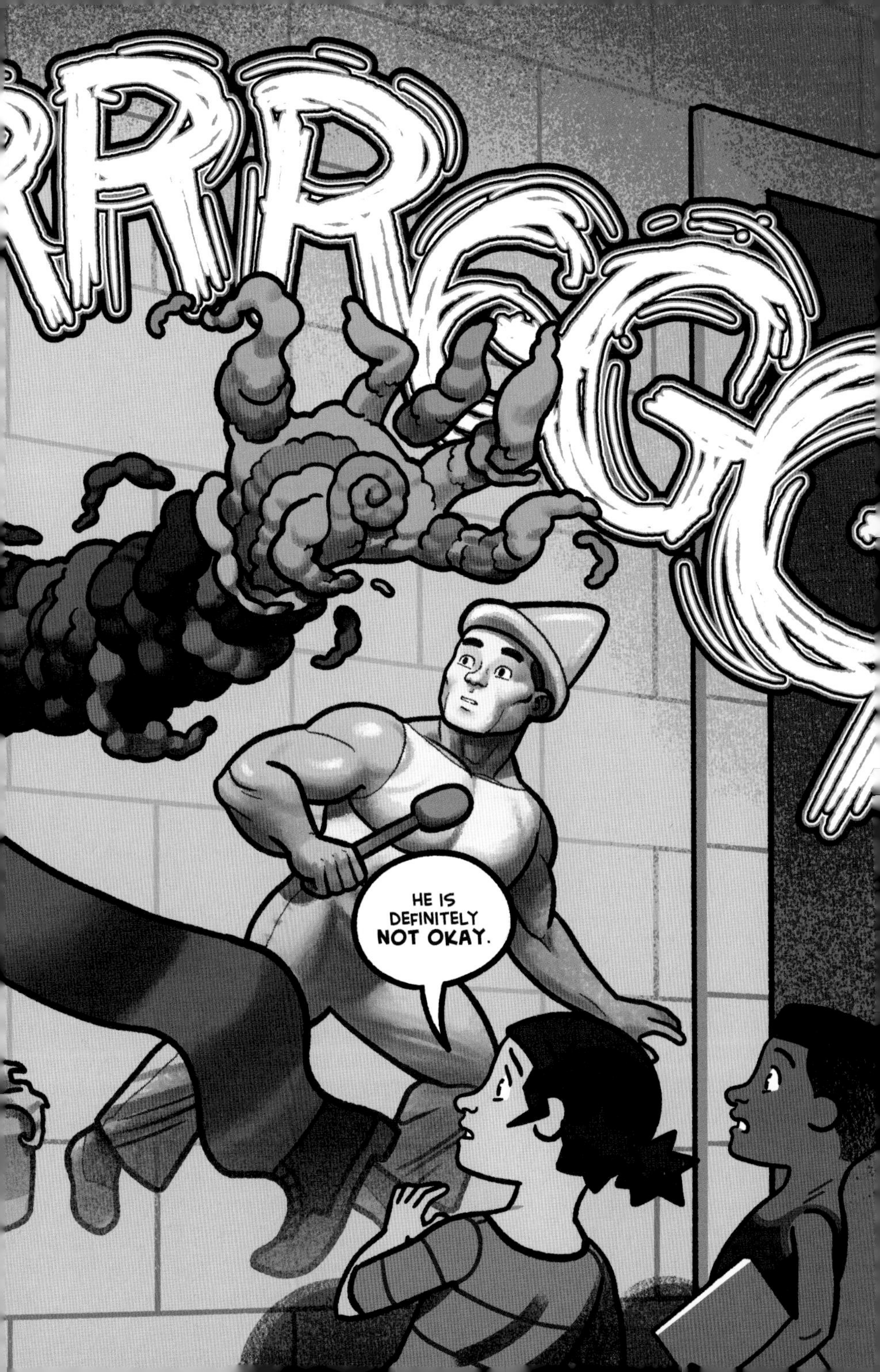
RRRGGG
HE IS DEFINITELY NOT OKAY.

CHAPTER 4: DEFINITELY NOT OKAY

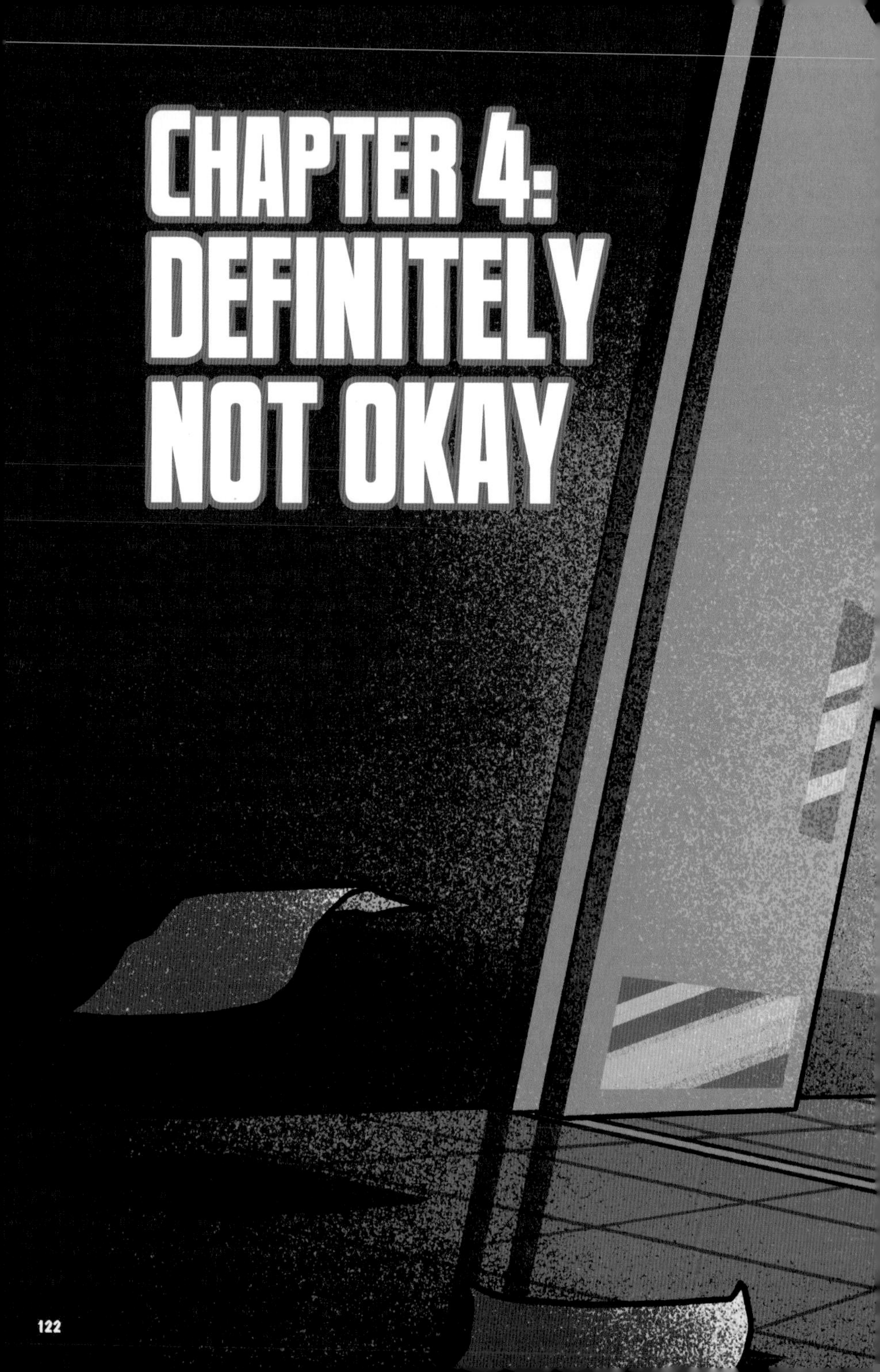

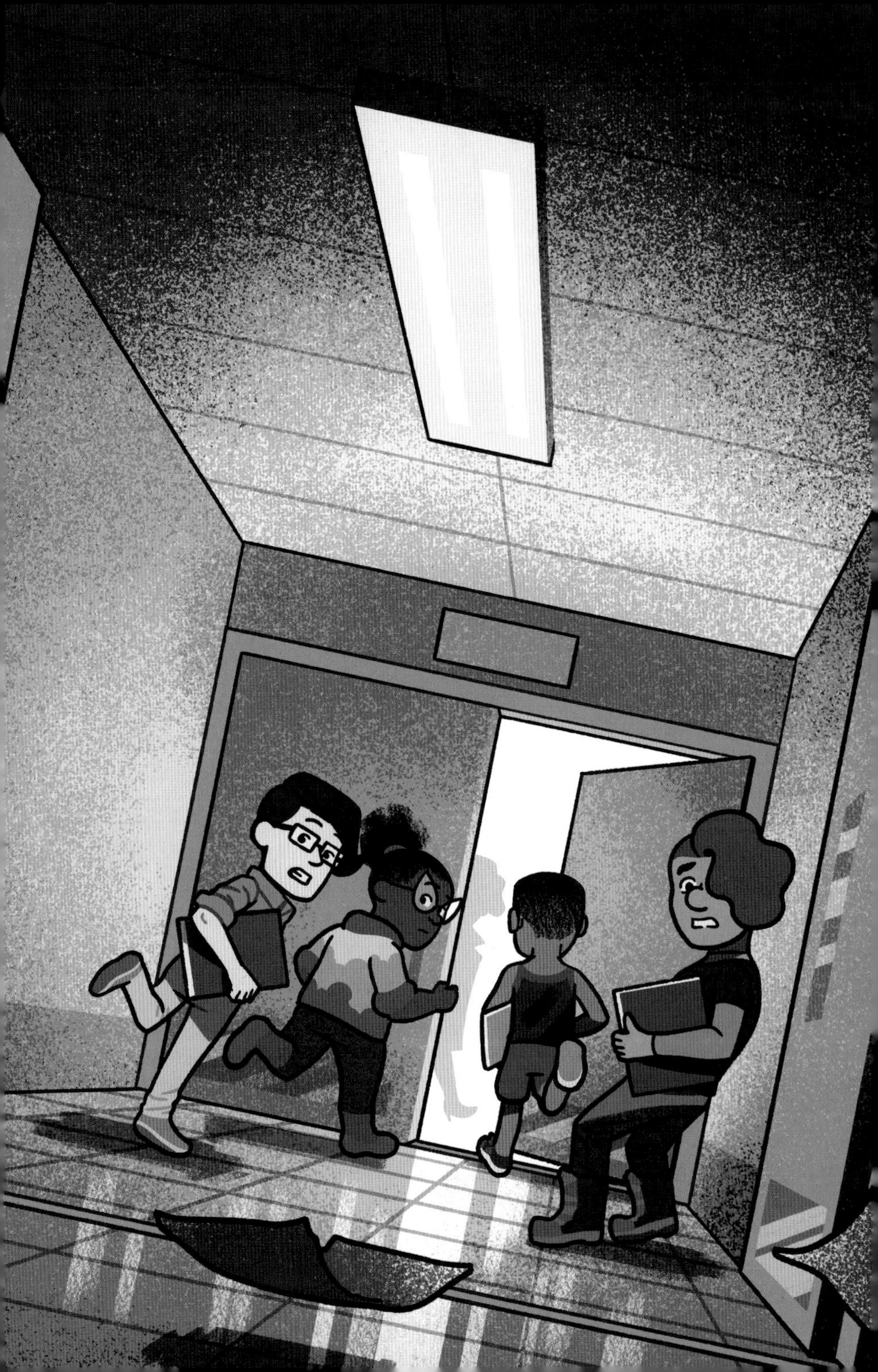

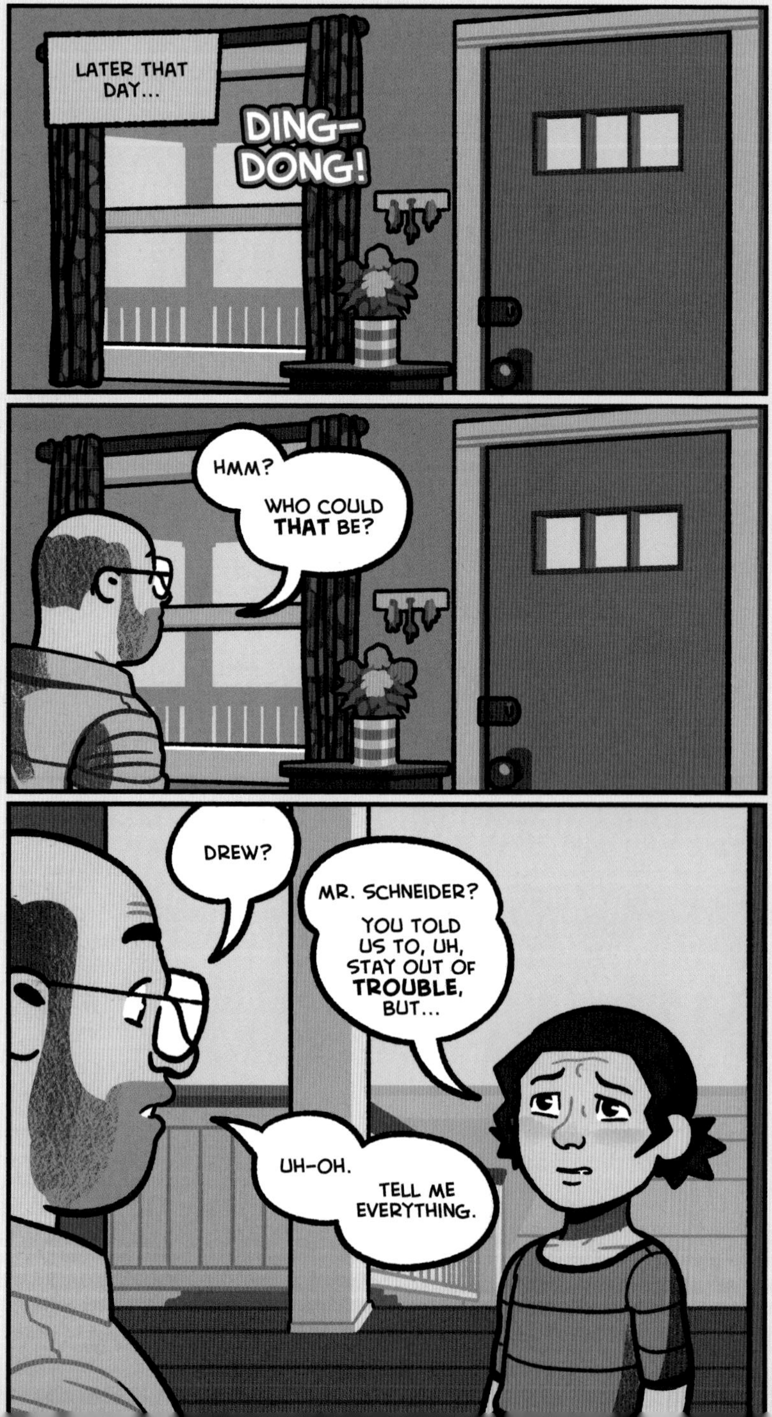
LATER THAT DAY...
DING-DONG!
HMM?
WHO COULD **THAT** BE?
DREW?
MR. SCHNEIDER?
YOU TOLD US TO, UH, STAY OUT OF **TROUBLE**, BUT...
UH-OH.
TELL ME EVERYTHING.

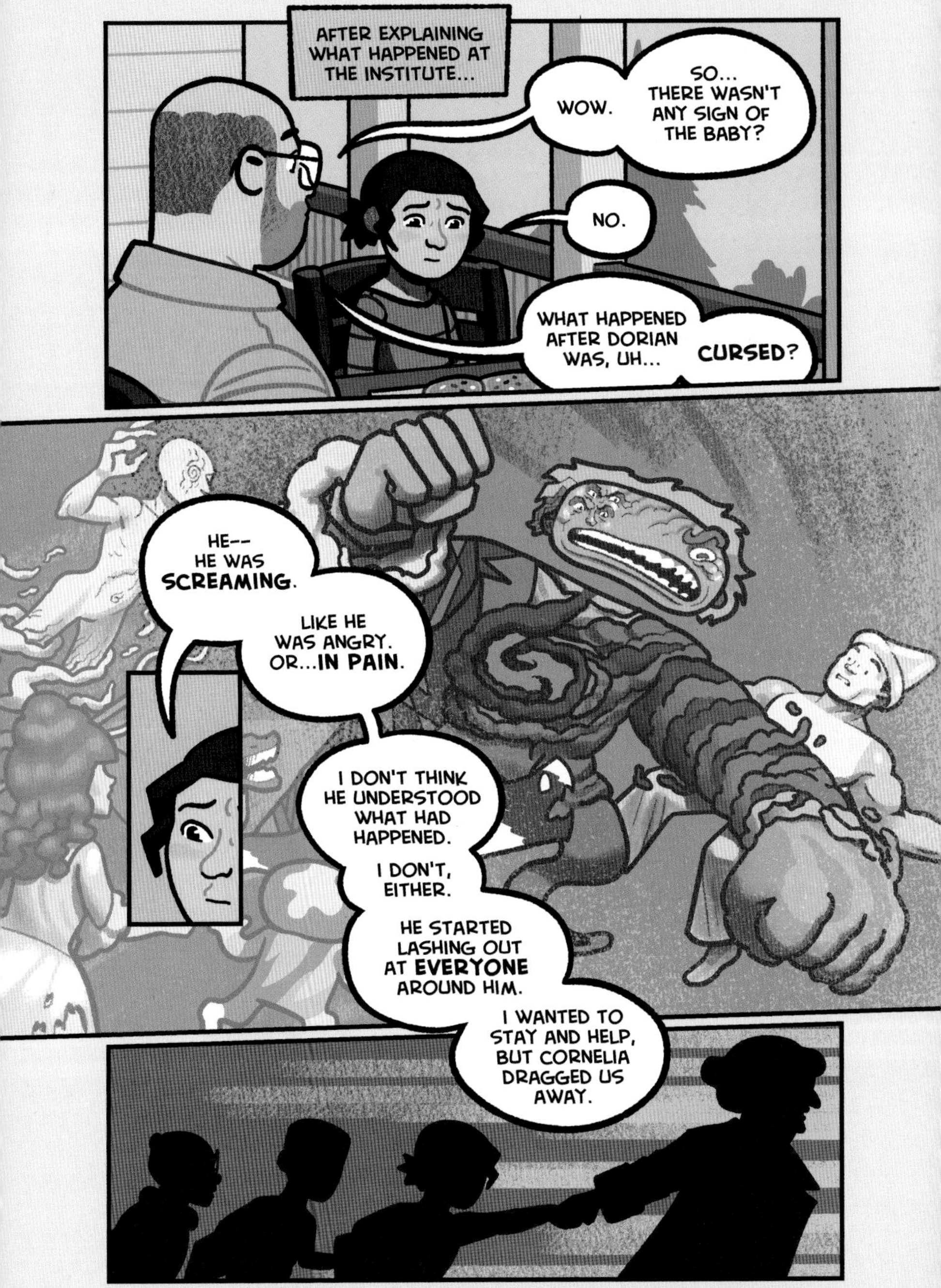
AFTER EXPLAINING WHAT HAPPENED AT THE INSTITUTE...
WOW.
SO... THERE WASN'T ANY SIGN OF THE BABY?
NO.
WHAT HAPPENED AFTER DORIAN WAS, UH... CURSED?
HE-- HE WAS SCREAMING.
LIKE HE WAS ANGRY. OR...IN PAIN.
I DON'T THINK HE UNDERSTOOD WHAT HAD HAPPENED.
I DON'T, EITHER.
HE STARTED LASHING OUT AT EVERYONE AROUND HIM.
I WANTED TO STAY AND HELP, BUT CORNELIA DRAGGED US AWAY.

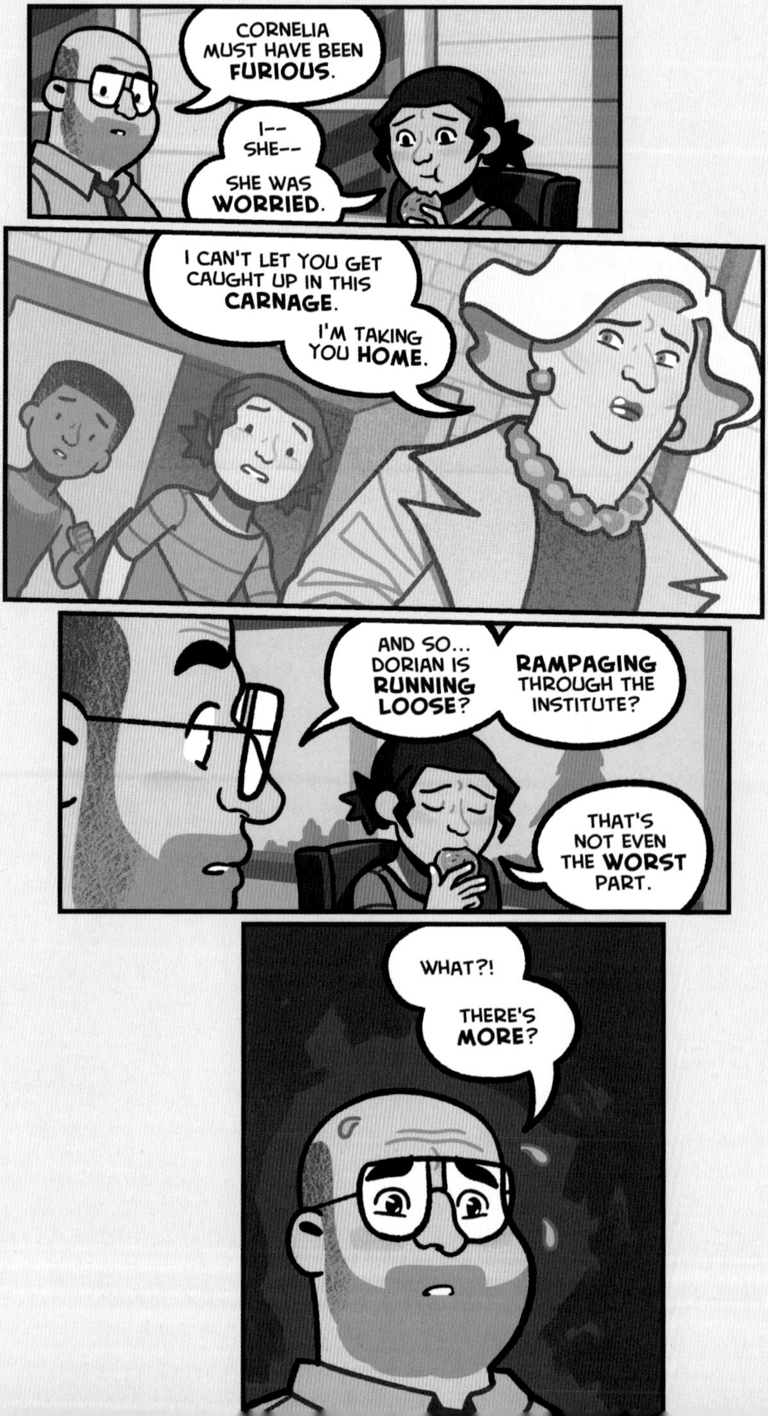
CORNELIA MUST HAVE BEEN **FURIOUS**.
I-- SHE--
SHE WAS **WORRIED**.
I CAN'T LET YOU GET CAUGHT UP IN THIS **CARNAGE**.
I'M TAKING YOU **HOME**.
AND SO... DORIAN IS **RUNNING LOOSE**?
RAMPAGING THROUGH THE INSTITUTE?
THAT'S NOT EVEN THE **WORST** PART.
WHAT?!
THERE'S **MORE**?

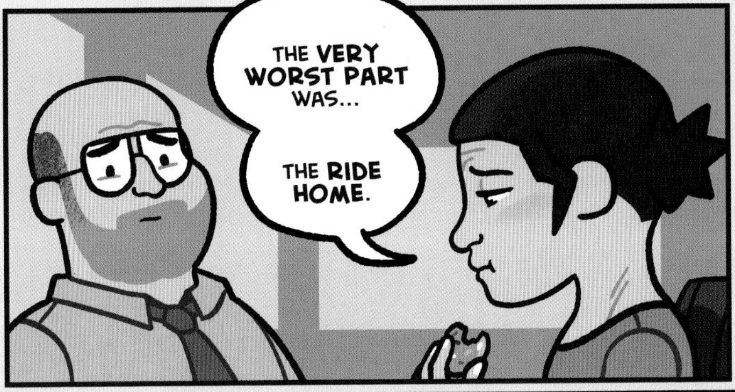
THE VERY WORST PART WAS...
THE RIDE HOME.

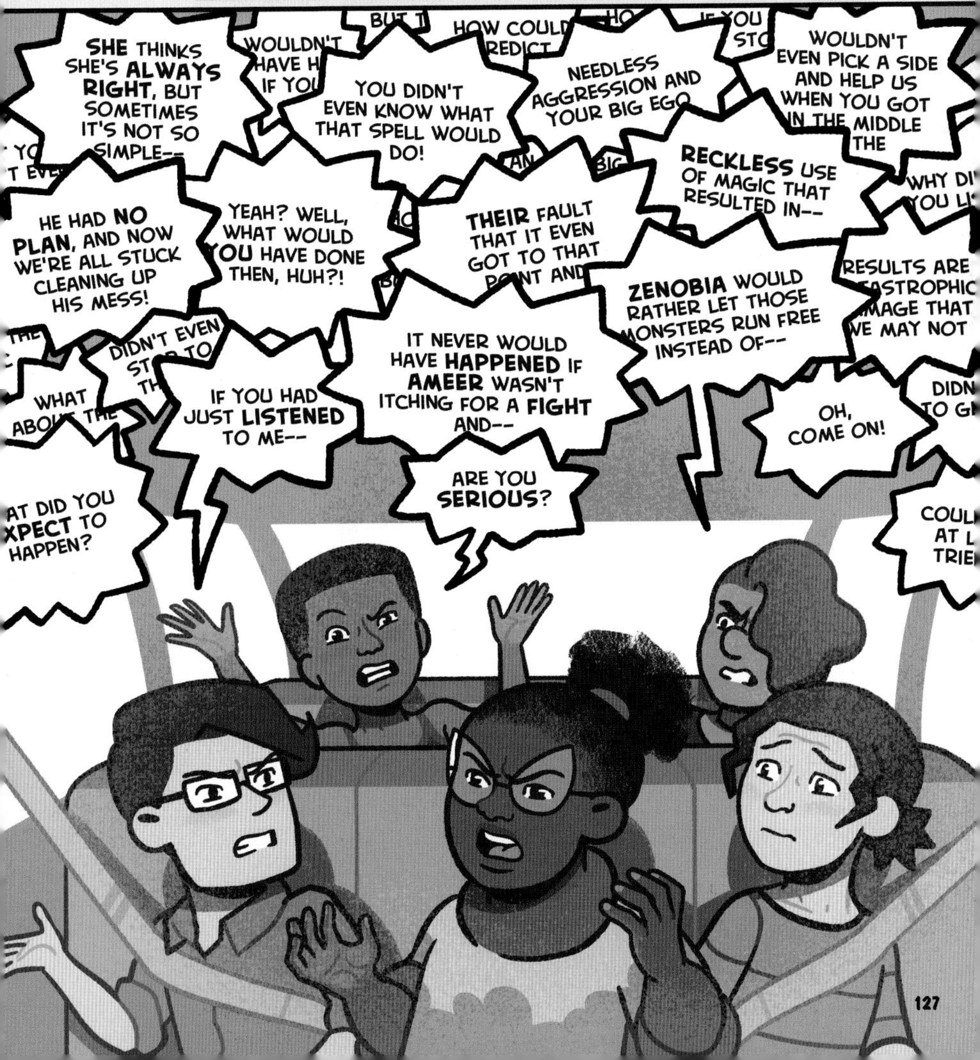
SHE THINKS SHE'S ALWAYS RIGHT, BUT SOMETIMES IT'S NOT SO SIMPLE--
YOU DIDN'T EVEN KNOW WHAT THAT SPELL WOULD DO!
NEEDLESS AGGRESSION AND YOUR BIG EGO
WOULDN'T EVEN PICK A SIDE AND HELP US WHEN YOU GOT IN THE MIDDLE THE
RECKLESS USE OF MAGIC THAT RESULTED IN--
HE HAD NO PLAN, AND NOW WE'RE ALL STUCK CLEANING UP HIS MESS!
YEAH? WELL, WHAT WOULD YOU HAVE DONE THEN, HUH?!
THEIR FAULT THAT IT EVEN GOT TO THAT POINT AND
ZENOBIA WOULD RATHER LET THOSE MONSTERS RUN FREE INSTEAD OF--
IT NEVER WOULD HAVE HAPPENED IF AMEER WASN'T ITCHING FOR A FIGHT AND--
IF YOU HAD JUST LISTENED TO ME--
OH, COME ON!
ARE YOU SERIOUS?
AT DID YOU XPECT TO HAPPEN?

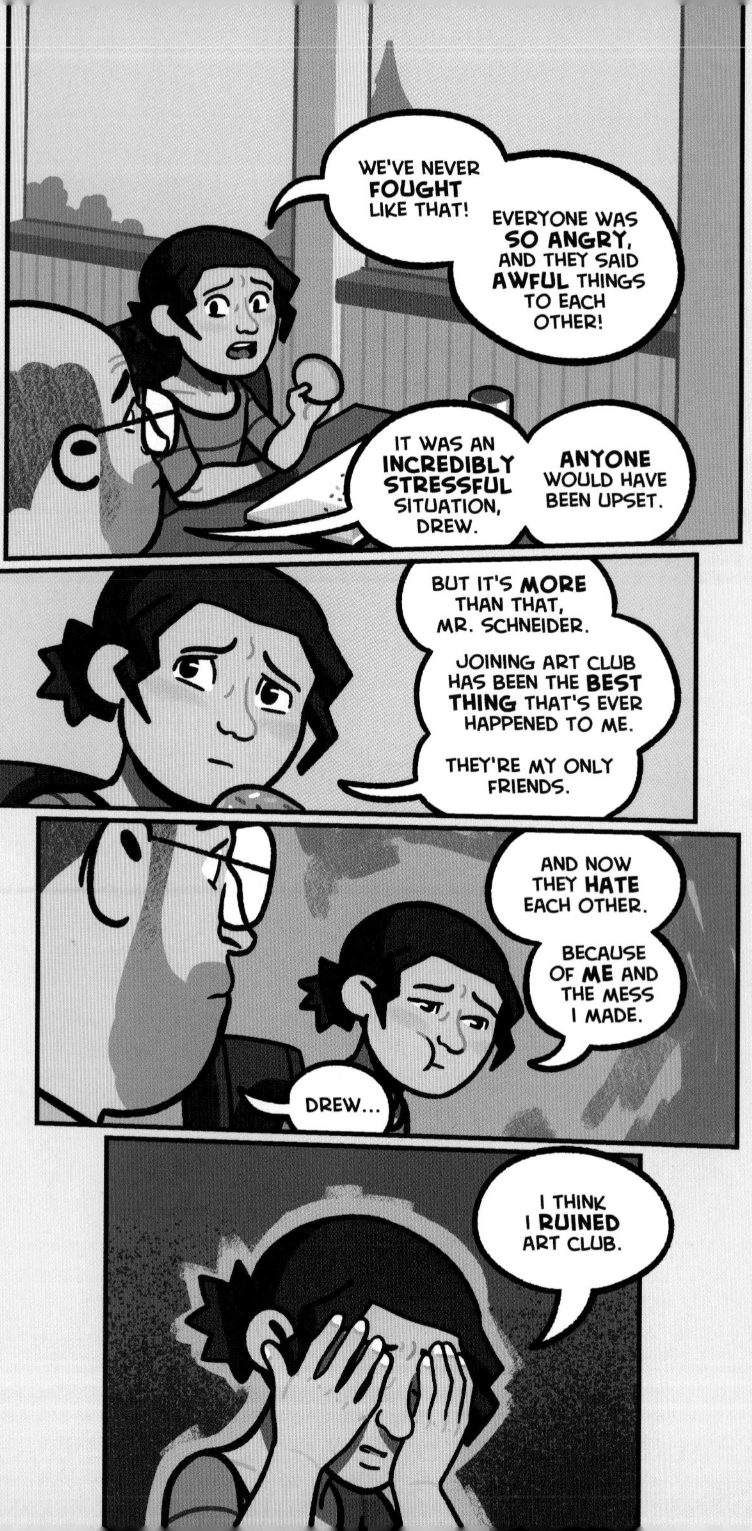
WE'VE NEVER FOUGHT LIKE THAT!
EVERYONE WAS SO ANGRY, AND THEY SAID AWFUL THINGS TO EACH OTHER!
IT WAS AN INCREDIBLY STRESSFUL SITUATION, DREW.
ANYONE WOULD HAVE BEEN UPSET.
BUT IT'S MORE THAN THAT, MR. SCHNEIDER.
JOINING ART CLUB HAS BEEN THE BEST THING THAT'S EVER HAPPENED TO ME.
THEY'RE MY ONLY FRIENDS.
AND NOW THEY HATE EACH OTHER.
BECAUSE OF ME AND THE MESS I MADE.
DREW...
I THINK I RUINED ART CLUB.

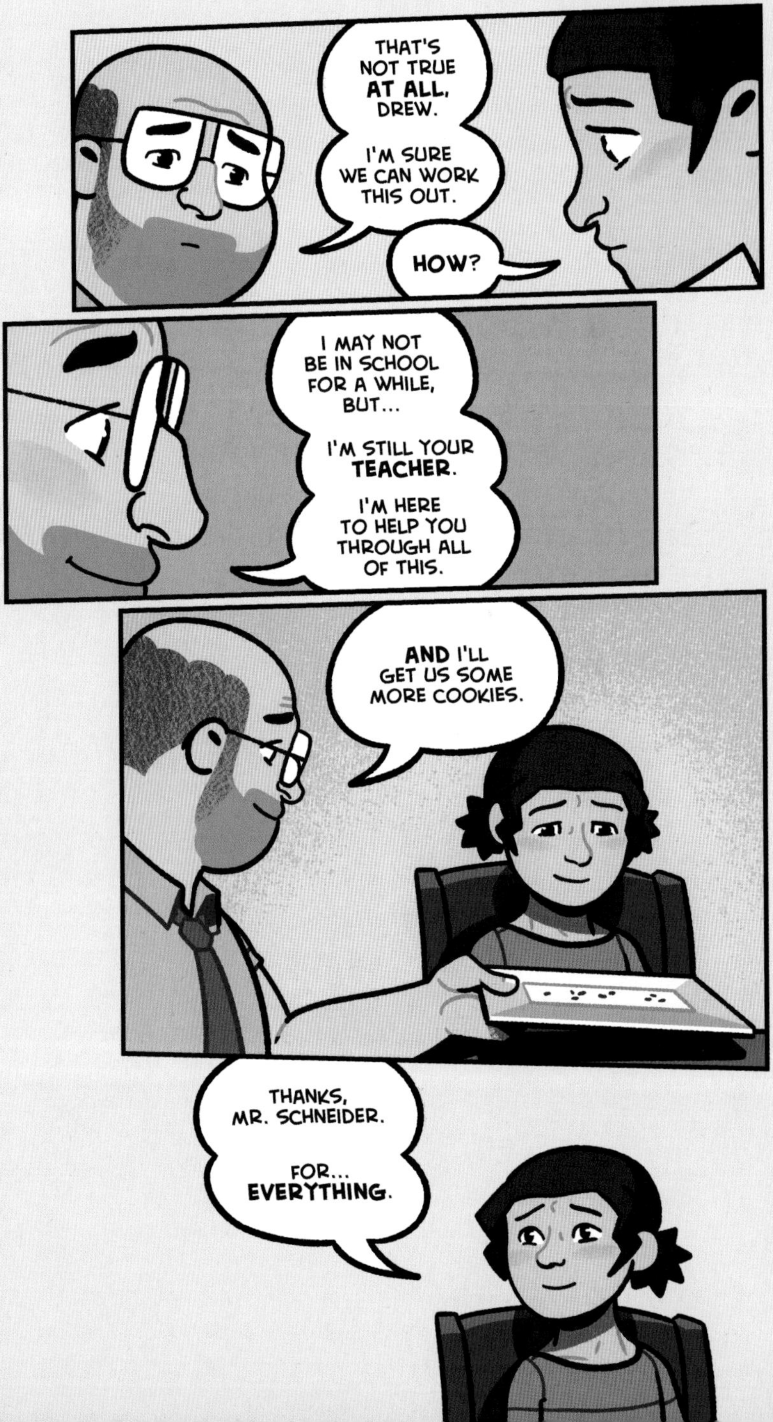
THAT'S NOT TRUE AT ALL, DREW.
I'M SURE WE CAN WORK THIS OUT.
HOW?
I MAY NOT BE IN SCHOOL FOR A WHILE, BUT...
I'M STILL YOUR TEACHER.
I'M HERE TO HELP YOU THROUGH ALL OF THIS.
AND I'LL GET US SOME MORE COOKIES.
THANKS, MR. SCHNEIDER.
FOR... EVERYTHING.

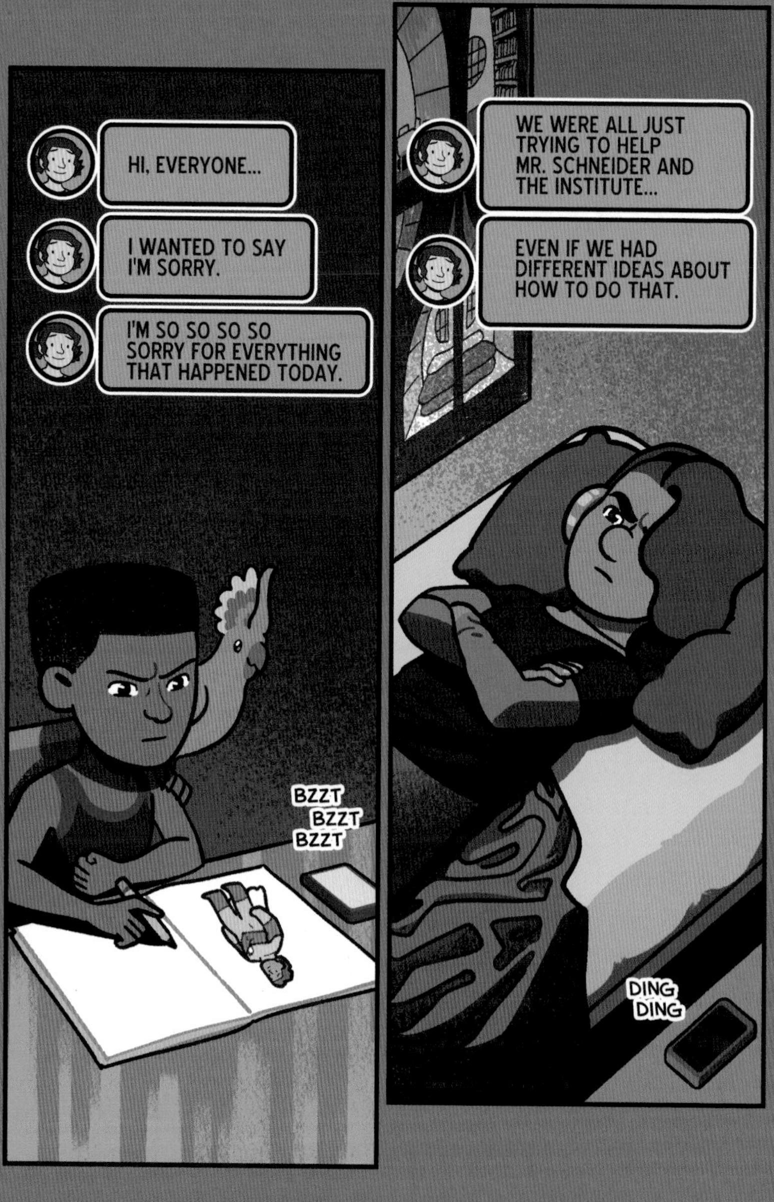
HI, EVERYONE...
I WANTED TO SAY I'M SORRY.
I'M SO SO SO SO SORRY FOR EVERYTHING THAT HAPPENED TODAY.
BZZT BZZT BZZT
WE WERE ALL JUST TRYING TO HELP MR. SCHNEIDER AND THE INSTITUTE...
EVEN IF WE HAD DIFFERENT IDEAS ABOUT HOW TO DO THAT.
DING DING

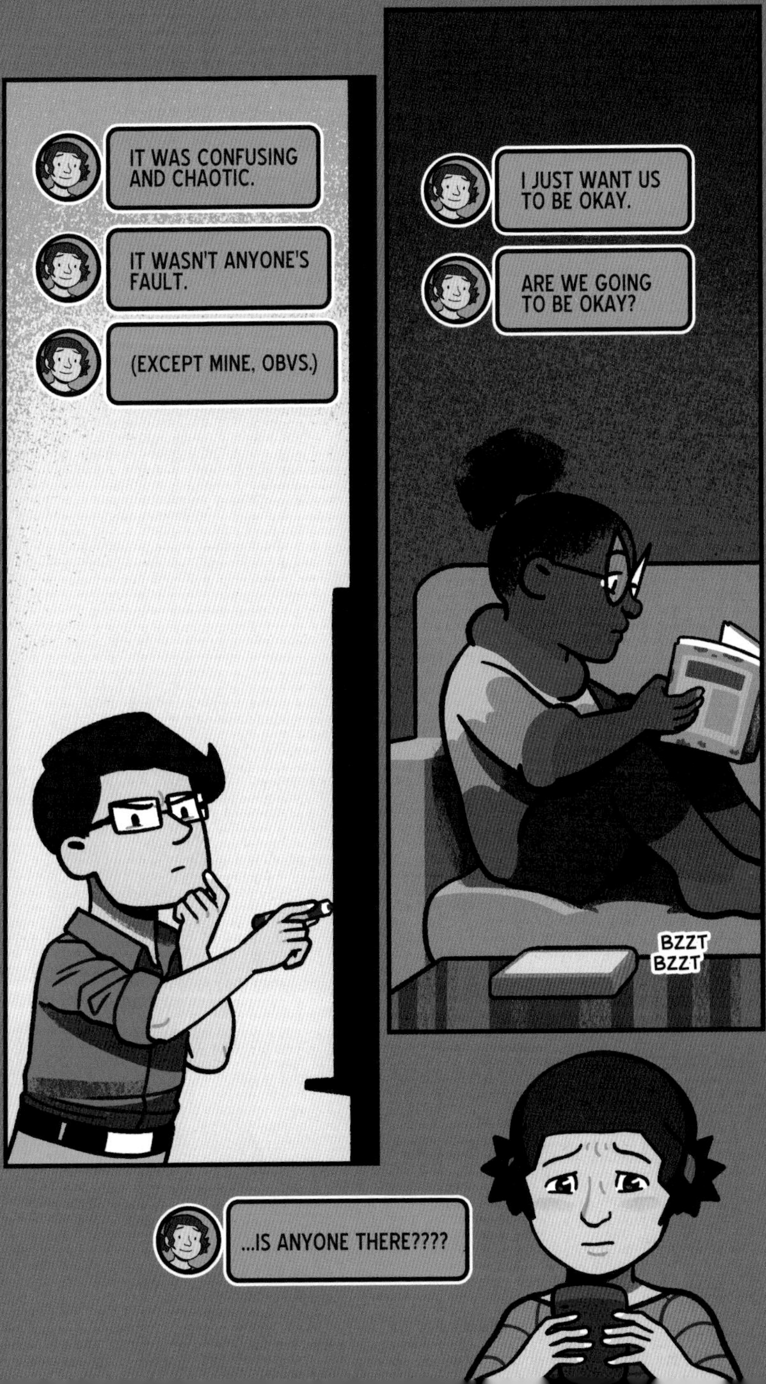
IT WAS CONFUSING AND CHAOTIC.
IT WASN'T ANYONE'S FAULT.
(EXCEPT MINE, OBVS.)
I JUST WANT US TO BE OKAY.
ARE WE GOING TO BE OKAY?
BZZT BZZT
...IS ANYONE THERE????

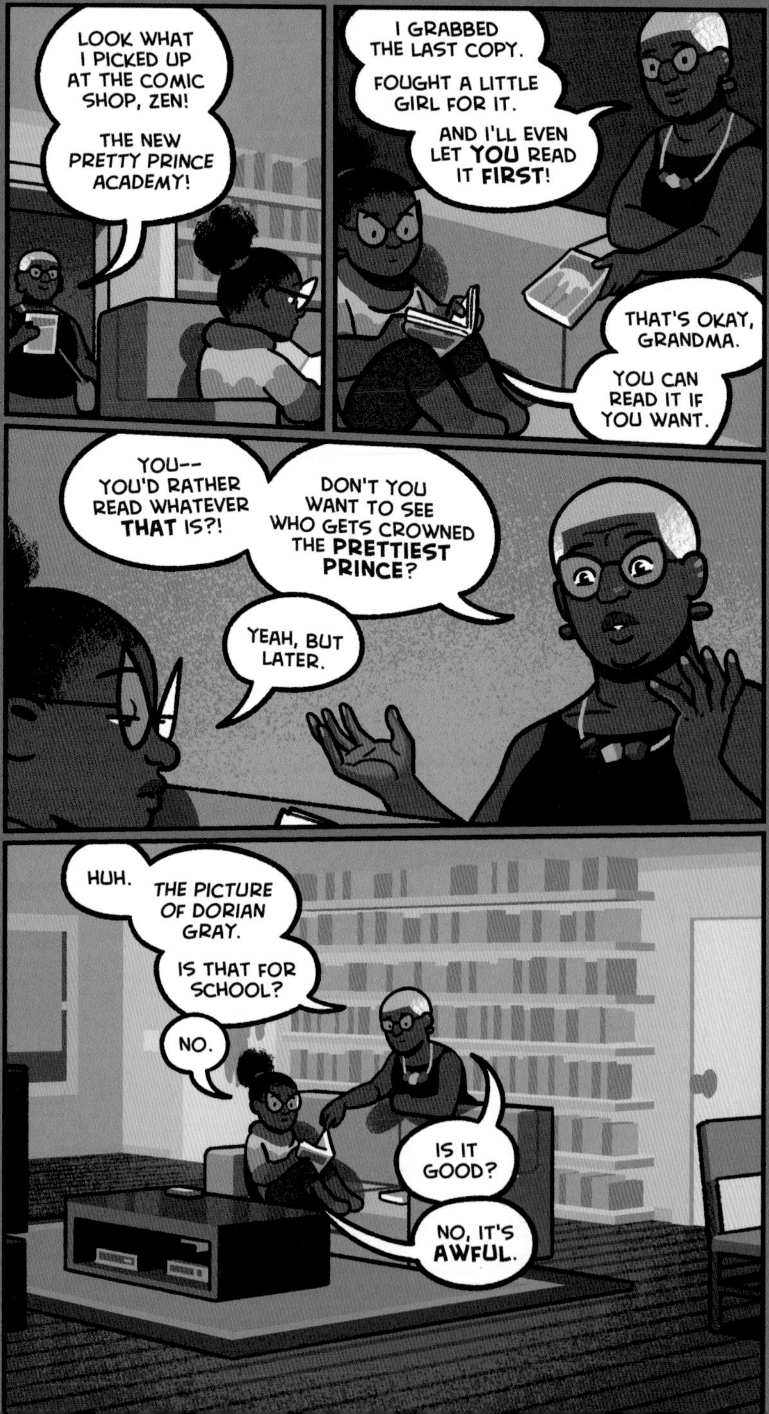

LOOK WHAT I PICKED UP AT THE COMIC SHOP, ZEN!
THE NEW PRETTY PRINCE ACADEMY!
I GRABBED THE LAST COPY.
FOUGHT A LITTLE GIRL FOR IT.
AND I'LL EVEN LET **YOU** READ IT **FIRST**!
THAT'S OKAY, GRANDMA.
YOU CAN READ IT IF YOU WANT.
YOU-- YOU'D RATHER READ WHATEVER **THAT** IS?!
DON'T YOU WANT TO SEE WHO GETS CROWNED THE **PRETTIEST PRINCE**?
YEAH, BUT LATER.
HUH.
THE PICTURE OF DORIAN GRAY.
IS THAT FOR SCHOOL?
NO.
IS IT GOOD?
NO, IT'S **AWFUL**.

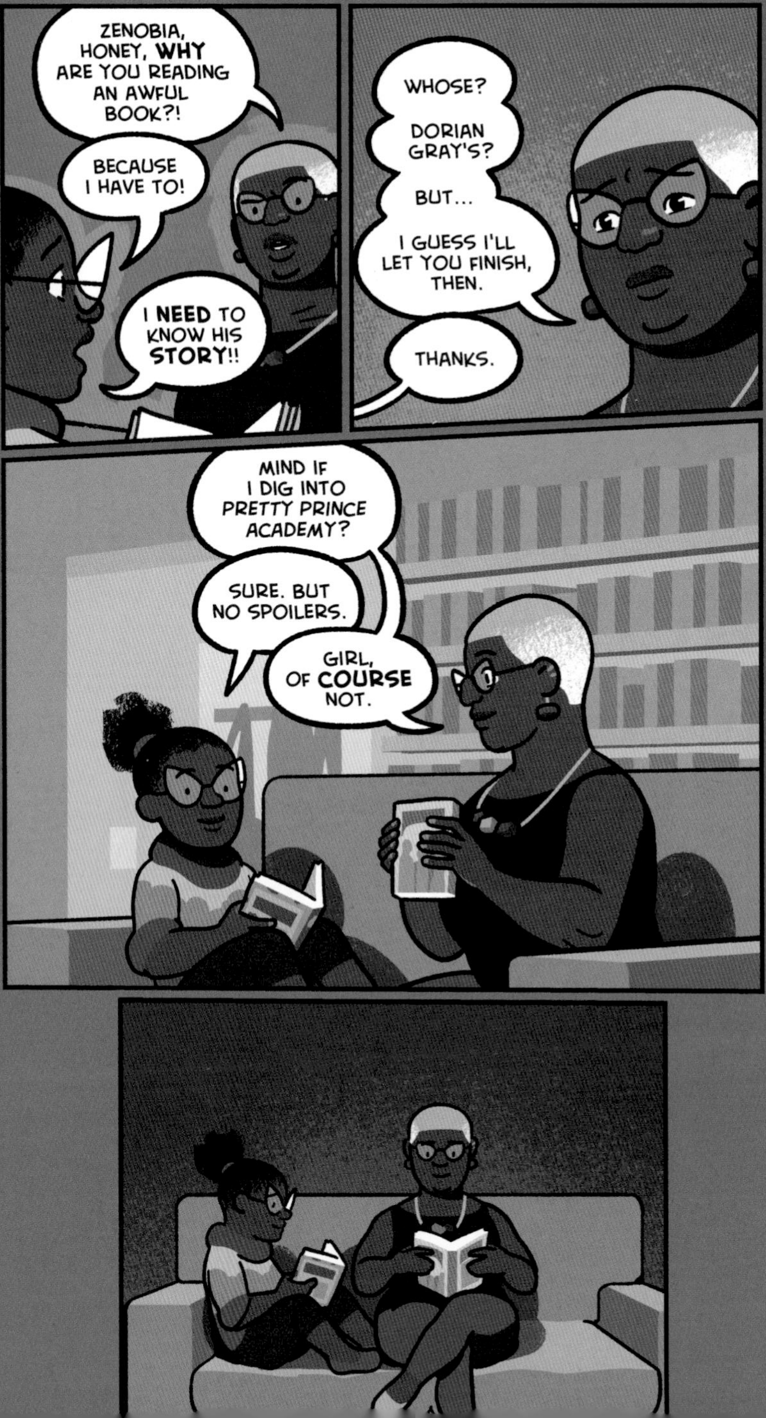
ZENOBIA, HONEY, WHY ARE YOU READING AN AWFUL BOOK?!
BECAUSE I HAVE TO!
I NEED TO KNOW HIS STORY!!
WHOSE?
DORIAN GRAY'S?
BUT...
I GUESS I'LL LET YOU FINISH, THEN.
THANKS.
MIND IF I DIG INTO PRETTY PRINCE ACADEMY?
SURE. BUT NO SPOILERS.
GIRL, OF COURSE NOT.

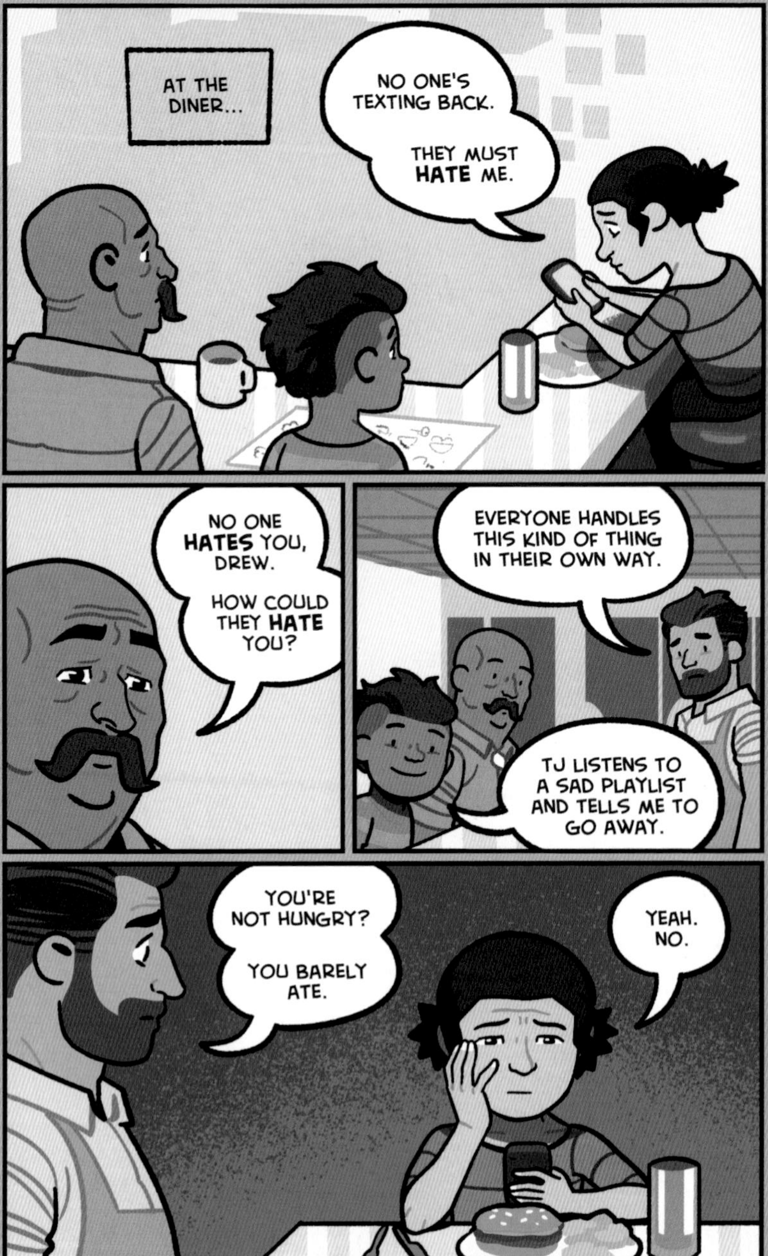
AT THE DINER...
NO ONE'S TEXTING BACK.
THEY MUST HATE ME.
NO ONE HATES YOU, DREW.
HOW COULD THEY HATE YOU?
EVERYONE HANDLES THIS KIND OF THING IN THEIR OWN WAY.
TJ LISTENS TO A SAD PLAYLIST AND TELLS ME TO GO AWAY.
YOU'RE NOT HUNGRY?
YOU BARELY ATE.
YEAH. NO.

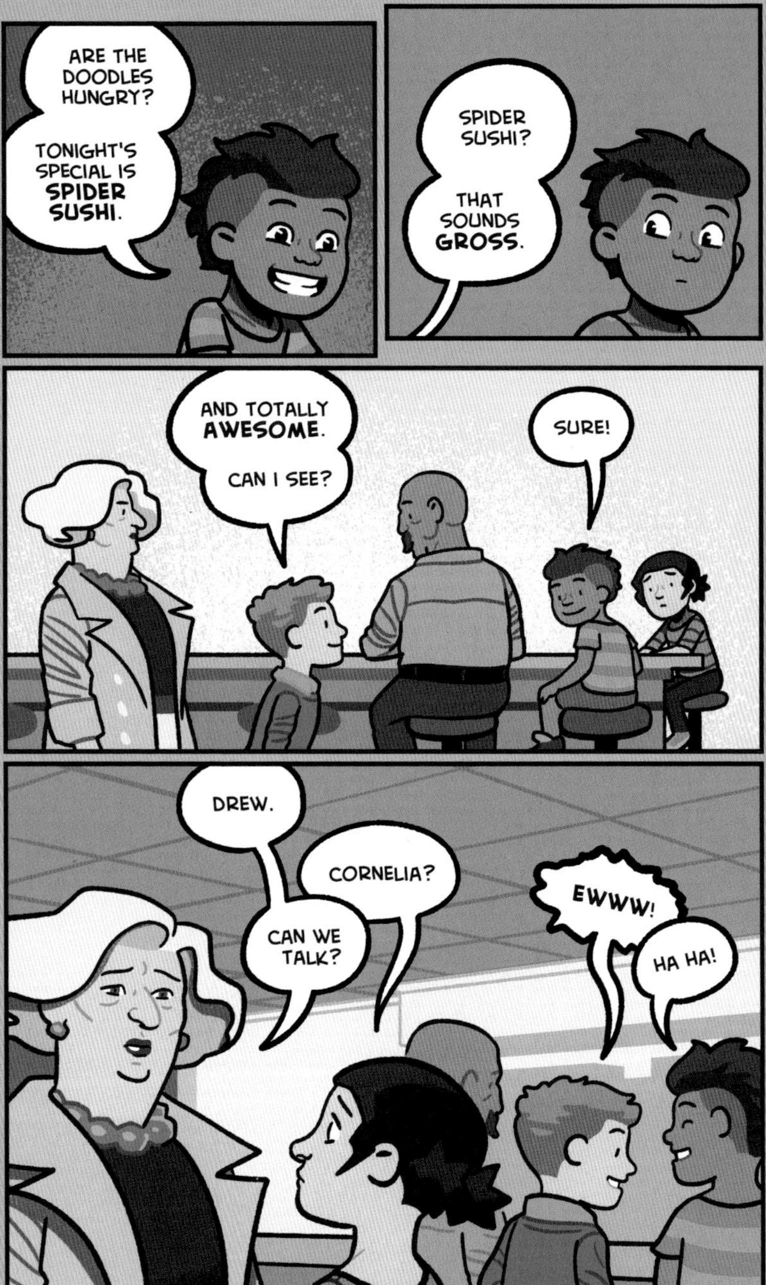
ARE THE DOODLES HUNGRY?
TONIGHT'S SPECIAL IS **SPIDER SUSHI**.
SPIDER SUSHI?
THAT SOUNDS **GROSS**.
AND TOTALLY **AWESOME**.
CAN I SEE?
SURE!
DREW.
CAN WE TALK?
CORNELIA?
EWWW!
HA HA!

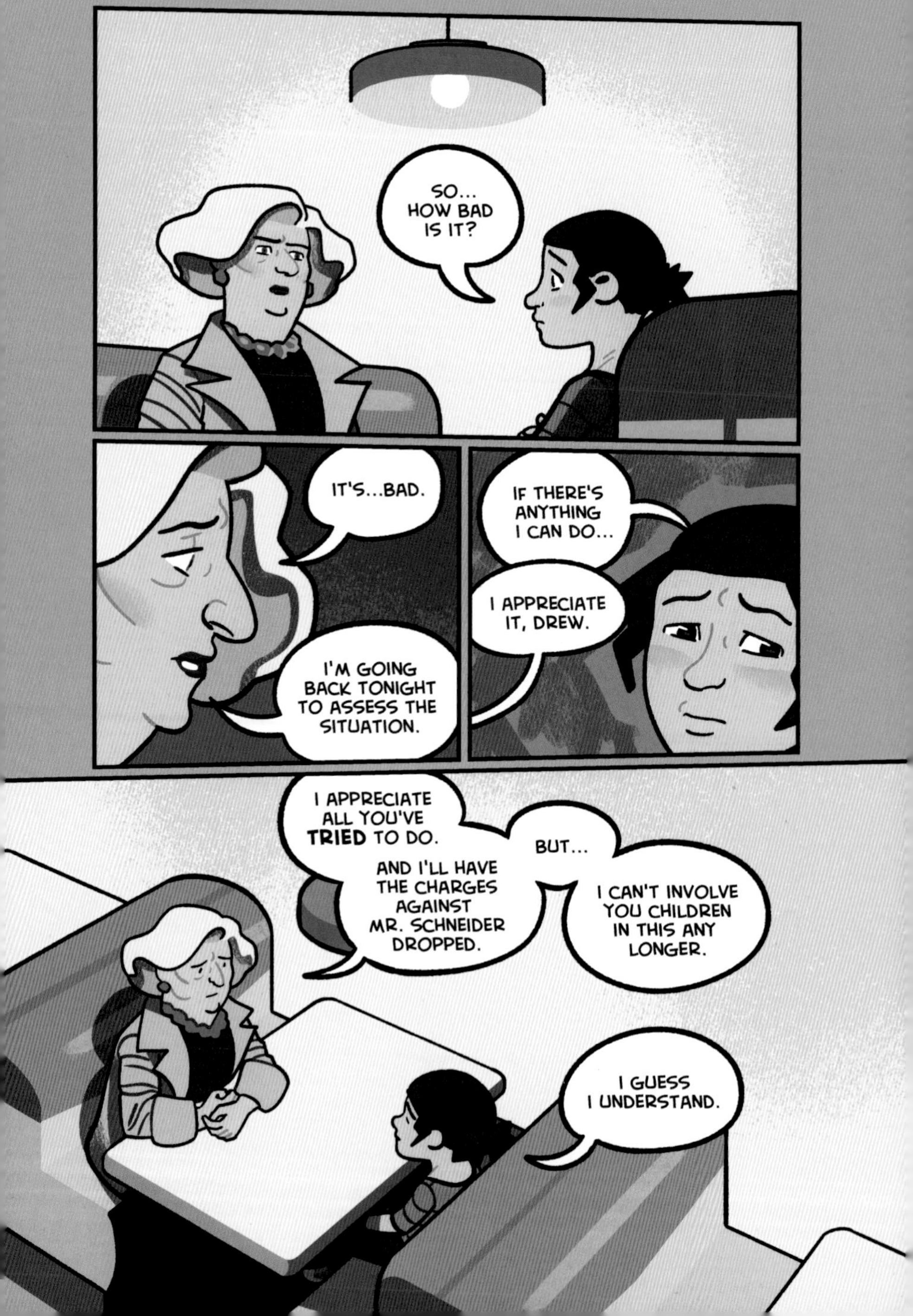
SO... HOW BAD IS IT?
IT'S...BAD.
I'M GOING BACK TONIGHT TO ASSESS THE SITUATION.
IF THERE'S ANYTHING I CAN DO...
I APPRECIATE IT, DREW.
I APPRECIATE ALL YOU'VE **TRIED** TO DO.
AND I'LL HAVE THE CHARGES AGAINST MR. SCHNEIDER DROPPED.
BUT...
I CAN'T INVOLVE YOU CHILDREN IN THIS ANY LONGER.
I GUESS I UNDERSTAND.

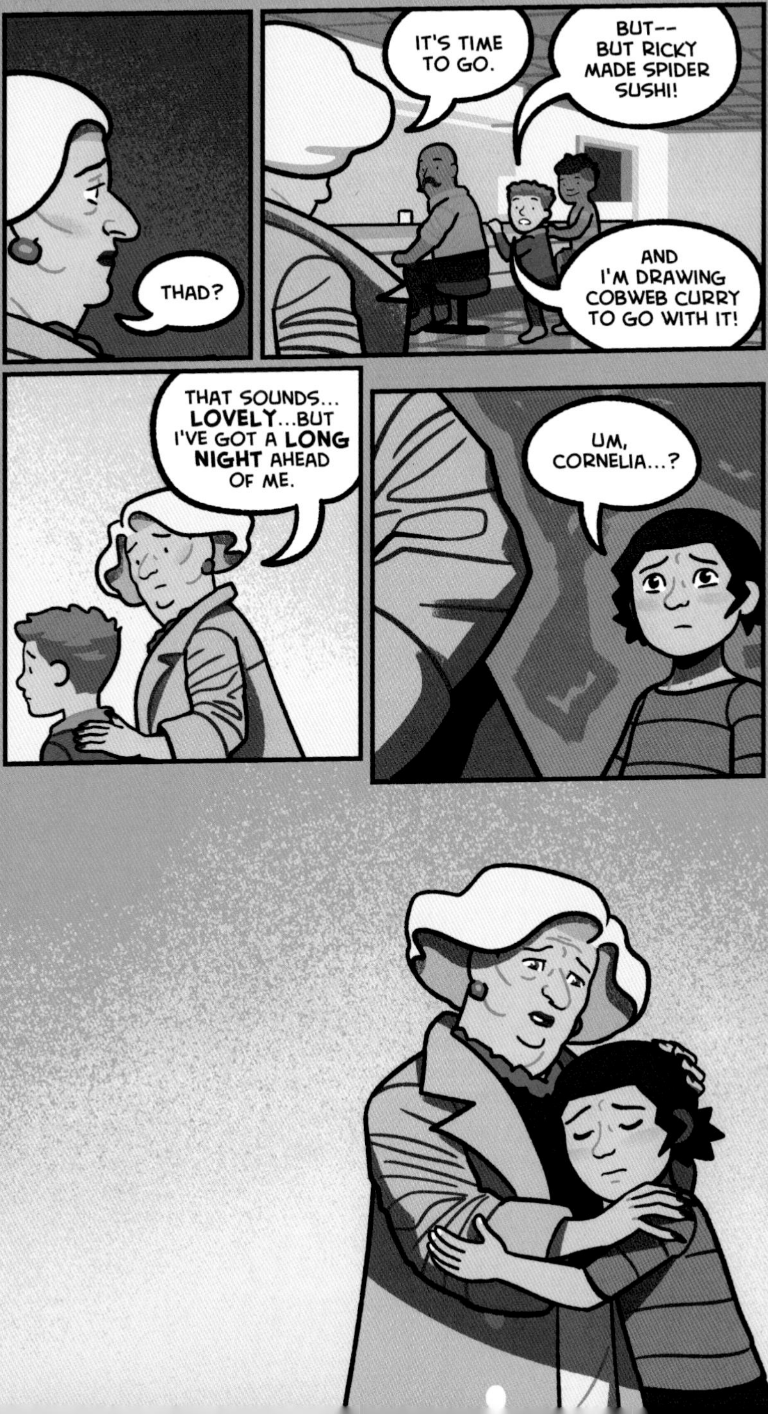
THAD?
IT'S TIME TO GO.
BUT-- BUT RICKY MADE SPIDER SUSHI!
AND I'M DRAWING COBWEB CURRY TO GO WITH IT!
THAT SOUNDS... LOVELY...BUT I'VE GOT A LONG NIGHT AHEAD OF ME.
UM, CORNELIA...?

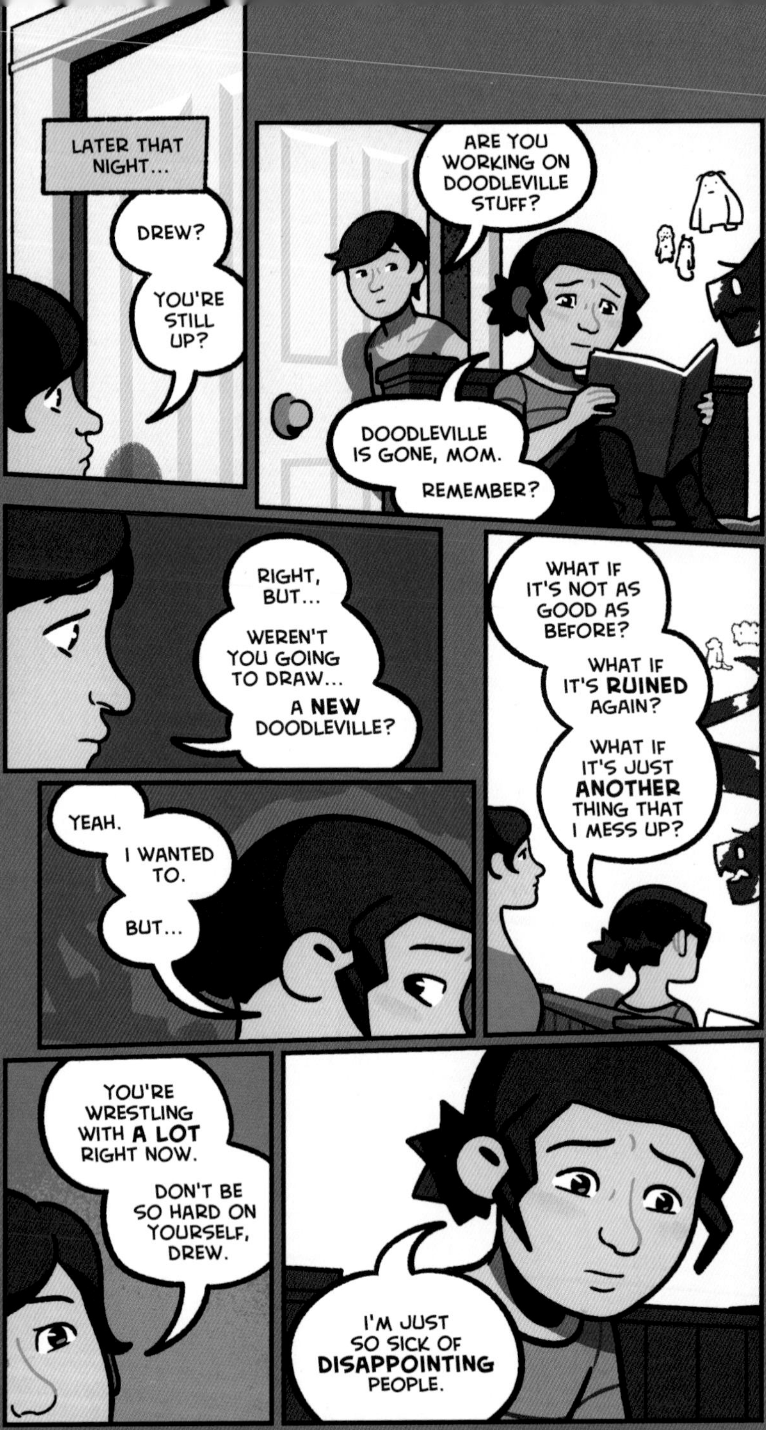

LATER THAT NIGHT...
DREW?
YOU'RE STILL UP?
ARE YOU WORKING ON DOODLEVILLE STUFF?
DOODLEVILLE IS GONE, MOM.
REMEMBER?
RIGHT, BUT...
WEREN'T YOU GOING TO DRAW...
A **NEW** DOODLEVILLE?
YEAH.
I WANTED TO.
BUT...
WHAT IF IT'S NOT AS GOOD AS BEFORE?
WHAT IF IT'S **RUINED** AGAIN?
WHAT IF IT'S JUST **ANOTHER** THING THAT I MESS UP?
YOU'RE WRESTLING WITH **A LOT** RIGHT NOW.
DON'T BE SO HARD ON YOURSELF, DREW.
I'M JUST SO SICK OF **DISAPPOINTING** PEOPLE.

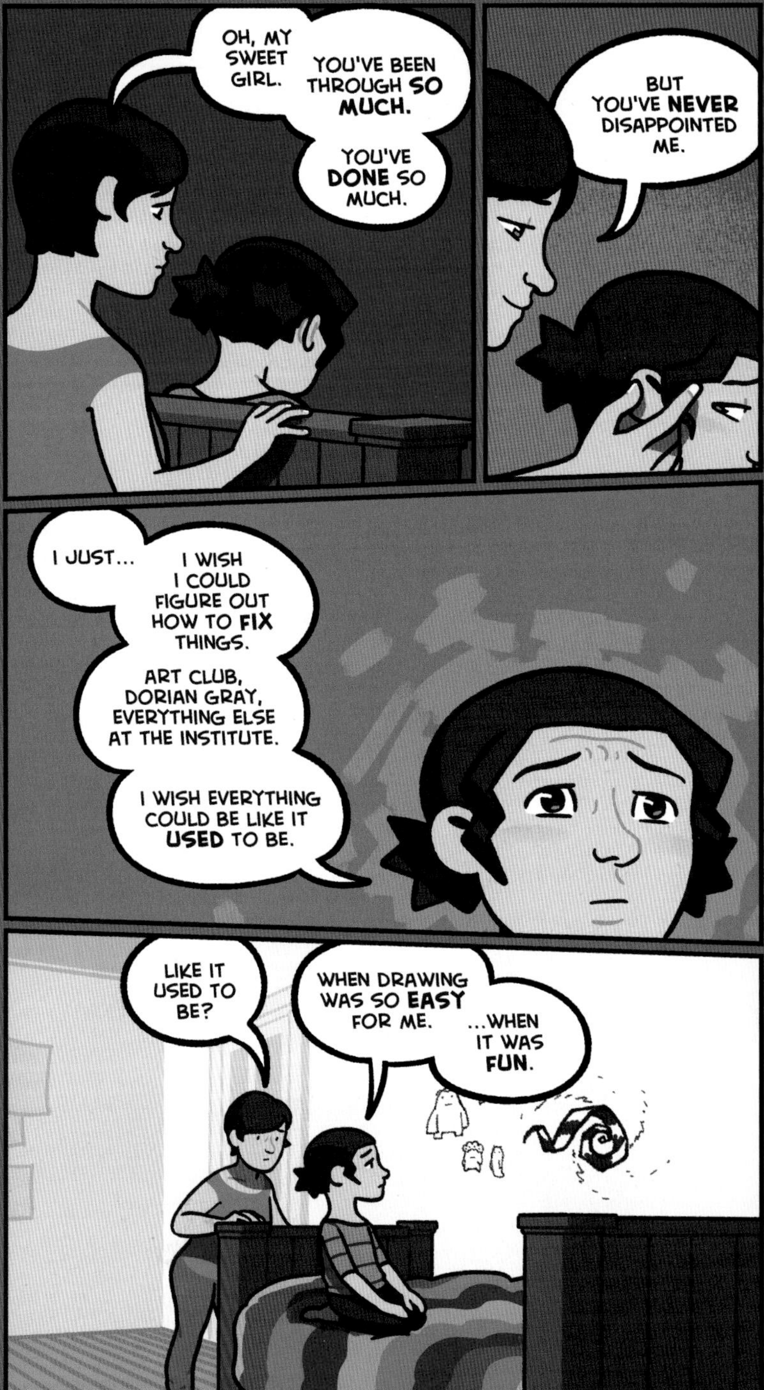
OH, MY SWEET GIRL.
YOU'VE BEEN THROUGH SO MUCH.
YOU'VE DONE SO MUCH.
BUT YOU'VE NEVER DISAPPOINTED ME.
I JUST...
I WISH I COULD FIGURE OUT HOW TO FIX THINGS.
ART CLUB, DORIAN GRAY, EVERYTHING ELSE AT THE INSTITUTE.
I WISH EVERYTHING COULD BE LIKE IT USED TO BE.
LIKE IT USED TO BE?
WHEN DRAWING WAS SO EASY FOR ME.
...WHEN IT WAS FUN.

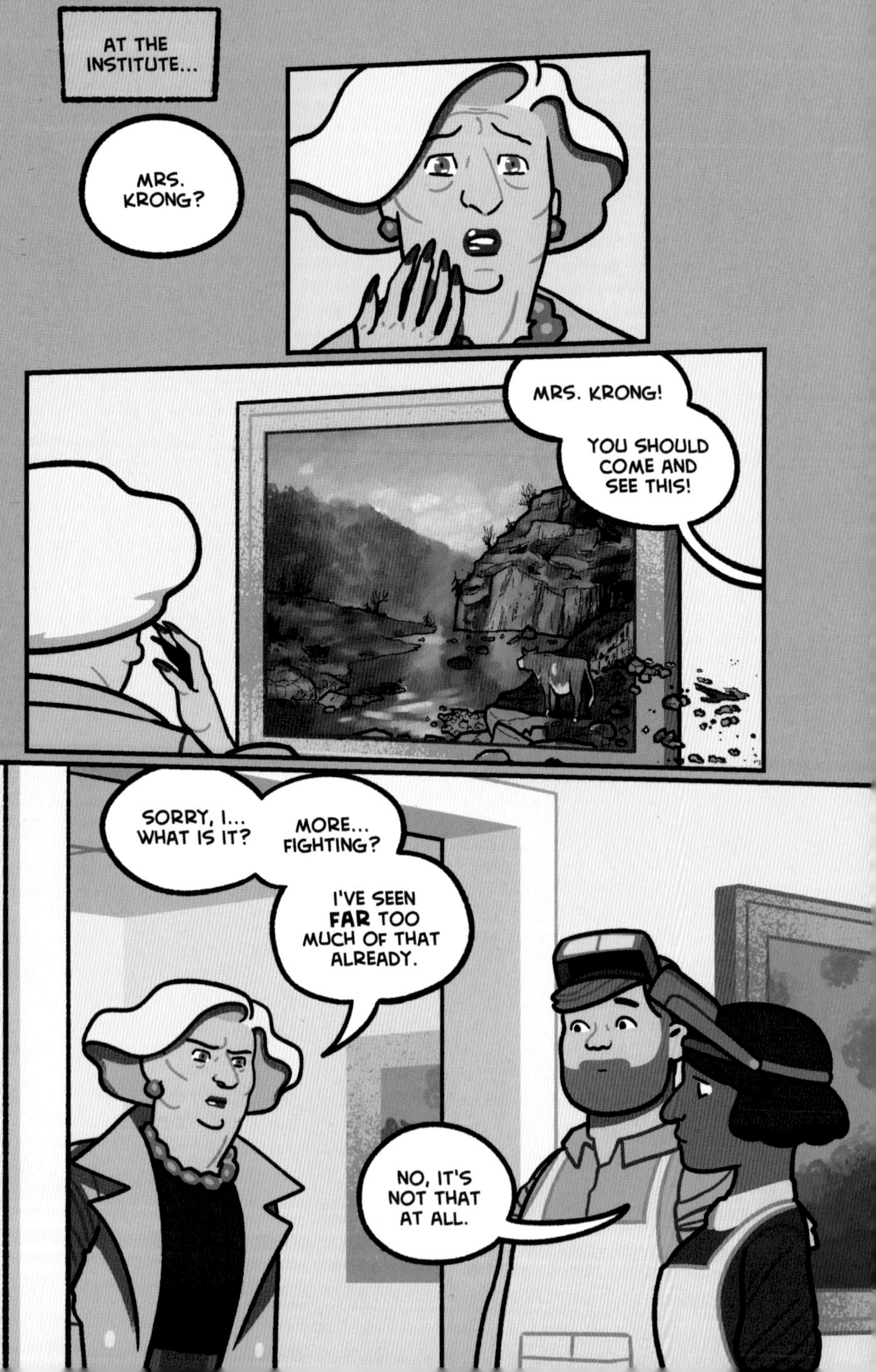
AT THE INSTITUTE...
MRS. KRONG?
MRS. KRONG!
YOU SHOULD COME AND SEE THIS!
SORRY, I... WHAT IS IT?
MORE... FIGHTING?
I'VE SEEN **FAR** TOO MUCH OF THAT ALREADY.
NO, IT'S NOT THAT AT ALL.

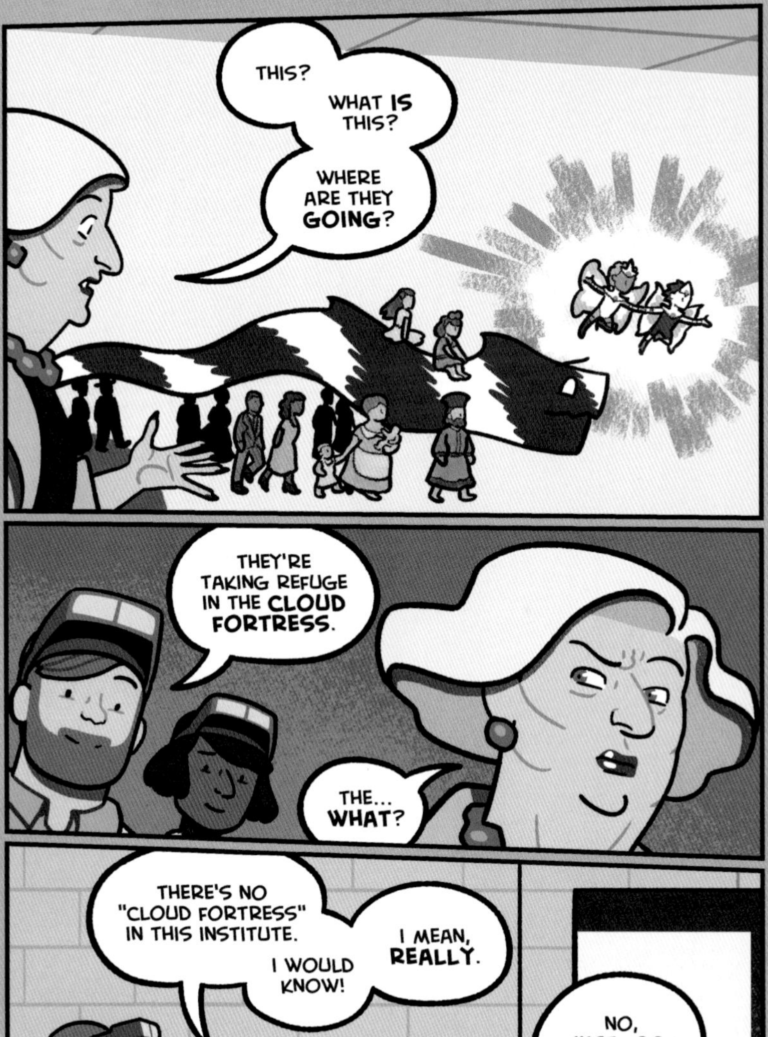
THIS?
WHAT IS THIS?
WHERE ARE THEY GOING?
THEY'RE TAKING REFUGE IN THE CLOUD FORTRESS.
THE... WHAT?
THERE'S NO "CLOUD FORTRESS" IN THIS INSTITUTE.
I WOULD KNOW!
I MEAN, REALLY.
NO, JUST LOOK. IN THERE.

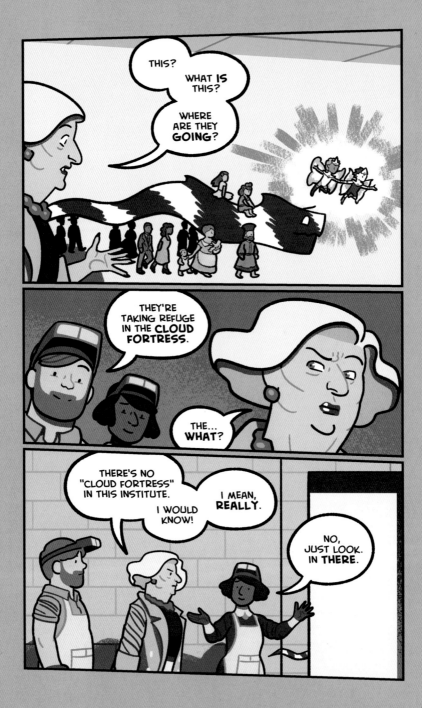

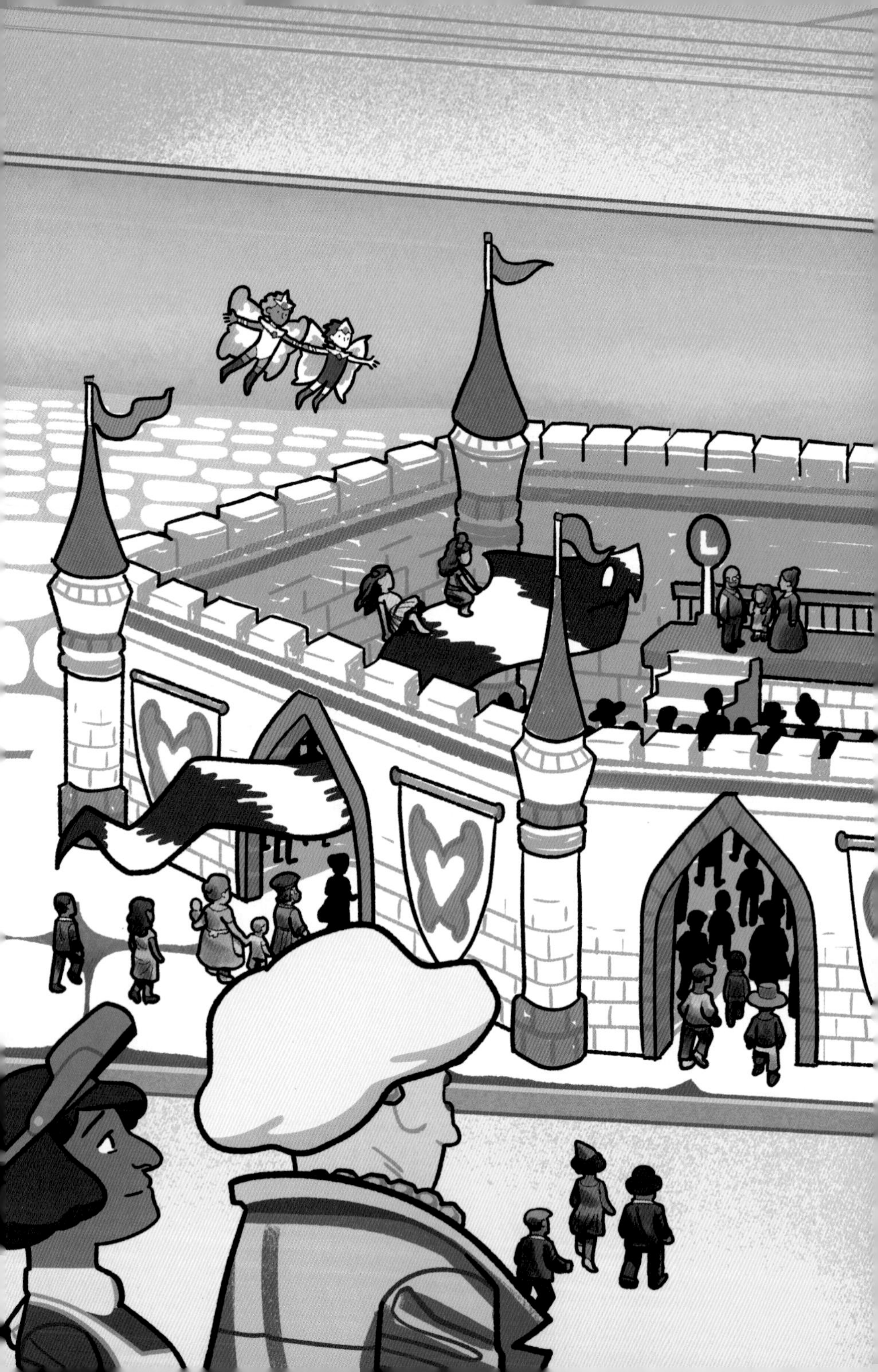
L

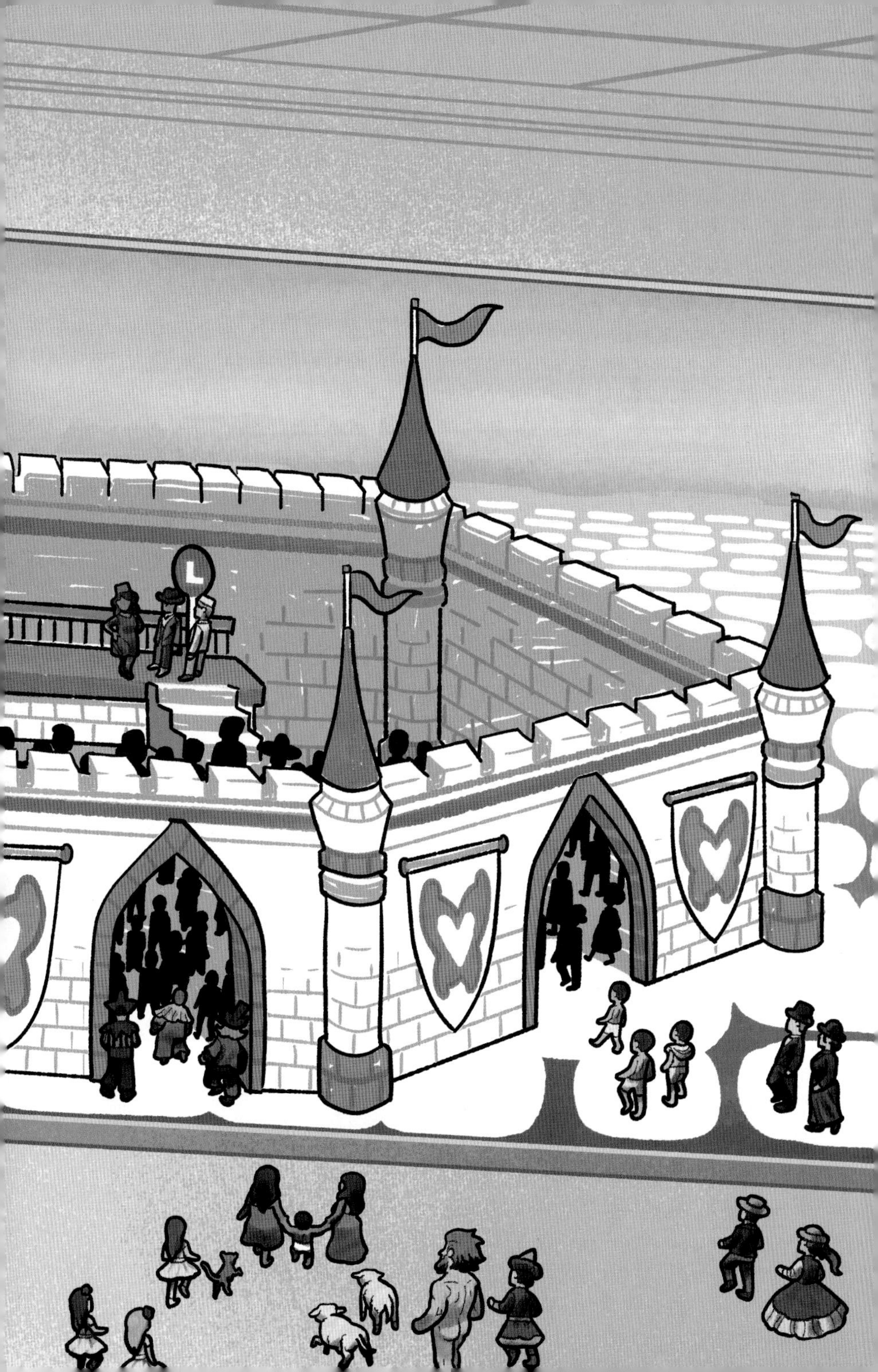
L

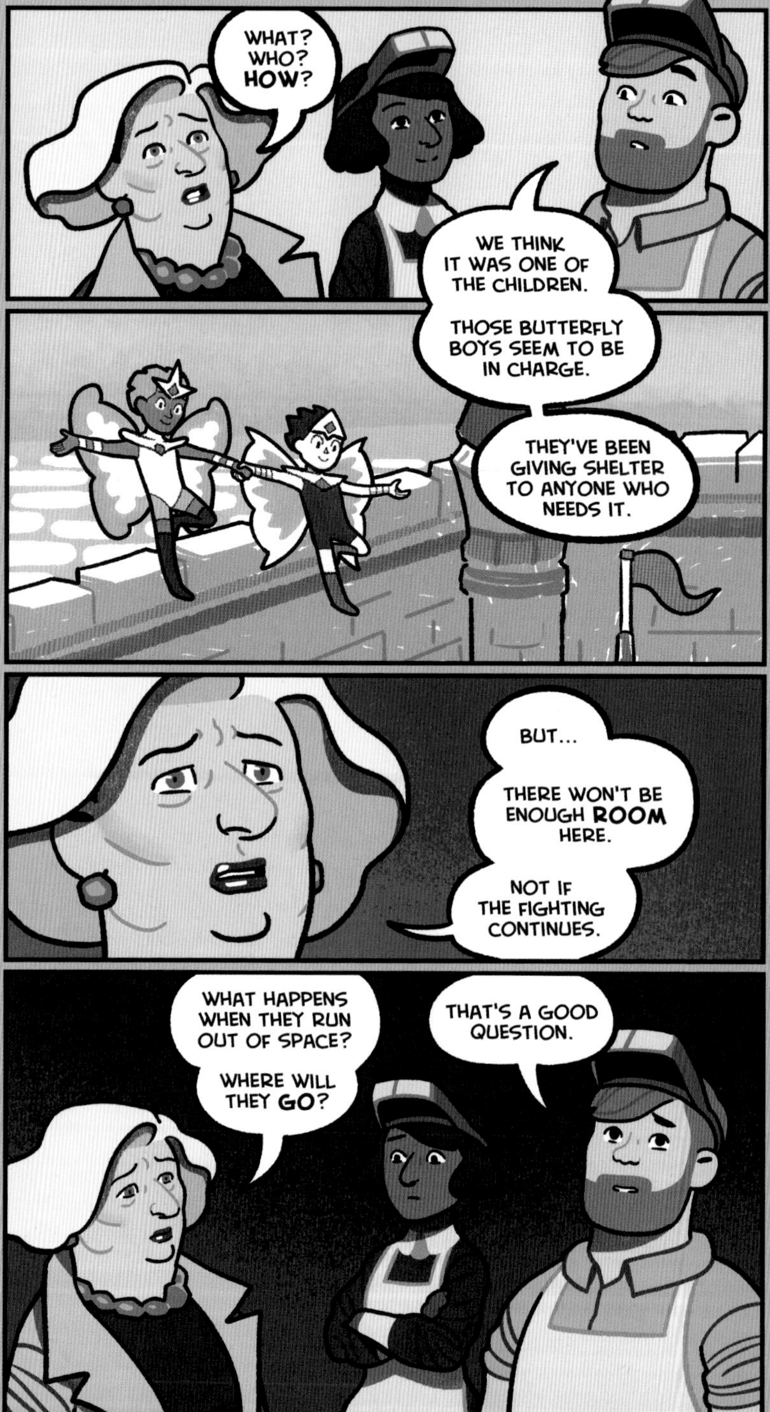
WHAT? WHO? HOW?
WE THINK IT WAS ONE OF THE CHILDREN.
THOSE BUTTERFLY BOYS SEEM TO BE IN CHARGE.
THEY'VE BEEN GIVING SHELTER TO ANYONE WHO NEEDS IT.
BUT...
THERE WON'T BE ENOUGH ROOM HERE.
NOT IF THE FIGHTING CONTINUES.
WHAT HAPPENS WHEN THEY RUN OUT OF SPACE?
WHERE WILL THEY GO?
THAT'S A GOOD QUESTION.

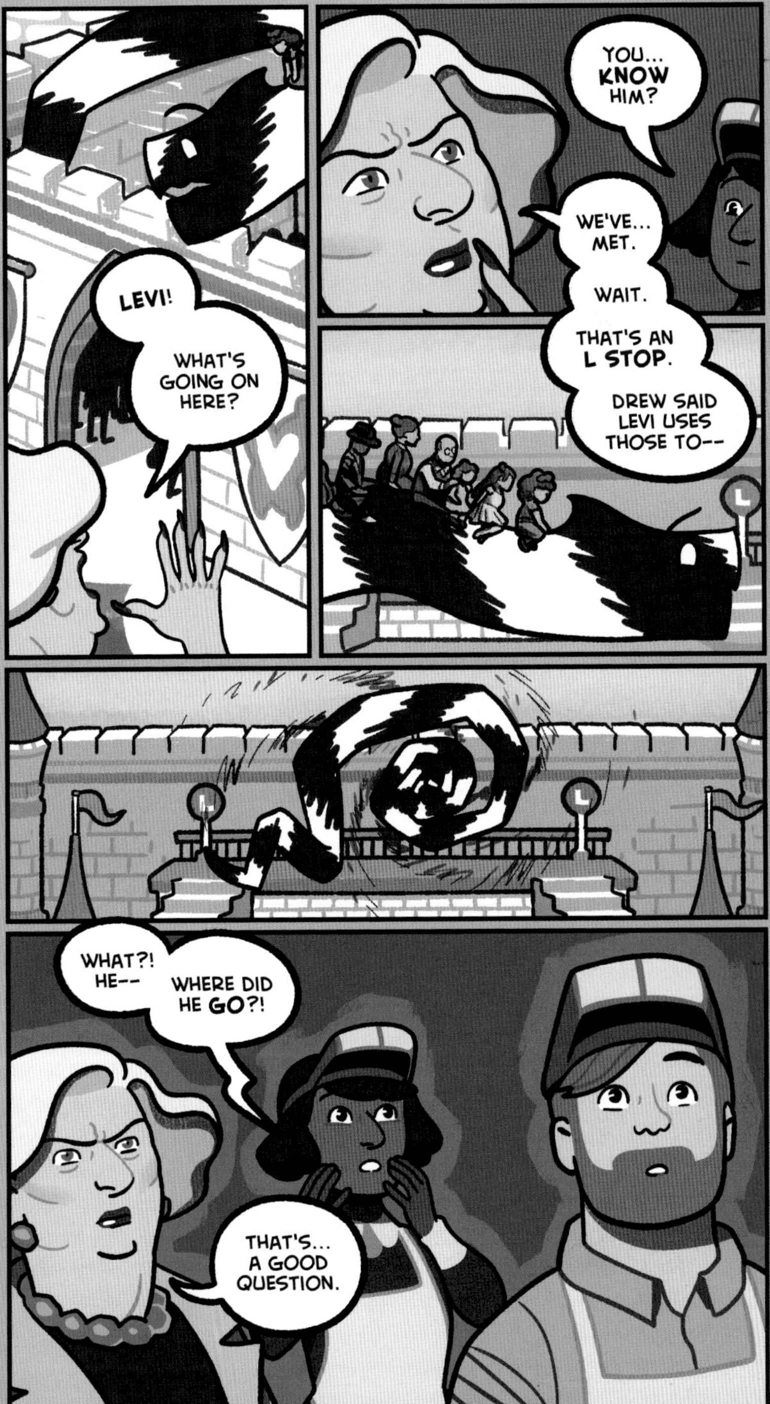
LEVI!
WHAT'S GOING ON HERE?
YOU... KNOW HIM?
WE'VE... MET.
WAIT.
THAT'S AN L STOP.
DREW SAID LEVI USES THOSE TO--
WHAT?! HE--
WHERE DID HE GO?!
THAT'S... A GOOD QUESTION.

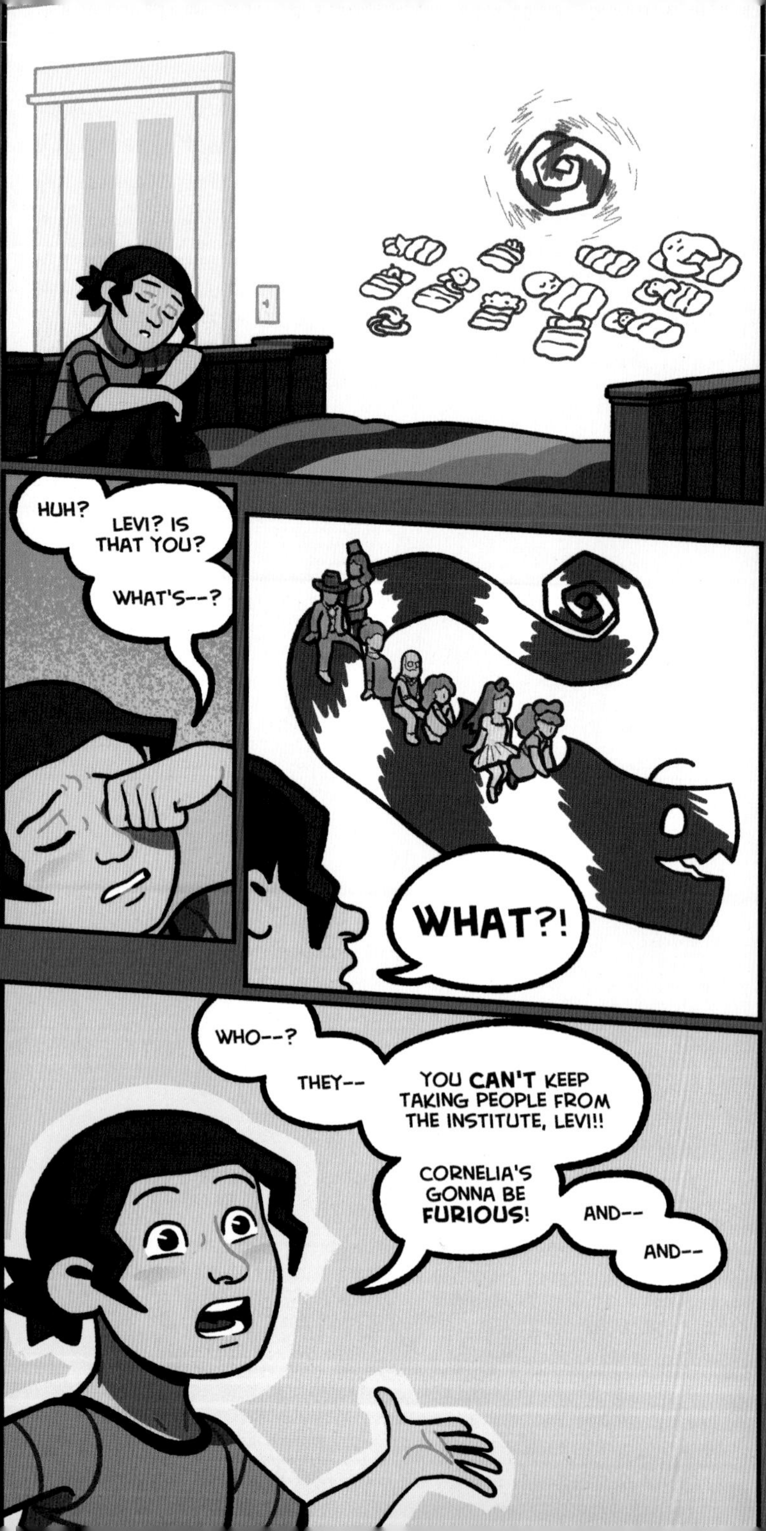
HUH?
LEVI? IS THAT YOU?
WHAT'S--?
WHAT?!
WHO--?
THEY--
YOU **CAN'T** KEEP TAKING PEOPLE FROM THE INSTITUTE, LEVI!!
CORNELIA'S GONNA BE **FURIOUS**!
AND--
AND--

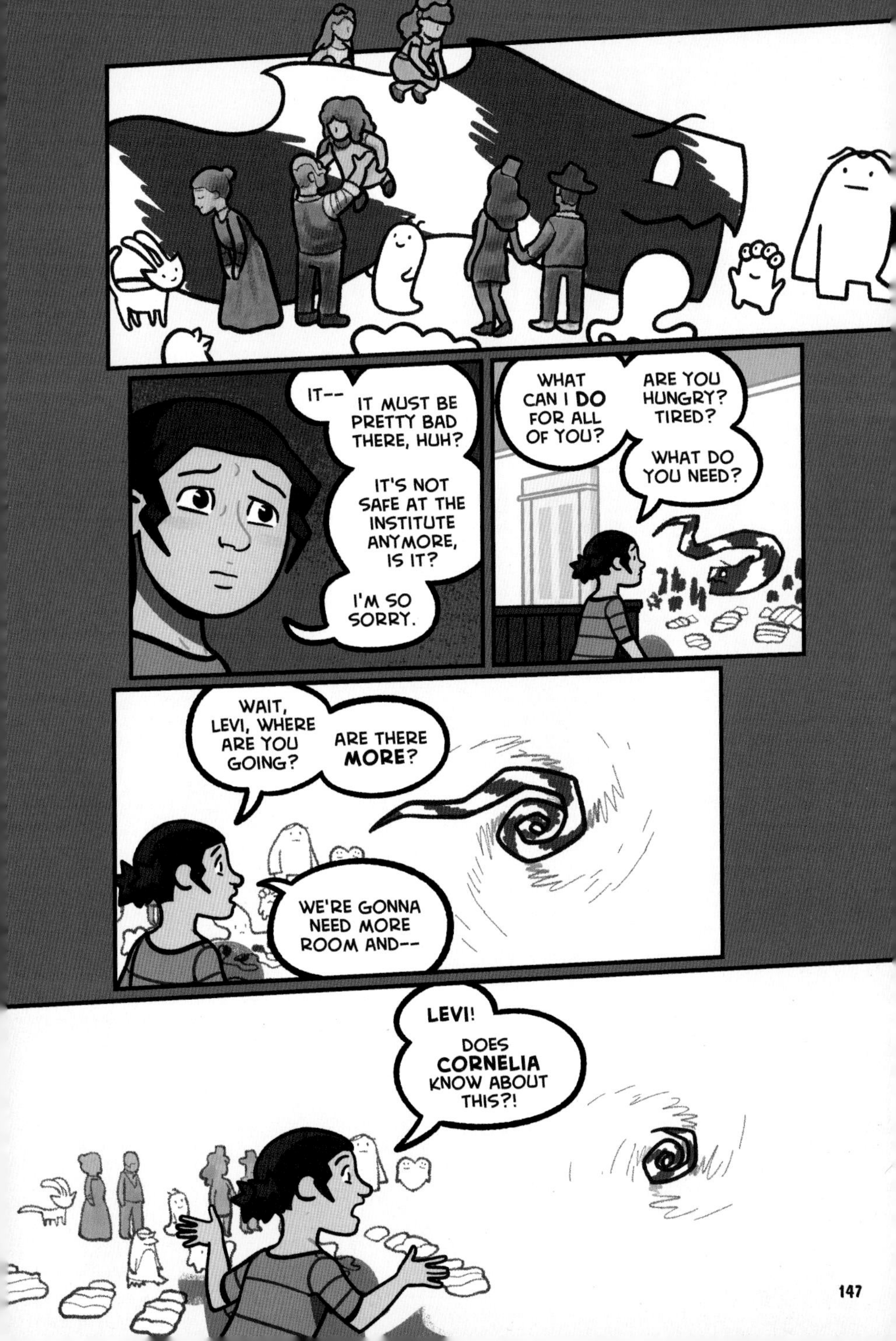
IT--
IT MUST BE PRETTY BAD THERE, HUH?
IT'S NOT SAFE AT THE INSTITUTE ANYMORE, IS IT?
I'M SO SORRY.
WHAT CAN I **DO** FOR ALL OF YOU?
ARE YOU HUNGRY? TIRED?
WHAT DO YOU NEED?
WAIT, LEVI, WHERE ARE YOU GOING?
ARE THERE **MORE**?
WE'RE GONNA NEED MORE ROOM AND--
LEVI!
DOES **CORNELIA** KNOW ABOUT THIS?!

CHAPTER 5: THE ART INSTITUTE EXODUS

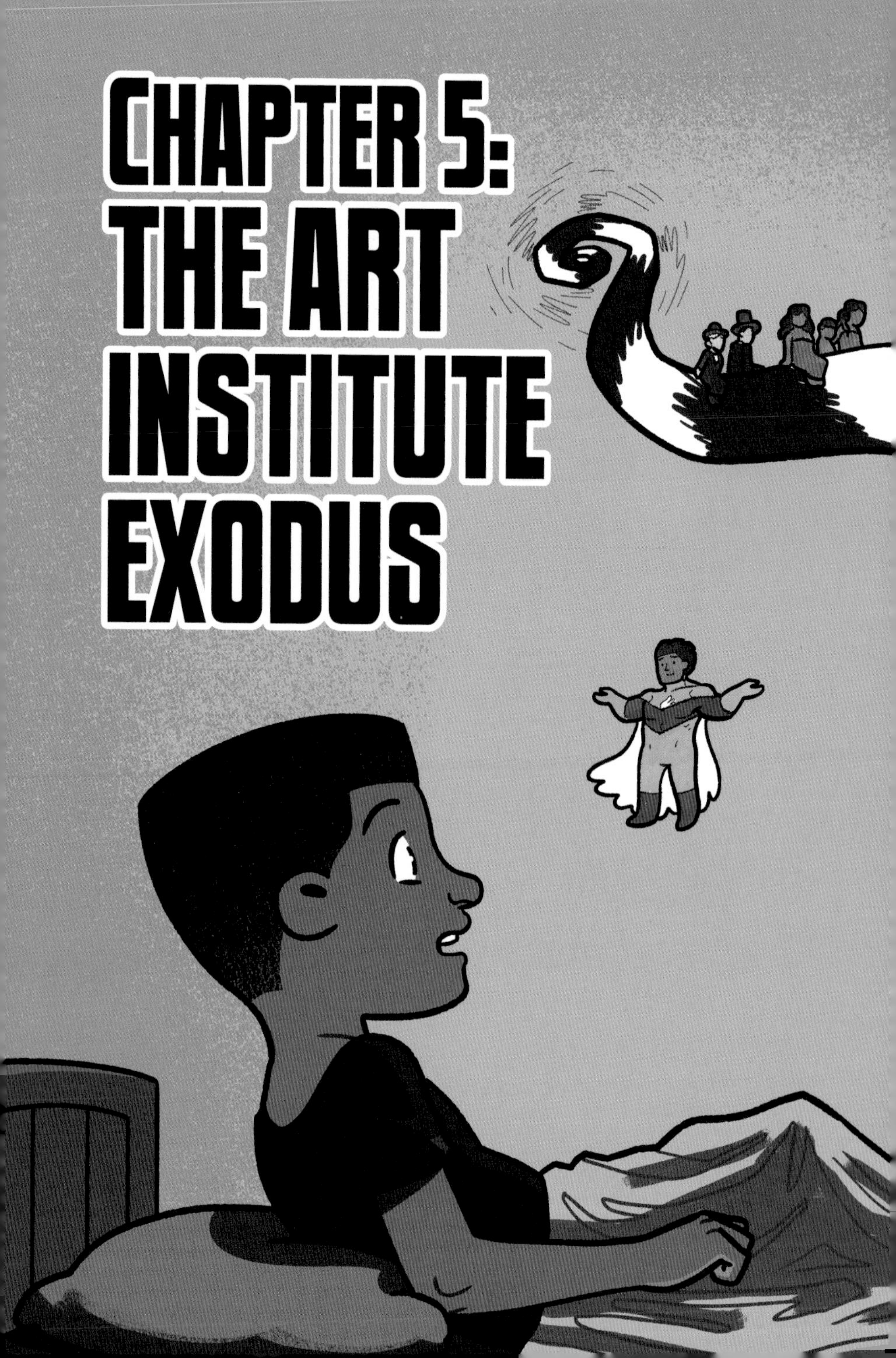

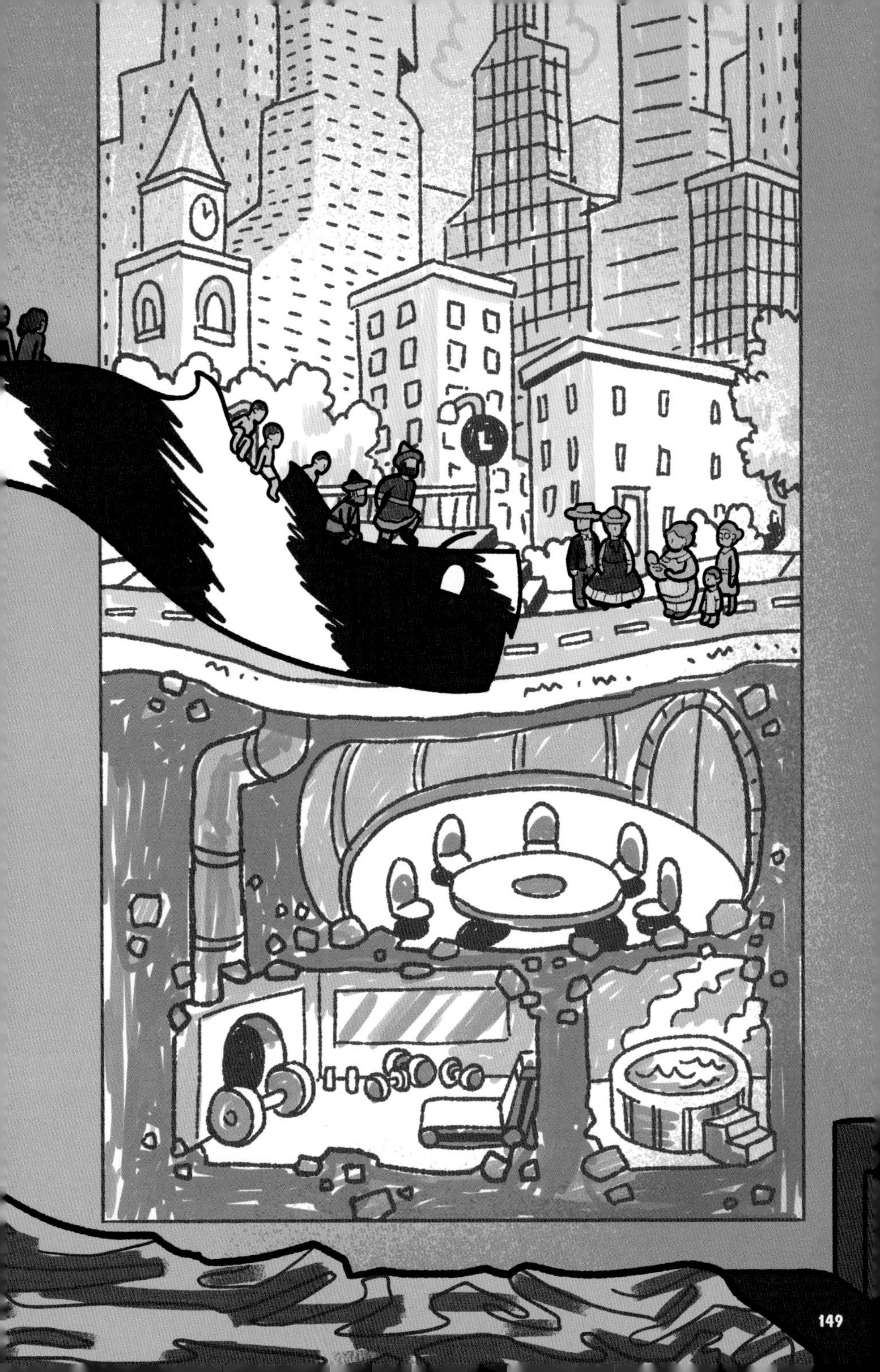
L

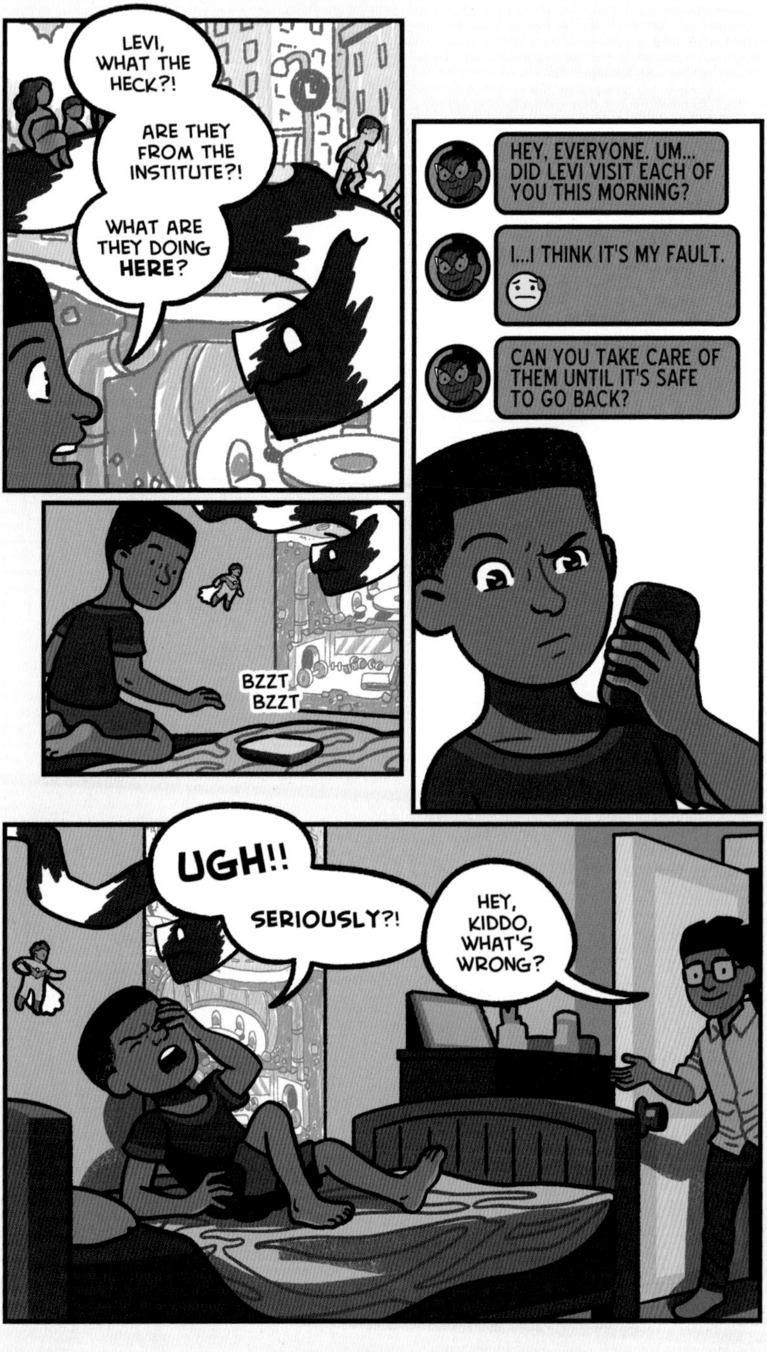
LEVI, WHAT THE HECK?!
ARE THEY FROM THE INSTITUTE?!
WHAT ARE THEY DOING HERE?
HEY, EVERYONE. UM... DID LEVI VISIT EACH OF YOU THIS MORNING?
I...I THINK IT'S MY FAULT.
CAN YOU TAKE CARE OF THEM UNTIL IT'S SAFE TO GO BACK?
BZZT BZZT
UGH!!
SERIOUSLY?!
HEY, KIDDO, WHAT'S WRONG?

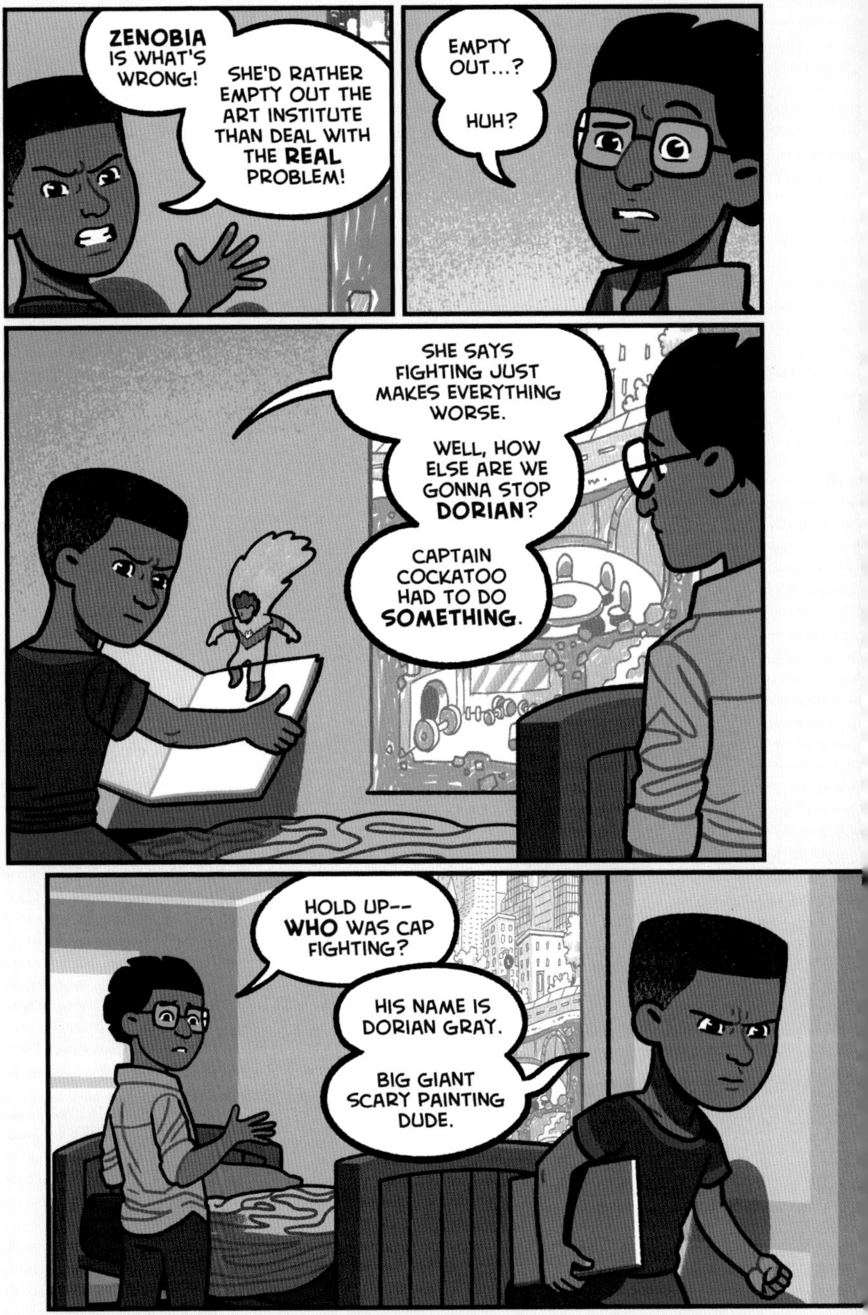
ZENOBIA IS WHAT'S WRONG!
SHE'D RATHER EMPTY OUT THE ART INSTITUTE THAN DEAL WITH THE REAL PROBLEM!
EMPTY OUT...?
HUH?
SHE SAYS FIGHTING JUST MAKES EVERYTHING WORSE.
WELL, HOW ELSE ARE WE GONNA STOP DORIAN?
CAPTAIN COCKATOO HAD TO DO SOMETHING.
HOLD UP-- WHO WAS CAP FIGHTING?
HIS NAME IS DORIAN GRAY.
BIG GIANT SCARY PAINTING DUDE.

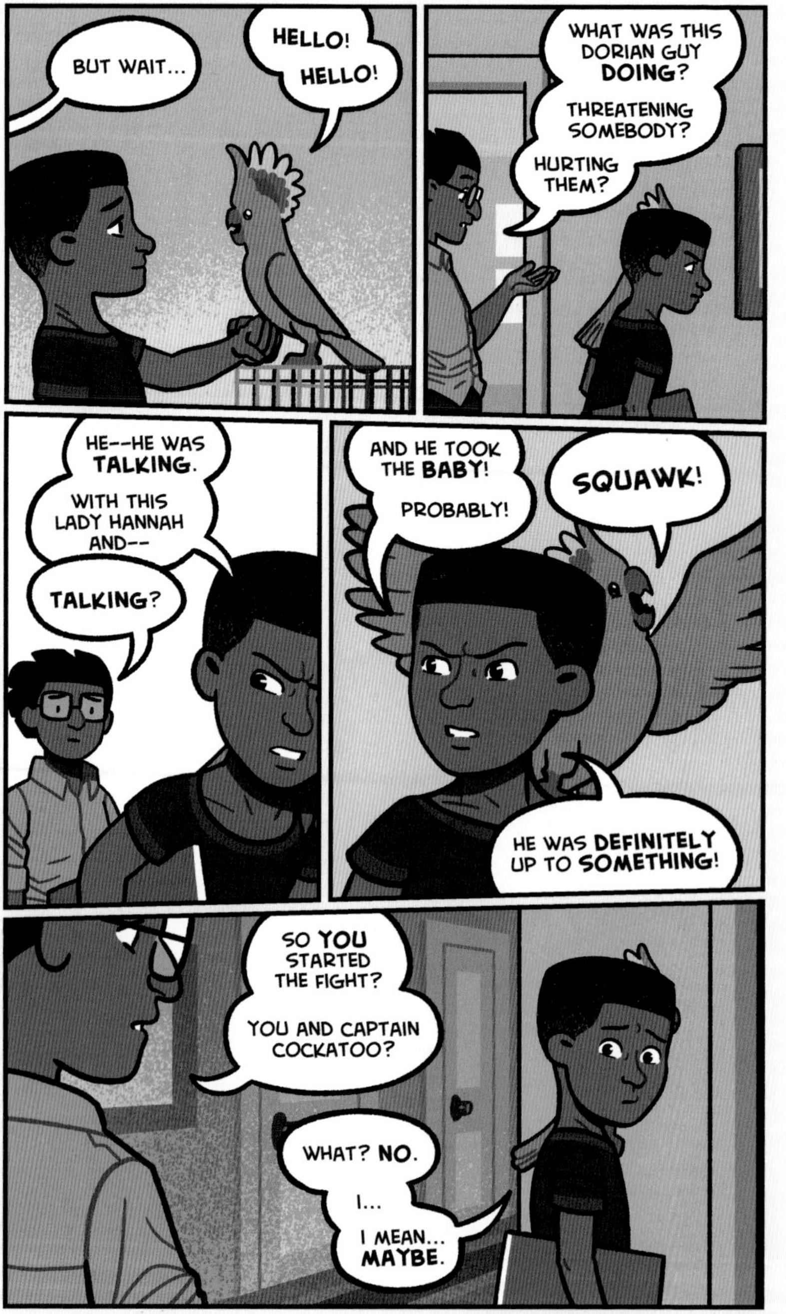
BUT WAIT...
HELLO! HELLO!
WHAT WAS THIS DORIAN GUY DOING?
THREATENING SOMEBODY?
HURTING THEM?
HE--HE WAS TALKING.
WITH THIS LADY HANNAH AND--
TALKING?
AND HE TOOK THE BABY!
PROBABLY!
SQUAWK!
HE WAS DEFINITELY UP TO SOMETHING!
SO YOU STARTED THE FIGHT?
YOU AND CAPTAIN COCKATOO?
WHAT? NO.
I...
I MEAN... MAYBE.

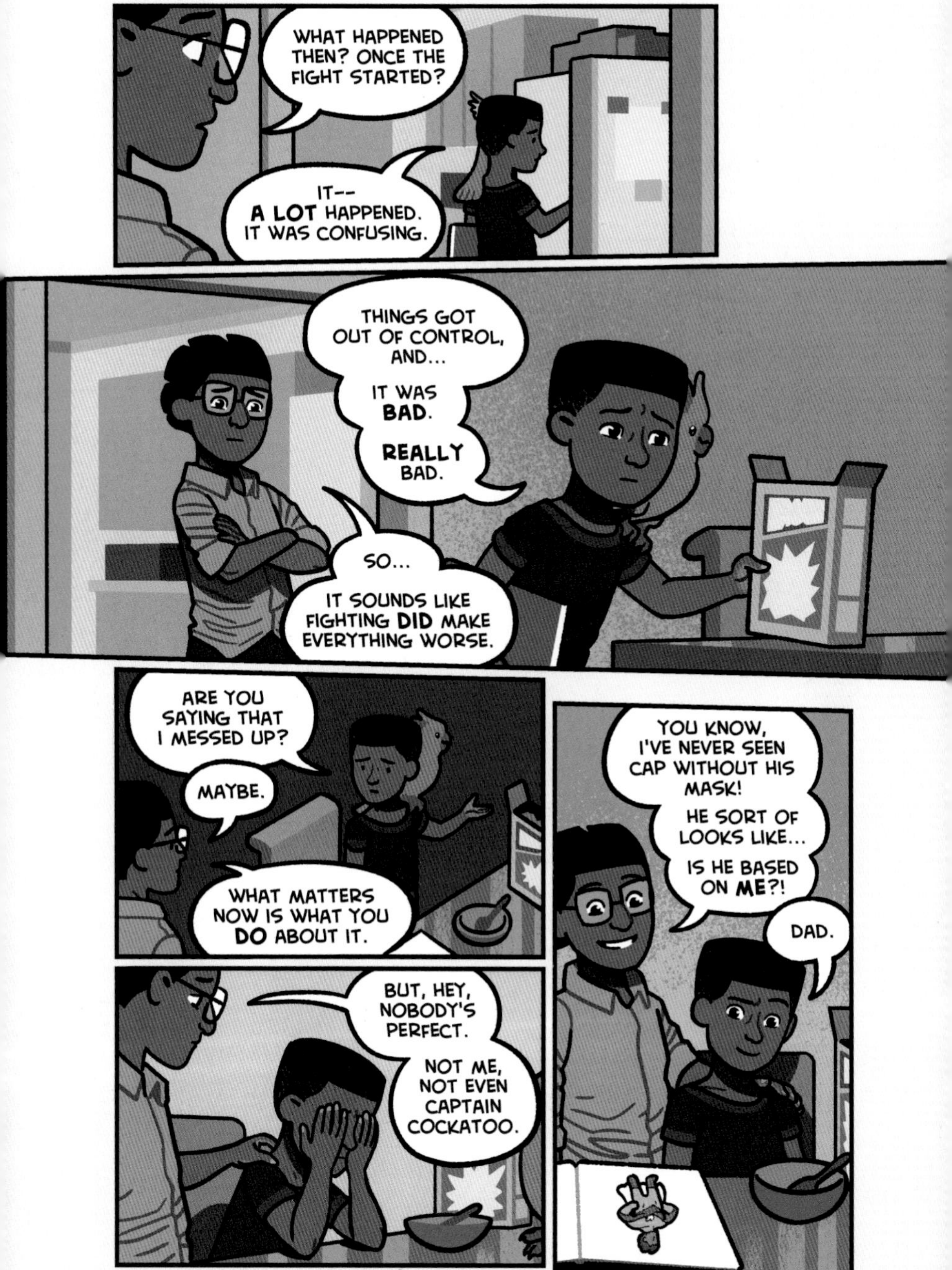
WHAT HAPPENED THEN? ONCE THE FIGHT STARTED?
IT-- A LOT HAPPENED. IT WAS CONFUSING.
THINGS GOT OUT OF CONTROL, AND...
IT WAS BAD.
REALLY BAD.
SO...
IT SOUNDS LIKE FIGHTING DID MAKE EVERYTHING WORSE.
ARE YOU SAYING THAT I MESSED UP?
MAYBE.
WHAT MATTERS NOW IS WHAT YOU DO ABOUT IT.
BUT, HEY, NOBODY'S PERFECT.
NOT ME, NOT EVEN CAPTAIN COCKATOO.
YOU KNOW, I'VE NEVER SEEN CAP WITHOUT HIS MASK!
HE SORT OF LOOKS LIKE...
IS HE BASED ON ME?!
DAD.

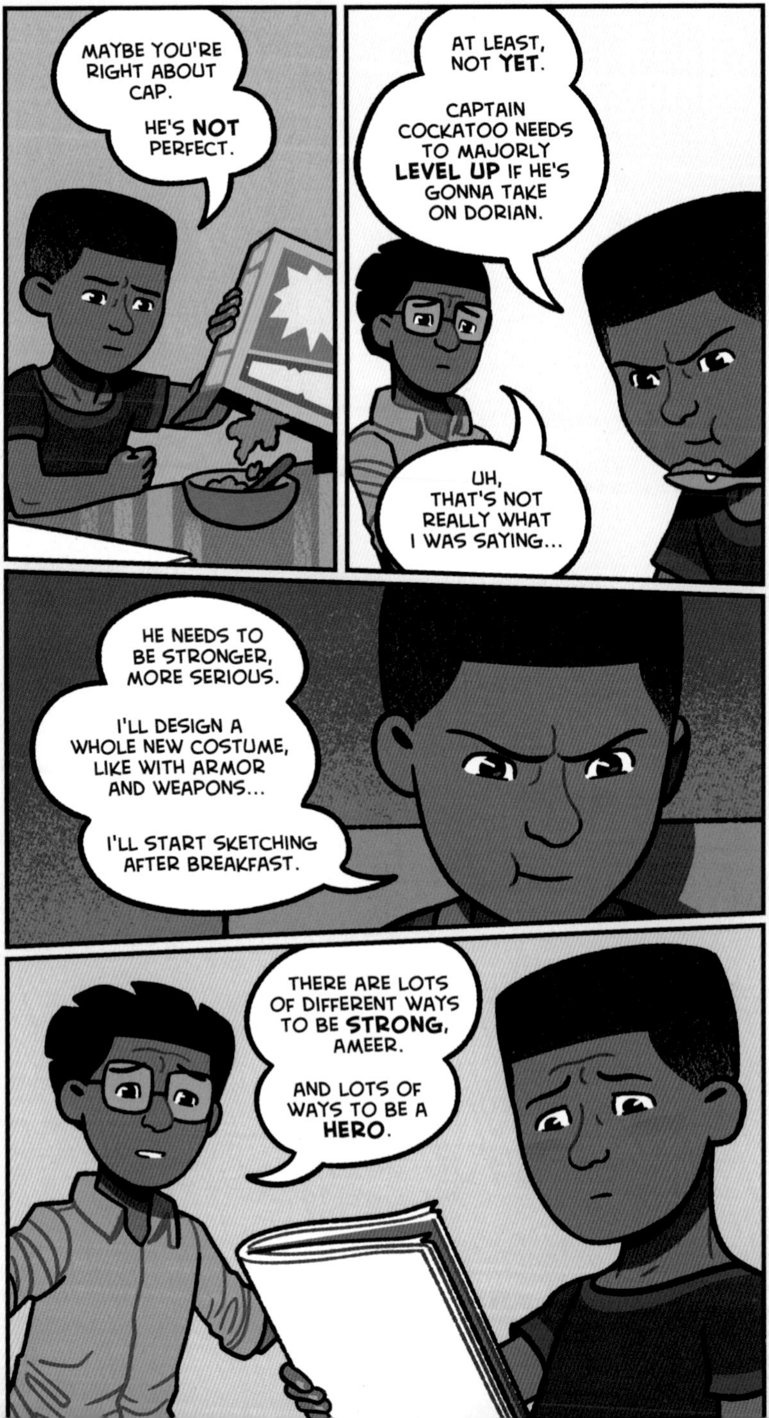
MAYBE YOU'RE RIGHT ABOUT CAP.
HE'S **NOT** PERFECT.
AT LEAST, NOT **YET**.
CAPTAIN COCKATOO NEEDS TO MAJORLY **LEVEL UP** IF HE'S GONNA TAKE ON DORIAN.
UH, THAT'S NOT REALLY WHAT I WAS SAYING...
HE NEEDS TO BE STRONGER, MORE SERIOUS.
I'LL DESIGN A WHOLE NEW COSTUME, LIKE WITH ARMOR AND WEAPONS...
I'LL START SKETCHING AFTER BREAKFAST.
THERE ARE LOTS OF DIFFERENT WAYS TO BE **STRONG**, AMEER.
AND LOTS OF WAYS TO BE A **HERO**.

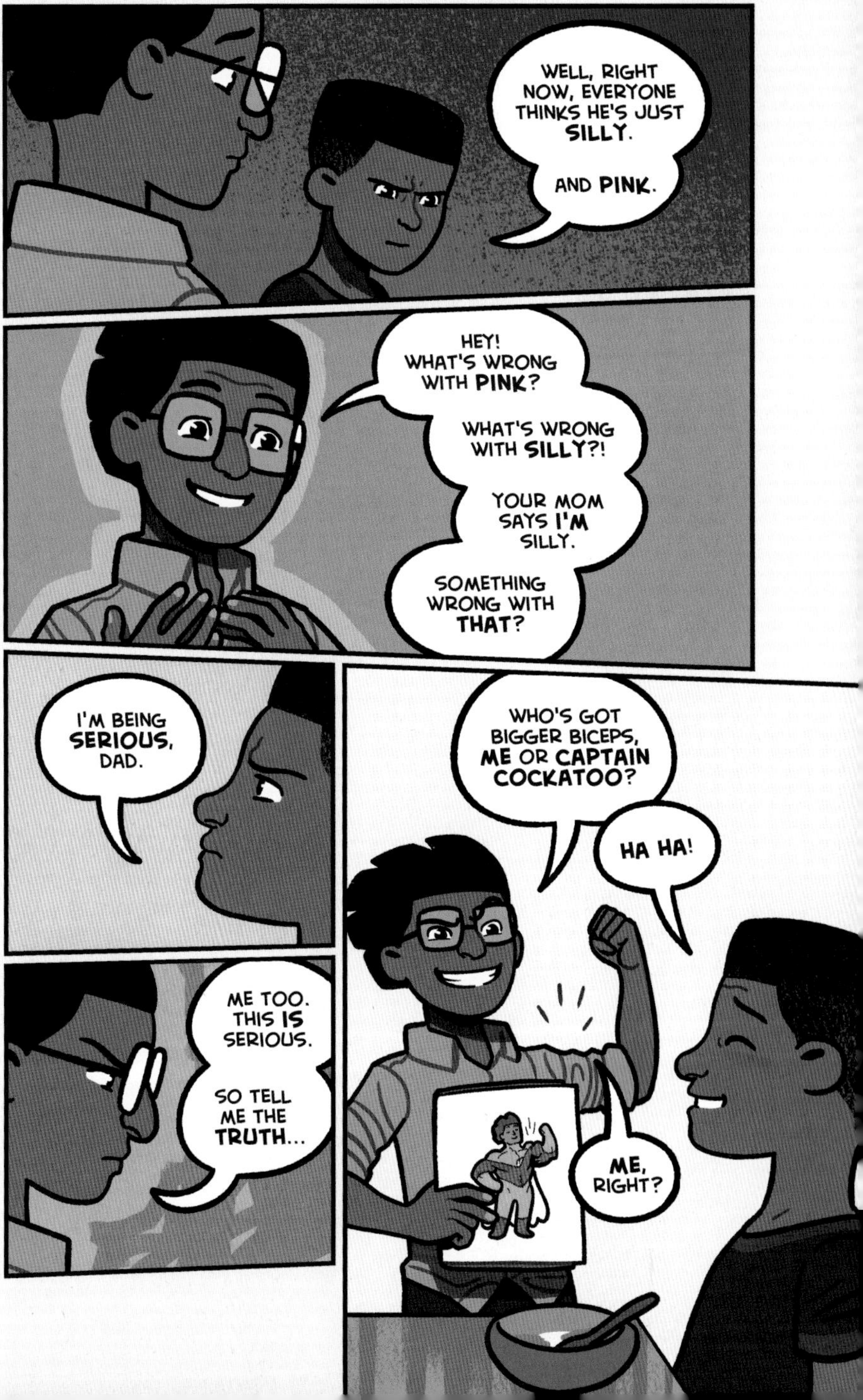
WELL, RIGHT NOW, EVERYONE THINKS HE'S JUST SILLY.
AND PINK.
HEY! WHAT'S WRONG WITH PINK?
WHAT'S WRONG WITH SILLY?!
YOUR MOM SAYS I'M SILLY.
SOMETHING WRONG WITH THAT?
I'M BEING SERIOUS, DAD.
ME TOO. THIS IS SERIOUS.
SO TELL ME THE TRUTH...
WHO'S GOT BIGGER BICEPS, ME OR CAPTAIN COCKATOO?
HA HA!
ME, RIGHT?

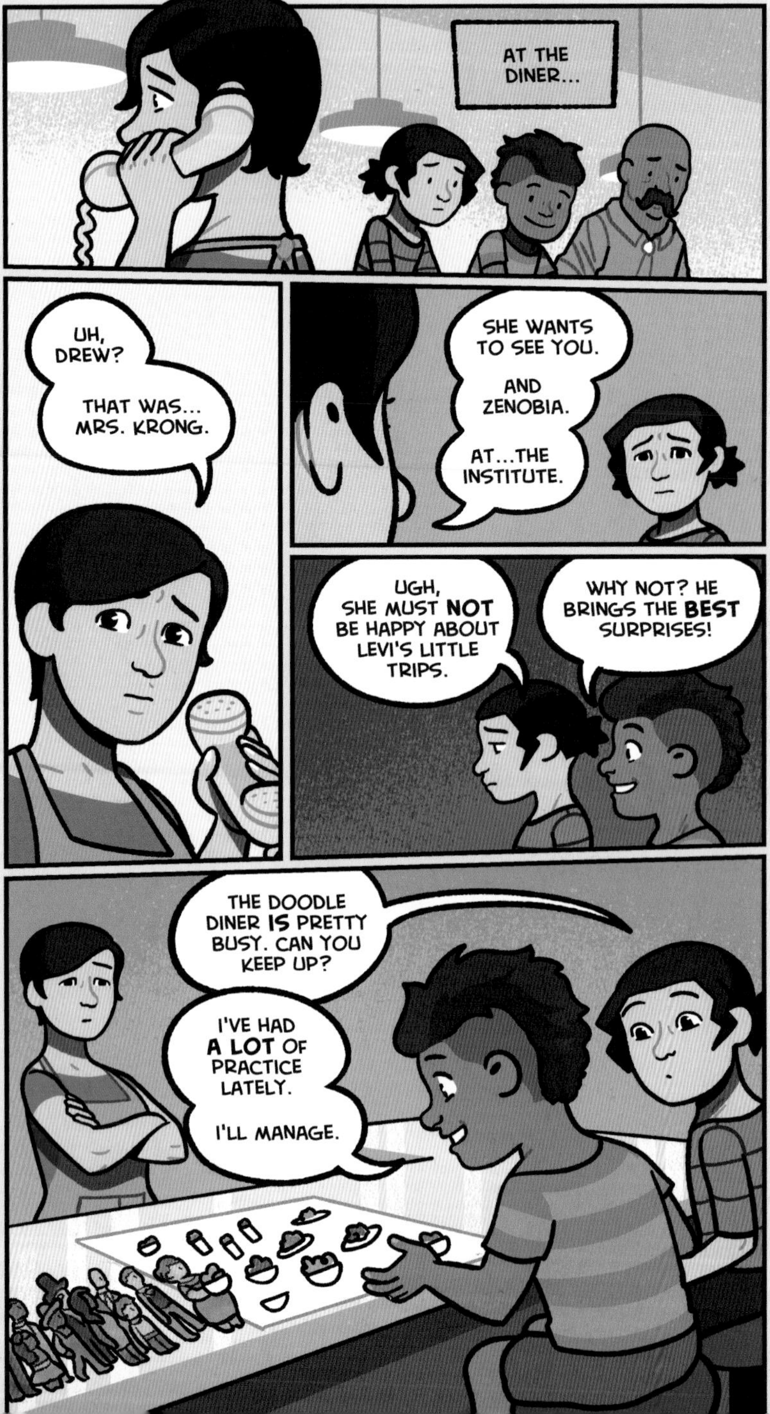
AT THE DINER...
UH, DREW?
THAT WAS... MRS. KRONG.
SHE WANTS TO SEE YOU.
AND ZENOBIA.
AT...THE INSTITUTE.
UGH, SHE MUST NOT BE HAPPY ABOUT LEVI'S LITTLE TRIPS.
WHY NOT? HE BRINGS THE BEST SURPRISES!
THE DOODLE DINER IS PRETTY BUSY. CAN YOU KEEP UP?
I'VE HAD A LOT OF PRACTICE LATELY.
I'LL MANAGE.

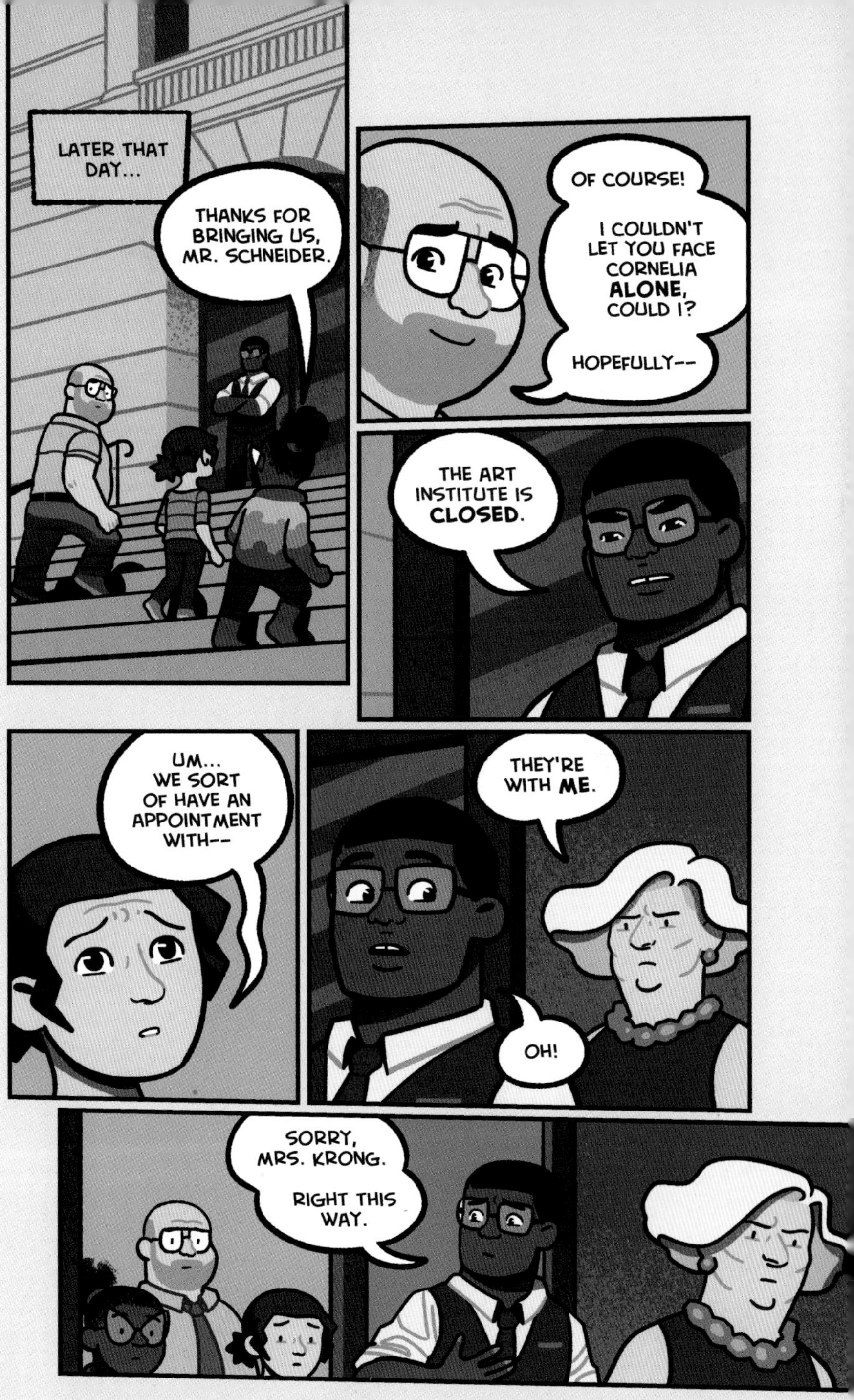
LATER THAT DAY...
THANKS FOR BRINGING US, MR. SCHNEIDER.
OF COURSE!
I COULDN'T LET YOU FACE CORNELIA ALONE, COULD I?
HOPEFULLY--
THE ART INSTITUTE IS CLOSED.
UM... WE SORT OF HAVE AN APPOINTMENT WITH--
THEY'RE WITH ME.
OH!
SORRY, MRS. KRONG.
RIGHT THIS WAY.

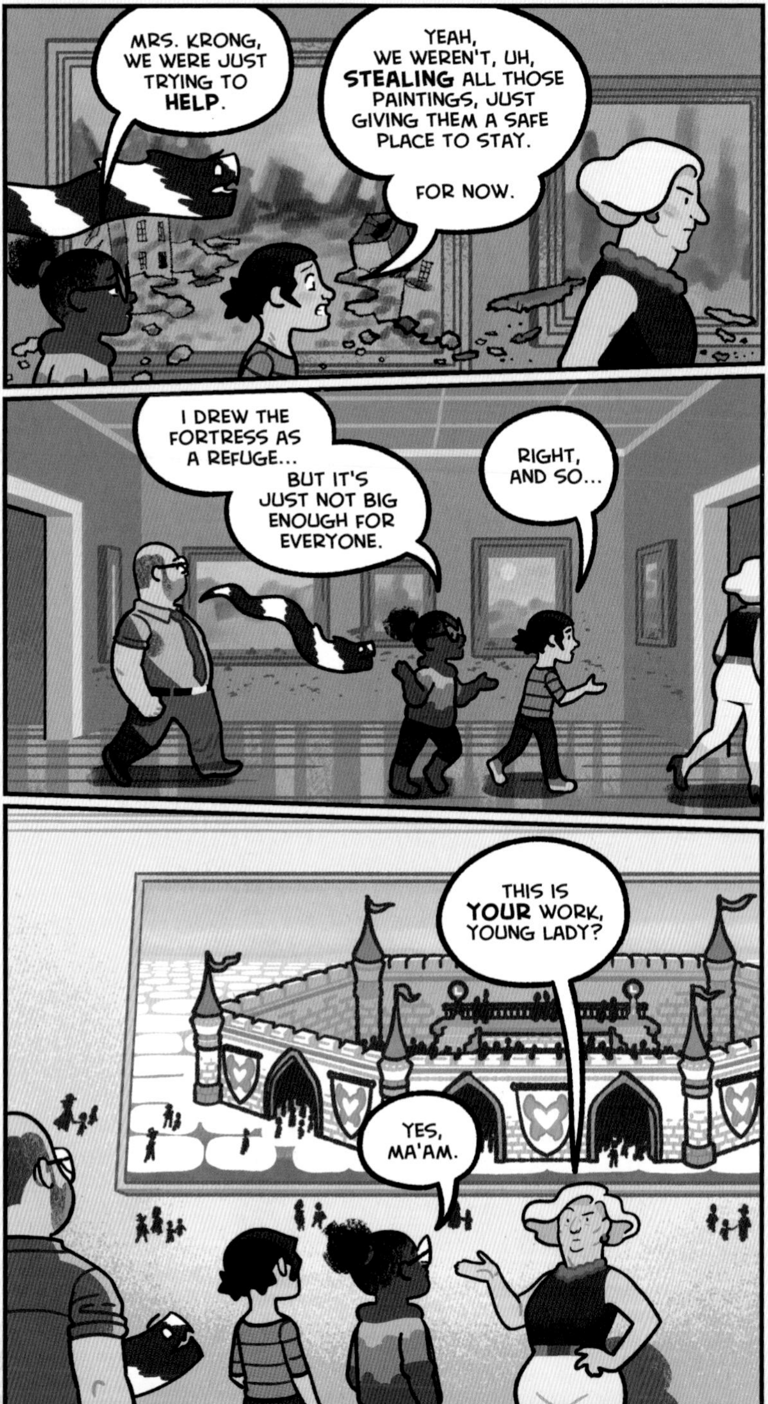
MRS. KRONG, WE WERE JUST TRYING TO **HELP**.
YEAH, WE WEREN'T, UH, **STEALING** ALL THOSE PAINTINGS, JUST GIVING THEM A SAFE PLACE TO STAY.
FOR NOW.
I DREW THE FORTRESS AS A REFUGE...
BUT IT'S JUST NOT BIG ENOUGH FOR EVERYONE.
RIGHT, AND SO...
THIS IS **YOUR** WORK, YOUNG LADY?
YES, MA'AM.

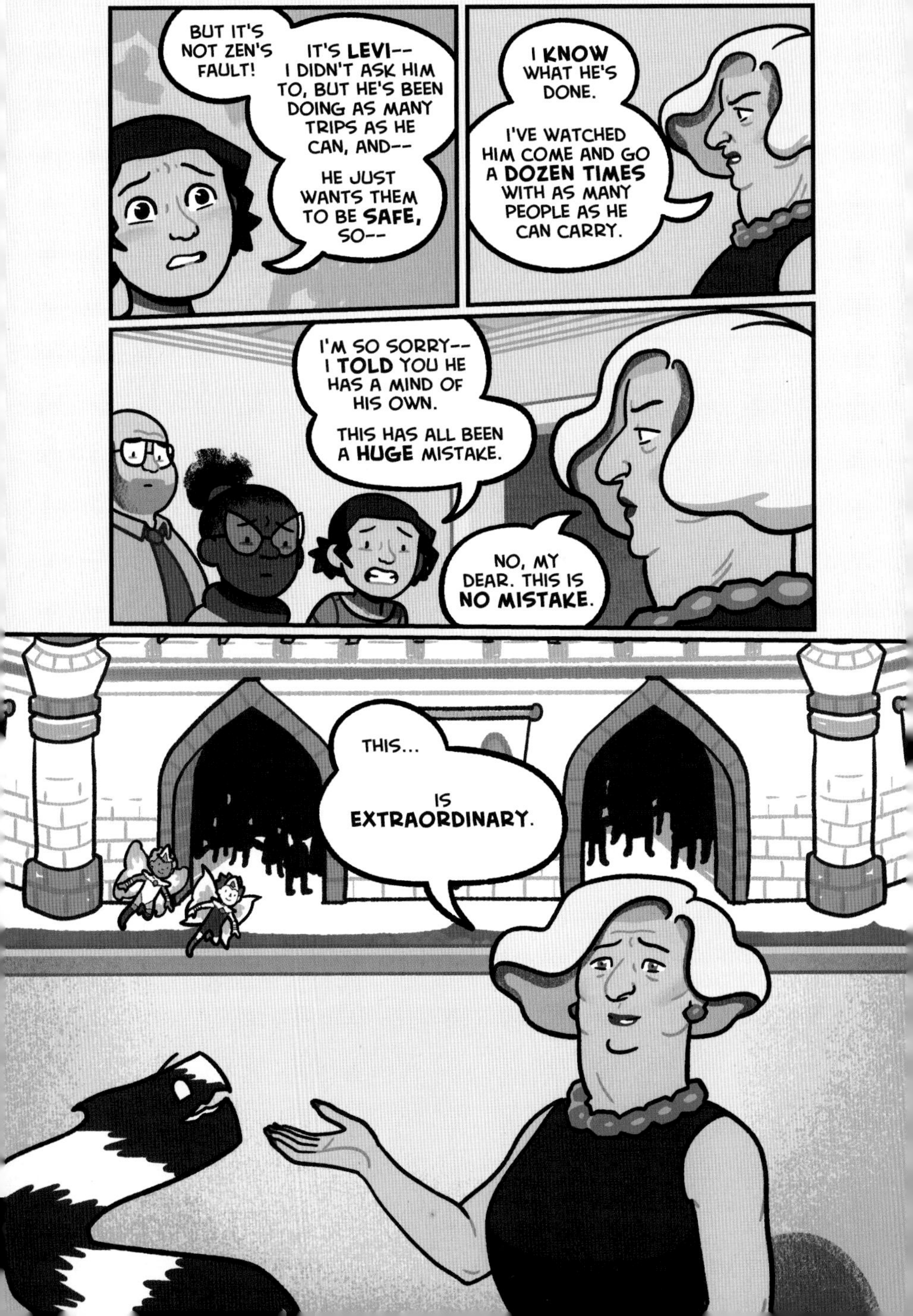
BUT IT'S NOT ZEN'S FAULT!
IT'S LEVI-- I DIDN'T ASK HIM TO, BUT HE'S BEEN DOING AS MANY TRIPS AS HE CAN, AND--
HE JUST WANTS THEM TO BE SAFE, SO--
I KNOW WHAT HE'S DONE.
I'VE WATCHED HIM COME AND GO A DOZEN TIMES WITH AS MANY PEOPLE AS HE CAN CARRY.
I'M SO SORRY-- I TOLD YOU HE HAS A MIND OF HIS OWN.
THIS HAS ALL BEEN A HUGE MISTAKE.
NO, MY DEAR. THIS IS NO MISTAKE.
THIS...
IS EXTRAORDINARY.

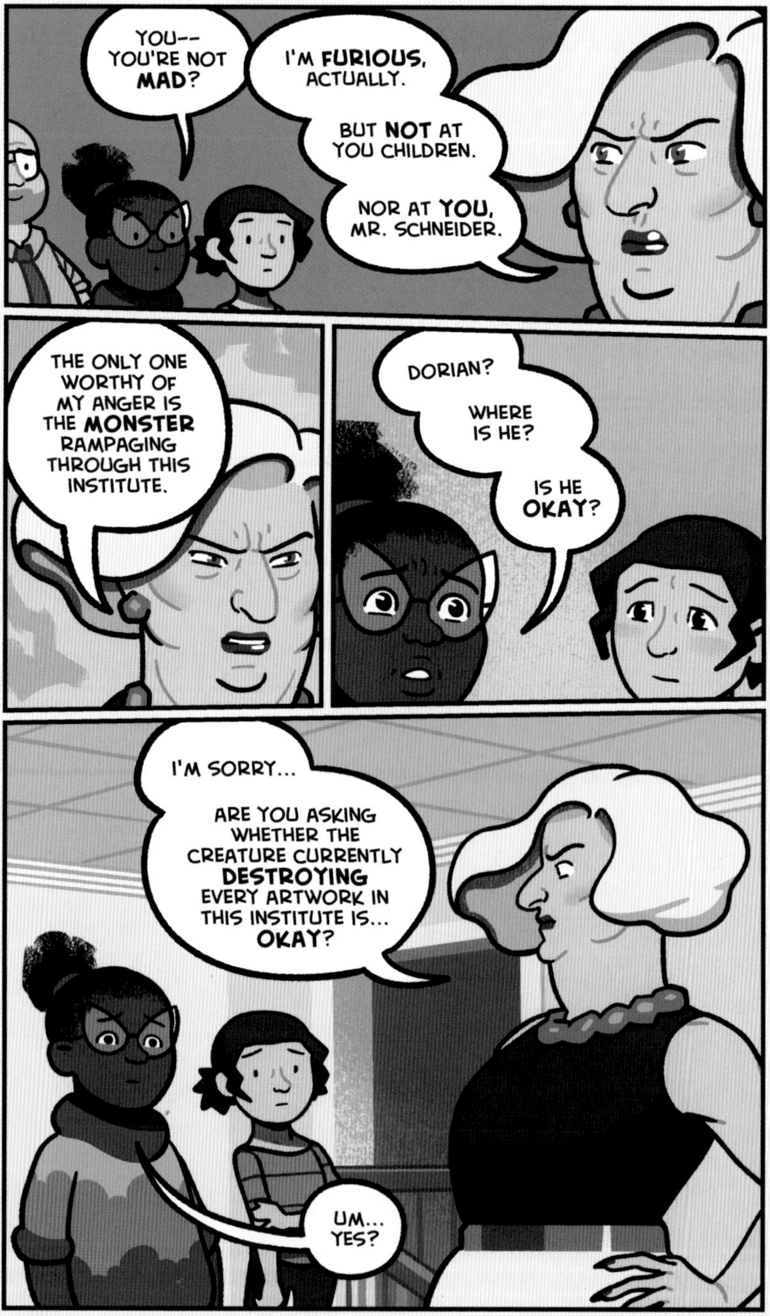
YOU--
YOU'RE NOT MAD?
I'M FURIOUS, ACTUALLY.
BUT NOT AT YOU CHILDREN.
NOR AT YOU, MR. SCHNEIDER.
THE ONLY ONE WORTHY OF MY ANGER IS THE MONSTER RAMPAGING THROUGH THIS INSTITUTE.
DORIAN?
WHERE IS HE?
IS HE OKAY?
I'M SORRY...
ARE YOU ASKING WHETHER THE CREATURE CURRENTLY DESTROYING EVERY ARTWORK IN THIS INSTITUTE IS... OKAY?
UM... YES?

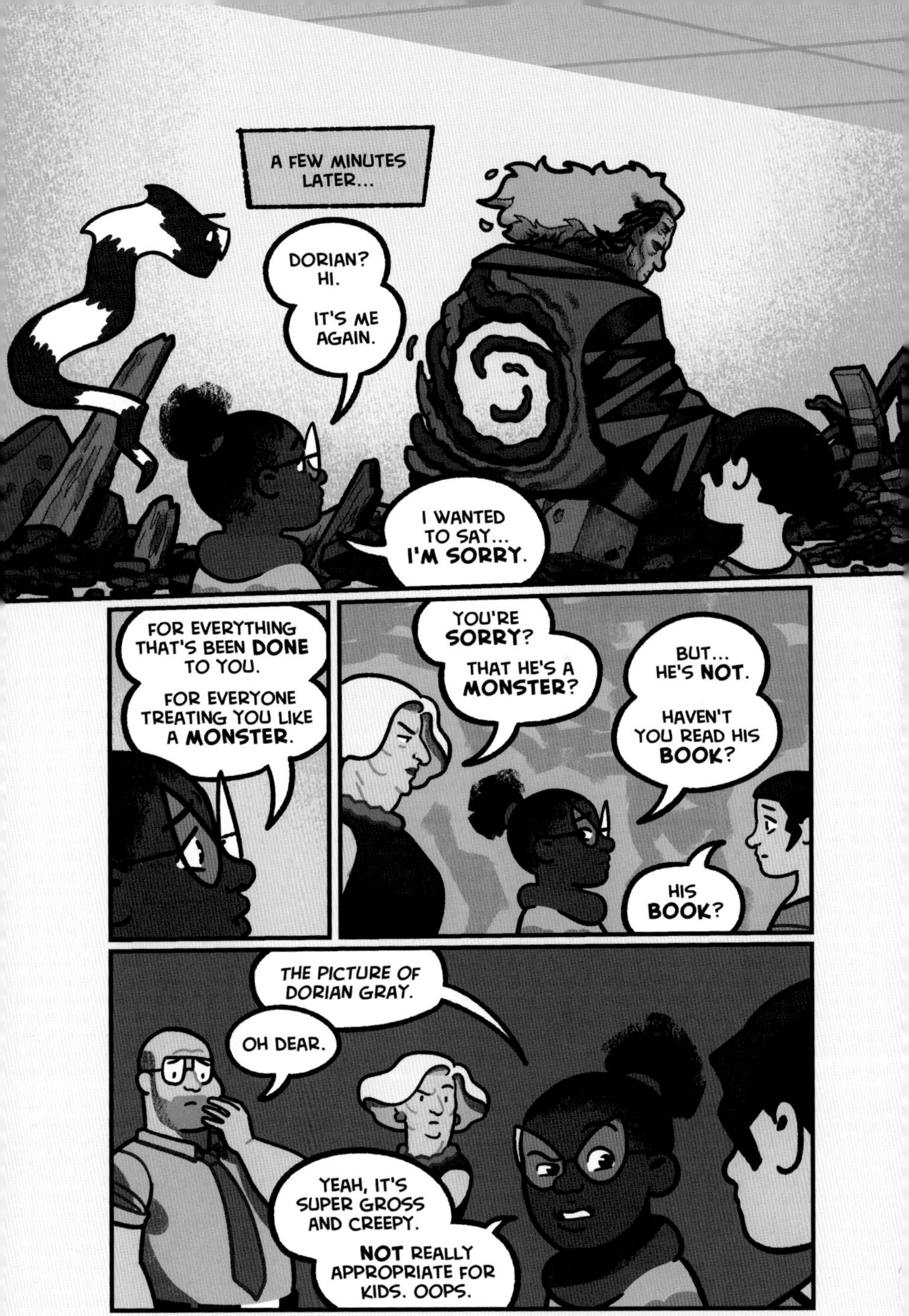
A FEW MINUTES LATER...
DORIAN? HI.
IT'S ME AGAIN.
I WANTED TO SAY... I'M SORRY.
FOR EVERYTHING THAT'S BEEN DONE TO YOU.
FOR EVERYONE TREATING YOU LIKE A MONSTER.
YOU'RE SORRY?
THAT HE'S A MONSTER?
BUT... HE'S NOT.
HAVEN'T YOU READ HIS BOOK?
HIS BOOK?
THE PICTURE OF DORIAN GRAY.
OH DEAR.
YEAH, IT'S SUPER GROSS AND CREEPY.
NOT REALLY APPROPRIATE FOR KIDS. OOPS.

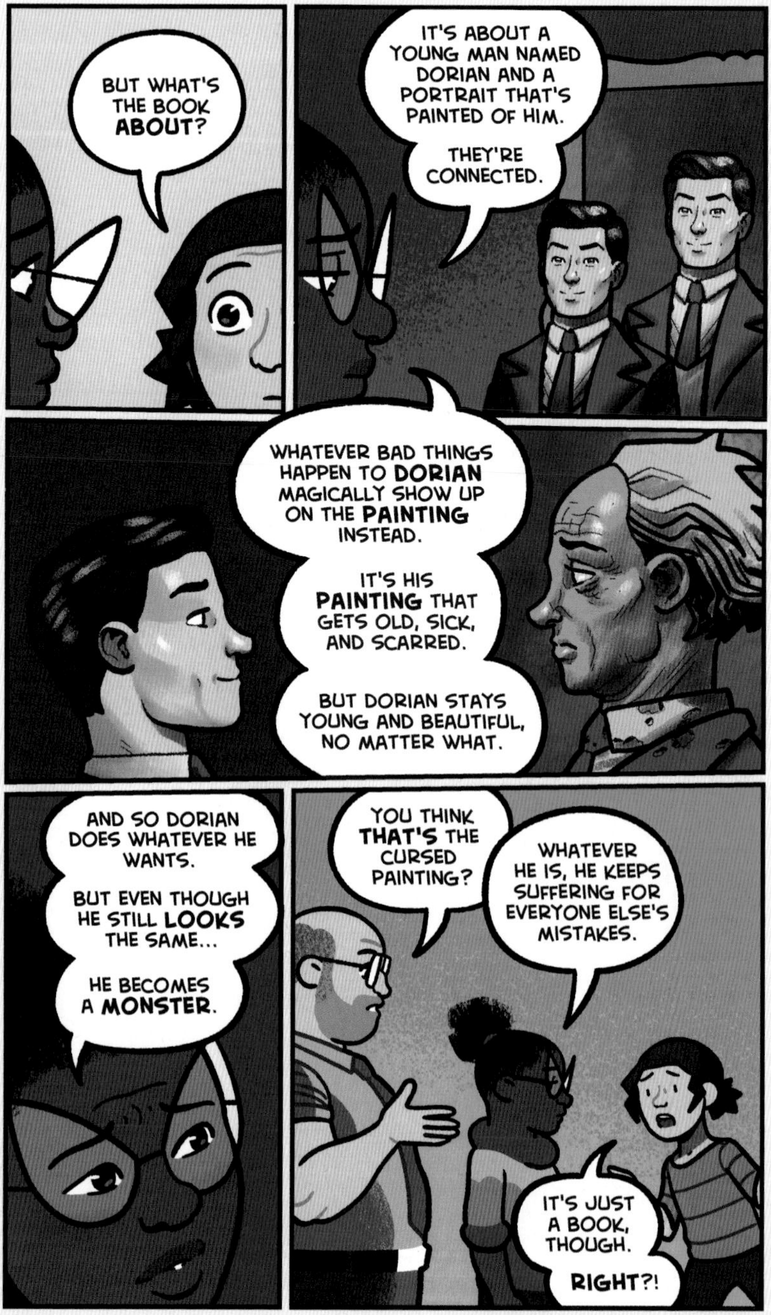
BUT WHAT'S THE BOOK **ABOUT**?
IT'S ABOUT A YOUNG MAN NAMED DORIAN AND A PORTRAIT THAT'S PAINTED OF HIM.
THEY'RE CONNECTED.
WHATEVER BAD THINGS HAPPEN TO **DORIAN** MAGICALLY SHOW UP ON THE **PAINTING** INSTEAD.
IT'S HIS **PAINTING** THAT GETS OLD, SICK, AND SCARRED.
BUT DORIAN STAYS YOUNG AND BEAUTIFUL, NO MATTER WHAT.
AND SO DORIAN DOES WHATEVER HE WANTS.
BUT EVEN THOUGH HE STILL **LOOKS** THE SAME...
HE BECOMES A **MONSTER**.
YOU THINK **THAT'S** THE CURSED PAINTING?
WHATEVER HE IS, HE KEEPS SUFFERING FOR EVERYONE ELSE'S MISTAKES.
IT'S JUST A BOOK, THOUGH.
RIGHT?!

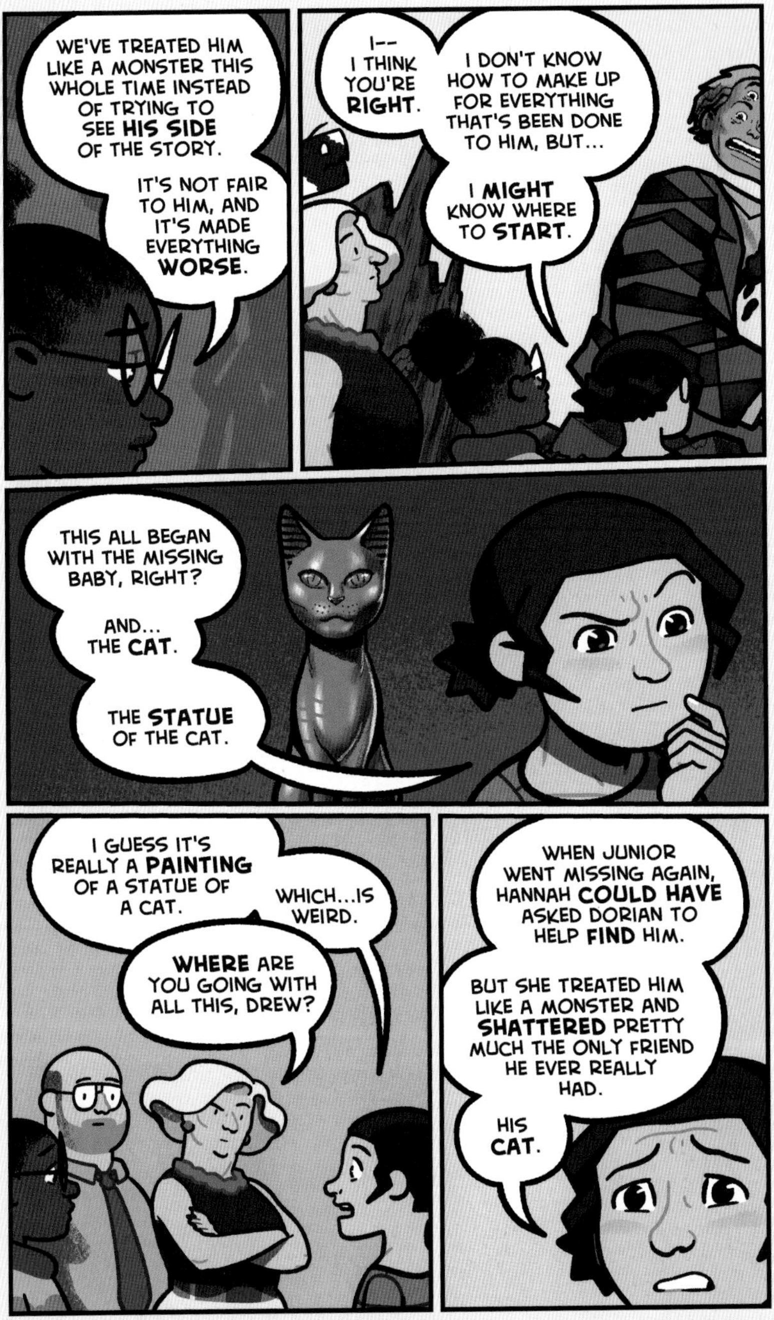
WE'VE TREATED HIM LIKE A MONSTER THIS WHOLE TIME INSTEAD OF TRYING TO SEE HIS SIDE OF THE STORY.
IT'S NOT FAIR TO HIM, AND IT'S MADE EVERYTHING WORSE.
I-- I THINK YOU'RE RIGHT.
I DON'T KNOW HOW TO MAKE UP FOR EVERYTHING THAT'S BEEN DONE TO HIM, BUT...
I MIGHT KNOW WHERE TO START.
THIS ALL BEGAN WITH THE MISSING BABY, RIGHT?
AND... THE CAT.
THE STATUE OF THE CAT.
I GUESS IT'S REALLY A PAINTING OF A STATUE OF A CAT.
WHICH...IS WEIRD.
WHERE ARE YOU GOING WITH ALL THIS, DREW?
WHEN JUNIOR WENT MISSING AGAIN, HANNAH COULD HAVE ASKED DORIAN TO HELP FIND HIM.
BUT SHE TREATED HIM LIKE A MONSTER AND SHATTERED PRETTY MUCH THE ONLY FRIEND HE EVER REALLY HAD.
HIS CAT.

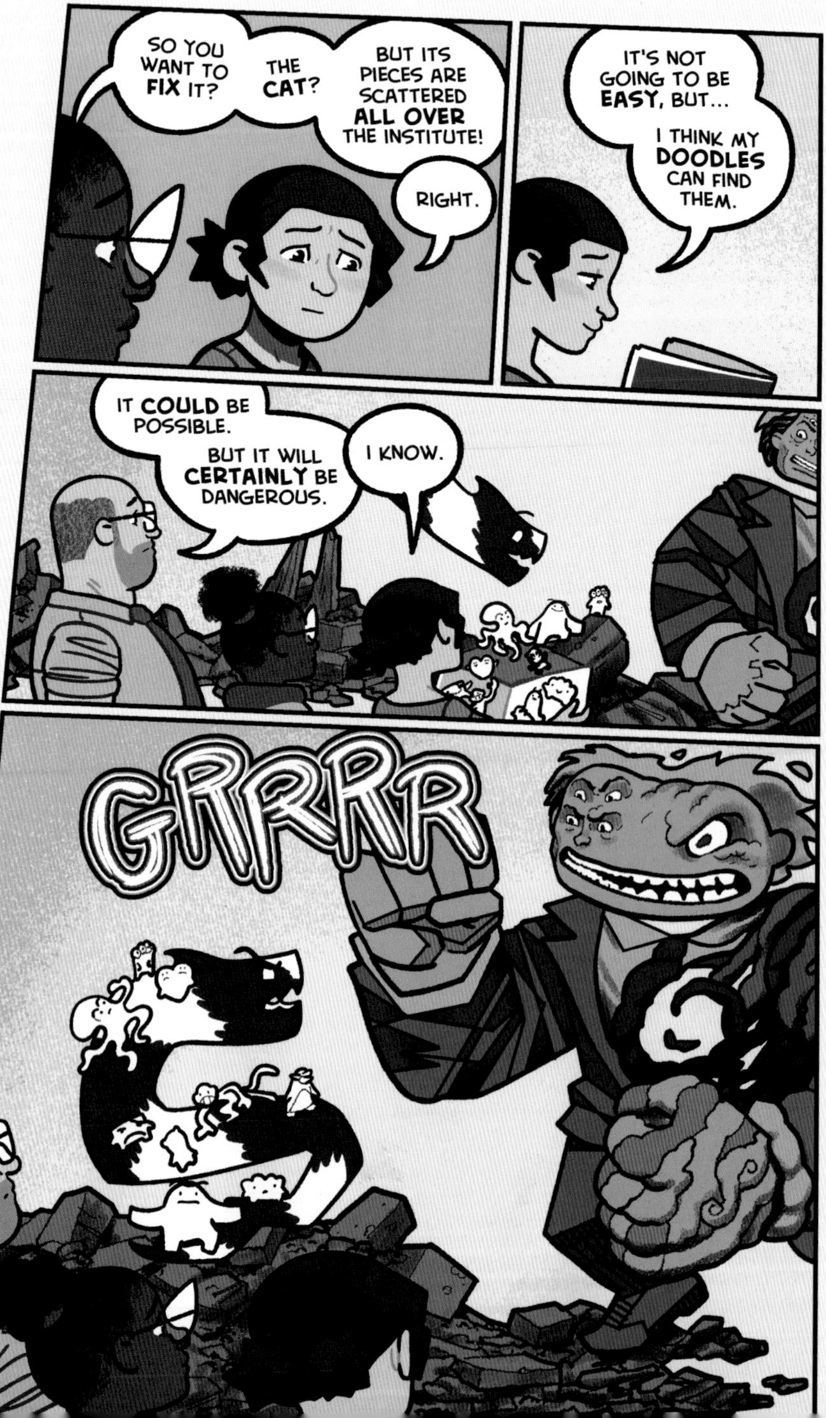
SO YOU WANT TO **FIX** IT?
THE **CAT**?
BUT ITS PIECES ARE SCATTERED **ALL OVER** THE INSTITUTE!
RIGHT.
IT'S NOT GOING TO BE **EASY**, BUT...
I THINK MY **DOODLES** CAN FIND THEM.
IT **COULD** BE POSSIBLE.
BUT IT WILL **CERTAINLY** BE DANGEROUS.
I KNOW.
GRRRR

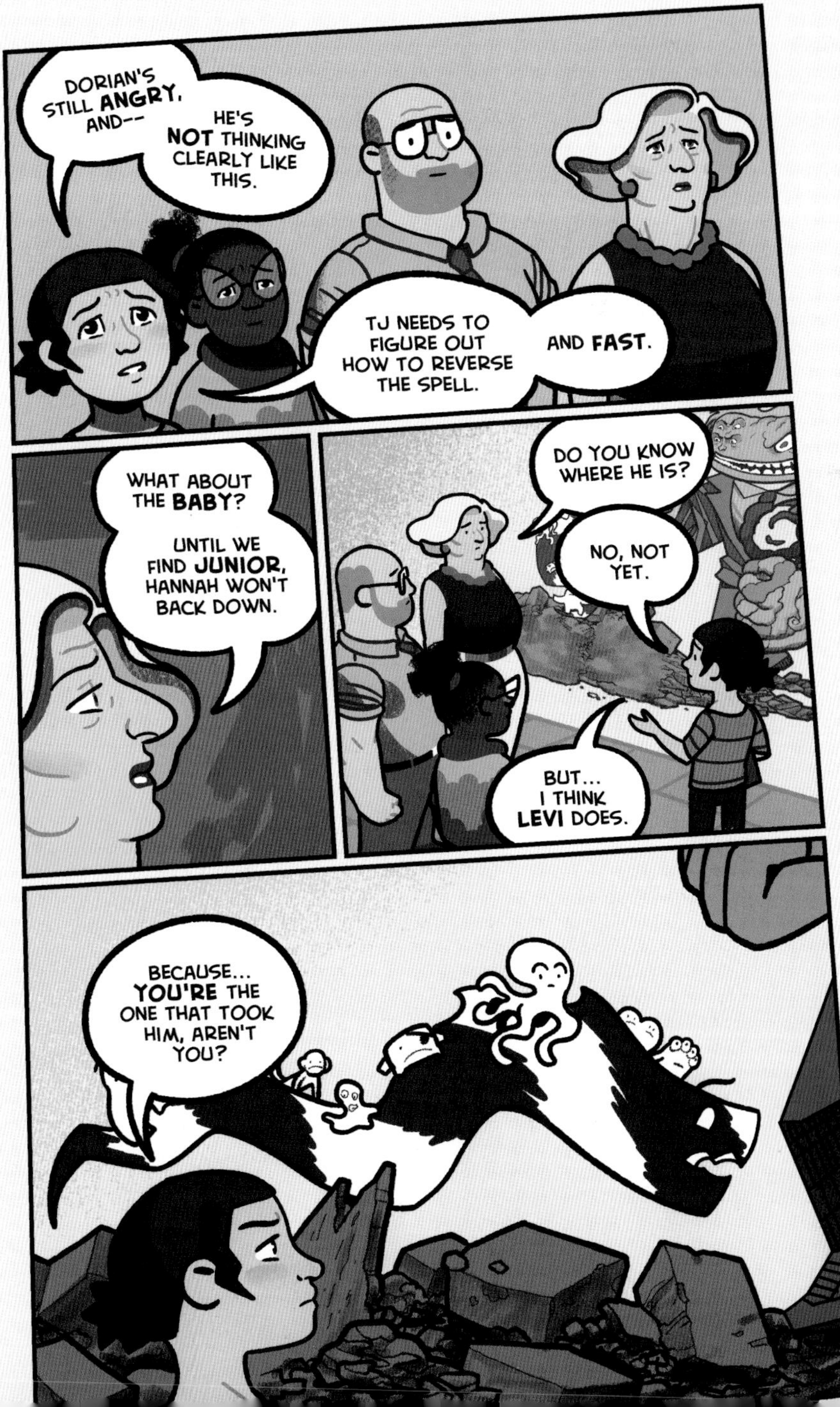
DORIAN'S STILL ANGRY, AND--
HE'S NOT THINKING CLEARLY LIKE THIS.
TJ NEEDS TO FIGURE OUT HOW TO REVERSE THE SPELL.
AND FAST.
WHAT ABOUT THE BABY?
UNTIL WE FIND JUNIOR, HANNAH WON'T BACK DOWN.
DO YOU KNOW WHERE HE IS?
NO, NOT YET.
BUT... I THINK LEVI DOES.
BECAUSE... YOU'RE THE ONE THAT TOOK HIM, AREN'T YOU?

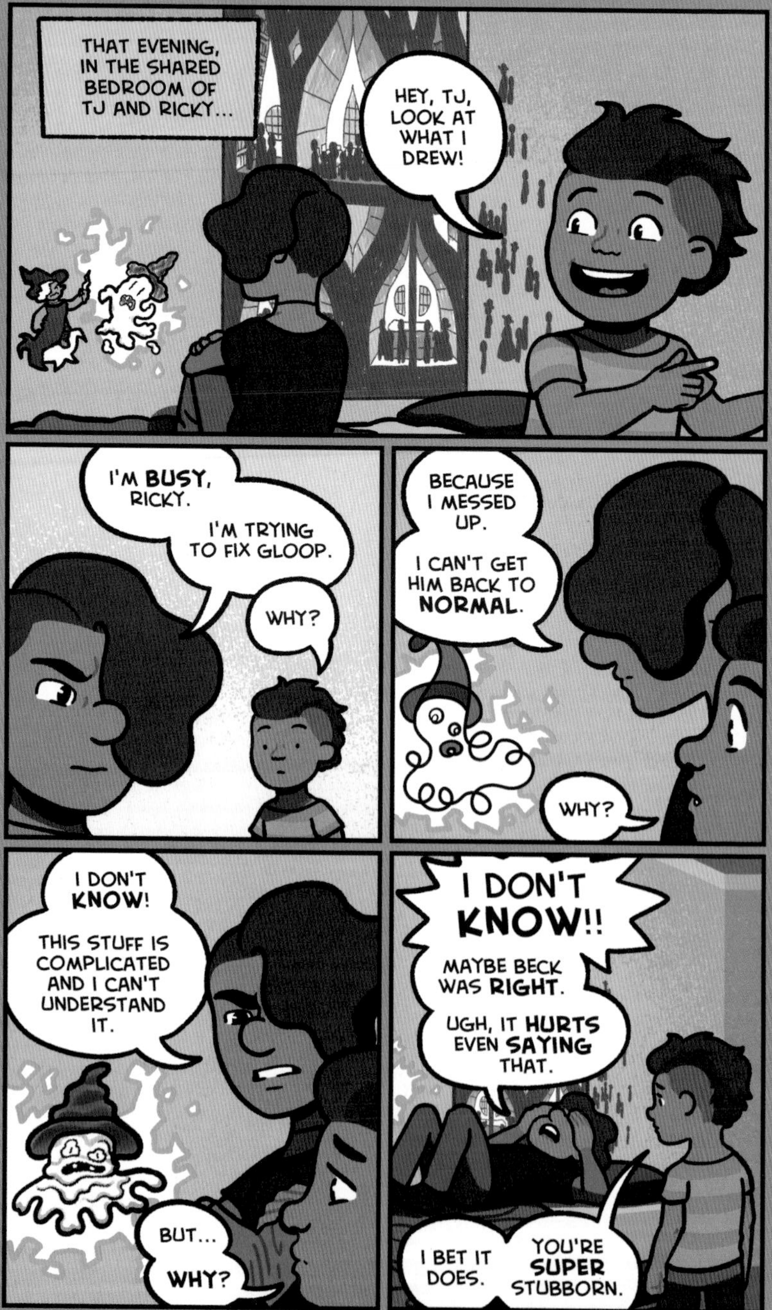
THAT EVENING, IN THE SHARED BEDROOM OF TJ AND RICKY...
HEY, TJ, LOOK AT WHAT I DREW!
I'M **BUSY**, RICKY.
I'M TRYING TO FIX GLOOP.
WHY?
BECAUSE I MESSED UP.
I CAN'T GET HIM BACK TO **NORMAL**.
WHY?
I DON'T **KNOW**!
THIS STUFF IS COMPLICATED AND I CAN'T UNDERSTAND IT.
BUT... **WHY**?
I DON'T **KNOW**!!
MAYBE BECK WAS **RIGHT**.
UGH, IT **HURTS** EVEN **SAYING** THAT.
I BET IT DOES.
YOU'RE **SUPER** STUBBORN.

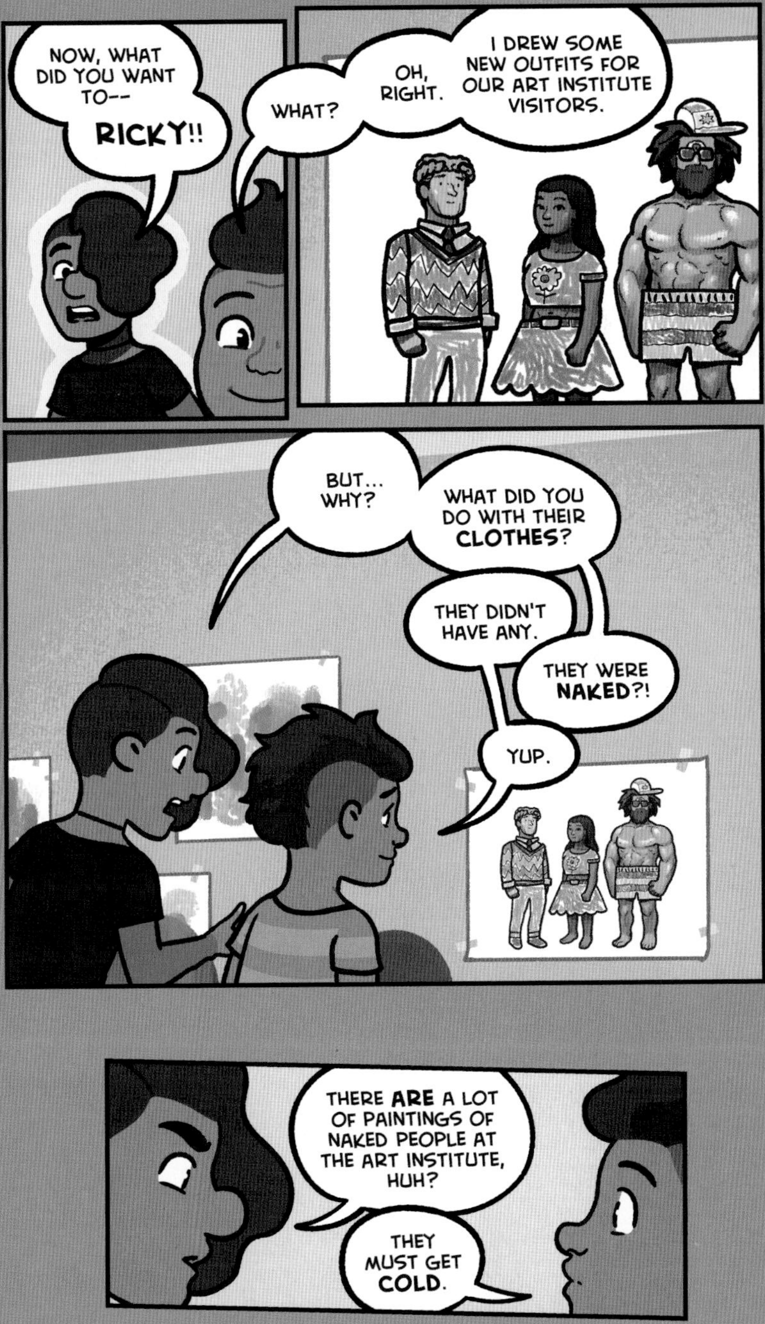

NOW, WHAT DID YOU WANT TO--
RICKY!!
WHAT?
OH, RIGHT.
I DREW SOME NEW OUTFITS FOR OUR ART INSTITUTE VISITORS.
BUT... WHY?
WHAT DID YOU DO WITH THEIR CLOTHES?
THEY DIDN'T HAVE ANY.
THEY WERE NAKED?!
YUP.
THERE ARE A LOT OF PAINTINGS OF NAKED PEOPLE AT THE ART INSTITUTE, HUH?
THEY MUST GET COLD.

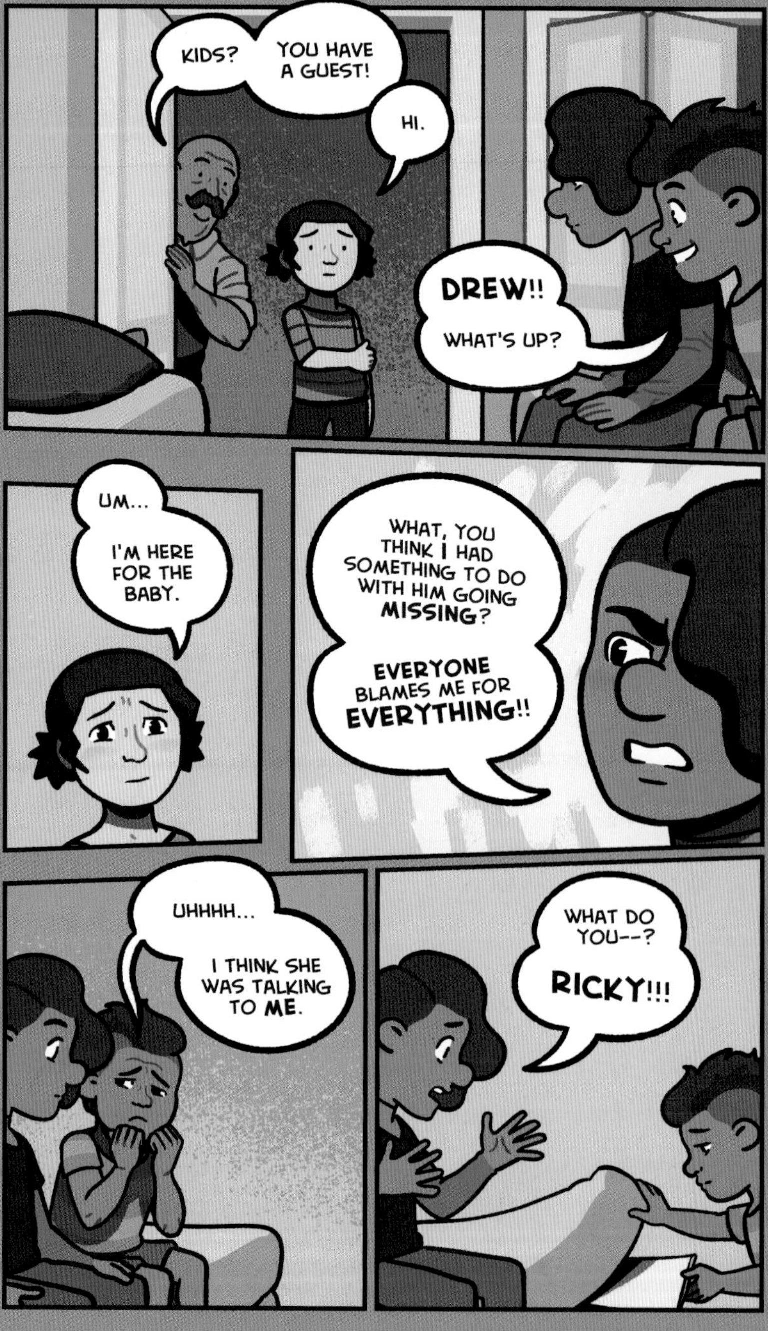
KIDS?
YOU HAVE A GUEST!
HI.
DREW!!
WHAT'S UP?
UM...
I'M HERE FOR THE BABY.
WHAT, YOU THINK I HAD SOMETHING TO DO WITH HIM GOING MISSING?
EVERYONE BLAMES ME FOR EVERYTHING!!
UHHHH...
I THINK SHE WAS TALKING TO ME.
WHAT DO YOU--?
RICKY!!!

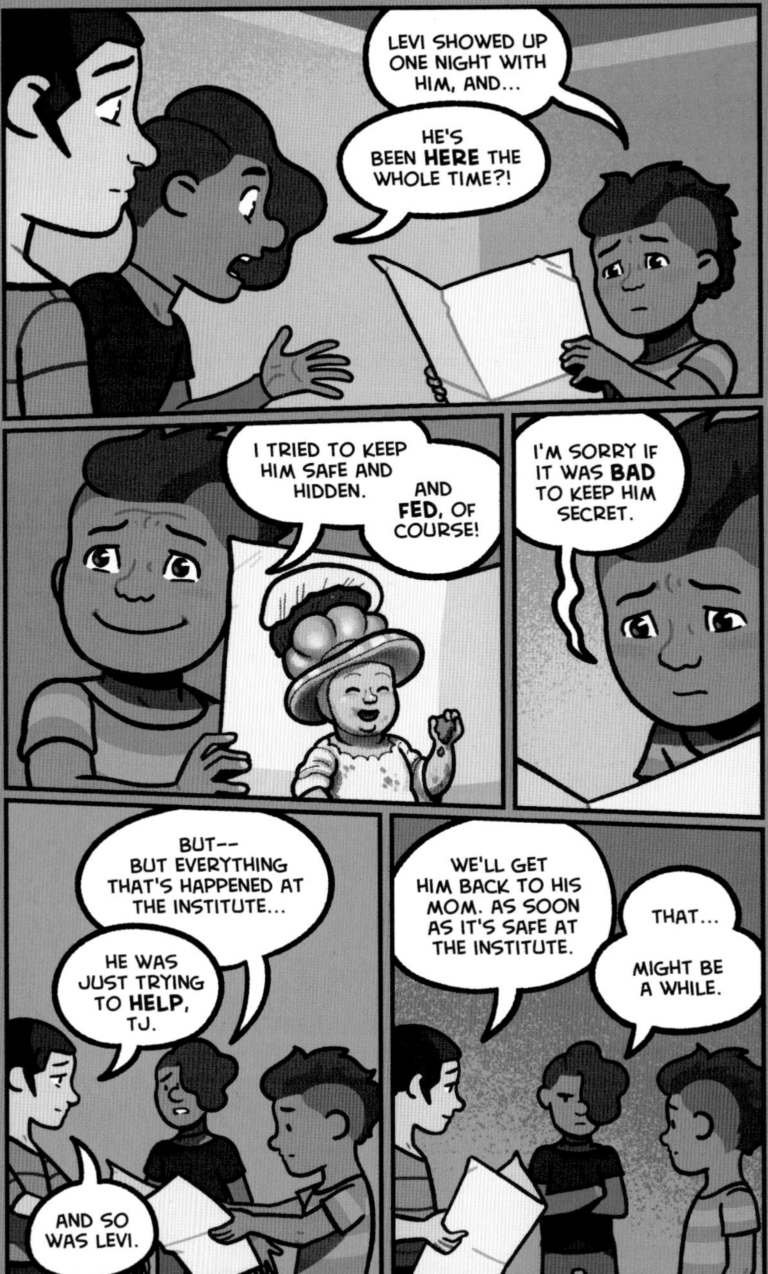
LEVI SHOWED UP ONE NIGHT WITH HIM, AND...
HE'S BEEN **HERE** THE WHOLE TIME?!
I TRIED TO KEEP HIM SAFE AND HIDDEN.
AND **FED**, OF COURSE!
I'M SORRY IF IT WAS **BAD** TO KEEP HIM SECRET.
BUT-- BUT EVERYTHING THAT'S HAPPENED AT THE INSTITUTE...
HE WAS JUST TRYING TO **HELP**, TJ.
AND SO WAS LEVI.
WE'LL GET HIM BACK TO HIS MOM. AS SOON AS IT'S SAFE AT THE INSTITUTE.
THAT...
MIGHT BE A WHILE.

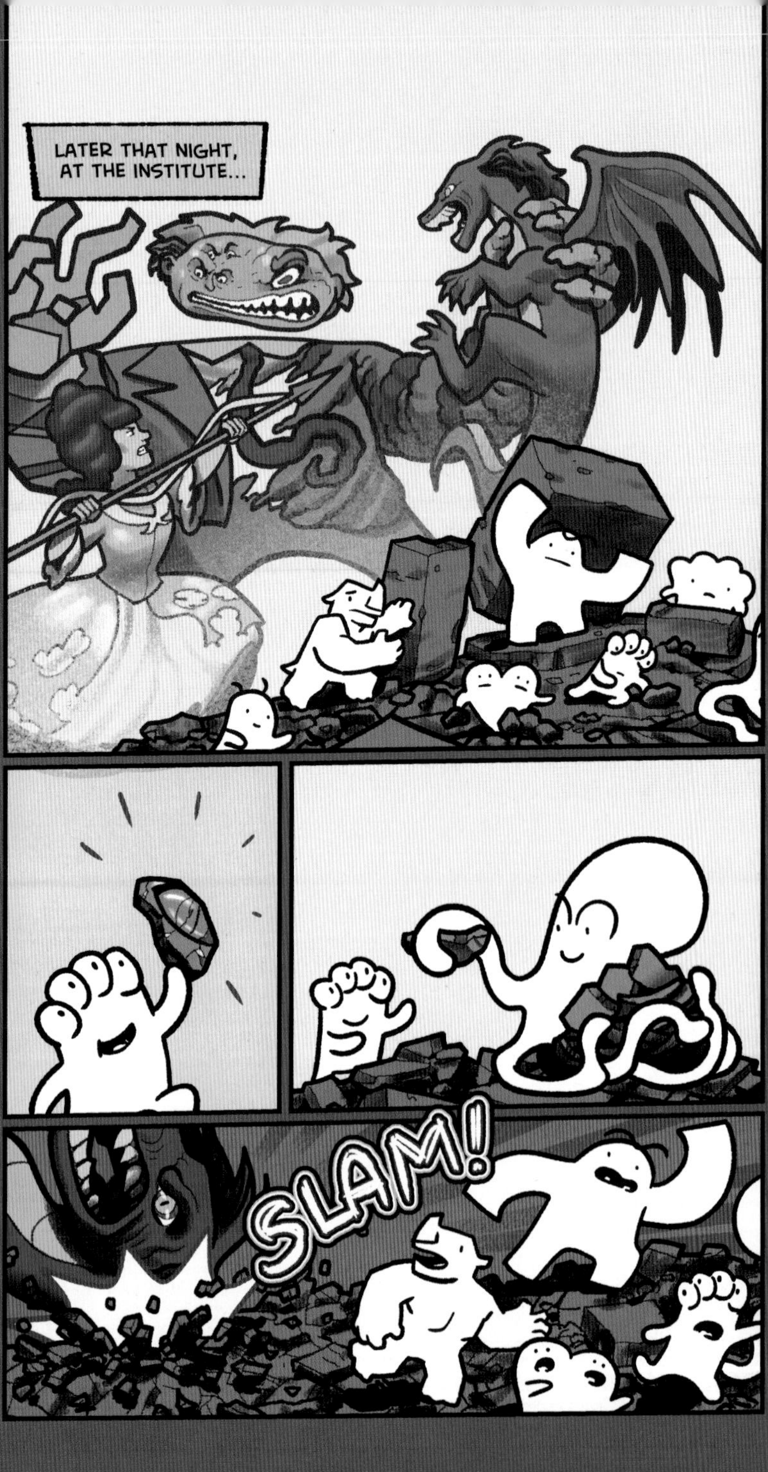
LATER THAT NIGHT, AT THE INSTITUTE...
SLAM!

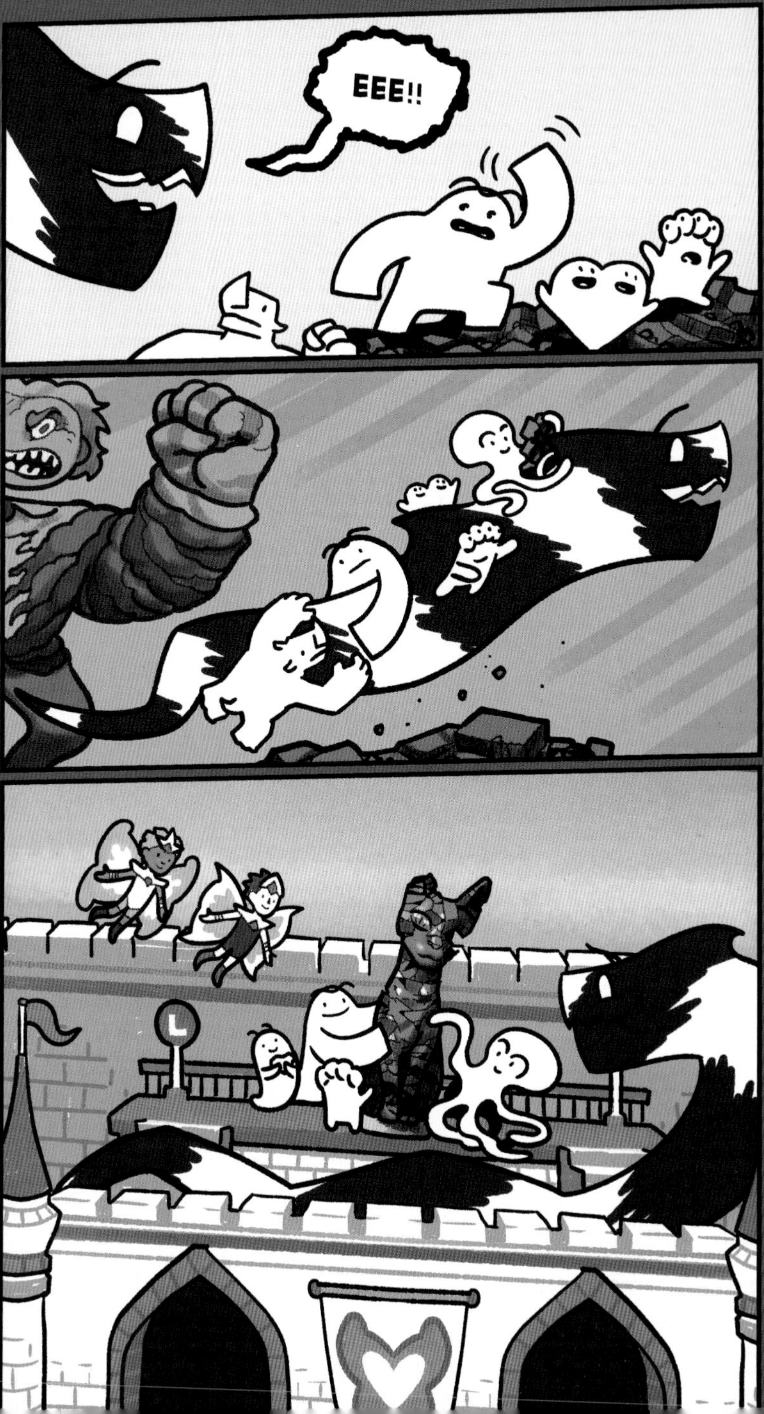
EEE!!

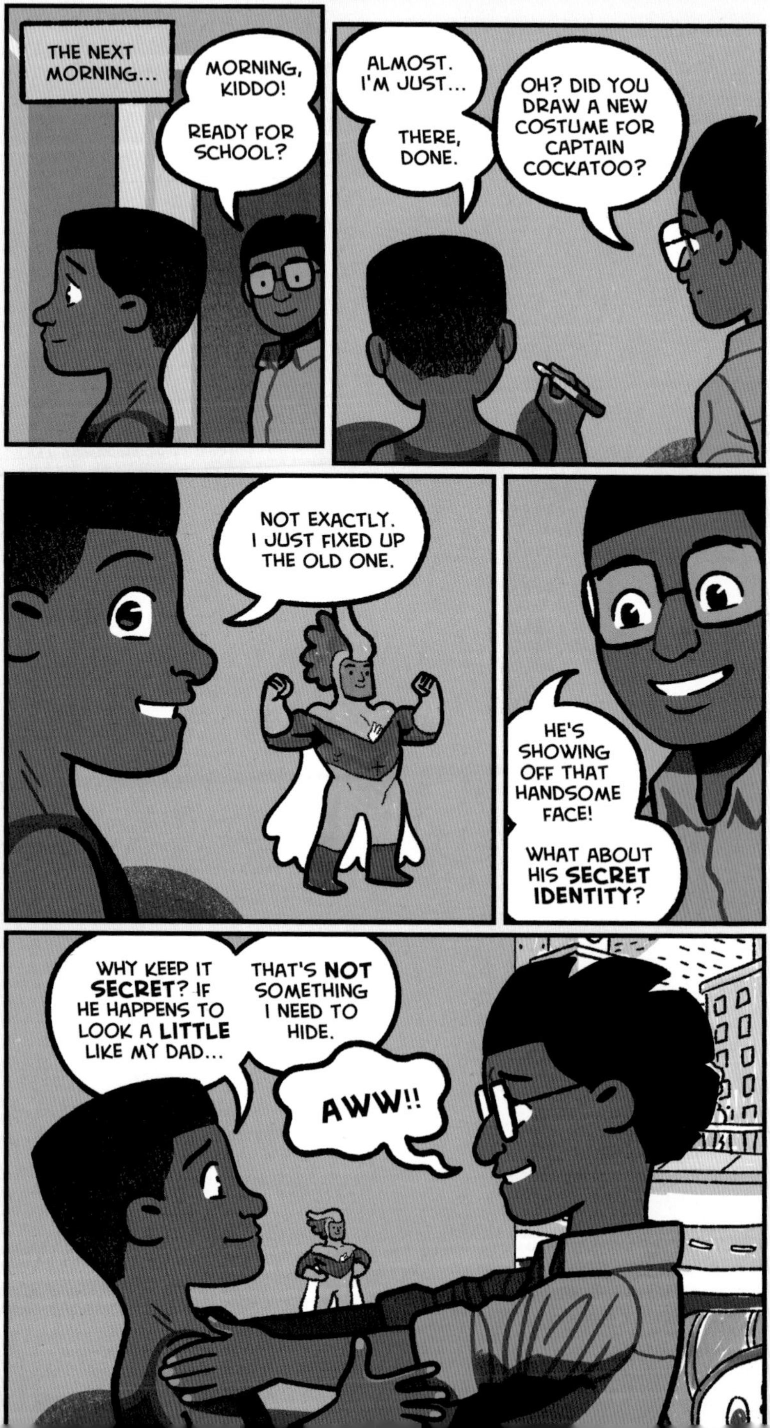
THE NEXT MORNING...
MORNING, KIDDO!
READY FOR SCHOOL?
ALMOST. I'M JUST...
THERE, DONE.
OH? DID YOU DRAW A NEW COSTUME FOR CAPTAIN COCKATOO?
NOT EXACTLY. I JUST FIXED UP THE OLD ONE.
HE'S SHOWING OFF THAT HANDSOME FACE!
WHAT ABOUT HIS SECRET IDENTITY?
WHY KEEP IT SECRET? IF HE HAPPENS TO LOOK A LITTLE LIKE MY DAD...
THAT'S NOT SOMETHING I NEED TO HIDE.
AWW!!

CHAPTER 6: MAKING PLANS

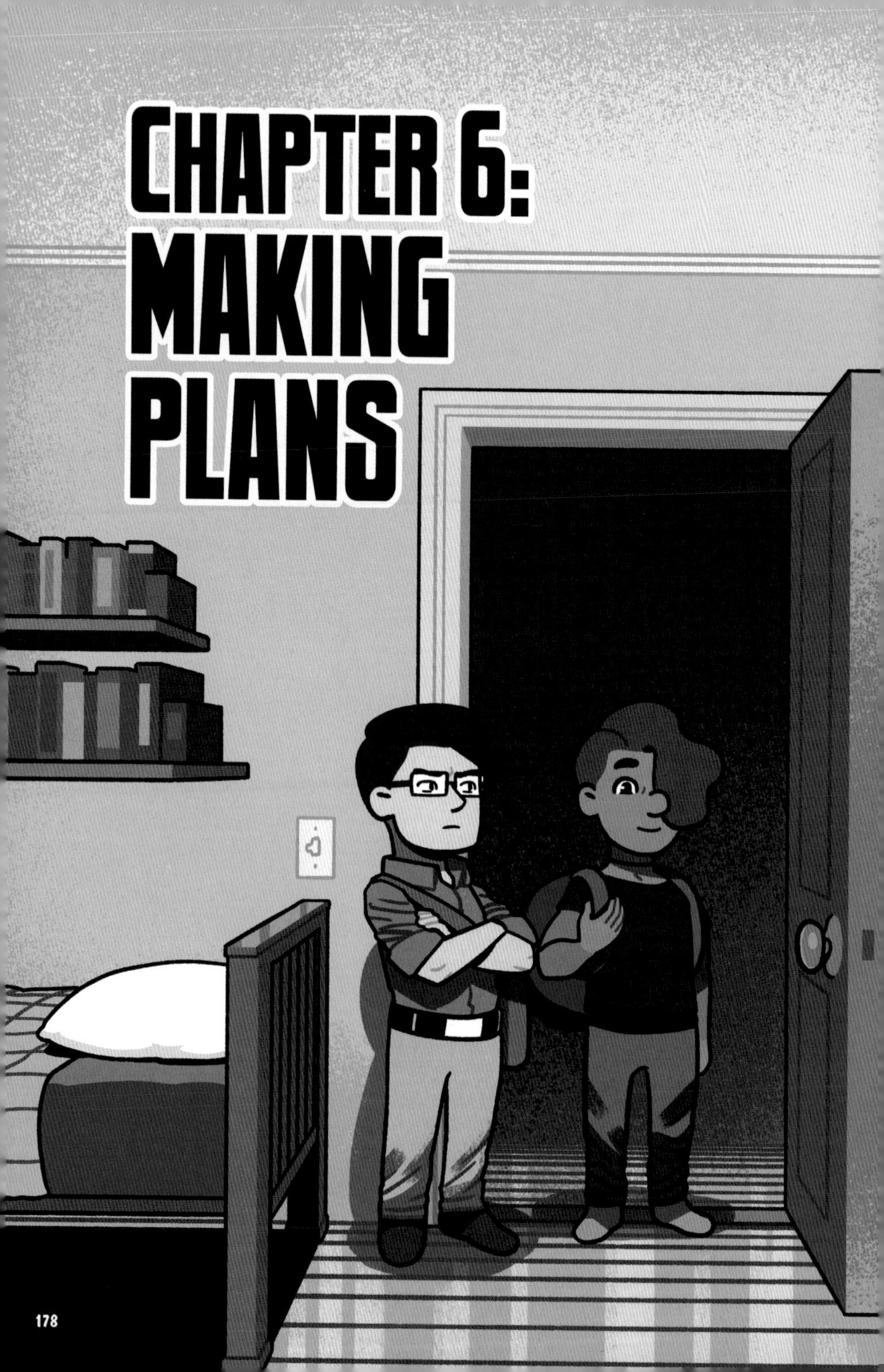

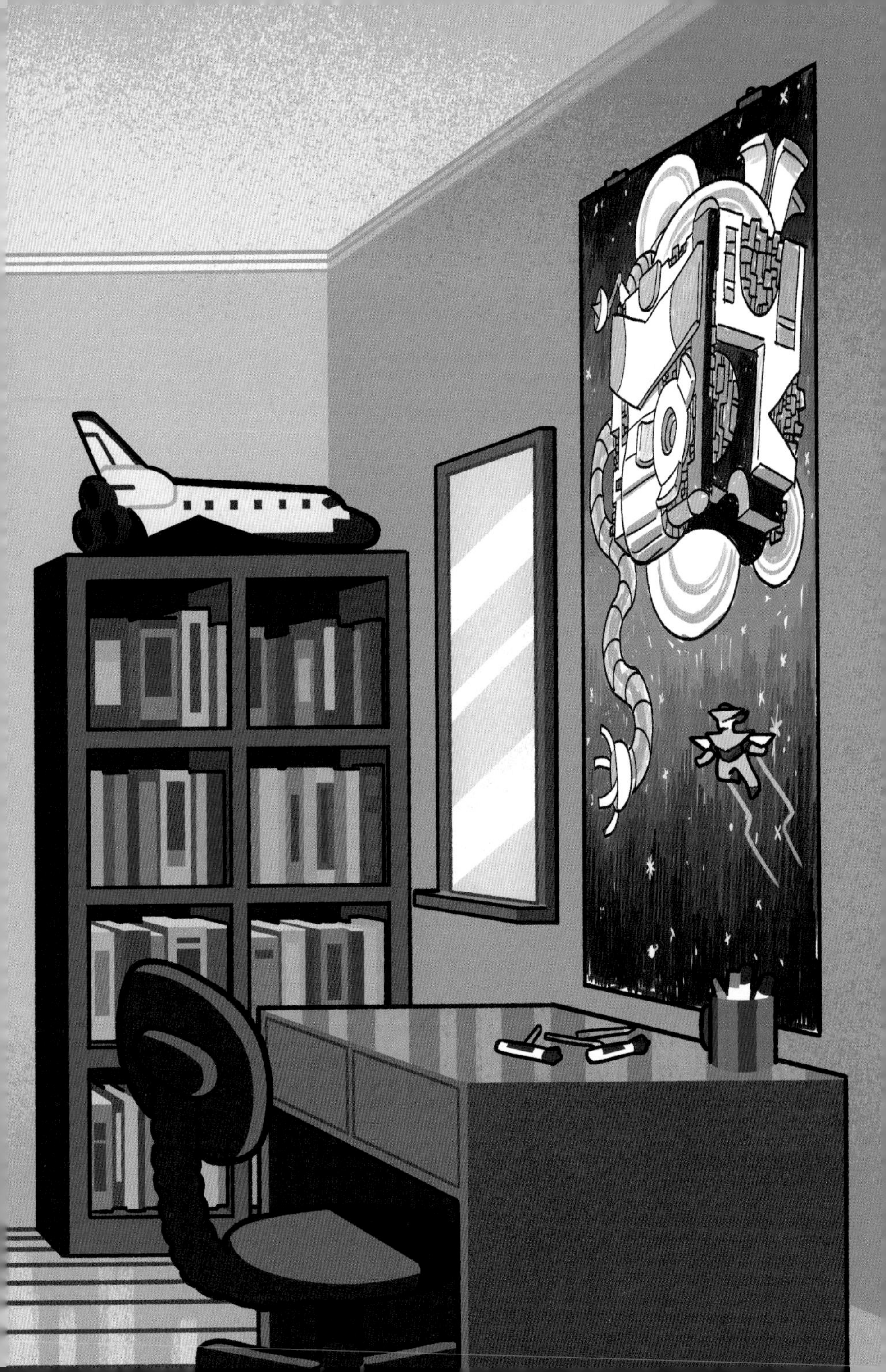

181

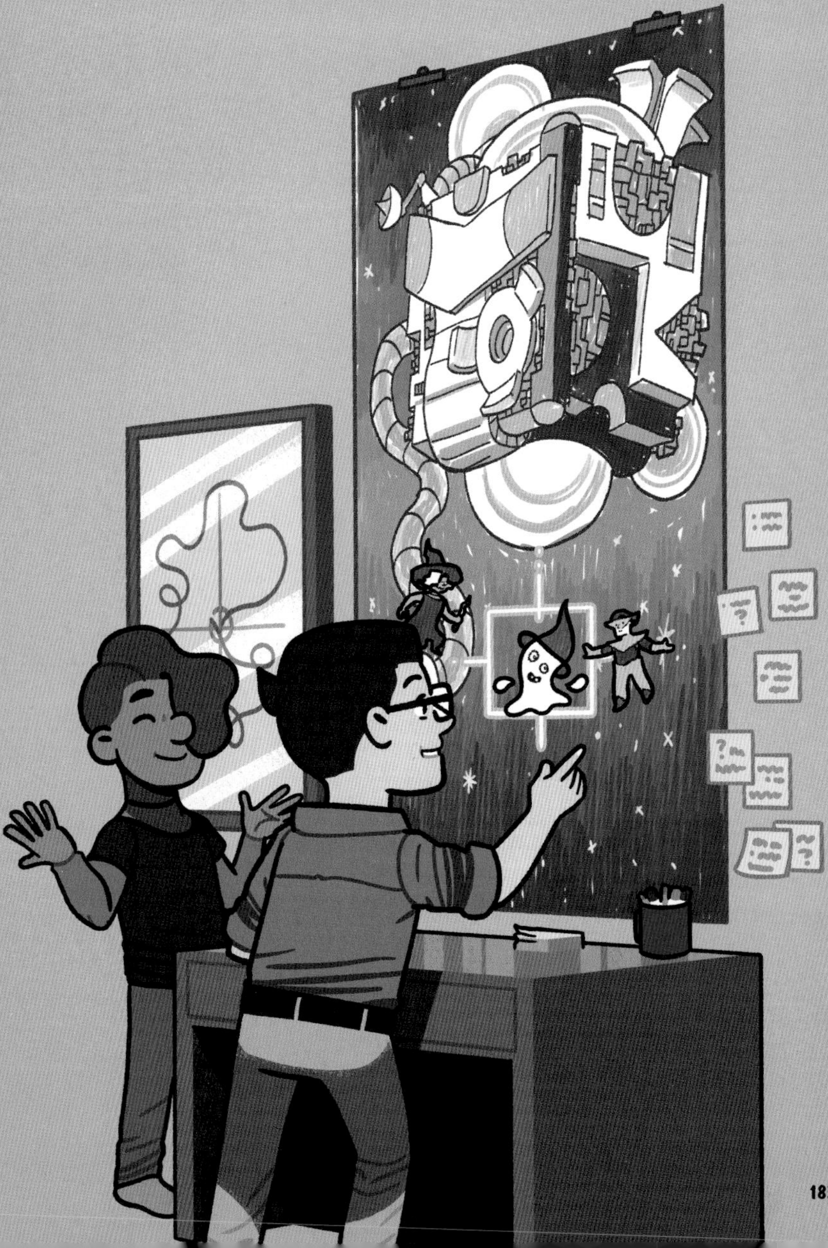

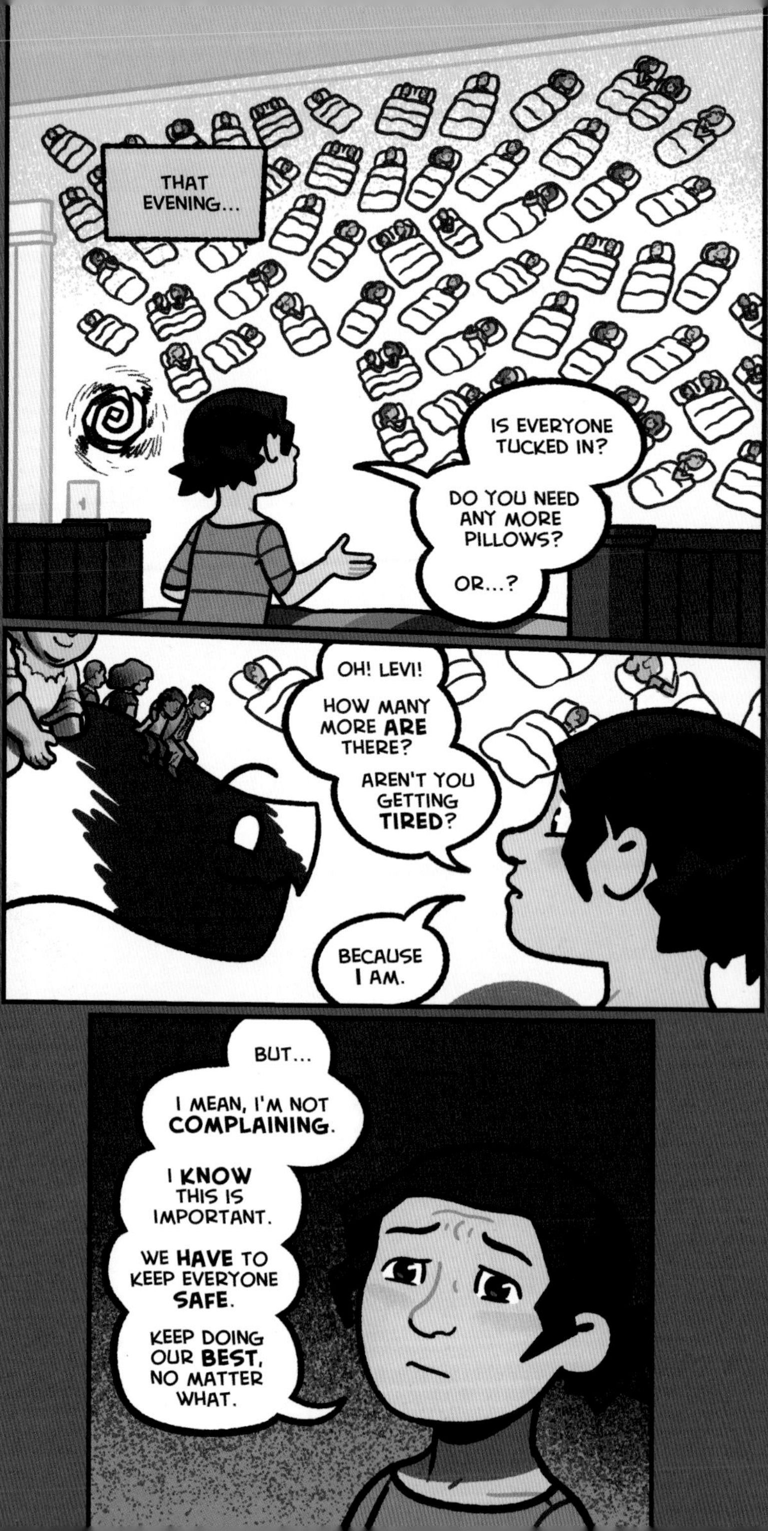
THAT EVENING...
IS EVERYONE TUCKED IN?
DO YOU NEED ANY MORE PILLOWS?
OR...?
OH! LEVI!
HOW MANY MORE ARE THERE?
AREN'T YOU GETTING TIRED?
BECAUSE I AM.
BUT...
I MEAN, I'M NOT COMPLAINING.
I KNOW THIS IS IMPORTANT.
WE HAVE TO KEEP EVERYONE SAFE.
KEEP DOING OUR BEST, NO MATTER WHAT.

185

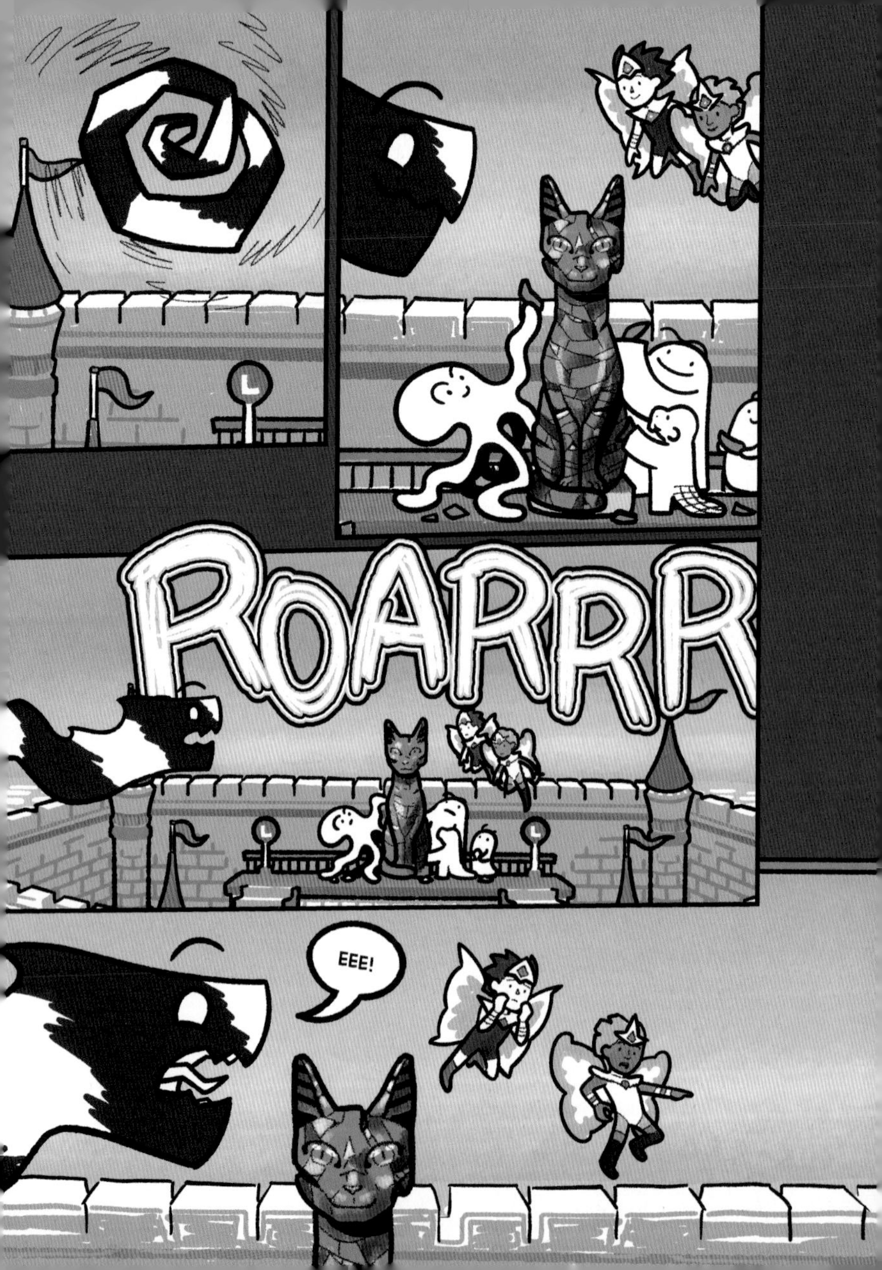
ROARRR
EEE!

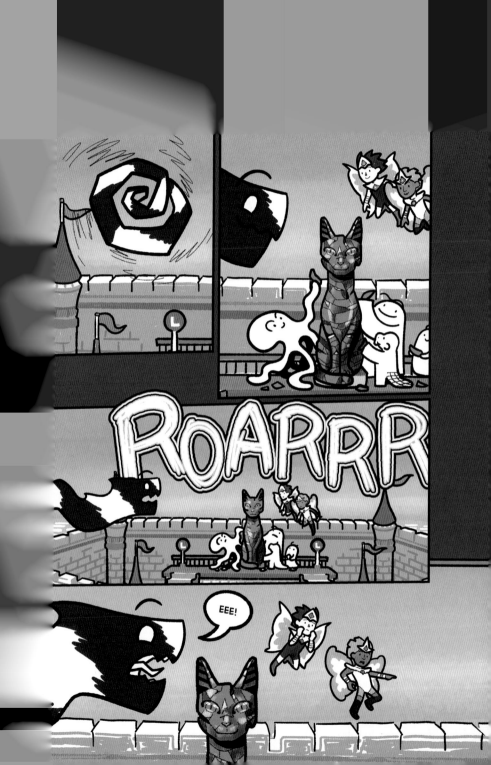

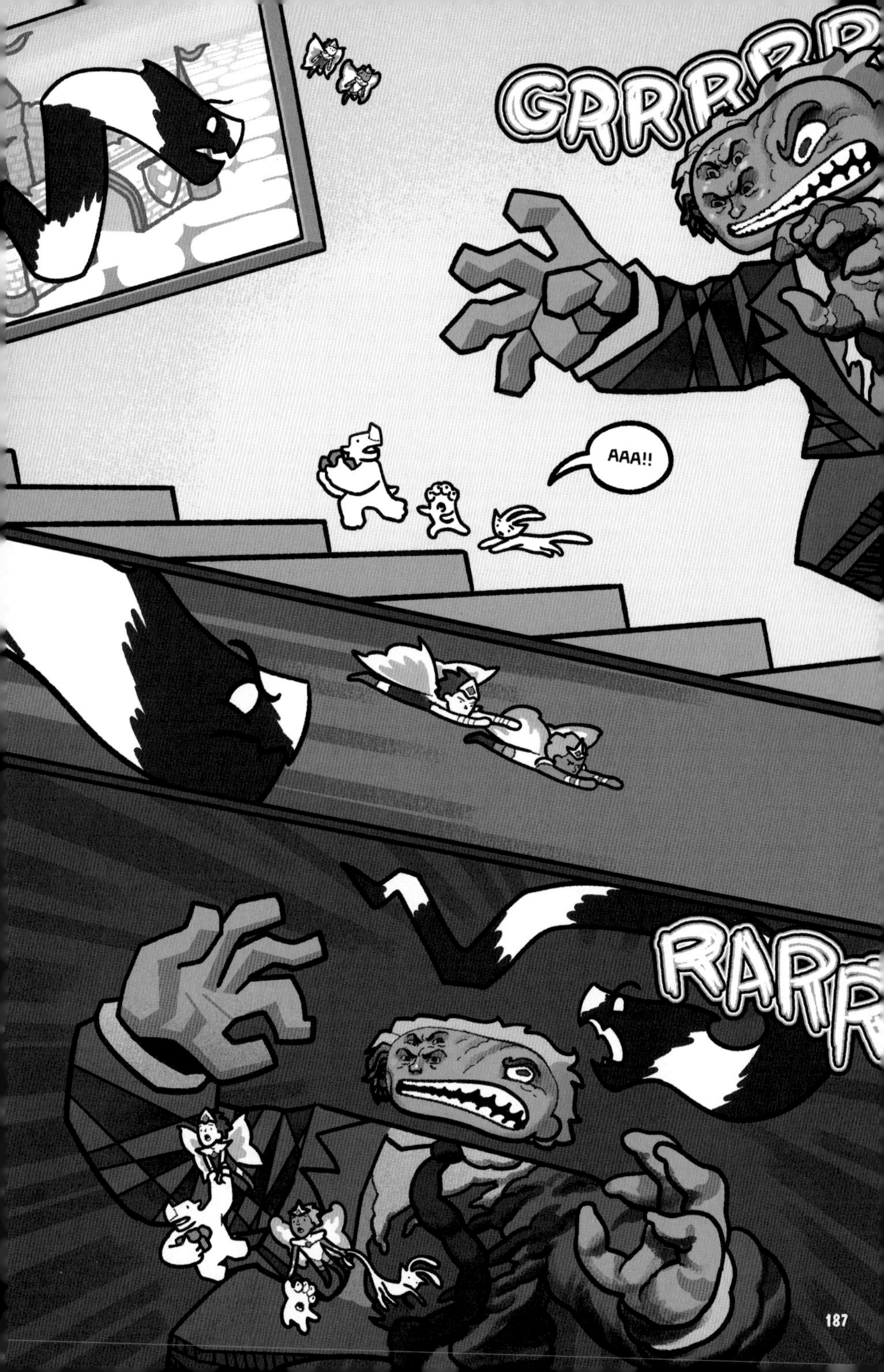
GRRRR
AAA!!
RARR

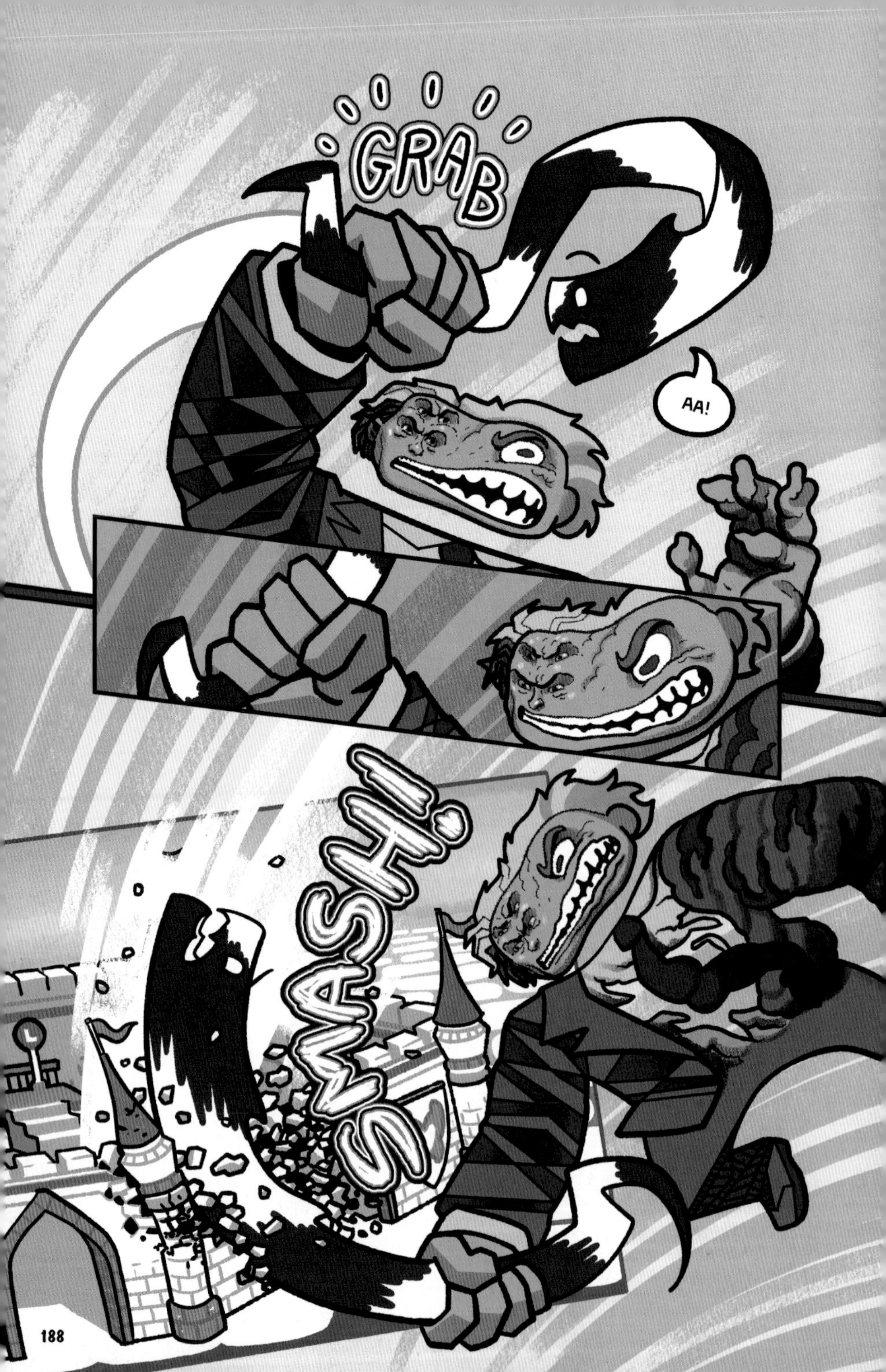
GRAB
AA!
SMASH!!

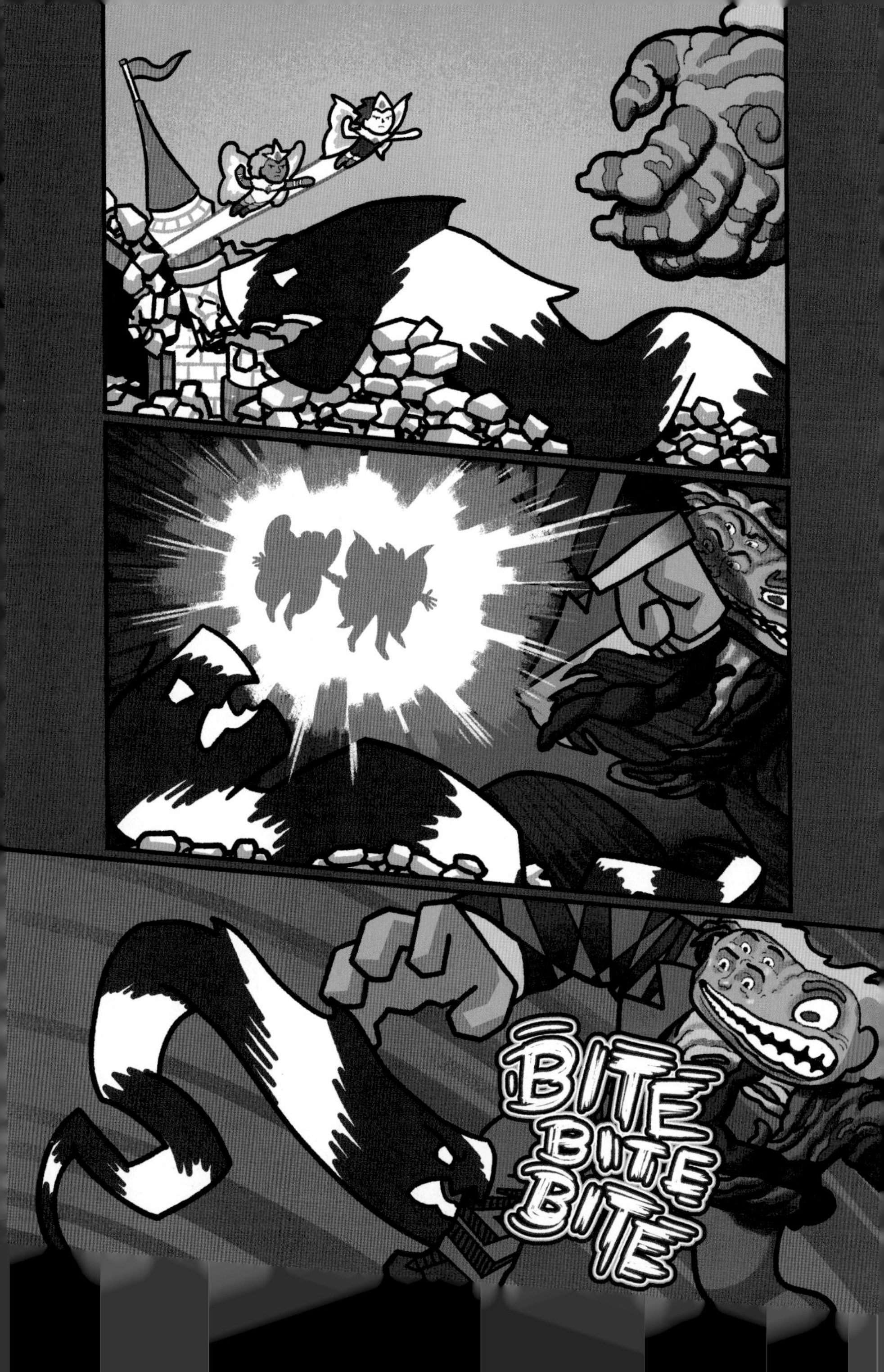
BITE BITE BITE

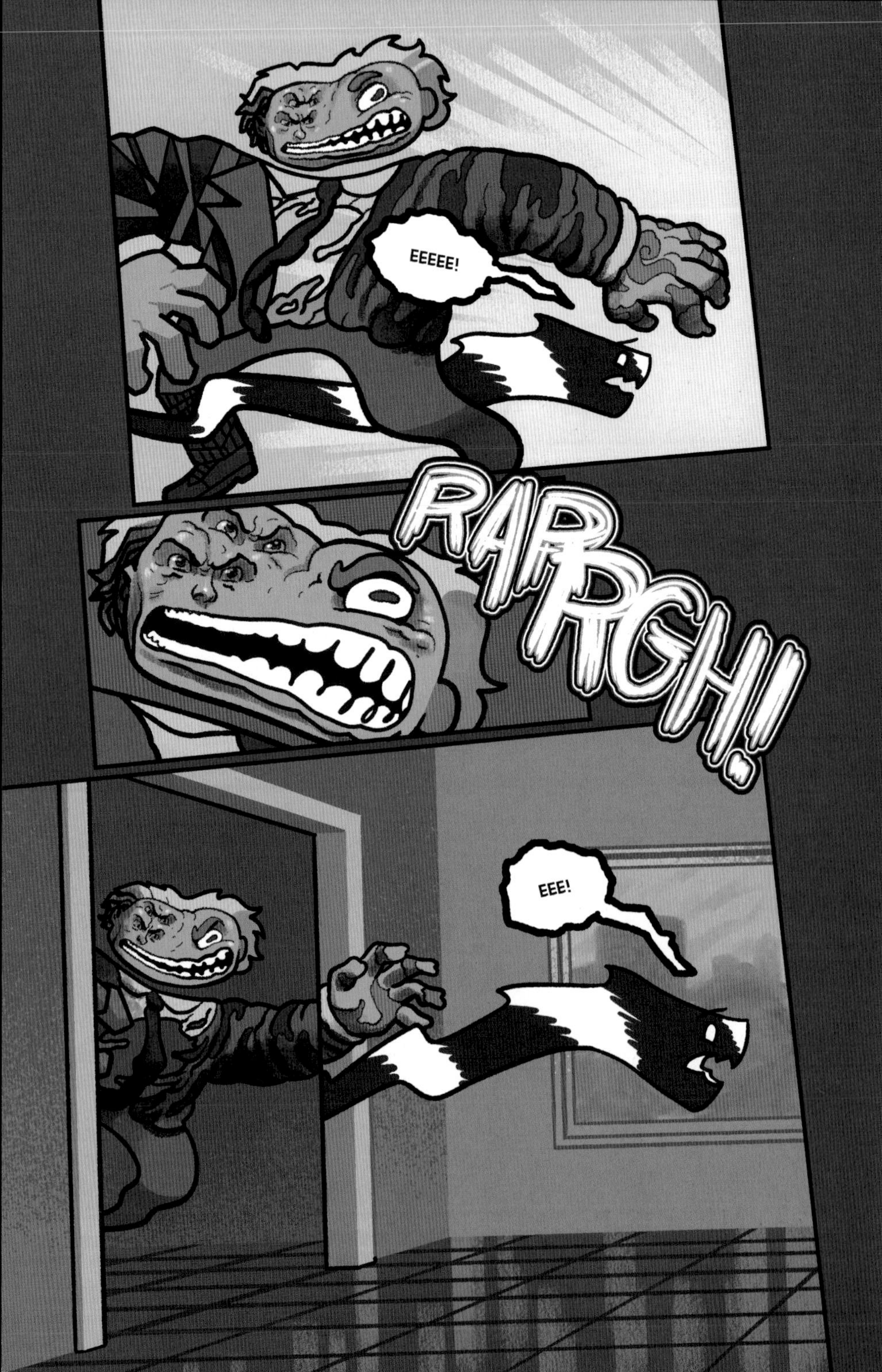
EEEEE!
RARRGH!!
EEE!

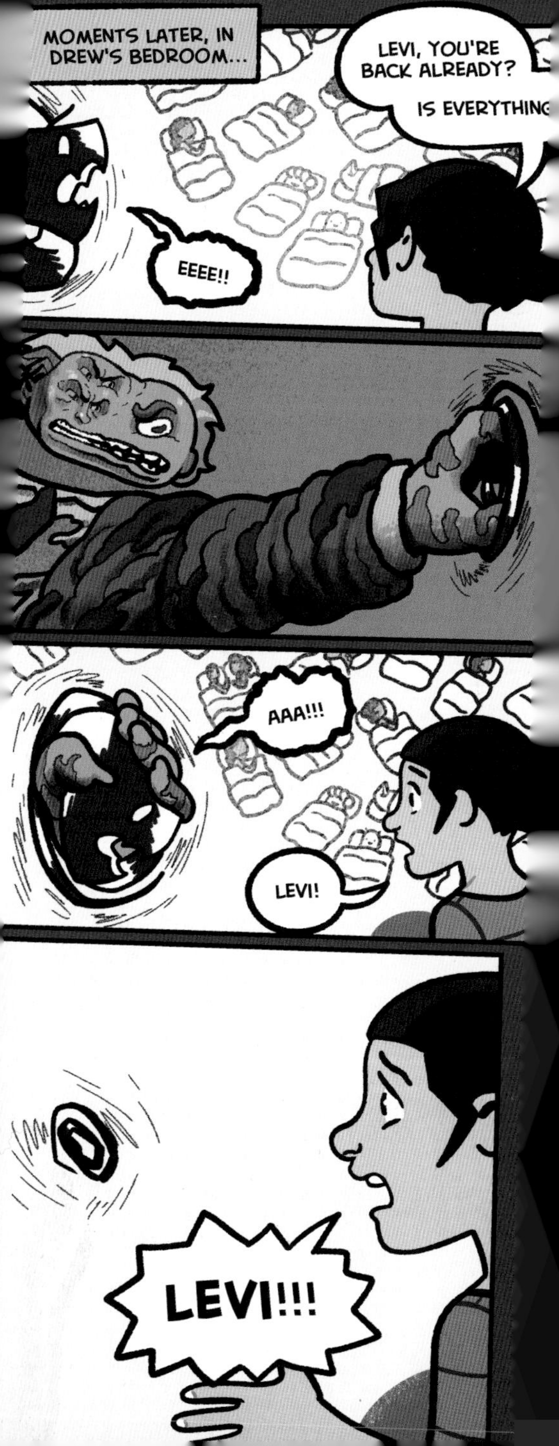
MOMENTS LATER, IN DREW'S BEDROOM...
LEVI, YOU'RE BACK ALREADY?
IS EVERYTHING
EEEE!!
AAA!!!
LEVI!
LEVI!!!

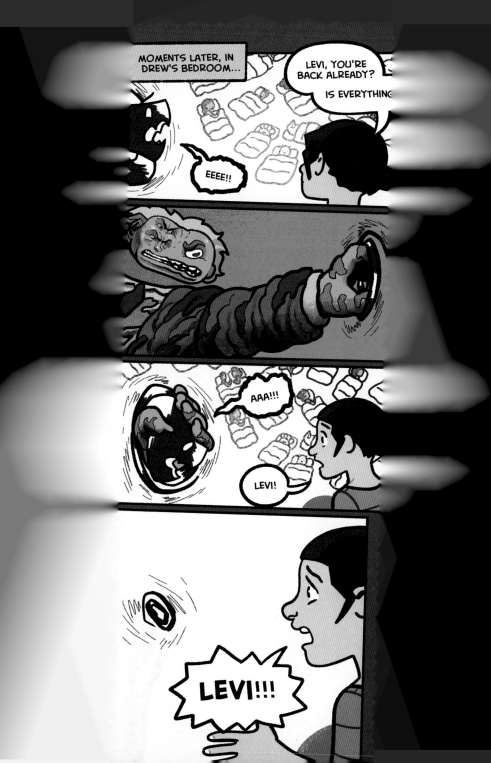

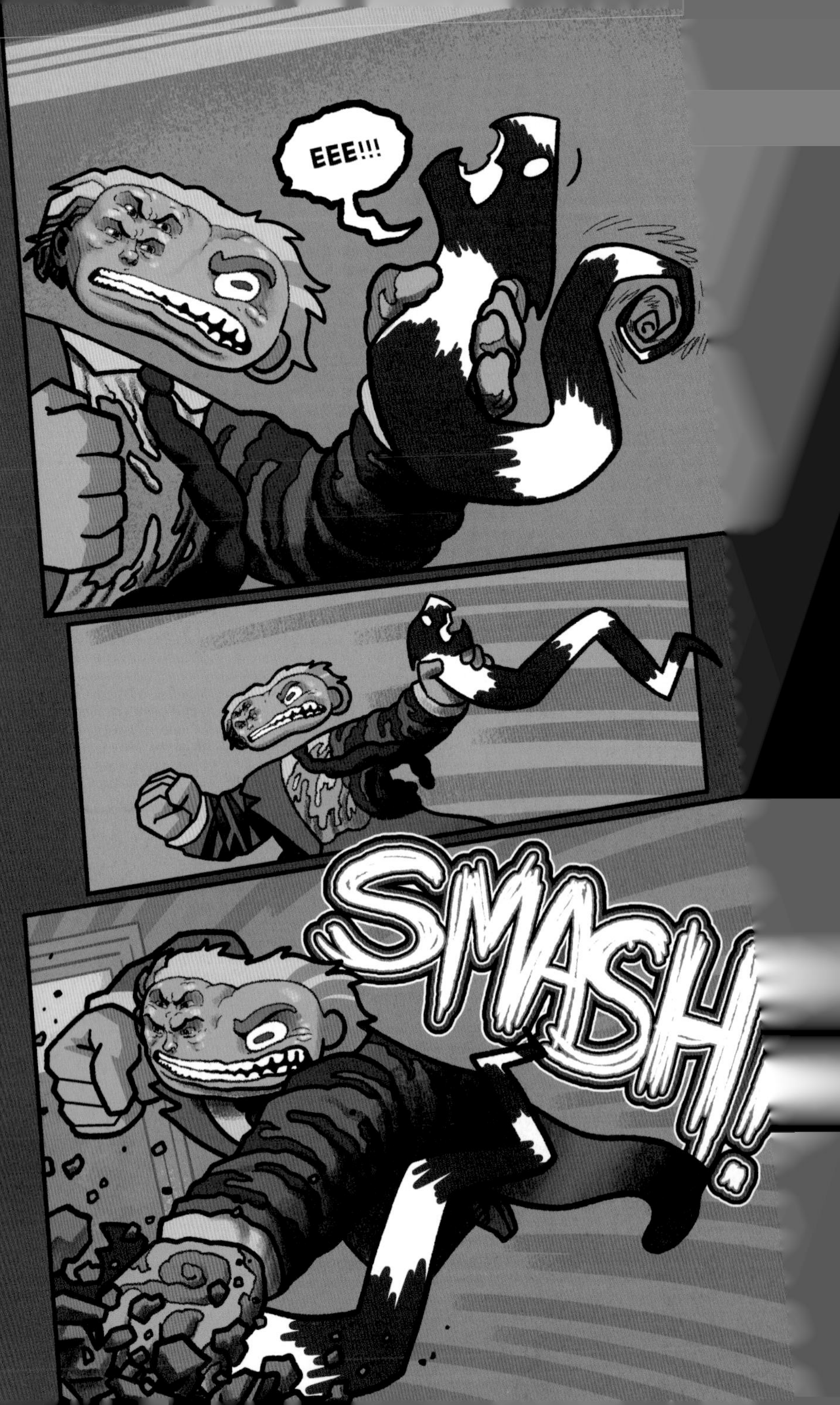
EEE!!!
SMASH!!

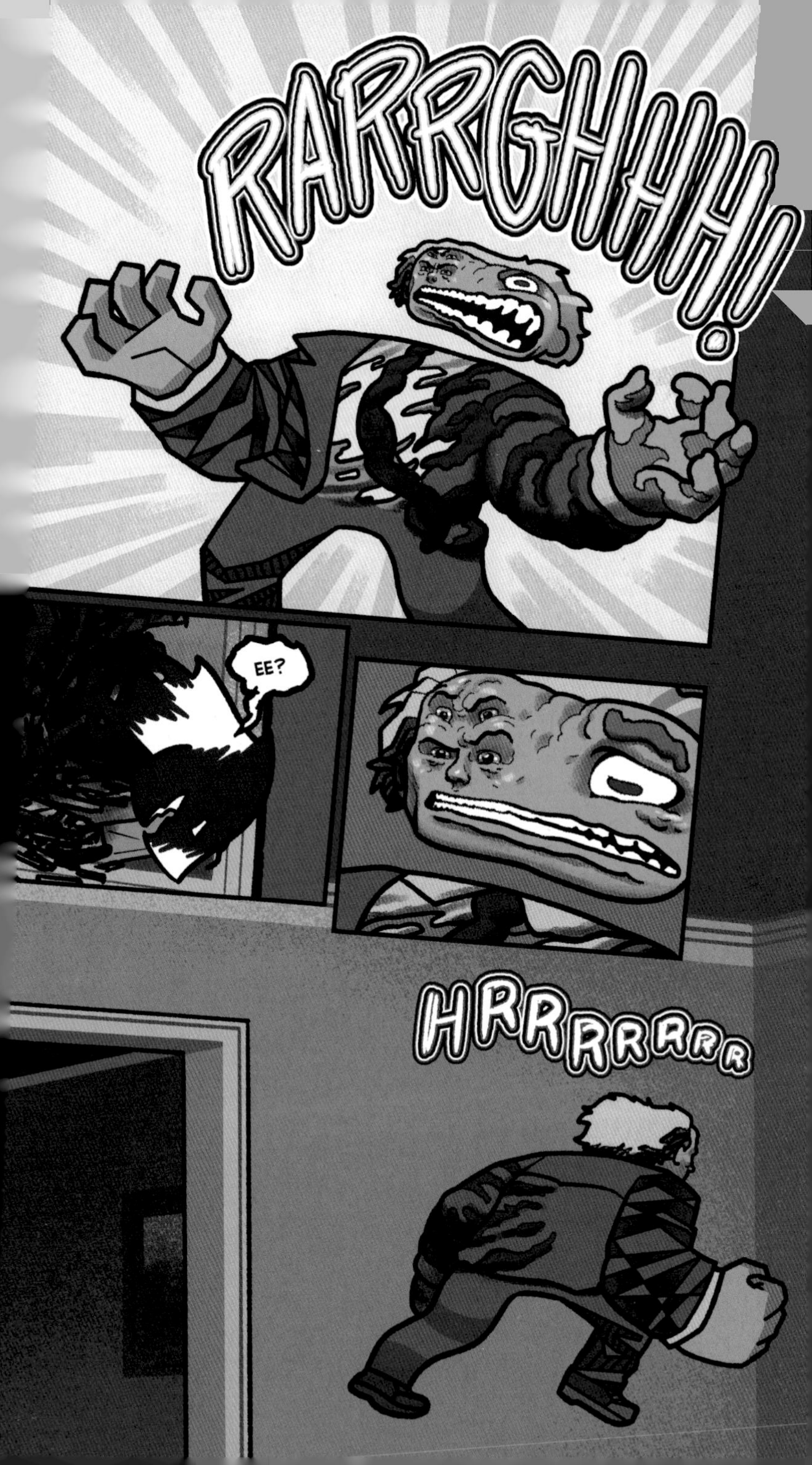
RARRGHHHH!
EE?
HRRRRRRR

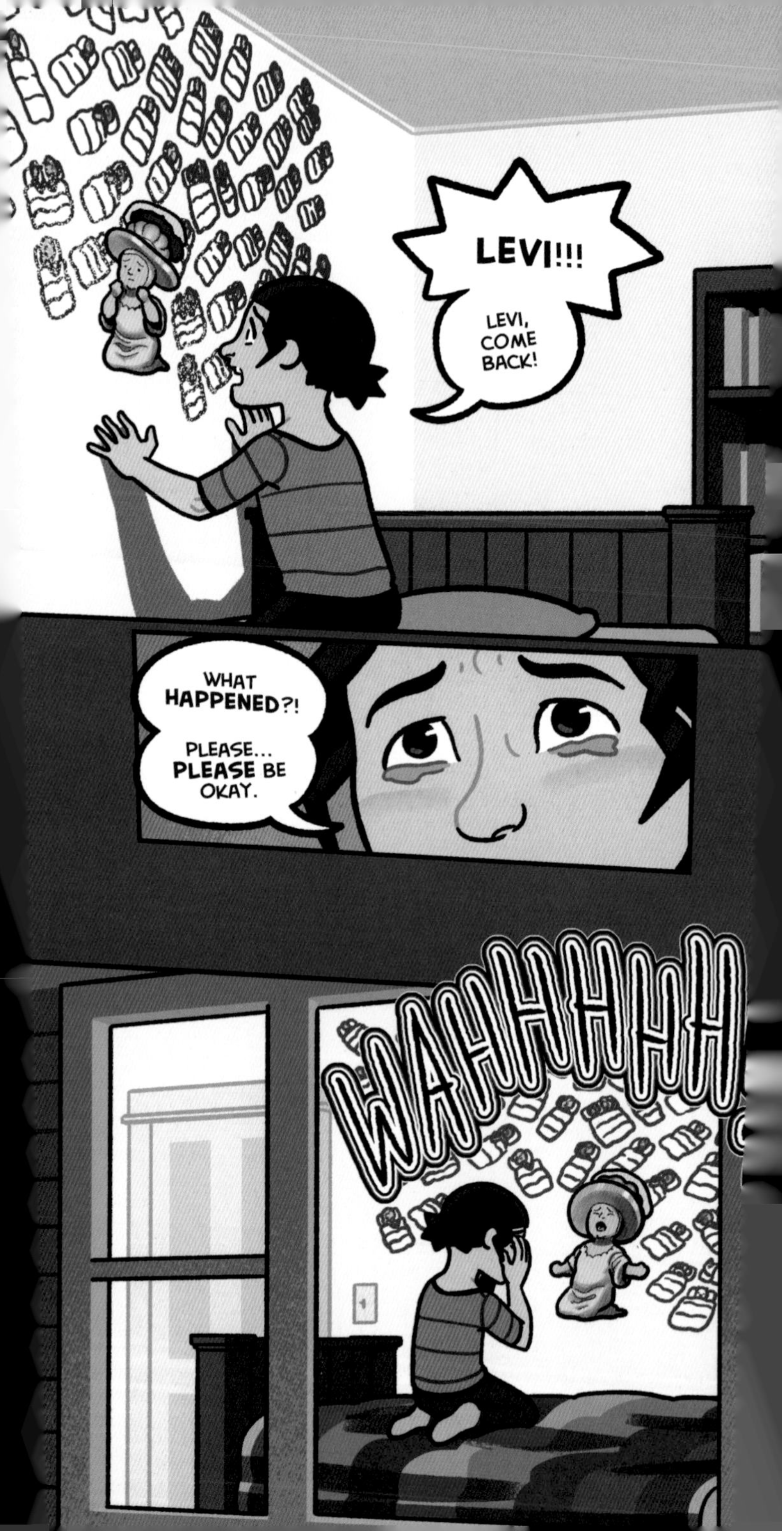
LEVI!!!
LEVI, COME BACK!
WHAT HAPPENED?!
PLEASE... PLEASE BE OKAY.
WAHHHHHH

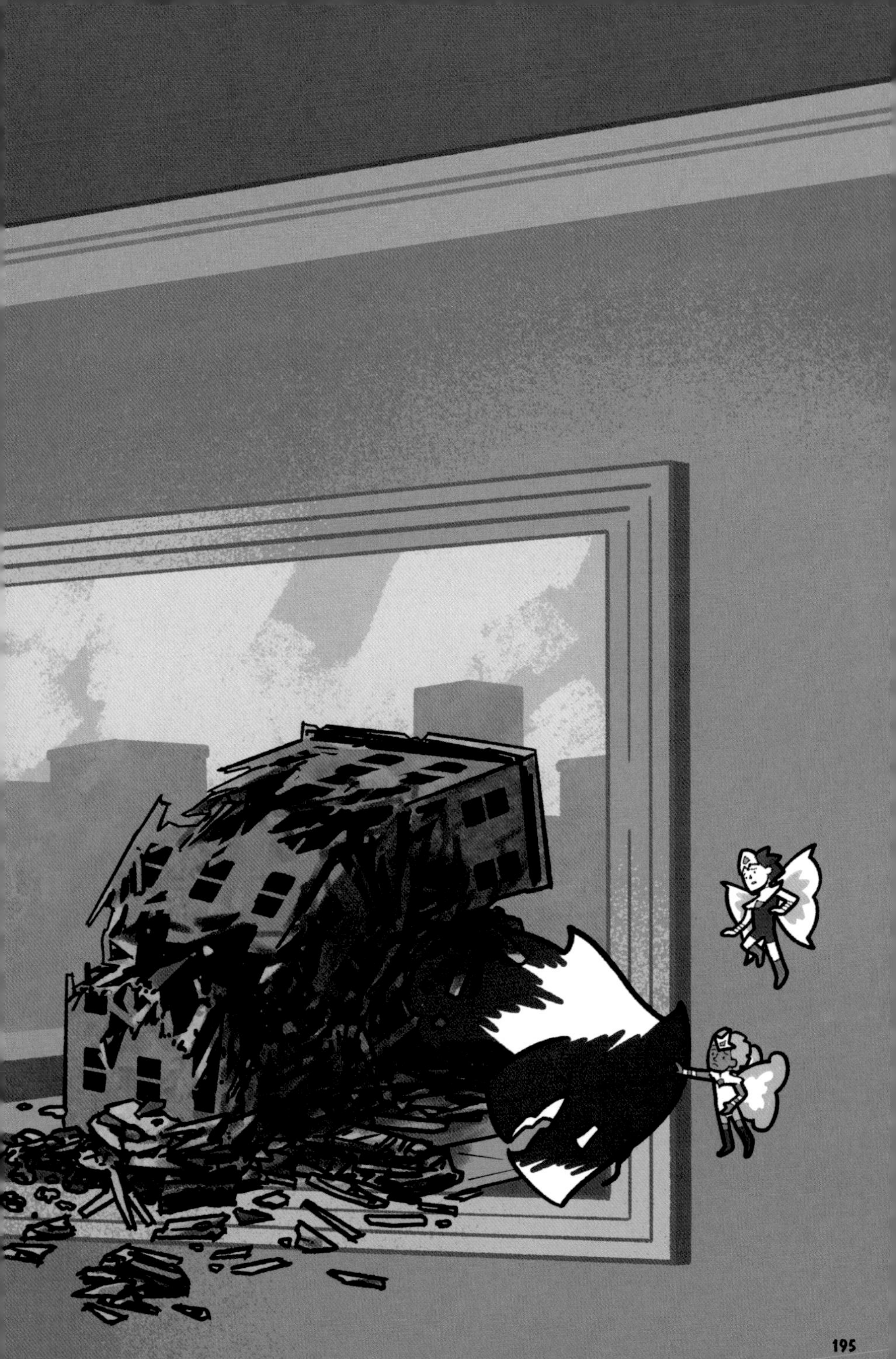

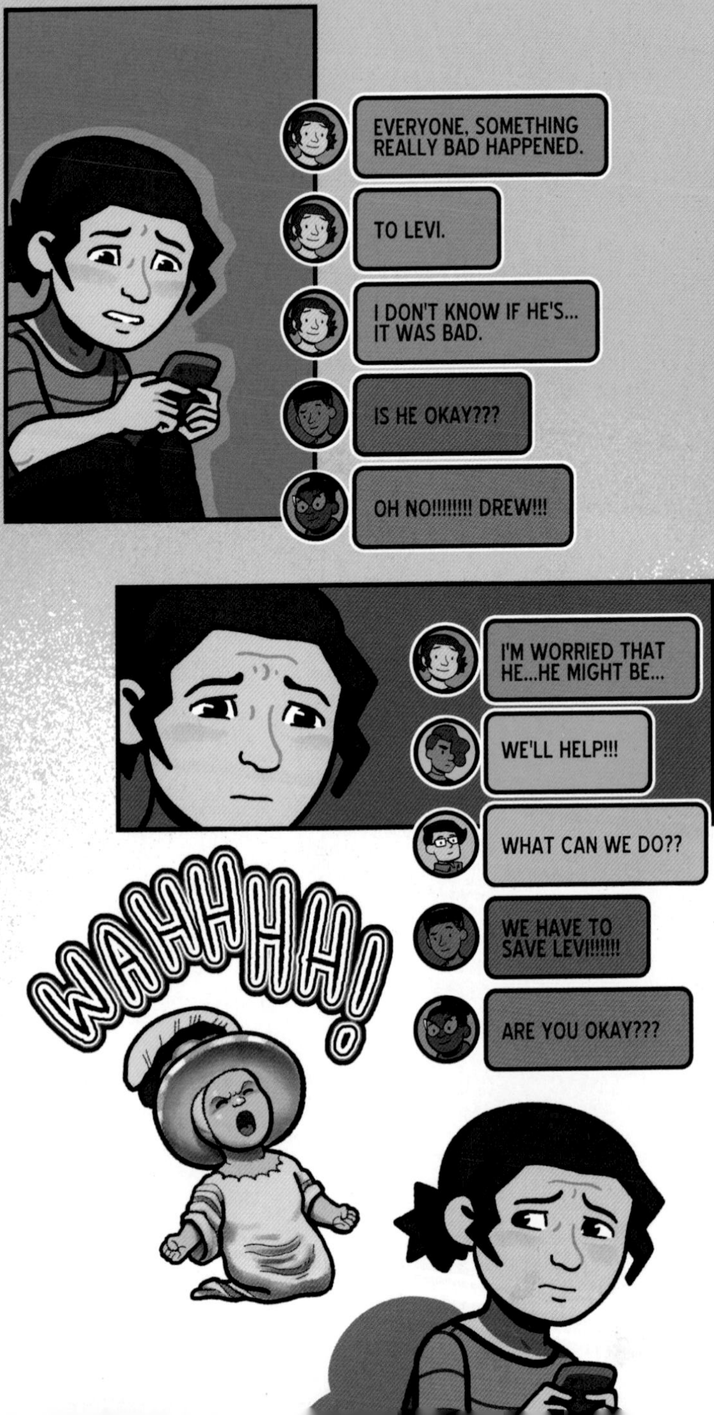
EVERYONE, SOMETHING REALLY BAD HAPPENED.
TO LEVI.
I DON'T KNOW IF HE'S... IT WAS BAD.
IS HE OKAY???
OH NO!!!!!!!! DREW!!!
I'M WORRIED THAT HE...HE MIGHT BE...
WE'LL HELP!!!
WHAT CAN WE DO??
WE HAVE TO SAVE LEVI!!!!!!
ARE YOU OKAY???
WAHHHH!

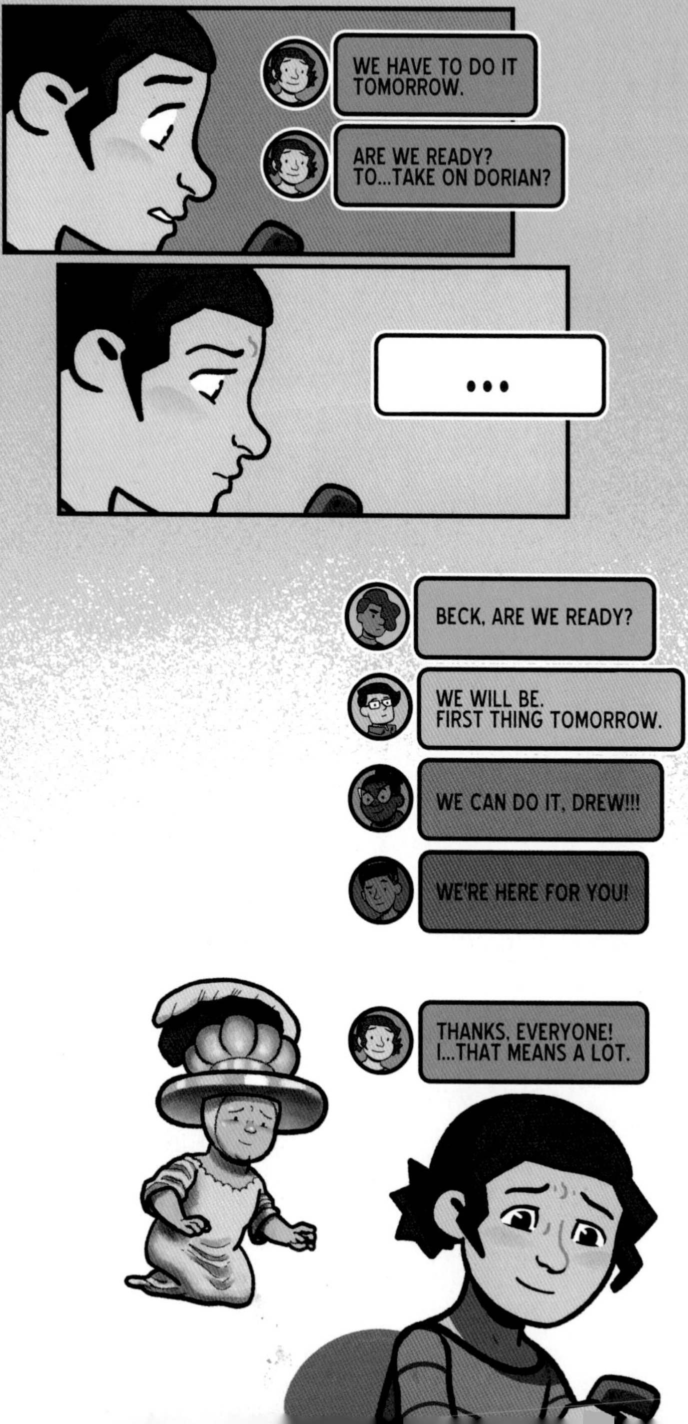
WE HAVE TO DO IT TOMORROW.
ARE WE READY? TO...TAKE ON DORIAN?
...
BECK, ARE WE READY?
WE WILL BE. FIRST THING TOMORROW.
WE CAN DO IT, DREW!!!
WE'RE HERE FOR YOU!
THANKS, EVERYONE! I...THAT MEANS A LOT.

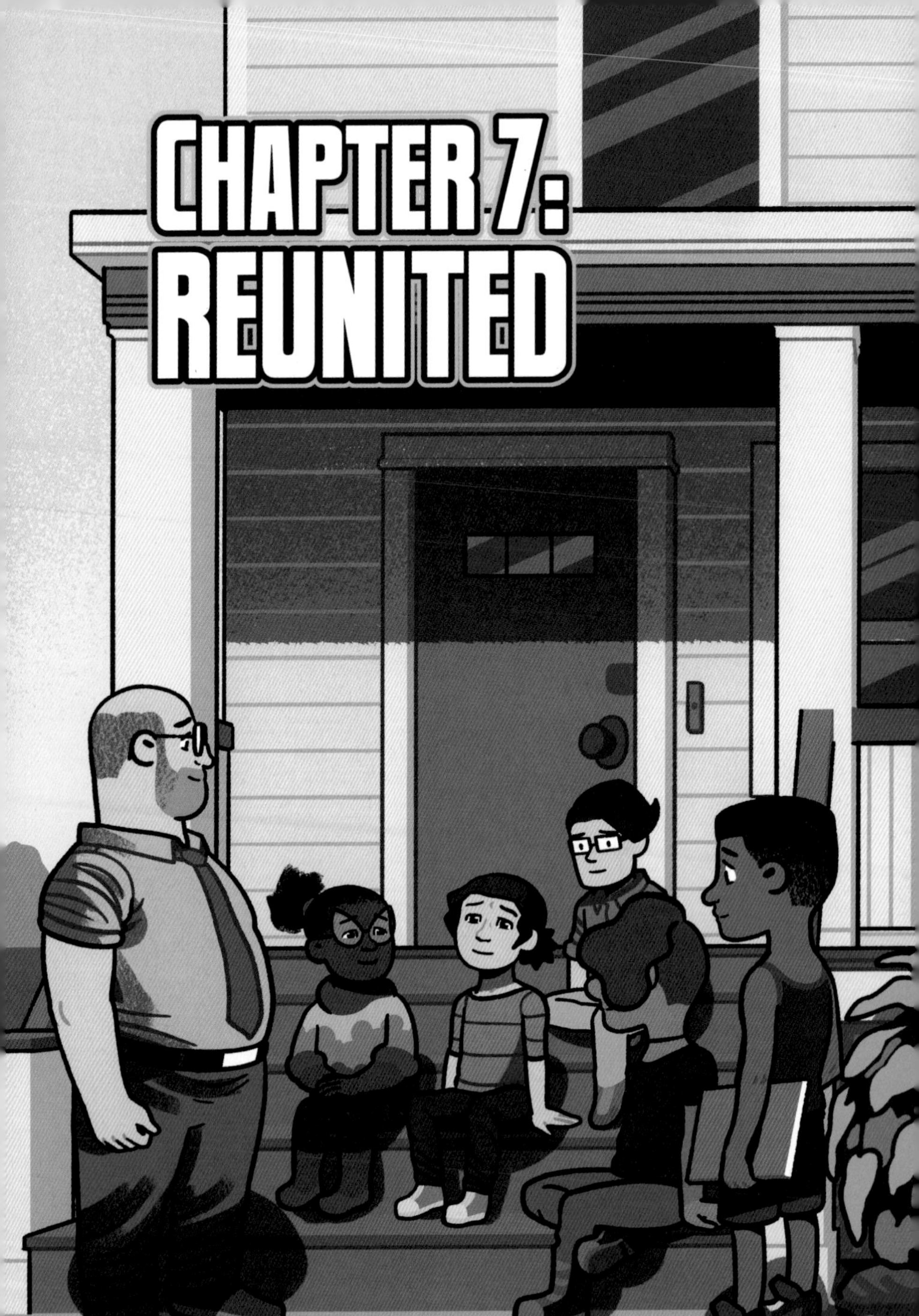
CHAPTER 7:
REUNITED

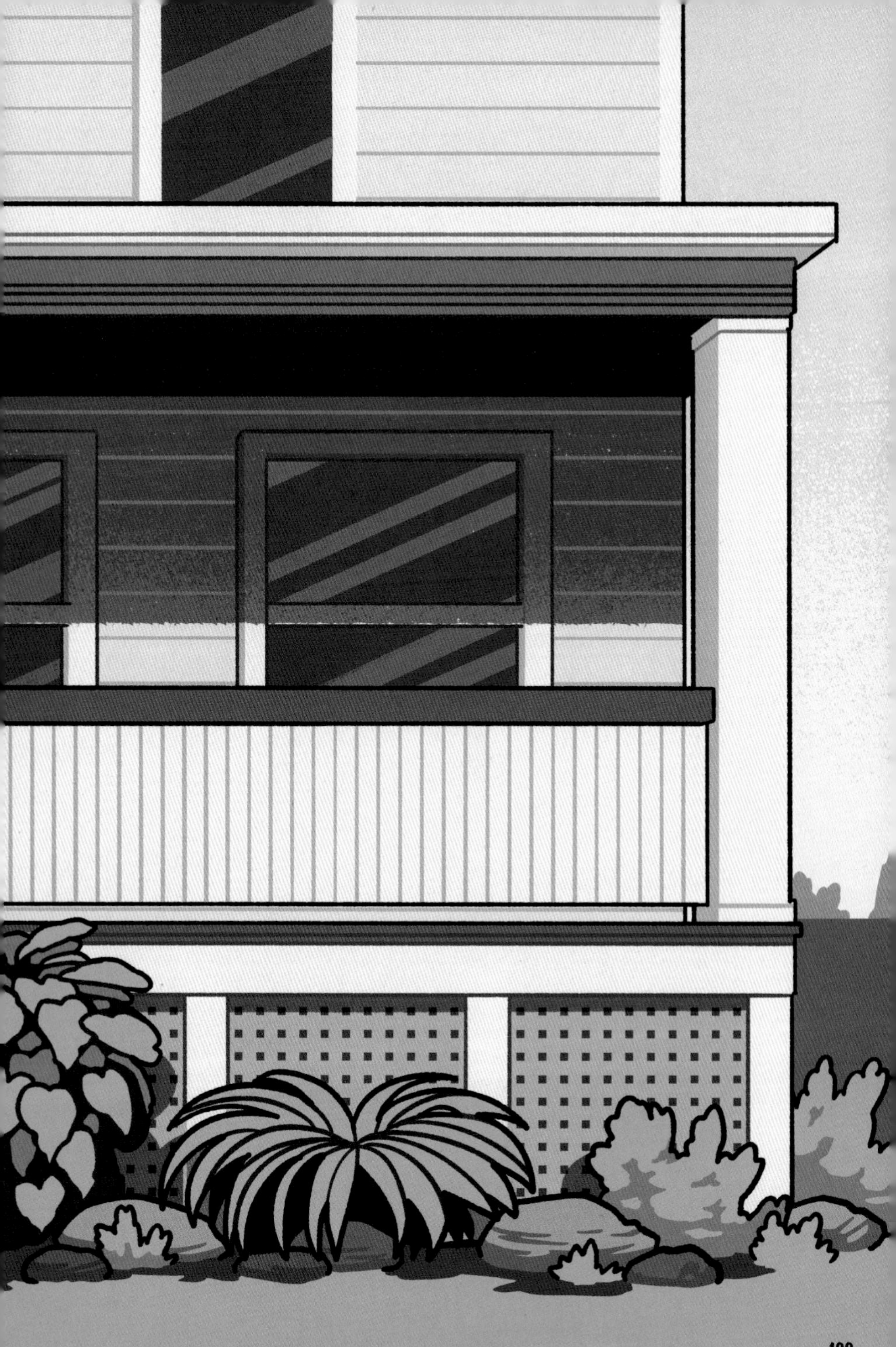

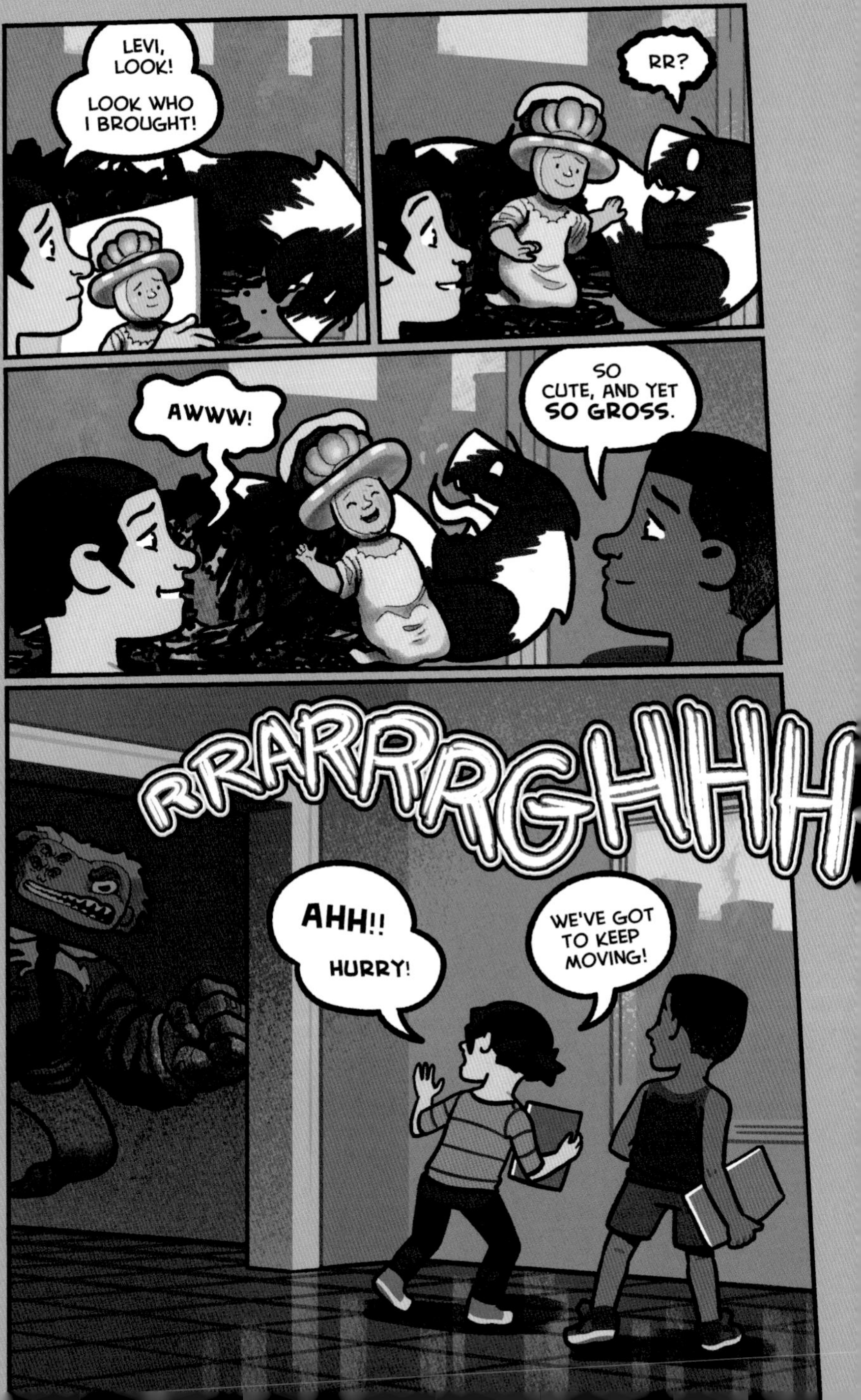
LEVI, LOOK!
LOOK WHO I BROUGHT!
RR?
AWWW!
SO CUTE, AND YET SO GROSS.
RRARRRRGHHH
AHH!! HURRY!
WE'VE GOT TO KEEP MOVING!

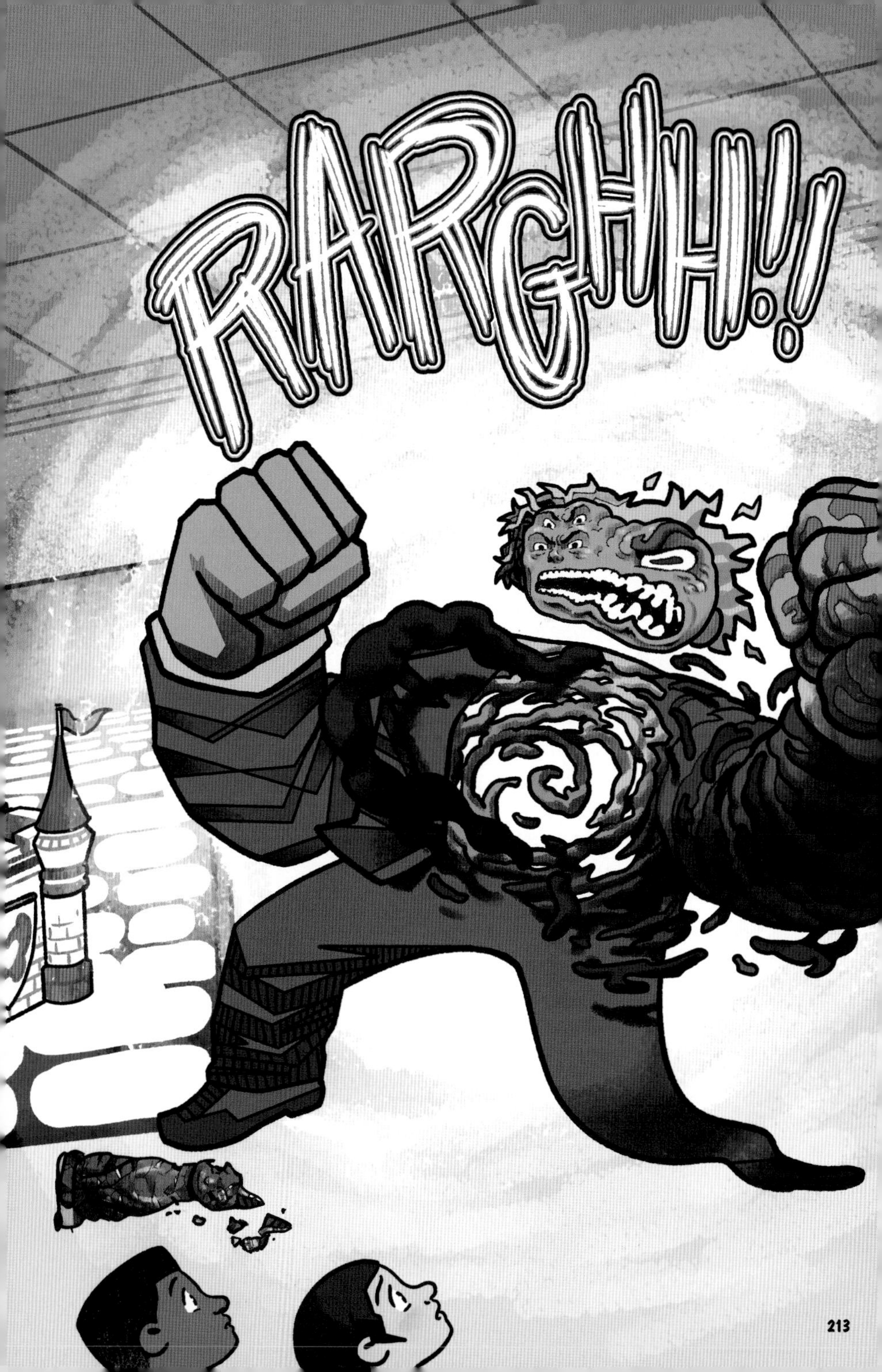
RARGHH!!

216

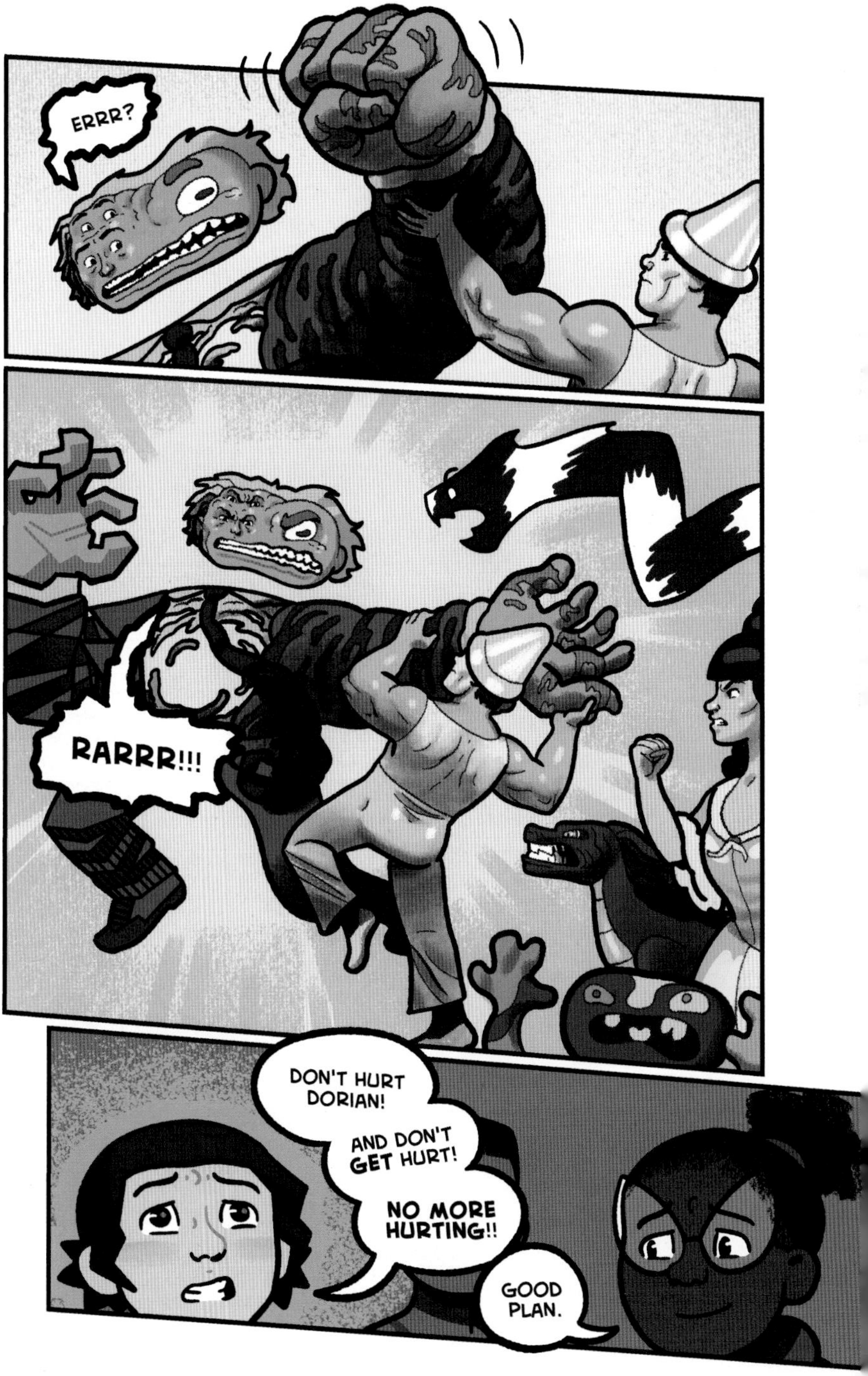
ERRR?
RARRR!!!
DON'T HURT DORIAN!
AND DON'T GET HURT!
NO MORE HURTING!!
GOOD PLAN.

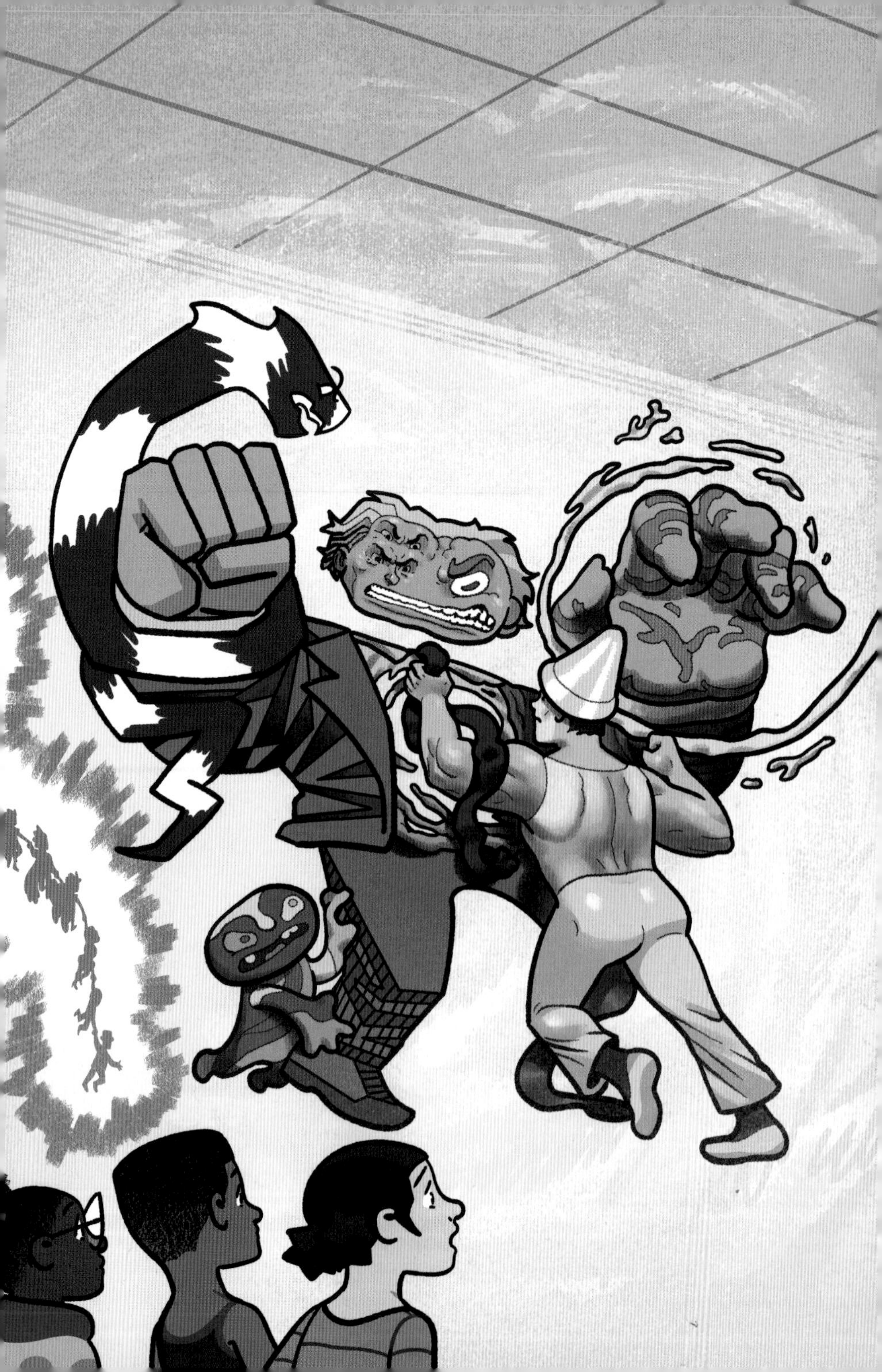

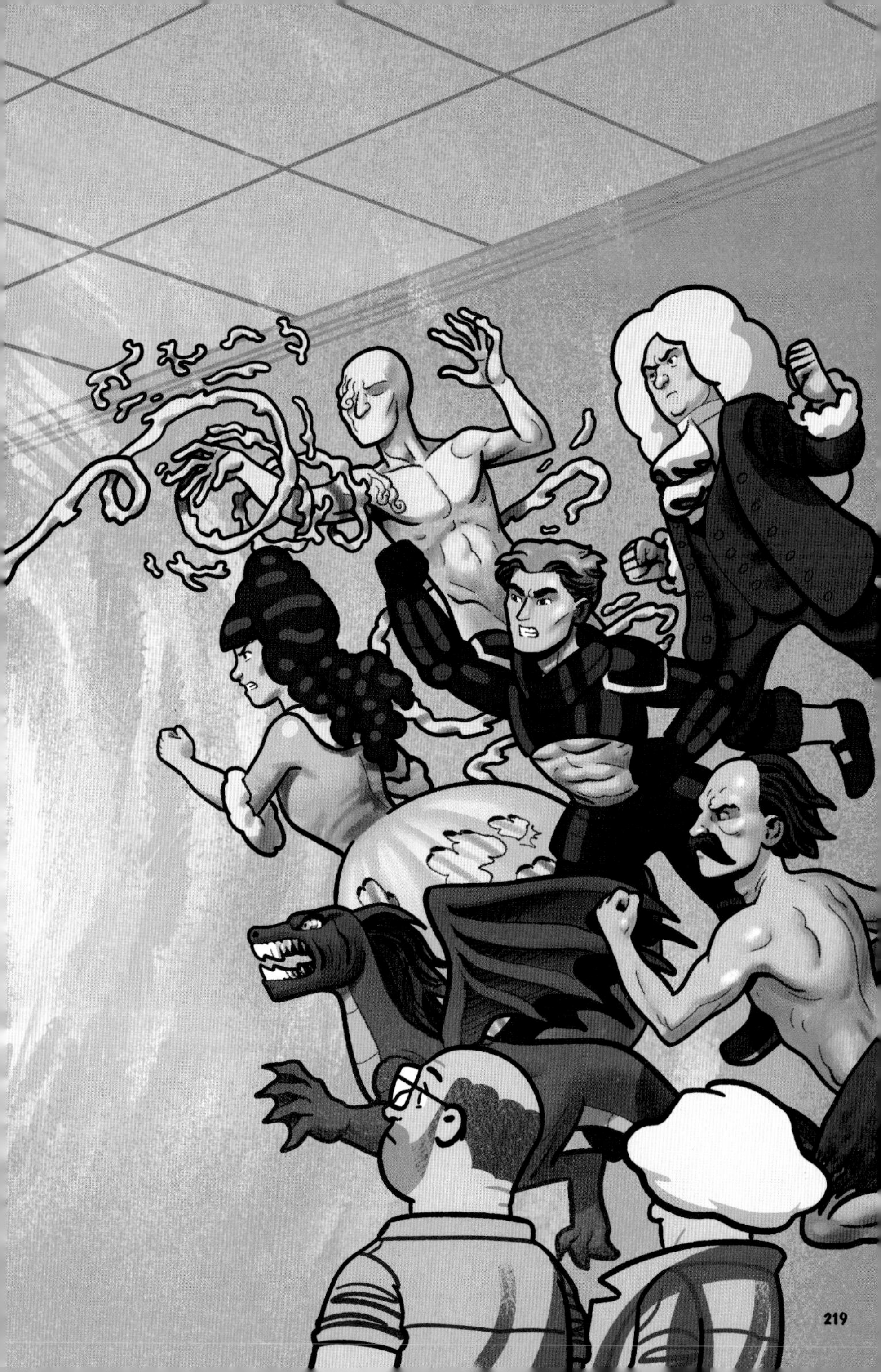

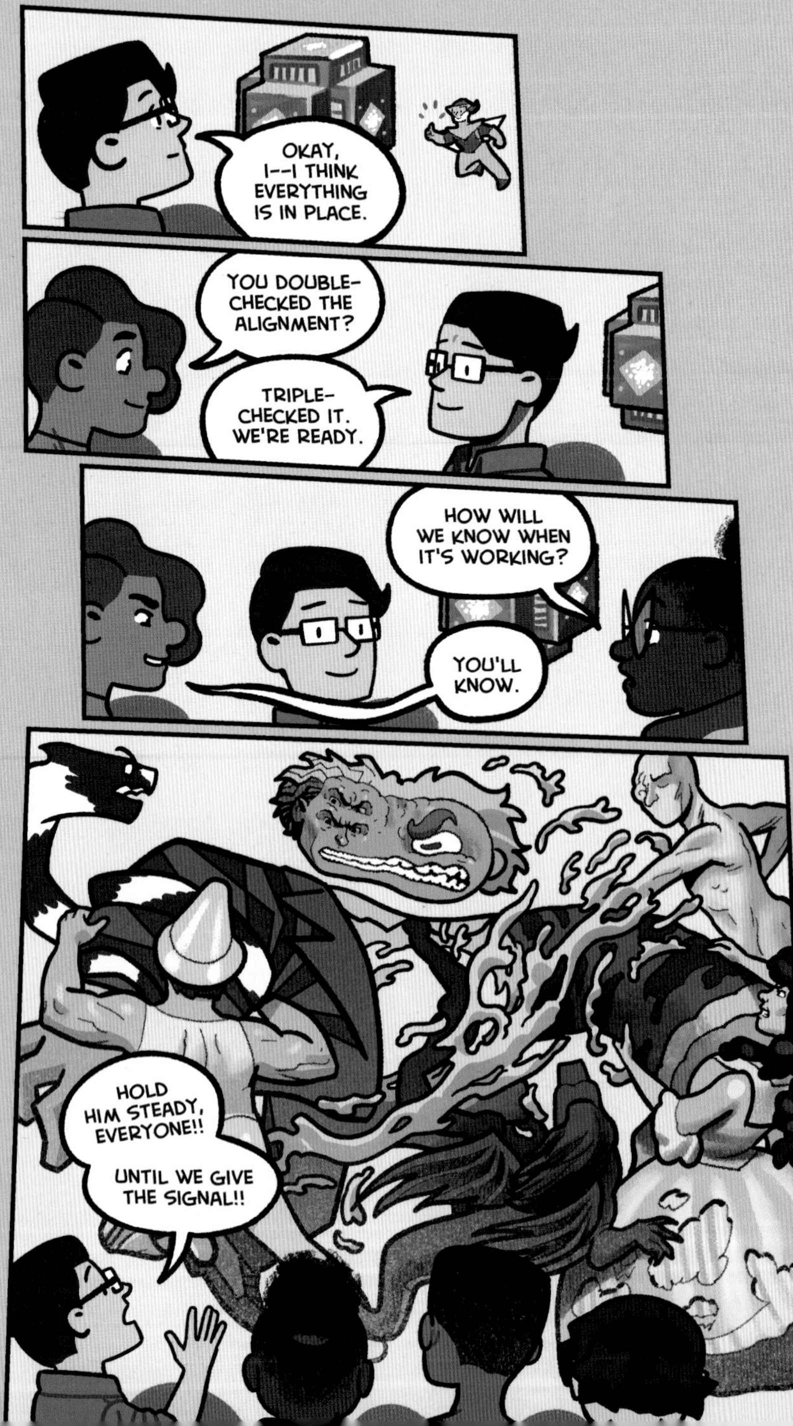
OKAY, I--I THINK EVERYTHING IS IN PLACE.
YOU DOUBLE-CHECKED THE ALIGNMENT?
TRIPLE-CHECKED IT. WE'RE READY.
HOW WILL WE KNOW WHEN IT'S WORKING?
YOU'LL KNOW.
HOLD HIM STEADY, EVERYONE!!
UNTIL WE GIVE THE SIGNAL!!

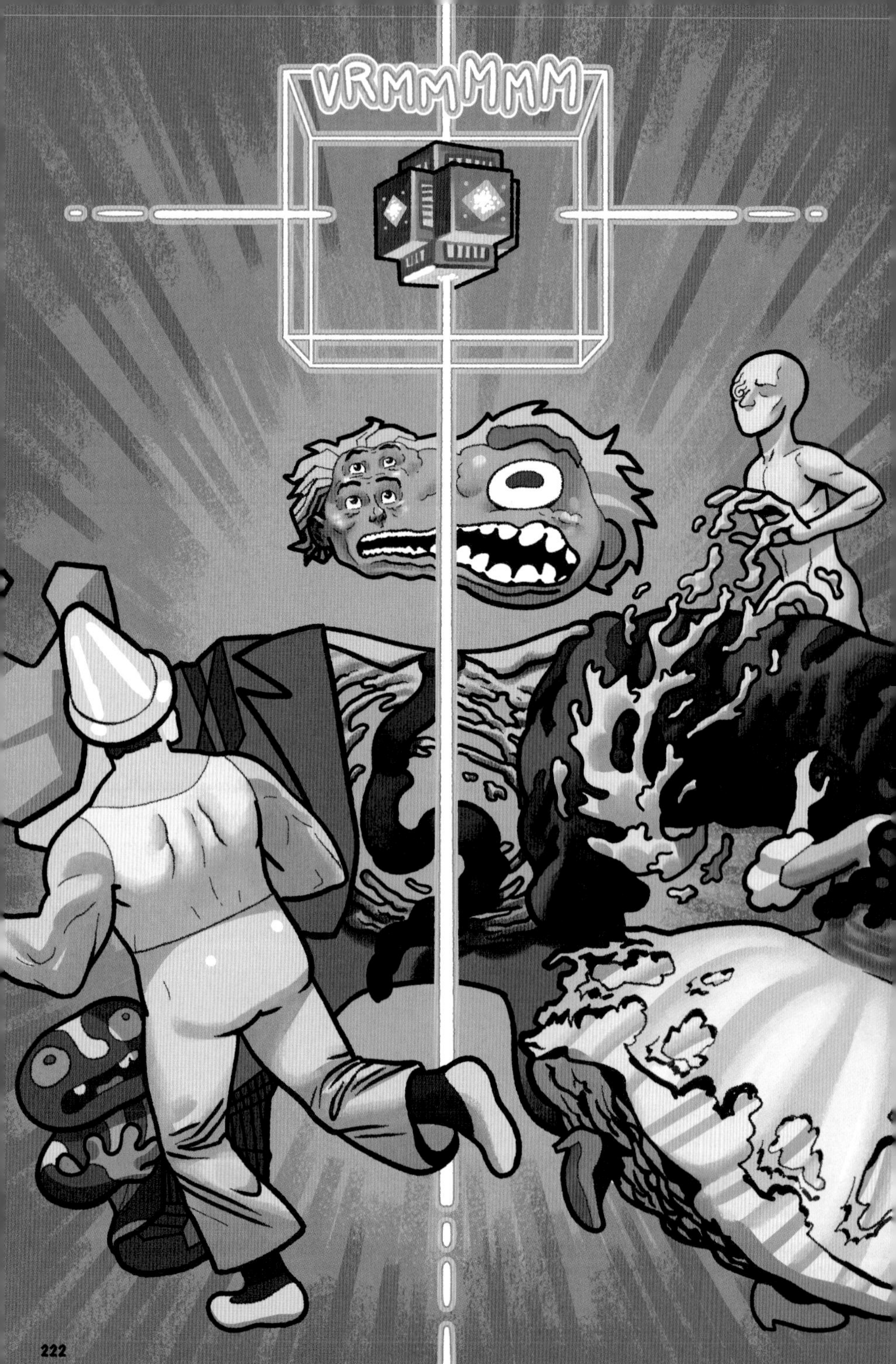
VRMMMMMM

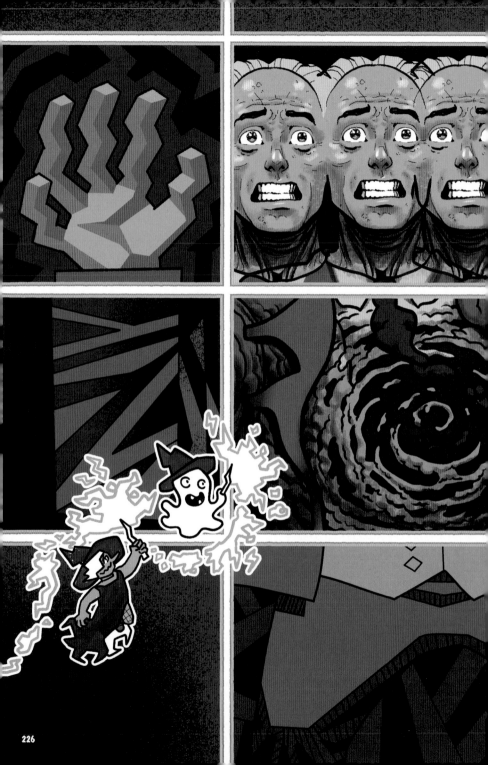

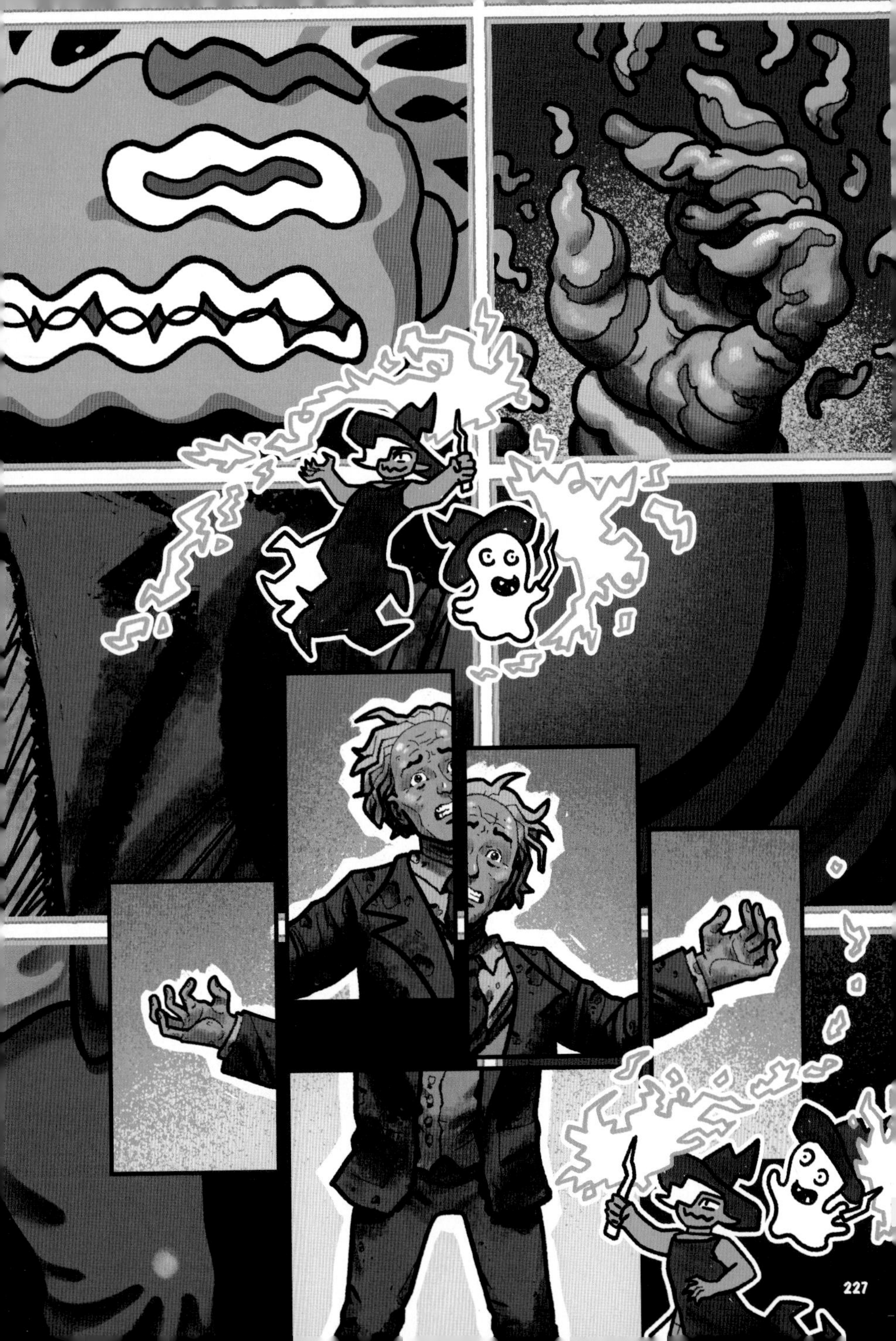

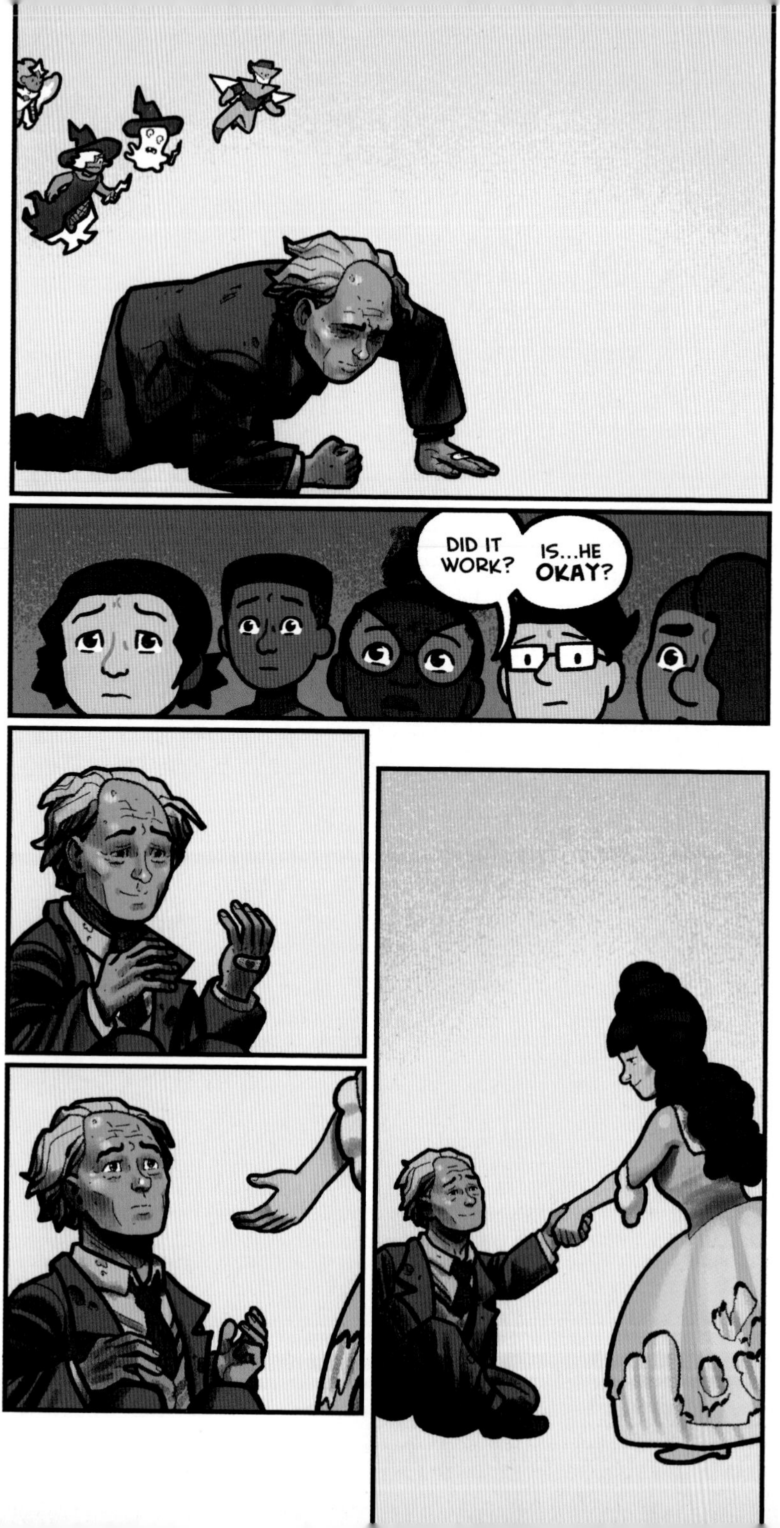
DID IT WORK?
IS...HE OKAY?

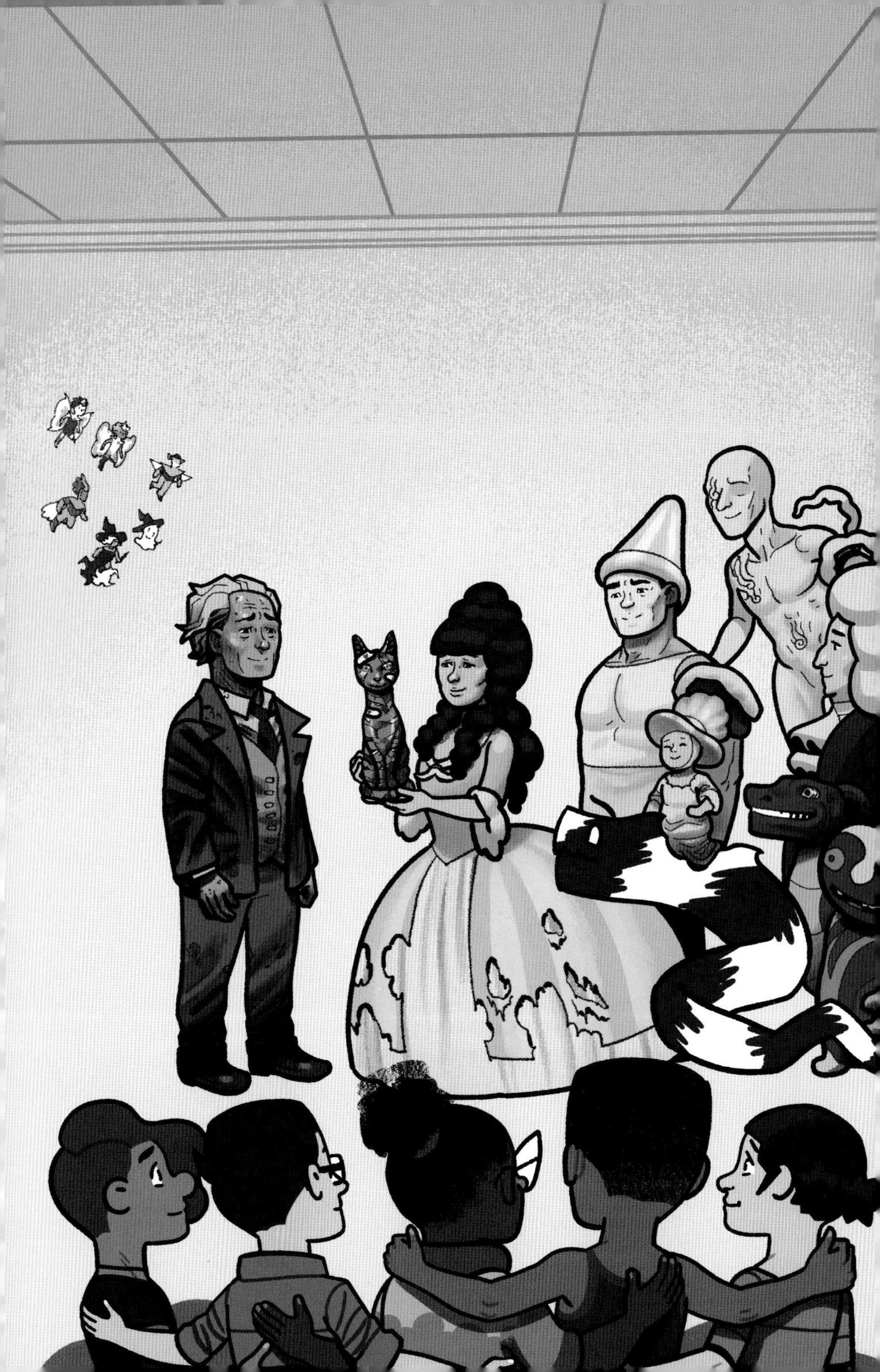

CHAPTER 8: GETTING STARTED

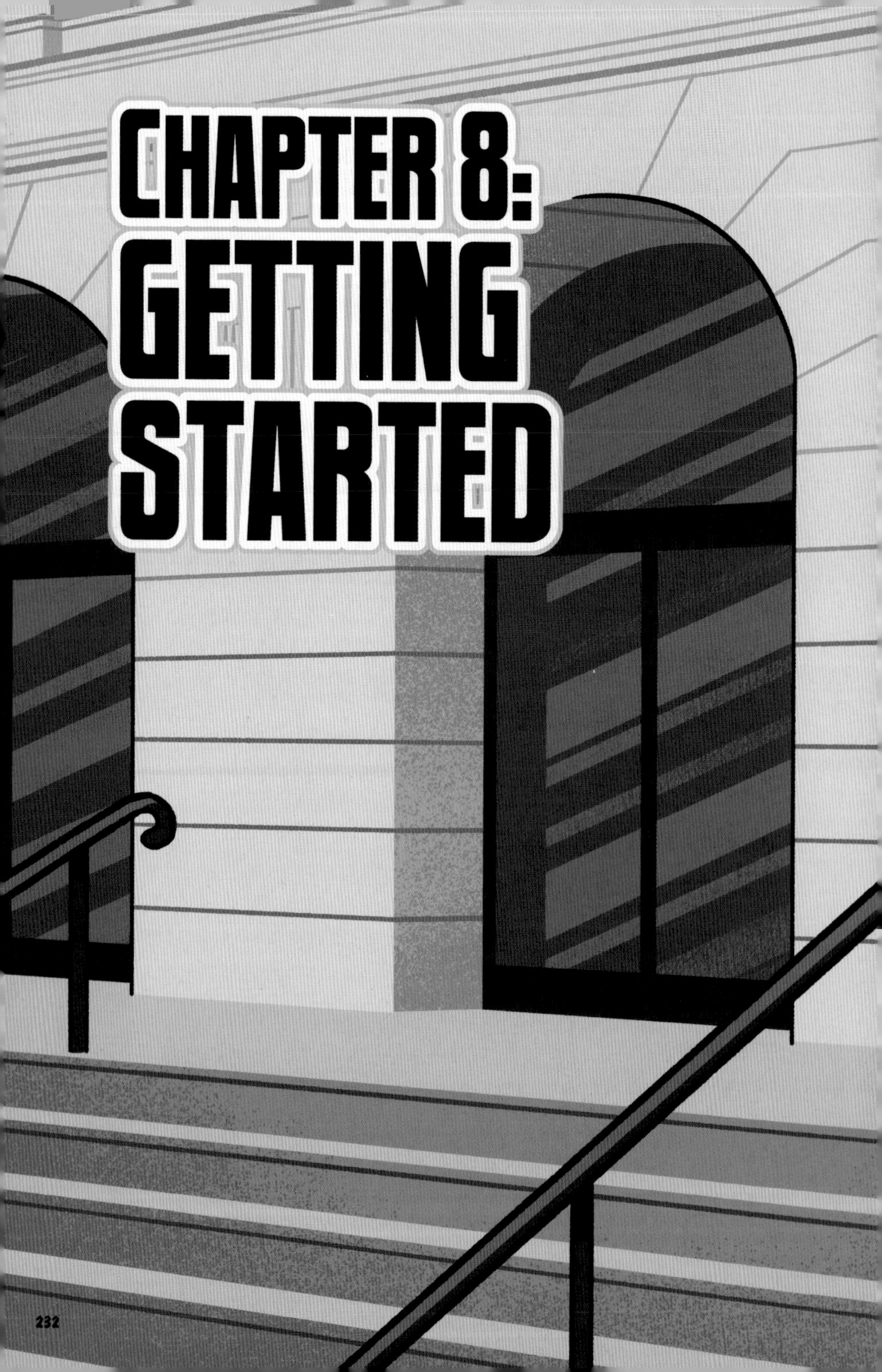

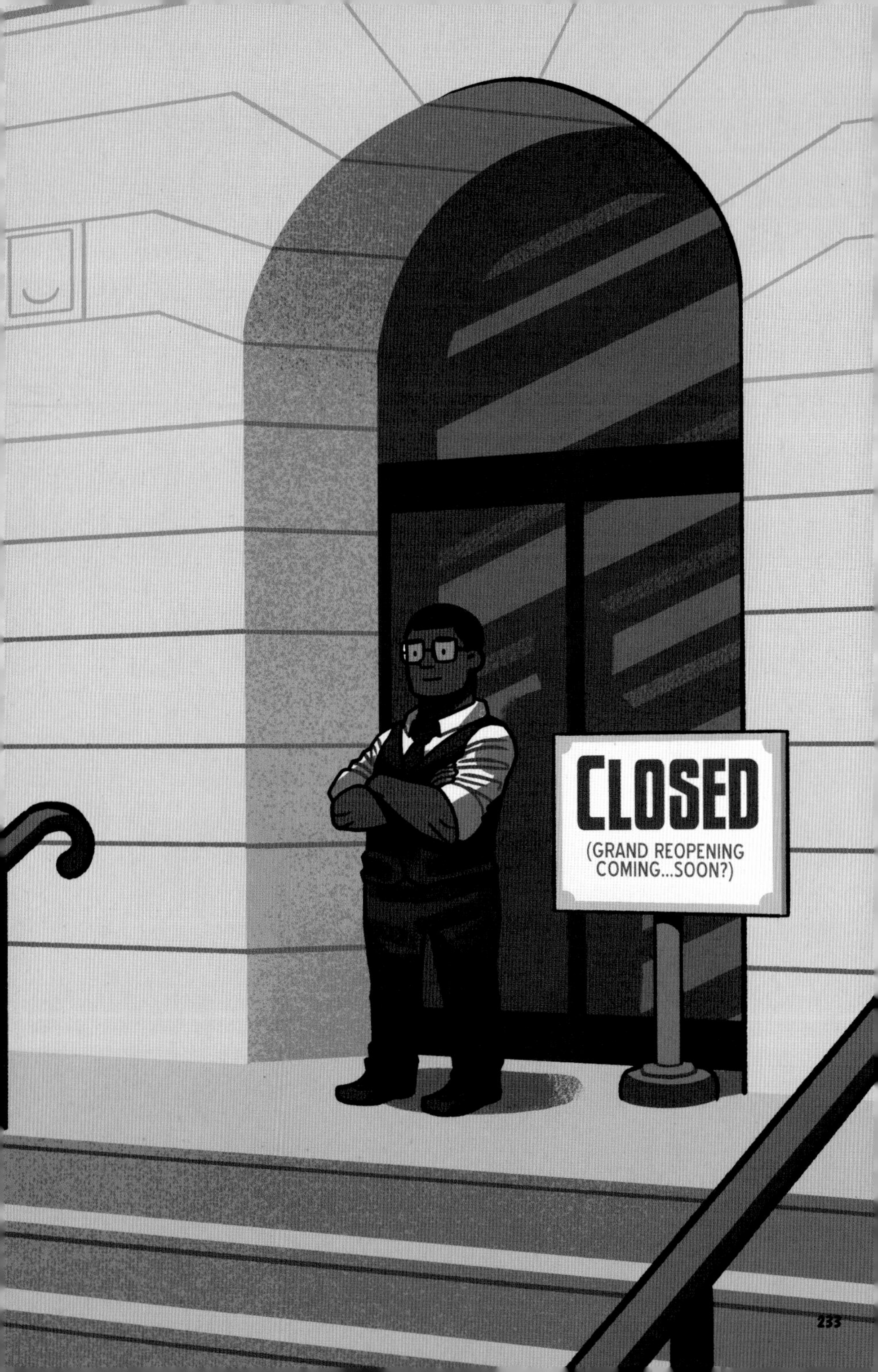
CLOSED
(GRAND REOPENING COMING...SOON?)

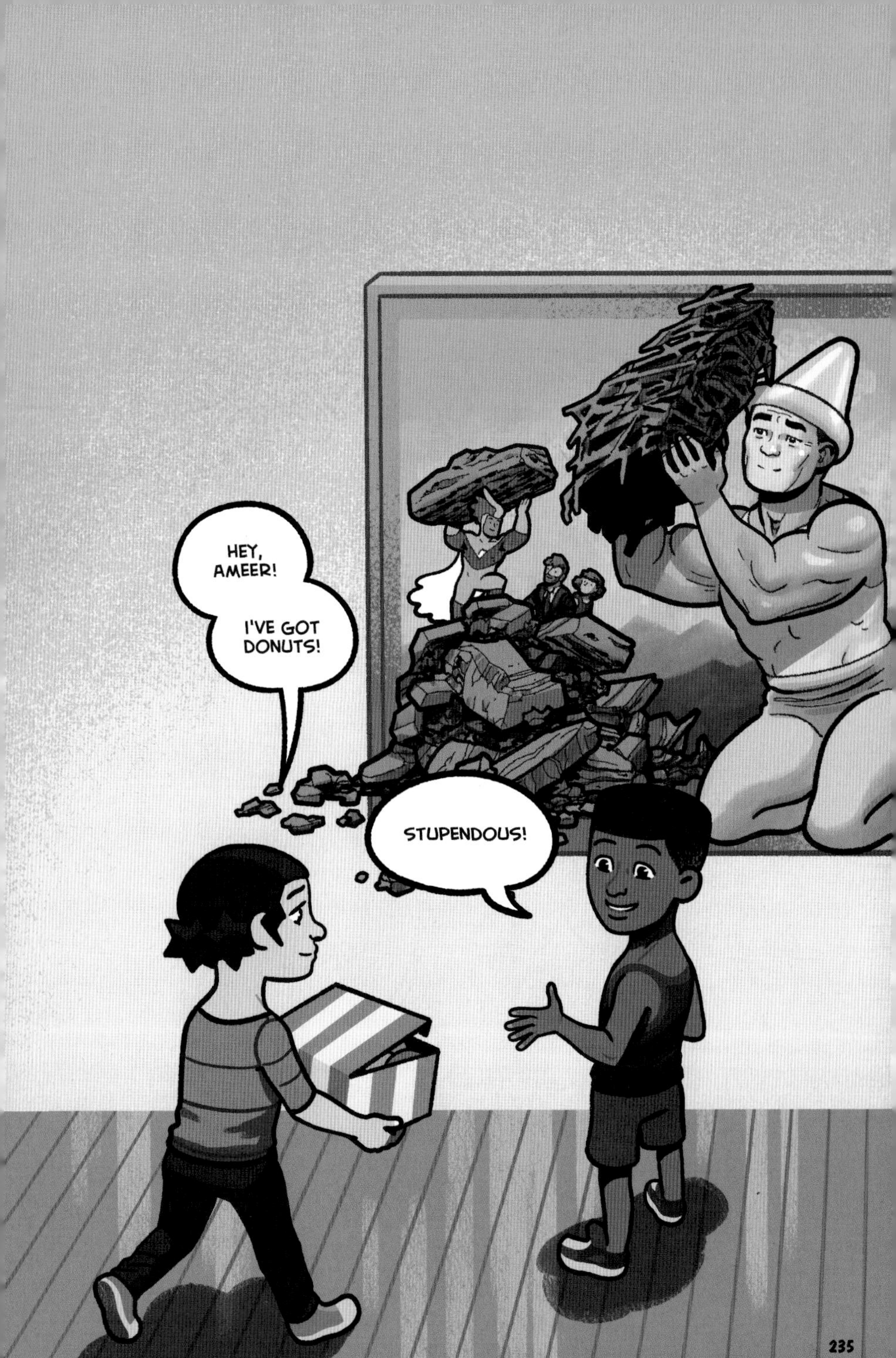
HEY, AMEER!
I'VE GOT DONUTS!
STUPENDOUS!

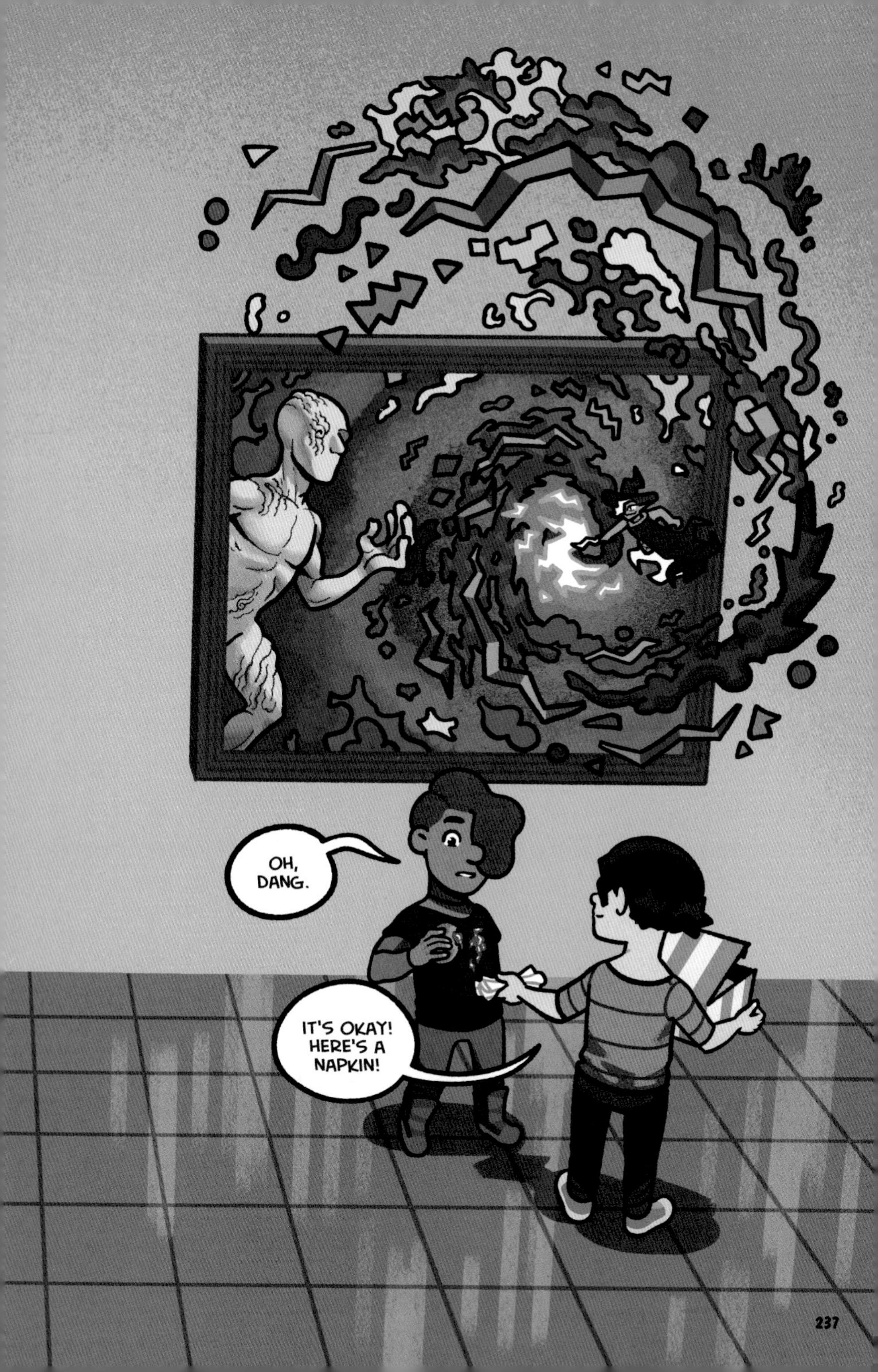
OH, DANG.
IT'S OKAY! HERE'S A NAPKIN!

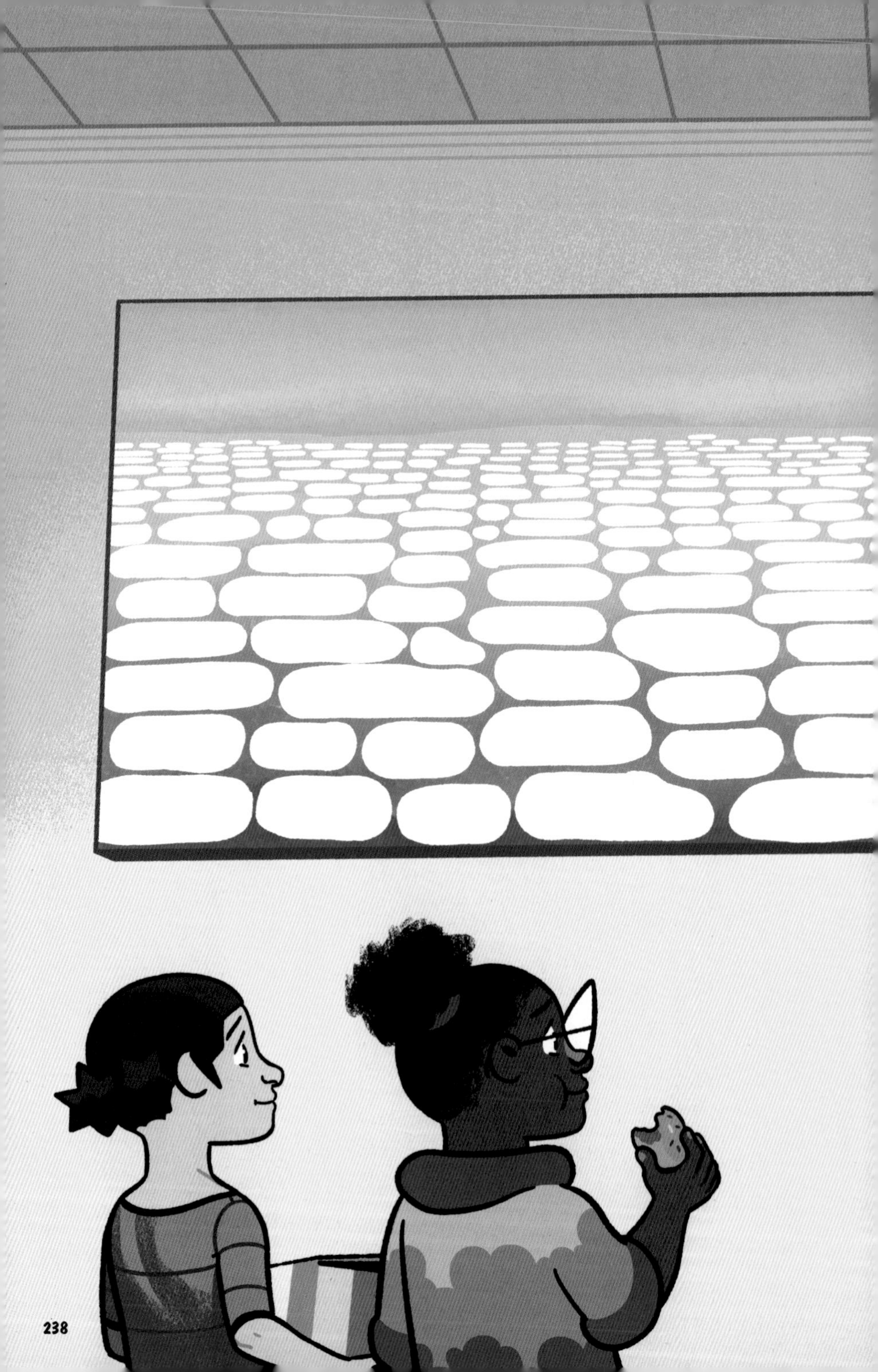

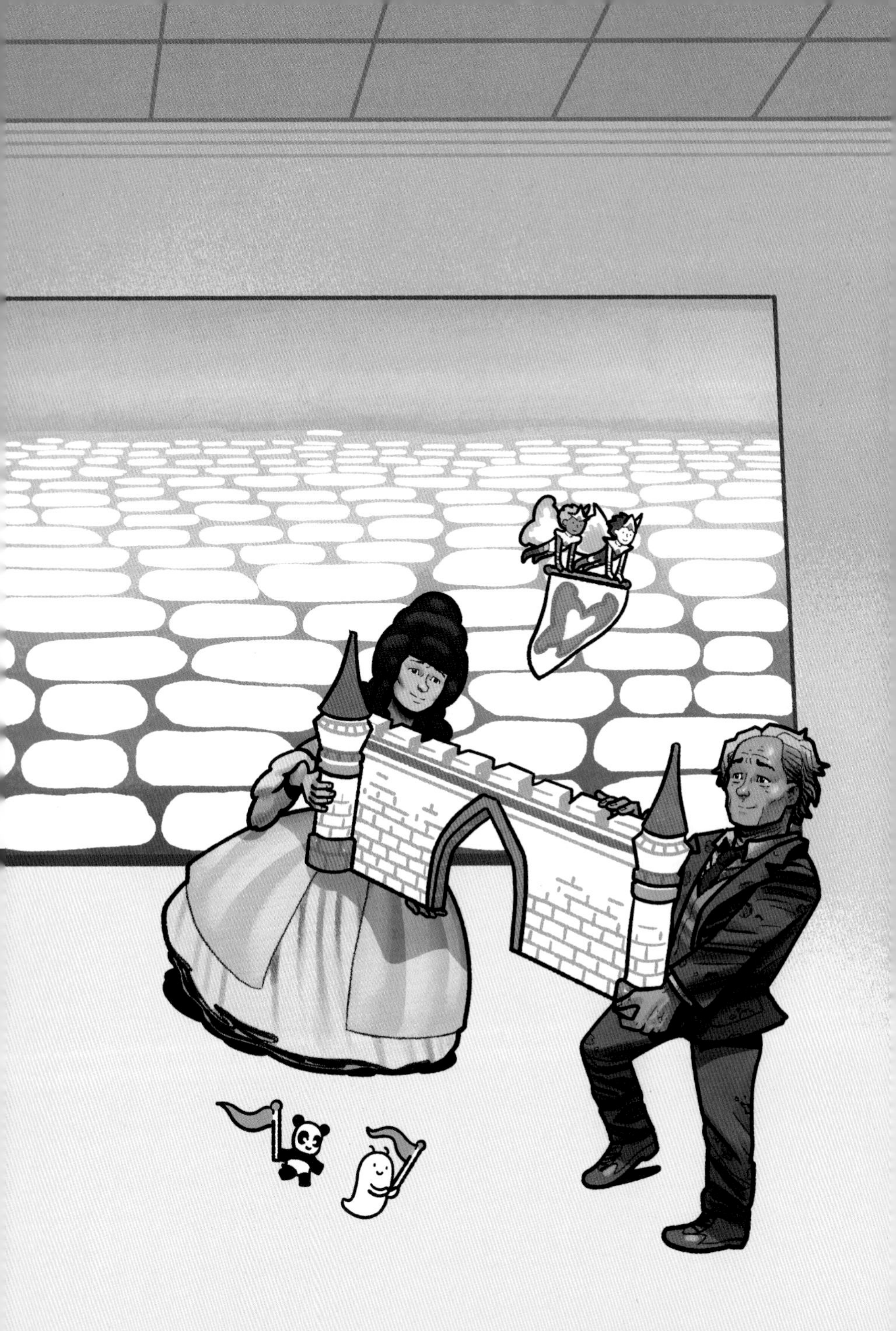

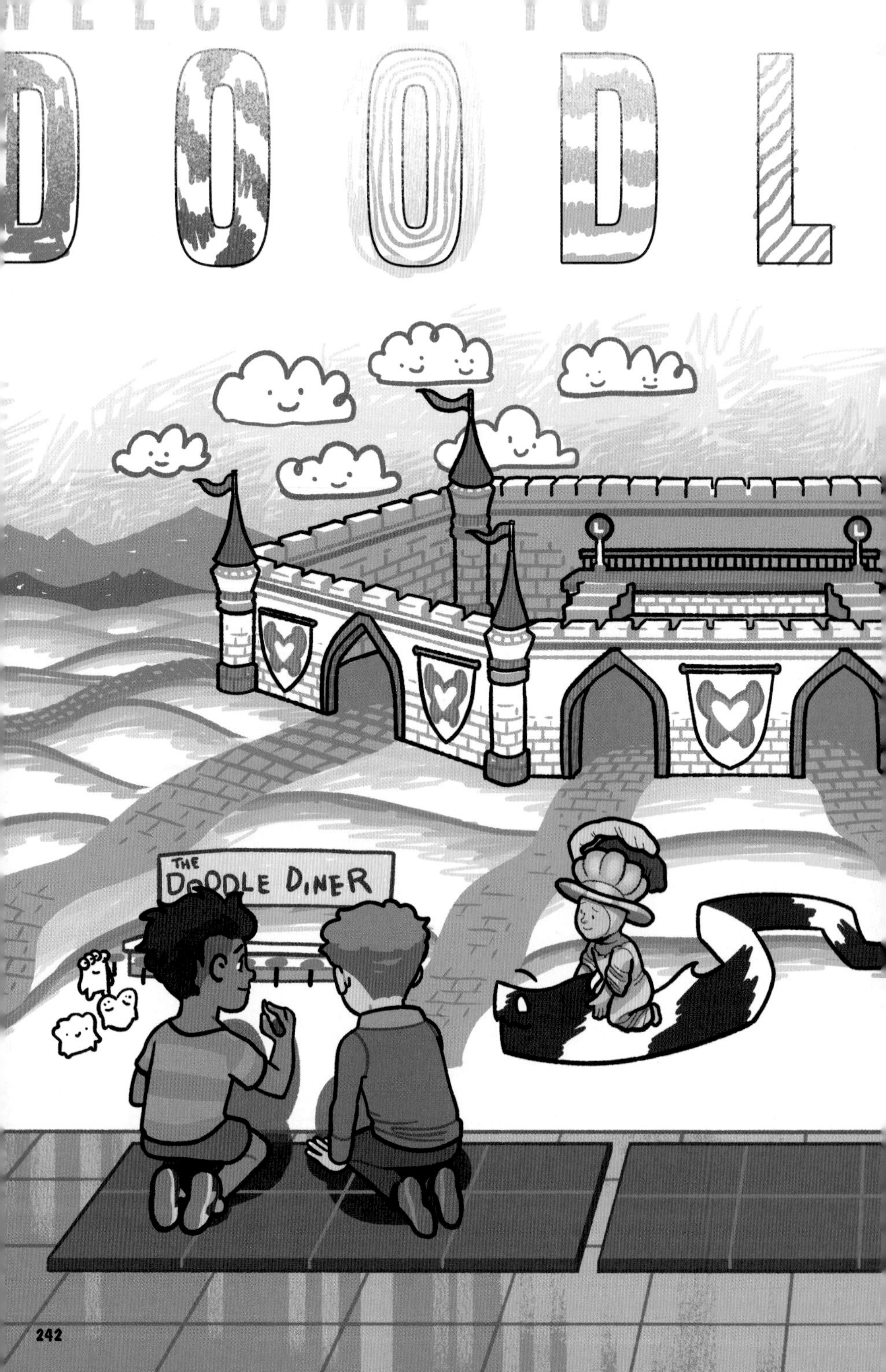
DOODL
THE DOODLE DINER

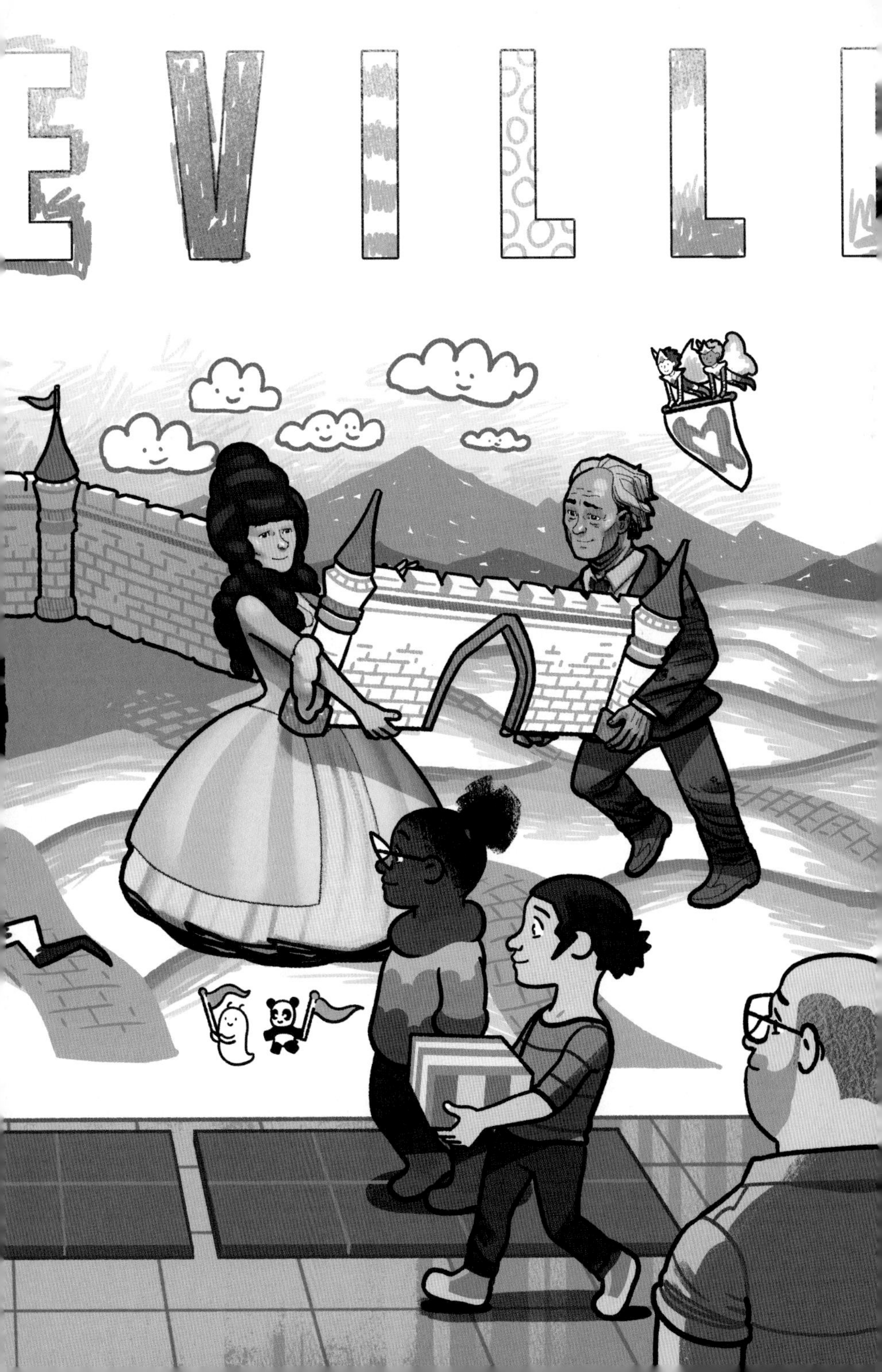
EVILL

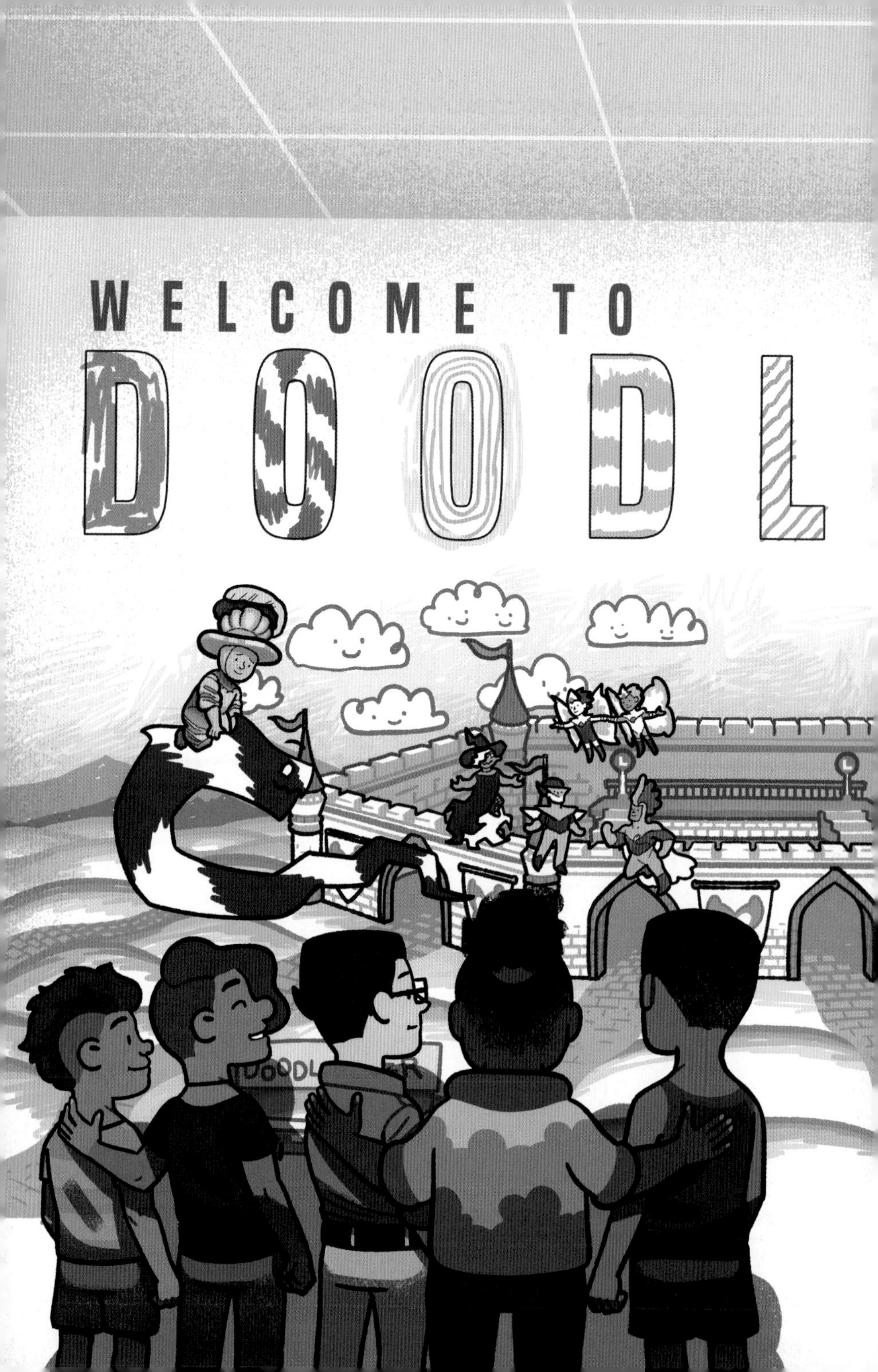
WELCOME TO
DOODL

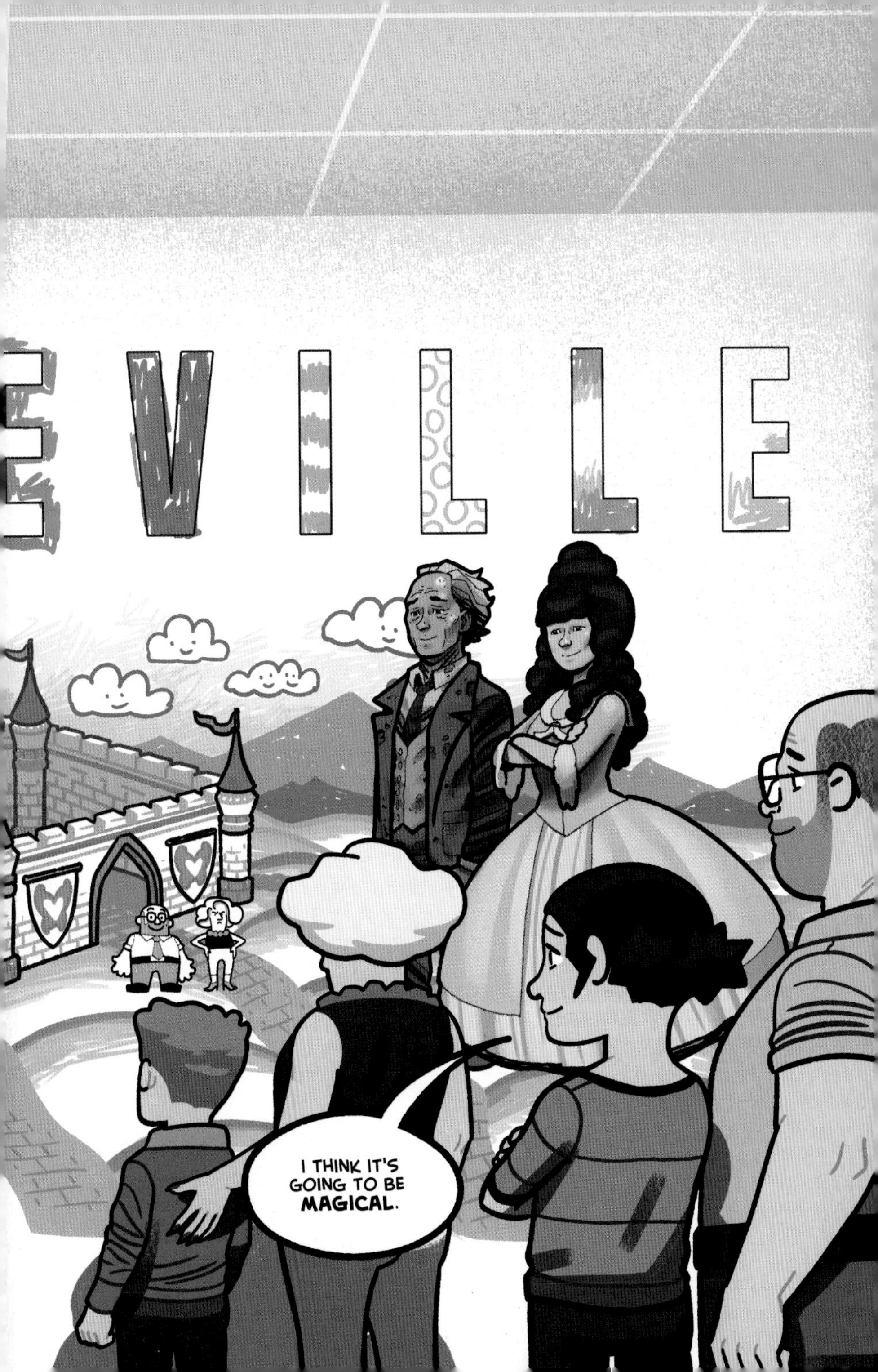
EVILLE
I THINK IT'S GOING TO BE MAGICAL.

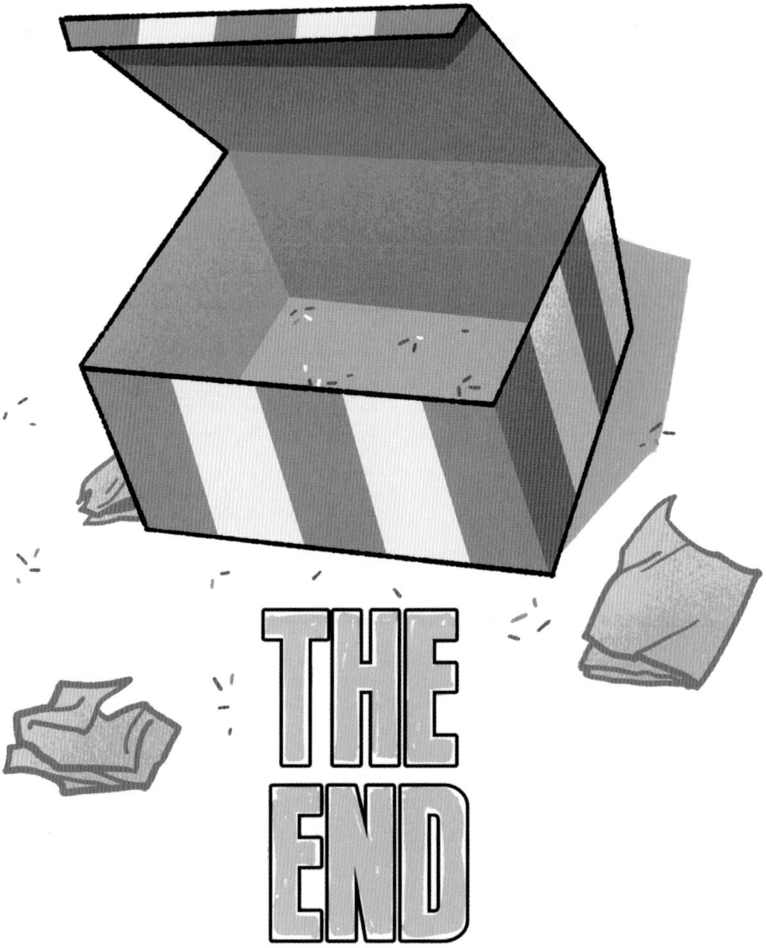
THE END